SHE'LL PUT

A SPELL ON YOU....

D0362525

continued . . .

Dark Emerald

"A complex medieval romance . . . moves forward on several levels that ultimately tie together in an exciting finish. The lead characters are a passionate duo while the secondary players strengthen the entire novel. Ms. Jackson has struck a gemstone mine."   —Painted Rock Reviews

"Snares the readers in an intricate plot and holds them until the very end."   —*Romantic Times*

Dark Ruby

"A true gem—a medieval masterpiece. Wonderfully compelling, filled with adventure and intrigue, sizzling sexual tension and a to-die-for hero, this one has it all."
                                        —Samantha James

"Rich, mysterious, passionate. It's a winner."
                                        —Alexis Harrington

"Fast-paced and fun from the start . . . a high-action adventure that will keep you turning the pages."   —Kat Martin

"A rich, unforgettable tale."   —Stella Cameron

SORCERESS

LISA JACKSON

A SIGNET BOOK

SIGNET
Published by New American Library, a division of
Penguin Group (USA) Inc., 375 Hudson Street,
New York, New York 10014, USA
Penguin Group (Canada), 90 Eglinton Avenue East, Suite 700, Toronto,
Ontario M4P 2Y3, Canada (a division of Pearson Penguin Canada Inc.)
Penguin Books Ltd., 80 Strand, London WC2R 0RL, England
Penguin Ireland, 25 St. Stephen's Green, Dublin 2,
Ireland (a division of Penguin Books Ltd.)
Penguin Group (Australia), 250 Camberwell Road, Camberwell, Victoria 3124,
Australia (a division of Pearson Australia Group Pty. Ltd.)
Penguin Books India Pvt. Ltd., 11 Community Centre, Panchsheel Park,
New Delhi - 110 017, India
Penguin Group (NZ), 67 Apollo Drive, Rosedale, North Shore 0745,
Auckland, New Zealand (a division of Pearson New Zealand Ltd.)
Penguin Books (South Africa) (Pty.) Ltd., 24 Sturdee Avenue,
Rosebank, Johannesburg 2196, South Africa

Penguin Books Ltd., Registered Offices:
80 Strand, London WC2R 0RL, England

First published by Signet, an imprint of New American Library,
a division of Penguin Group (USA) Inc.

First Printing, September 2007
10   9   8   7   6   5   4   3   2   1

To Roz Noonan.
Wow. I couldn't have done it
without you. Thanks!

ACKNOWLEDGMENTS

Thanks to everyone who helped me with this book. It was truly a group effort. First and foremost, I would like to thank Roz Noonan, who worked tirelessly with the characters. Roz's upbeat personality and persistence were a godsend. Also, I have to give credit where credit is due to my editor, Claire Zion, whose clear thinking and detailed revisions helped me through some of the difficult points of the plot.

I can't forget my agent, Robin Rue, who insisted we could get this done and done right, and promised drinks with umbrellas when the book was finished.

At home, I have an incredible support team behind me and would like to thank Nancy and Ken Bush, Marilyn Katcher, Kathy Okano, Alexis Harrington, Matthew Crose, Niki Wilkins, Michael Crose, and Ken Melum, along with probably a dozen other people I've forgotten to mention.

PROLOGUE

North Wales
Winter 1273

*R*un, *Tempest, run!*
Frigid air tore at Kambria's hair and whistled past her ears as she silently spurred her mount onward through the bare trees and snow-crusted ground. The poor mare was struggling, gasping for air as she gamely plunged forward through the scraggly thicket of yew and pine. Hot air plumed from the horse's nostrils and her hooves tore into the hard, icy earth, but her shaggy coat was covered in sweat, and despite all of Kambria's prayers to Morrigu, the Mother Goddess, the beast was losing ground.

Soon the hunters would be upon them. So-called holy men, dressed in black. Intent upon seeing their own twisted justice meted out upon her, they chased her with a wrathful, vengeful fire that no amount of reason or persuasion could dampen.

"Faster!" Kambria leaned over her mare's shoulders, hearing the poor horse labor, its breath whistling. Strong equine muscles began to flag. Her mission was surely lost. Nightfall was too far off. Even then, beneath the shroud of night, the hunters would track her, follow her, run her to the ground. There was no darkness deep enough to hide her.

"Give me strength. Lay your hands upon my mare," Kambria prayed as icy fingers of wind snarled her hair. Up ahead she caught a glimpse of another horseman darting through the frigid undergrowth. The dark riders were everywhere.

Even as she tugged on the reins and veered west, toward the mountains, she knew with a sinking heart that she was trapped. There would be no turning back, no circling around. The five horsemen had fanned out through the bare trees, cutting off all chance of escape, all roads returning her to her home, to safety.

Frantic, she pulled on the reins, guiding the mare to a narrow twisting path that climbed upward, through the lower hillocks toward a ridge. The territory was new. Foreign. Forbidden. But she had no other choice.

She heard their shouts.

Terror cut like shards of ice through her heart.

Tempest struggled, her hooves slipping, her flanks quivering, foam beginning to spot her gray, wet coat. "Please . . . you can do it."

Upward, ever more slowly, the beast ran on as snow began to fall, and Kambria felt a sharp cramp. She glanced down at her skirts, bundled high, and noticed the warm ooze of blood that dripped down her leg and splattered to the ground, bright red upon the frozen snow.

Her heart plummeted.

Not only would the blood leave a perfect trail—it would also strengthen the hunters' purpose.

"God's teeth," she said, placing the reins in her mouth and trying vainly to staunch the flow. From the corner of her eye she saw movement, black-robed figures upon fleet steeds climbing the ridge, flashing past a thicket of spindly trees. By the saints, they were upon her!

And all the while drops of blood spotted the ground, caught by the wind.

Somehow she had to stop this madness.

At the top of the ridge, she spurred her horse onward and the mare, finding footing, took off, cutting along a narrow deer trail. Heart pounding, skirts billowing, Kambria thought for a second that she would prevail, that her sure-footed jennet was more than a match for their bulkier steeds, which would scramble upon this narrow mountain spine. "Good girl," she whispered, barely believing her luck.

She prayed that the mountain would slow their steeds. If not, if they caught her, at least the dagger was safe; she had seen to that. A weapon possessed of great magick, the Sacred Dagger was destined to be in the hands of the Chosen One, as the age-old prophecy prescribed:

Sired by Darkness,
Born of Light,
Protected by the Sacred Dagger,
A ruler of all men, all beasts and beings,
It is he who shall be born on the Eve of Samhain.

The dagger could not fall into the hands of men with hearts of darkness, men like those who pursued her now.

As her horse galloped into the thin icy wind of the mountain, she felt a clutch of pain in her abdomen, a reminder of her baby, the child she'd had to leave behind. There was no pain like a mother's loss, but she'd had to see to the baby's safety, her child of Light.

At the crest of this hill, the trail split as neatly as a snake's tongue and, if she was far enough ahead, she might be able to tear off a bit of bloody clothing to lead her pursuers on the wrong course. She glanced over her shoulder and saw no one, none of the dark horsemen following.

Had she lost them?

Nay.

They would not give up. Their purpose was too strong. She dug her heels into the gasping gray's sides and wound through the trees. Blood sang through her veins when she caught sight of the fork in the path, one trail leading downward toward the village and river, the other following the backbone of these sheer mountains. Surely those behind her would expect her to take the lower path to the town. . . .

Suddenly her horse shied.

Stumbled.

Kambria's heart clutched.

She fell forward, nearly toppling over Tempest's bowed neck. Bristly black hairs from her jennet's mane stung her eyes and blinded her for a heartbeat. As the horse regained her footing and Kambria's eyes focused again, she saw him: a single dark predator upon a white steed. His head was covered with a black cloak, only the cleric's collar visible in the darkness, but she felt his eyes upon her, sensed his hideous intent.

She tried to pull her horse around, but it was too late. The others had closed in and she was trapped upon her panting mare.

Doom, it seemed, had found her.

"There is no escape for sinners," the horseman blocking the fork stated bluntly.

"I've not sinned."

"Have you not?" His dark eyes were slits deep in his cowl as he pointed a long, accusatory finger at the ground, where blood stained the icy snow. "Proof of your perfidy, Kambria, descendant of Llewellyn," he said. "Of your heresy and adultery. You are a harlot and a whore of the worst order, a daughter of the devil."

She felt the other horsemen drawing closer, circling her tightly, and for a second she felt as if she couldn't breathe. The mare beneath her quivered and Kambria laid a calming hand upon the frightened horse's shoulder. Was there no way out? Could she force her little mare to break through this ring of soulless men? She turned her thoughts inward, to the strength that lay deep in the marrow of her bones, the faith and courage that had brought her this far. *There are ways to defeat these monsters, means not physical, forces you have only to call upon.*

As if he read her thoughts, the leader snagged the reins from her hands and dropped to the ground. "Dismount," he ordered.

When she hesitated, he nodded to one of the others. A large hooded man with shoulders as broad as a woodcutter's ax hopped lithely off his bay, his boots hitting hard against the frozen terrain. Though she held on fiercely to the pommel of her saddle, it was no use. The big brute of a man dragged her from her horse and pinned her arms roughly behind her back, causing her shoulders to scream in pain. She felt the blood drain from her face but didn't cry out, determined to confront the fury of these lying thugs with a fire of her own.

The leader was the worst—a zealot who spoke of piety and divinity but was, in truth, an abomination to all of mankind.

He was known as Hallyd, and his cloak was but a disguise to hide the legacy of evil he'd inherited from his father, a man rumored to be half demon himself.

Aye, she knew this man who posed as a priest by day but was known to be quite a swordsman with women in the village by night. Had he not tried to bed her? Even threatened her when she'd refused him? But she'd seen the eerie light in his eyes. She could smell the smoky darkness of his soul. She sensed the yawning abyss of hatred that threatened to devour all light from the sky. She'd known what he really wanted, and she could not let it fall into his hands, even if she died protecting it.

If only the other hunters knew of his evil . . . but the men seemed all too willing to follow his orders as Hallyd gave a quick nod and they too slid to the ground, surrounding her.

Please, Great Mother, hear my prayer. If you do not save me, at least spare the life of my babe.

"Hypocritical spawn of Arawn," she whispered defiantly, "go back to Annwn, the underworld of the dead. May you never see the light of day again!"

He froze, thunderstruck.

"Silence!" Hallyd ordered.

"I know you," she whispered, holding his gaze. Even as he accused her of practicing the dark arts, beneath his Christian cloak and collar, he, too, was familiar with the old ways. Evil was apparent in the eerie, ethereal glow within his brown eyes—wild, determined eyes of a man who was not yet twenty years. "I know of your own sins, Hallyd, and they be many."

For an instant he hesitated.

"Harm me now and you will forever look over your shoulder, chased by your own guilt and my vengeance." As if to add credence to her words, lightning split the sky. The forest trembled.

"Mother of God," one of the men whispered nervously.

But the leader would not back down. Through lips that barely moved as the day darkened, he hissed, "You, Kambria of Tarth, daughter of Waylynn, descendant of Llewellyn, are an adulteress as well as a witch. The only way to save yourself is to tell me where you've hidden the dagger."

She didn't respond, though in her mind she caught an image of a wicked little knife covered in jewels.

"You know where it is," he accused, leaning closer.

She spat upon his face, the spittle sliding down his cheek and neck, lodging behind his clerical collar.

Enraged, he yanked a rosary from a pocket, then forced it over her head, its sharp beads tangling in her hair. "For your sins against God and man, you are hereby condemned to death."

She saw it then, the traitorous gleam in his eye. Oh, he was a fraud, a man with a soul black as the darkest night. He was doing this, sentencing her to die, to protect himself and his true mission. Her destruction had little to do with her, but all to do with his ambition to seize the Sacred Dagger.

"No amount of killing will save you," she said, then closed her eyes and began to chant, conjuring up a dark and deadly spell. She sensed the wind shift as it rattled the branches of the trees and swept across the icy ridge. Without seeing, she knew that thick clouds were suddenly forming, coming together, roiling toward the heavens, turning the color of aging steel. Far in the distance, thunder boomed.

"God in heaven," one man whispered, his voice raspy, "what is this?"

"Is she really the progeny of Llewellyn the Great?" another asked, and Kambria felt their fear.

"Ignore her cheap tricks," Hallyd said, though his voice was void of conviction. "She is using your fear against you."

"Save us all," the other man cried, falling to his knees and crossing himself.

Lost in her chant, Kambria barely heard their words. Pressing fingertips to her forehead, she prayed, summoning the spirits, whispering for the safety of her child and the destruction of her enemies.

"Stop! Jezebel! Call not your demons!"

And yet her words would not stop, the prayers of the old ones springing from her lips.

"Nay!" the dark horseman cried, enraged at her calm, her inner peace. He wanted to see her fear, to feel her terror. He received no satisfaction from her serenity. "Tell me, witch!"

Through her fluid chant she felt his vexation swell, sensed the growing fear that he couldn't hide.

"Curse you, Hallyd, and may your darkest fears be known." Her eyes opened and she stared into the mask of rage upon his face. "Your black soul shall be condemned for all eternity and you shall live in darkness forever, the pain of day too much to bear. From this day forward you will become a creature of the night." She saw it then—the fear, causing the pupils of his eyes to dilate to holes dark as the blackest dungeon, black swirls that would never shrink. His would be a blindness not only of the soul but of all daylight. And he would be marked, the very ring of color of one of his eyes turning to a pale gray.

Roiling with fury, he curled his fingers into fists until every knuckle turned white.

But she would not be deterred. "Go back to the bowels of hell from whence you were spawned," she said, staring into his black eyes, dark mirrors that reflected her own image.

"Tell me where the dagger is," he railed. "Tell me, whore!" Enraged, he struck, his fist slamming into her face.

Her nose splintered. Blood sprayed over the earth, yet she didn't flinch.

When he saw she was unmoved, he said, "So be it. You are to die, now. Do you hear me, whore? You cannot be saved. Go thee to Satan!" He shook her and more blood spewed from her body, streaking his white collar red, speckling his chin.

Jaw clenched, his pulse pounding at his temple, he reached into the voluminous folds of his robe and withdrew a sharp-edged rock.

In that instant, still chanting, she closed her eyes again and gave herself over to the Great Mother. In a heartbeat, she felt her spirit rise into the tempest of clouds. As she looked down, far below, she spied her body standing defiantly upon the jagged cliff, her skirts billowing. She watched from above as he hurled the stone with a fury born of fear. The rock crashed hard against her face, splintering her jaw, slicing her pale skin. Blood sprayed upon the ground as she stumbled back. Another stone smashed against her forehead and she fell, the group of men upon her, demons dressed in black pounding at her flesh.

There was no pain.

Only peace.

Her child, Kambria knew, was safe.

And vengeance would be hers.

CHAPTER ONE

North Wales
February 1289

On hands and knees, Gavyn slid through the undergrowth, moving stealthily, praying dusk would come quickly. His pursuers were nearby, ever closer. He heard the snort of their horses, the rumble of the great steeds' hooves, smelled their horsehide and sweat. Above all else, he sensed the eyes of his pursuers scouring the woods, searching. Always searching. For him.

But he heard no dogs. No furry sentinels ready to bay to the heavens upon smelling his scent. For that alone he was grateful.

His body ached from the beating, and he knew, if he were to look into a mirror, he would see bruises and welts criss-crossing his skin. They came to him compliments of Craddock, the sheriff of Agendor, a ruthless son of a cur if ever there was one.

And now a dead man.

Gavyn had no time to think of that now. He would not let his mind wander to the fight, the battering of flesh, the smell of sweat or the oaths of fury. He refused to revisit the crack of bone as it shattered and Craddock fell, his head twisted at a horrid angle upon his broken neck.

Fingers digging into the wet earth, he dragged himself

beneath the bracken and scrub brush, hoping the shadows of the massive yew and oak trees would hide him as he crept toward the edge of the cliff, where a narrow path cut down the sheer face. No sane man nor intelligent beast would follow, and 'twas all he had, his only way of escape.

Jaw set, he edged toward the ridge where the switchback was perilous, but it was safer than risking close proximity to the Lord of Agendor.

"Hey! What's this?" a man shouted.

Gavyn froze.

Held his breath and dared not move a muscle.

"What?"

"I thought I saw something in the . . . Ach, 'twas only a skunk."

A horse neighed in distress and the stench of a skunk's defenses seeped through the ivy and ferns. Gavyn's eyes began to water.

"Aye, Seamus. What did ye do? Christ Jesus, that stinks! Oh, fer the love of God."

"Holy Jesus!" one man cried while another coughed from somewhere close, though he was hidden in the gloom.

Maintaining silence, Gavyn watched the offending skunk waddle quickly into the shadows of a fallen log.

"Shh!" An order.

Gavyn's heart stilled as the putrid smell settled over the area. He knew his father's hiss as surely as if he'd grown up with the snake, though of course he'd never set foot in the Lord of Agendor's keep and had, instead, been raised by one of the old man's mistresses. He forced back the bile in his throat, for the hatred between them was strong.

"He's near." His father's voice again.

That much was true. Through the dense foliage Gavyn noticed the shadowy outline of a horse's legs, close enough that were he to reach forward, he could touch the beast and startle it. 'Twas his father's mount, a stallion with one odd stocking. Gavyn's heart knocked in his chest at the thought of being mere inches from the man who had sired him, the baron who detested him, the goddamned warrior who wanted him dead.

"Eww, but, m'lord, the smell."

"'Twill not kill you, Badden," Deverill said impatiently as several men farther away coughed but were smart enough not to argue. Badden, his father's guard, was a big, burly man who wasn't afraid to say what he thought, though he'd felt the back of Deverill's hand or the insidious ridicule from his lord more often than not.

Gavyn took in a quick, hideously smelling breath.

The horse shifted, kicking up dry leaves and dirt as it turned, bridle jangling in the ever-darkening air. Were Gavyn to look up, he was certain he would find the angry countenance of his father, so like his own, glaring at the darkness, defying the night from falling so that he could finish his task.

"Damn but it's dark," Deverill admitted. "Find him! Find the murderer, now!"

"Leith should be back soon, with the dogs and fresh torches." Again Badden had the nerve and lack of brains to speak up.

Gavyn's heart turned to ice. Fear crawled up his spine. His father's hunting mastiffs were trained to be vicious. Weighing his chances, he heard the first distant bays of the huge dogs with their long fangs.

He had no choice but to edge closer to the cliff and risk detection. With one eye on the white stocking of his father's steed, he inched forward noiselessly. Jaw set, body screaming in pain, he dragged himself upward through the twilight and stench.

As he did, a dry leaf rustled and the horse flinched.

Gavyn didn't dare breathe.

"Shh," the lord hissed again.

And the air grew quiet, as still as a dead man's heart.

And then the horses began to move, to circle. Gavyn knew that the Baron of Agendor had motioned to his men without a word, silently instructing them to entrap him.

He had to move. Even if it risked exposure.

Squinting into the darkness, he spied the large split trunk of an oak that stood at the head of the path.

Now.

On his feet in an instant, Gavyn threw himself toward the cliff and the treacherous path that zigzagged down to the canyon floor.

"There," Badden shouted. "Over there!"

Phhhht. An arrow zipped by his ear.

He dove.

Ssst. Another deadly missile passed him in the gathering dark.

His feet found the end of the path, dirt crumbling beneath his boots.

"Traitor," his father roared.

A hissing sound . . . and suddenly he was propelled forward by a burning pain that struck his shoulder. He spun around just in time to see, in the shadows, the Lord of Agendor's bow raised, evidence that it was he who had found his mark.

Was that a smile that curved across his lips?

It was too dark to tell. In a heartbeat, Gavyn fell into the yawning darkness of the ravine.

Isa's death had been the beginning, Bryanna thought as she rode beneath the portcullis of Castle Calon's gate, leaving the keep that had become her home in the past few months. When she'd first traveled through these gates, Bryanna had never anticipated the odd turn of events that would take the life of the woman who'd nearly raised her . . . or the haunting strains of Isa's voice thrumming through her head.

Bryanna had been born and raised in Penbrooke with four siblings: brothers Tadd and Kelan, and sisters Morwenna and Daylynn. Upon the death of their father, Alwynn, Kelan had ascended to the barony at Penbrooke, but Castle Calon, still in his holdings, became a keep without a lord. At first many had looked to Tadd, who was off fighting for the king. But young, reckless Tadd was hardly ready to rule a keep.

Then Bryanna's older sister, Morwenna, had dared to defy convention. She'd insisted she was capable of running Calon, and their brother had grudgingly given her the chance. Bryanna had journeyed there to be with her older sister, a headstrong woman with ebony hair, so different from Bryanna. Through a recent spate of murders at Calon, Morwenna had proven to be a brave, insightful lady of the keep. That came as no surprise to Bryanna. However, no one had anticipated that Morwenna would find true love at Calon and marry. Now she and her husband shared the rule.

And now Isa was dead, one of the victims of the terror that had besieged Calon. Her violent end was the point when the madness had really begun. When she'd visited the nurse-maid—poor Isa, dead and cold, her eyes staring sightlessly toward the dark rafters—Bryanna had heard her nursemaid's voice. As clear as rainwater rushing through the gutters, the old woman's voice had flowed, instructing Bryanna, and she had listened.

I will be with you always, Isa's spirit had insisted. *You alone, of all your siblings, have the sight. Trust me and I will teach you. You, Bryanna of Penbrooke, will be called Sorceress.*

Now, nary a fortnight later, Bryanna, upon her fleet mare, thought there was a good chance she was making the biggest mistake of her life. And that was not an idle musing. In her sixteen years she'd erred often and had just as often been caught up in her foolishness. But this—riding away from the warmth and safety of Castle Calon—seemed suddenly rash and foolish, and she had to wonder if she were truly going mad.

If the vision had not been so real, the images so strong, the voice inside her head so loud, she might have pushed thoughts of this journey aside, but she could not. And then there were the dreams that had been with her since childhood, dreams of gems raining from a night sky, dreams laced with that hauntingly familiar chant:

An opal for the northern point,
An emerald for the east,
A topaz for the southern tip,
A ruby for the west.

She'd never understood the words until now. . . .

"God help me," she whispered under her breath as a cold winter wind bit at her nose and earlobes. Alabaster's hooves dug into the hard-packed road, carrying her off on this truly mad journey.

Her sister's voice caught up with her, chillingly echoing her own desperate prayer. "Bryanna, God be with you," Morwenna called, her voice floating high on the brisk winter wind.

From astride her horse Bryanna forced a smile upon her cold lips and glanced over her shoulder to wave at Morwenna with one gloved hand, all the while holding the reins in a death grip. She spied her tall, dark-haired sister and the man she'd married. Bryanna's heart tore a little at the sight of him, taller than his wife, his shoulders strong and wide, his near-black hair falling over a strong forehead and eyes as blue as a summer sky. *Dear God, do* not *let me want him. Please. Do* not. But it was already too late for prayer. She was half in love with him already.

Foolish, foolish girl.

After a quick look ahead, she glanced back again to spy the thick stone walls of Castle Calon rising behind Morwenna and her new husband. Although the heavy gates were clogged with the traffic of peasants, servants, and peddlers leaving and entering, Bryanna's gaze was held by the sight of this man at her sister's side.

So strong.

So masculine.

So disturbing.

He stood at his wife's side, one strong arm wrapped protectively around Morwenna's waist.

How had she let herself grow so close to him when he was

so obviously in love with Morwenna? Why did she ache just at the thought of him, long for the feel of his hand in her hair, his lips brushing her cheek? Sweet Mother Mary, how could she be so vile, so despicable as to actually lust after her sister's husband? Bryanna's stomach turned at the thought and she silently vowed that no one would ever know her secret. She would take it with her to her grave.

"Godspeed, sister!" As he stood at the castle gates, his voice rose over the hills and sliced straight through Bryanna's black heart.

Sister. He thought of Bryanna as one of his wife's siblings, nothing more.

Of course he does. He's in love with his wife. His wife, *Bryanna. You are a wicked woman to want it any other way. Maybe, just maybe, those voices in your head, the ones that insist you're a witch, maybe they're true. Maybe your heart is as black as obsidian.*

Her throat was suddenly thick. Envy slid through her blood and Bryanna hated herself for her wayward thoughts.

Despite the warring emotions burning through her obviously damned soul, she pretended all was as it should be, that she was embarking upon a great adventure and would soon return safely. She gave a final wave and blinked back the tears of regret that burned her eyes.

Urging her jennet to a quicker pace, she felt the mare, Alabaster, a gift from her sister, respond by flattening out, ground-eating strides ever lengthening. Bryanna pushed all thoughts of Calon and Morwenna and *him* out of her head. With resolve, she turned in her saddle and faced forward, her eyes focused on the frozen road leading north, though she knew it would not be an easy path. The wind whistled in her ears and tugged at her hair as the sturdy stone walls of Calon faded behind her.

Away from her sister.

Away from Calon.

Away from *him.*

And into the unknown.

For, according to a voice as clear as a night bell, the voice of a woman already in her grave, north was where her destiny lay.

If she could believe such rot.

Sixteen years.

Cursed for sixteen long, unforgiving years since he'd stoned the witch to death and seen her spirit rise to mock him. Sixteen years spent enduring the bloody curse that had been a weight upon his back. 'Twas as if he'd been living in uffern, his own private hell.

And yet he'd survived.

Hallyd's fingers curled into tight fists as he stood upon the battlements of Chwarel and stared into the thick night. He was alone, the guard for the east wall asleep at his post in the tower. A lazy one was Afal, with bad teeth and a penchant for ale. Yet, the man was loyal, and that trait, above all others, secured his job.

Frowning, Hallyd looked to the south, from whence she was riding. He felt his blood stir with a fever reminiscent of his youth. With the passing of years he was no longer young, no longer hotheaded or so easily enraged. With the passing of time came patience, strength, and stamina, honed by a conviction so deep it filled his soul.

And now, at last, the time had come.

His dreams of the dagger had not faded and his ambitions, as double-edged as the blade, would serve two purposes: to cast off the black spell and absorb the vast power of the Sacred Dagger.

She was approaching.

Bryanna.

Daughter of the witch.

Squinting through the crenels of the thick curtain wall, he noticed the rising fog and heard the sound of distant hoof-beats, their steady rhythm echoing through his brain like a heartbeat.

She was drawing near, her horse galloping toward him.

Quicksilver warmth fired his blood and he licked his lips. His nostrils flared and he swore he smelled her scent on the slow-moving wind. Fresh and touched with lavender and musk, it rose to greet him, to cause a hardening of his cock, to burn erotic images deep into his brain.

The winter wind was harsh, an icy blast promising more snow as it chased away the fog. His lips were chapped as he licked them again and thought of her with her alabaster skin, eyes as clear and sharp as cut emeralds. She was the one.

He smiled to himself and dared to touch his thickening member. Oh, what he would do to her. He'd waited so long and now, soon . . . so very soon . . . he would have his way with her. He imagined first touching her firm, yielding flesh, then considered how it would feel to scrape his teeth and tongue down her back to her buttocks, where he would nip at her before turning her over and finding her breasts. She would buck up to him, wanting more, panting, snarling as he grazed her nipple with his teeth. Crying out, she would feel the first hint of his punishment when he drew a little blood before he spread her legs and forced himself into her.

Then there was the rutting. Hard. Fast. As animals. In his mind's eye he envisioned her backside, moving beneath him, his thumbs nearly touching as his hands spanned her waist, his cock pummeling her hot wetness. And then, that one moment when the Fates crossed paths and he spilled his seed deep into her. He would toss back his head and scream in ecstasy with the effort, claiming her as his.

Rightfully his.

But that would not be the end of it. Oh no. He would take her again and again, until she was gasping and spent. And then, by God, he'd take her again. She would learn what it meant to be a slave to unholy desire. Just as he had.

He smiled a little, the wind cool against his heated flesh as he considered how much she would want him. Again and again she would beg him to mount her. She would hate herself for the wicked, heated need that was powerful enough to make her ache for more. He would do what he wanted to her and would not stop until he'd planted his seed deep within her.

"M'lord?"

Startled, he jumped and whirled on the soldier, who apparently had awoken and decided to come prying.

"'Tis sorry I am for bothering you," Afal said carefully, "but I wondered if something was wrong. 'Tis not like you to be up here at night."

"I'm not an old woman," Hallyd snapped. The nerve of the mongrel!

"Nay, m'lord, I know, and yet, 'tis not your usual manner to brood in the middle of the night—"

"Brood?" he repeated, one hand fisting and a tic forming beneath his eye. "Bloody hell, Afal, is this not my keep? Can I not take a walk upon my battlements at my whim?" He should cuff the idiot here and now.

And the man was lying, for it was always at night when Hallyd was about. Ever since the curse had been cast upon him, daylight burned his eyes and drove him inside. Only on the darkest days of winter did he dare venture from the shadow of the tall walls of the keep before the sun set.

"Of course you may walk wherever you want, but—"

"But *what*?" Hallyd demanded, irritated that this pathetic excuse for a guard would have the nerve to approach him, even challenge him.

"Not a thing," Afal said, realizing belatedly that he'd overstepped his station. He lowered his head and began backing up, like the whipped dog he should be. "I was just inquiring as to your health. And now, I'll be off to my post."

And good riddance, Hallyd thought, eyes narrowing as the beefy soldier hustled back to the bastion and took up his post, ramrod stiff, as if he didn't doze through the night watch. Hallyd was quite aware of that. He also knew Afal kept a small jug of ale tucked into a spot in the tower where the mortar had broken free and a rock had loosened.

Fool.

Hallyd considered pummeling the guard and casting him

headfirst over the wall, but he could ill afford to lose another soldier. He also didn't want to explain the death to the visiting priest, a reverent man who was suspicious enough as it was.

Gritting his teeth, Hallyd turned in the opposite direction and strode to the south tower, where he hurried down the spiraling stairs amid dusky smoke from the rushlights burning low. His own shadow chased him and a rat scurried away, tiny claws scraping as he reached the ground level and walked into the darkened bailey. Beneath the few scattered stars in the misting heavens he surveyed the darkened huts and steep walls.

Once this keep had been a magnificent castle, a shining fortress crawling with servants, peasants, freemen, and soldiers. Now 'twas decaying, half dead, the skeleton of a once robust fortress, filled only with the whispering curse that Kambria had laid upon him. Still, after all these years, that wretched curse cut him to the bone and echoed in the parapets.

He crossed the yellowed grass of the bailey, nearly tripping over a slinking cat that yowled, hissed, then shot into the darkness to hide behind the mason's hod. "Miserable beast." He hurried up the steps to the great hall, stung with rage that, like the cat, he had become a creature of darkness.

"Good evening, m'lord," a guard greeted him as he opened the door. Hallyd strode inside to the smells of smoke, garlic, and pork fat, scents lingering from the last meal. Up the stairs he strode, his long legs taking the steps two at a time, his black mantle billowing behind him. 'Twas now, in the middle of the night, when he felt most alive, most vital.

He hurried along the corridor as the candles burned low and his boots rang hollowly on the stone floors. At the end of the long hall, he turned into his chamber, a large high-ceilinged room where the rafters were exposed and a feeling of emptiness pervaded. The fire had turned to embers and in the bloodred half-light he strode to an alcove where his old cleric's robes hung by a peg, gathering dust, the rosary dull and still stained with Kambria's blood.

"Liar," he whispered now, his fingers curling over the sharp beads as her image invaded his mind. By the gods how she had haunted him, her curse forever ringing in his ears.

You shall live in darkness forever. . . . *Your black soul condemned for all eternity.* . . .

Nay, not forever, though the past sixteen years had seemed several lifetimes.

Think not of the past.

Consider what is to come.

Starting with Bryanna . . .

Remember what you will do to her, how much pleasure you will find, all upon her tender flesh. . . .

His bad mood dissipated into the cold night air as he disrobed and returned to envisioning the pleasures he would force from her body, the satisfaction he would gain.

He tossed his mantle over a corner bench, then worked at the lacings of his breeches. He was getting hard again, his cock straining against the leather at the thought of the ways this sorceress would transform his life. She would restore magick to the dagger, thus ending his painful blindness. She would deliver the Sacred Dagger unto his hands, bringing him power over all of the kingdoms in Wales.

He rubbed the tips of his fingers on his thumbs at the thought, and his cock swelled ever more thickly.

The dagger.

The power.

And another red-haired sorceress to defile.

The image of their primitive mating was so clear he had to bite down hard upon his lip, drawing blood. Desire pulsed through his eager body, but he fought his own searing lust.

'Twas not yet time.

"Bryanna," he whispered, tasting his own blood as through the window he heard the creak of the windmill and the call of a night bird.

His breathing was shallow and fast, nearly a pant.

He'd waited what seemed a thousand years for this . . . for her.

Bryanna.

Chosen by the Fates.

Only she had the power to lift the curse of darkness.

Only she could deliver the charmed weapon that would elevate him to the highest throne.

His fingers played lightly upon his hardness. Sweat dampened his brow. Closing his eyes, he felt her heartbeat in his own, heard the thunder of her horse's hooves racing ever nearer, and oh, so distinctly, as if she were truly lying with him at this moment, he imagined her hot, sweet breath against his skin.

Aye, the pleasure would come soon enough.

As would the power.

CHAPTER TWO

B ryanna rode on, ever northward.

Her teeth chattered and her fingers turned icy as she held her cowl tightly over her head against the cold winter wind.

After three days of riding away from Calon, Bryanna knew that if it weren't for the ugly fact that she was running away because she was half in love with her sister's husband, she would never have listened to the voices in her head. Never!

But what about the visions? The strange dreams?

She gritted her teeth and pushed away thoughts of the images that flowed through her head. Gems raining from the sky and a red-haired woman on a galloping horse. Absently, gloved fingers holding tight to the reins, she made the sign of the cross over her chest.

Guiding her mare along the rutted road, she considered for the hundredth time if she were slowly but surely going out of her mind. As Alabaster raced easily past a fallow field where the earth was already turned, she wondered why she was haunted by such vivid nightmares of dark omens and jeweled daggers.

"Bother and broomsticks," she muttered, angling northwest at a fork in the road, where two runny-nosed boys in woolen caps were throwing punches at each other as their pregnant mother tugged on the leather rein of a tired donkey carrying bundles of sticks.

This curse, as she thought of it, had been with her for as long as she could remember, an oddity that set her apart from others, especially her siblings. Though she'd never actually heard words issued from the grave before, she'd experienced more than her share of premonitions. As a child she had played with friends only she had seen, people and animals she was certain were as real as those visible to others.

Her brothers, older and ready to tease at a moment's notice, had chided her mercilessly when she'd spoken of the friends they couldn't see. Tadd and Kelan had taken great pleasure in taunting her and embarrassing her to the point that she'd been near tears but smart enough to staunch their flow rather than suffer another onslaught of laughter.

Her sisters had been no better. Daylynn, the baby, had giggled, though Bryanna suspected the younger girl hadn't really understood the joke. But Morwenna, the eldest daughter, had made Bryanna regret confiding in any of her siblings.

"That's such rot," Morwenna had admonished as they'd been walking their horses through the orchard and plucking a few forgotten winter apples still dangling from a tree devoid of leaves. They'd been in the outer bailey of Penbrooke Keep. The winter sky had been the color of steel, the air crisp but smelling of smoke and horse dung. The farrier's forge had burned bright, his hammer clanging loudly through the bailey as he'd shaped horseshoes upon his anvil. A stable boy had been sweating as he pushed a cart piled high with dirty straw and manure toward the gates.

"Is anyone near you now?" Morwenna had asked from astride her larger gelding, a big brown beast with a single white stocking. "I mean, any of those friends you were talking about?"

Bryanna, slowly realizing that her sister, too, might mock her, had nodded slowly. "Aye," she'd said, lifting her chin defiantly. "A few."

"Really?" The older girl had taken a bite from her apple, then wrinkled her nose and spit out a wormy piece. "Well, *I* can't see her or him or them, so they aren't there."

Morwenna's eyes had narrowed as a crow had fluttered onto one of the bare branches. "You're not teasing me, are you? Not making this up for your own amusement at my expense?"

Bryanna had swallowed hard under her older sister's steady glare, but shook her head, her reddish curls bobbing defiantly. "They are here with me. With us."

One of Morwenna's dark eyebrows had arched in disbelief. "Here? Where?" Morwenna had asked. "On the horse with you?"

"Of course not," Bryanna had scoffed. "Why would they be on my horse?"

"Well, I don't know, goose. Why don't you tell me?"

Bryanna had sighed in long-suffering boredom. "Wolf . . . she's there, peering out from behind the bole of that tree. No, not that one . . . over there, by the sheep pen." She'd pointed to the gnarled trunk of a tree. "And then there's Lil. She's shy and hiding over there, near the well."

When Morwenna had turned her gaze to the well near the stables, Bryanna was certain that Lil, her silent friend, would show herself. Instead she peered shyly from behind the wooden bucket that dangled from a thick rod and creaked as it swayed in the wind.

"Lil?" Morwenna repeated, her voice thick as cook's porridge. "Is she a wolf, too?"

"Of course not! Don't be a ninny." Bryanna tossed her hair from her eyes. "Lil's a girl." Impatient with her older sister's open mockery, Bryanna had motioned to her friend. "Lil, come out from behind there." But the girl, as had been her wont, disappeared when Bryanna hadn't been looking. "Oh, now she's gone and hidden herself again."

"By the gods, Bryanna, you *are* daft." Morwenna had been as cross as she had been concerned. "There is no wolf, nor a girl hiding behind the well like a thief." To make her point, Morwenna had tossed her half-eaten apple at the well, knocking the pail and sending it downward, its rope uncoiling and twisting like a dying snake.

Wolf scuttled away from the well. Bryanna looked beseechingly after the little she-wolf, the distinctive ring of shaggy black fur around her neck in stark contrast to her silver coat. The boy she hadn't mentioned, with his thick shock of black hair and disturbing silver eyes, had looked at her before diving behind a hayrick piled high with straw. Not that Morwenna had been able to see him, of course. When it came to friends, it seemed, Morwenna was as blind as the old hermit monk in the south tower.

"Listen, Bryanna. I don't know why you insist you see these people and animals, but it's got to stop. It's embarrassing. You're seven years old now, nearly eight, and everyone in the keep is talking about how strange it is . . . how strange you are."

Bryanna had bristled.

"I don't mean to be unkind, but—"

"Yes, you do."

Morwenna had rolled her eyes to the sky, as if contemplating the thickening clouds. " 'Tis true. I want you to stop this. You worry Mother and Isa as well. Come now, don't be cross with me. Just, please, for Mother's sake, do not be crazy."

"I'm not." But Bryanna had felt more than a little stab of guilt when she thought of her mother.

"Good." Morwenna had nodded, as if satisfied. Then she'd yanked on the reins of her horse. The big gelding sidestepped. "Race you to the portcullis!"

"The captain of the guard won't like it."

Morwenna's eyes had sparkled and a wicked little grin had slid across her lips. "I know. All the better. Sir Hennessy is such an old bore."

Bryanna had laughed as Morwenna had leaned forward, pressing her knees hard against the horse's flanks. Her mount shot forward, taking off at a dead run.

On her smaller horse, Bryanna had been quick to follow, her hair streaming behind her, the thrill of the race causing her heart to pound.

She'd lost, of course. She'd lost all competitions when it came to her older sister. But Bryanna had learned her lesson.

From that day forward, she had held her tongue about the special friends who would visit her. She pretended to see only what her siblings confirmed, and over the years those ethereal friends—the wolf, Lil, and the boy—had faded to the point that she'd decided they had been nothing but a creation of her own bored mind.

Until recently.

When Isa, the old nursemaid had died and had begun speaking to Bryanna.

Worse yet, Isa was just as bossy dead as she had been while she was alive!

"'Tis a curse," Bryanna muttered under her breath as Alabaster flew over the frozen earth, her hooves thundering, throwing up bits of mud as they passed two huntsmen heading in the opposite direction. Over the back of one man's steed was a gutted stag, while the other man had a thick pack that no doubt held rabbits, squirrels, and perhaps a pheasant or dove.

Oh, this was surely a fool's mission. *"Worry not, Bryanna, 'tis your destiny."* Isa's voice rang clear as a church bell in Bryanna's head.

"'Tis naught but a batty woman's folly," she groused under her breath.

The woman came to Gavyn at night, in his dreams. When he was close to consciousness but hadn't quite awakened.

She was a woman with pale skin and burnished hair and eyes that gleamed the deep aqua of the sea. Riding through the clouds upon a horse as pale as moonlight, she whispered a soft chant that flowed through his brain and eased the pain that tore through his muscles.

Young and beautiful, vital and rare, she seemed unaware of him as the horse galloped past, gray stockings cutting through the filmy clouds and striking something rock-hard and flinty, causing sparks to appear and stars to shine for but a second before fading in her wake.

Did he know her? Why did he feel they had met before? As

she disappeared the clouds roiled and blackened, turning purple and silver until there was only darkness, a gathering gloom in which no stars shined. In the darkness, the agony tore through him once again.

And something else skulked in the obsidian depths.

An evil presence lurked in the shadows, a malevolent being that was silent and hidden, but ever nearer, getting closer to the woman who sped by.

Gavyn tried to cry out a warning, to tell her that she was being followed, nay, stalked, but his voice would not speak and his legs were dead to him, unmoving. He could not so much as lift a finger. Never in his life had he been weak or impotent, but lying still as death, he was useless. To himself. To *her*. And the evil one knew it. He feared nothing, this entity without shape that brought a sweeping coldness with him. His presence, his halo of imminent terror, clawed at Gavyn's heart and froze his soul.

Not a man easily frightened, not a man who feared death, not a man who would back down from a challenge, Gavyn knew terror and desperation for the first time in his life.

And he could do nothing.

Nothing.

Bryanna and Alabaster had traveled far this day, riding through fields where the grass was dry and yellow.

"'Tis a good girl you are," she said to the horse.

For the past few nights they had taken refuge in inns along the way. Though many an innkeeper's eyebrows raised as she'd approached alone and asked for a room, she'd always found lodging, a bowl of warm water to wash with, and a meal of beans, meat, and dry bread. No one had asked why she was unescorted, a woman whose clothes and manner spoke of nobility, nor had any thief stolen into her room at night, attempting to rob her.

The first night, as she wrapped herself in the inn's rough blanket and fell into an exhausted sleep, she had heard the sound of musical notes, a backdrop for Isa's voice as clear as

the rain pounding upon the roof. Isa told her she would meet
a lone minstrel traveling in the opposite direction. She was to
veer right over a bridge after the meeting.

Of course she'd thought the dream was nothing more than
a silly enchantment. But at midday, when the heavens threatened to open with more cold rain, she came upon a musician
riding upon a donkey, his long hornpipe slung across his back.
At the next crossroads, she turned right and soon crossed a
short bridge spanning a rushing creek.

The next night, Isa came to her dreams again, and this time
her instructions were less clear, but she mentioned a hawk and
the turn of his wing.

Rot and rubbish, Bryanna thought the following morning.
After a breakfast of tasteless porridge, she collected Alabaster
from the stable and again rode north. Although there was no
rain peppering the ground, the wind was fierce, keening down
from the mountains and whistling through the canyons. The
countryside was more rugged than she'd seen, the towns and
castles spaced far apart. As the day wore on not only was she
hungry, but lonely as well, and as she spied a hawk in the
cloudy sky, she silently cursed Isa and the visions.

Yet as she guided Alabaster into the woods, she kept her
eye on the hawk soaring overhead, his speckled breast hardly
discernible. With no other guide, she followed the hawk,
which flew above a little-used path that cut deeper into the
gathering gloom of the forest.

Little more than a deer trail, it seemed a ridiculous course.
Bryanna told herself she should turn around, go back to
Calon, admit that she was in love with Morwenna's husband
and suffer being banished to Penbrooke again. Would it be so
bad to be under her brother Kelan's rule?

*And what then? Let him marry you off to some neighbor-
ing baron? So that you can do whatever he wants and bear
him heirs? Is that what you want, to be the lady of a castle,
shackled to a man you do not love?*

Oh, Morrigu, surely Kelan wouldn't be so unkind.

And yet, what would he want with her and her visions, her

dreams of dead women speaking to her? Even Kiera, his wife, would think Bryanna was addled.

Nay, she could not return to Penbrooke.

Nor Calon.

As the horse walked steadily through the twilight, her thoughts turned again to her sister's husband. Dear Lord, why could she not stop thinking of him? Why did she have to suffer these torturous feelings? Why, in all of God's kingdom, was she chasing this lunatic dream when she could so easily turn around and return to her home? Her stomach rumbled and she thought of the cook's pheasant pyes, and jellied eggs, and roasted eel. Her mouth watered and she considered the laughter and gaiety of the Christmas Revels, the dancing and singing and her large chamber with its warm, glowing fire and soft, canopied bed. She should return. In the daylight, she should forget this fool's mission and turn back to Calon, head south and—

"Nay, Bryanna, fail me not. You must save the child," Isa's voice said, reverberating in Bryanna's head and stilling her heart.

So now it was a child.

'Twas nonsense.

"What child?" she said aloud, her own voice ricocheting off the canyon walls. Why had she followed the hawk, anyway? She'd just followed a bird down an overgrown, little-used path. Had her senses completely abandoned her? "I asked you what child, Isa!"

But, of course, Isa chose not to answer and Bryanna's question bounced back to her again. Alabaster snorted and the wind picked up, as if the old nursemaid had ordered it to slap at Bryanna's face and ruffle her hair.

Her pride had stopped her from seeking the shelter of other keeps and imposing upon family friends. Nay, she was on a mission that many might construe as pure folly. How could she explain herself if she were to show up without a guard or companion at a friendly keep? The lord would be suspicious, the lady posing questions, the servants listening at keyholes.

"Fie and feathers," she grumbled, as she spied what had once been a woodsman's hut and was now falling into ruin, the roof collapsed, one wall missing. 'Twas a pitiful shelter, but it would provide some protection against the sleet that had begun to pepper the ground.

She dismounted, yanked off the saddle, the horse's blanket, and her own rolled blanket. Then she untied the leather bags she'd bound to the saddle before tending to the mare. The grass here at the edge of the woods was sparse, but Bryanna carried with her a little grain from the stores at Calon and had bought a small satchel at the stable.

She offered Alabaster water from the stream that passed near the dilapidated hut, as well as a ration of feed that would last until the morrow, when she would find more sustenance for them both. She was not destitute. In truth, she carried far more coin with her than was safe, but she would be careful with it, for when it ran out, she would have nothing.

Oh, this was a bad idea, one born of a dead woman.

Or the demons in your mind, Bryanna.

Did they not come to you whilst you were hiding deep in the dark corridors of the keep? Yes, you were keeping your vigil, waiting to strike, praying to Morrigu for strength when the visions appeared.

Truth?

Or but a trick of your mind?

"Stop!" she shouted at herself.

Alabaster nickered softly from the spot where she was tethered, inside the small hut.

The wind raged as Bryanna found some dead moss and dry twigs and made a pathetic little fire in the pit within the hut. Then she walked to the stream, splashed some icy water upon her face and hands, all the while wondering what it would feel like if she were truly losing her mind. Would she even know it? Could it be any worse than the last few weeks of madness?

Upon returning to the hut, she poked at her meager fire. Watching shadows play upon the weathered, sagging walls, she heard Isa's voice as clearly as if she were standing beside her.

"Fear not, Bryanna," the old woman said.

"Humph. Easy for you to say. You're already dead."

"And now you must fulfill your quest."

Bryanna pulled a piece of dry meat from her leather pouch. "How do I know to trust you?"

"Oh, child, was I not your nursemaid? Your companion? Did I not care for you?"

"But you're dead. I saw you myself. I touched your cold body. Stared into your sightless eyes." Bryanna shivered, remembering the night she'd viewed the old nursemaid lying upon the physician's table. Isa's pale eyes had stared upward to the rafters. 'Twas then the voice had first spoken to Bryanna, instructing her to take the items Isa had secreted away.

"Take them—they are yours," Isa had told her, though, of course, the dead woman's lips hadn't moved and the voice had whispered only within Bryanna's mind.

Isa had been wearing a pouch around her waist and a necklace with her own special talisman around her neck. The voice had instructed Bryanna to remove those items from Isa's dead body and keep them as her own.

Within the pouch had been vials of herbs, bits of candles, and pieces of colored string. Bryanna had taken them all, along with the things she'd found secreted in Isa's hut. Isa's voice had directed her to prop a ladder against the post supporting the roof, and there, on the top of a crossbeam, invisible to the room below, was a false panel. Behind the panel, cut into the heavy wood, was a private little alcove. In this secret niche, Bryanna had discovered the dagger wrapped tightly in deer hide and tied with a leather thong. The knife was little more than a dull, cast-iron blade, the hilt tainted and rusting with empty holes where there had once been jewels.

Now, as the night wind seeped through the thin slats of the walls, she recalled how she'd first feared the old woman's words, how she'd recoiled at touching Isa's cold flesh, how she'd only done Isa's bidding out of curiosity, and how that curiosity had become this journey.

By the light of the fire, she opened one of the bags she carried with her and dug inside. Her fingers touched the pouch of coins, but she pushed it aside, searching further until she found the soft doeskin she sought. Seated on a smooth stone, she pulled out the rolled piece of hide and unlaced its tie. Within the folds of the doeskin was a dagger, ugly and small, with a wicked curved blade. If her dreams were to be believed, this weapon had once been beautiful, with precious gems embedded upon its bone handle.

She held the hilt in one hand as if testing its weight. Then, swiftly, she thrust the little weapon out, as if attacking someone or something. Aye, she'd seen this dagger often enough in the dream that came to her night after night. But in her imaginings the blade had always been polished and smooth, the handle decorated with gems that glittered brilliantly.

Enticingly.

Not so now.

When Bryanna was but a child, Isa used to tell her stories of a magickal dagger, a weapon mentioned in a prophecy of the old ones. How did it go? "Sired by Darkness, born of Light . . ." Something like that.

Vexed as always by the blade, Bryanna set the knife aside and smoothed the doeskin open to stare at the faded markings upon it. Her brow furrowed as she concentrated, for she was certain the etchings upon the odd-shaped piece of hide were a map, but one she could not decipher aside from the point marking a way north. She bit her lip and tried to make sense of the squiggles and marks. A river, perhaps, here in the eastern edge? Mountains to the northwest? It was impossible to tell.

But somehow, this flap of doeskin was her confounded destiny.

CHAPTER THREE

Morwenna felt like a traitor.

Nay, she *was* a traitor.

Biting her lip, she stared down at her sleeping husband, then eased out of the bed. 'Twas long before dawn and the man she married was sleeping deeply, snoring gently, unaware that she was about to go against his word.

Mort, her dog, rose to follow her, but she shushed him and pointed back to the bed, where he reluctantly curled up again. The mutt's dark eyes followed her every move, and she prayed that he wouldn't bark or stir again. It was imperative that her husband not waken.

Mayhap there was something inherently wrong with her that she could not meekly accept a man's authority. Mayhap she'd been mistress of Calon, this very keep, too long, for though she loved her husband with all her heart, in this instance he was wrong. Perhaps dead wrong.

Morwenna wasn't going to take a chance with her sister's life. She slid into an old woolen tunic and dark mantle, then grabbed the pouch she'd tucked into a pocket earlier in the day. The coins within clinked a bit and she froze, certain that her husband would awaken. Hardly daring to breathe, she waited until his even snores assured her that even Pwyll, god of the underworld, could not waken him. Then, with a silent but stern order for the dog to remain upon the bed, Morwenna slipped out to the corridor.

A few candles smelling of tallow and sheep fat still burned in their sconces. They flickered as she passed, her movement disturbing the thin streams of black smoke that curled toward the ceiling. Stuffing her arms into her mantle, she crept down the stairs to the great hall, where one of the speckled dogs lifted his head before spying Morwenna and settling back with his mate near the dying fire.

She didn't have much time.

Soon the laborers would be rising, the servants drawing water, tending the fires, replacing the candles, and gathering eggs.

Pulling her hood over her head, she crept down a long hallway and past the kitchen to a door leading out to the garden. Outside a fine mist was falling, the winter air cool and wet, and she was careful to step on the flagstones leading past the dirt, where, in the spring, flowers and herbs would abound. Now the wet ground had only thorny remembrances of last year's roses and the scent of rain-washed rosemary as she brushed against the overgrown shrub's stiff branches.

Glancing skyward, she saw dark forms upon the curtain wall, the sentries guarding the keep. Their eyes were trained to the exterior of the castle walls and rarely would they search the bailey. Clutching her cloak, she hurried past through the garden gate to the chapel, which was still dark, the priest not yet risen for his morning prayers.

She slipped inside and hastily made the sign of the cross over her chest. Her prayers were fragmented and filled with doubt. Oh, that she was doing the right thing. Oh, that she wasn't lying. Oh, that she would learn to be an obedient wife.

'Twas never to be, of course.

In all her years she had never been able to accept authority without reason, forever unable to bend to any man's will, be that man her father or brother. She had spent all of her life trying to be equal to Kelan and Tadd, proving herself as a huntswoman, a swordswoman, and eventually ruler of her own keep. And now . . . now she was married to a man who loved her with all his heart, who listened to her counsel as if

she were a wise woman, who would die for her without thinking twice.

And yet she was going against his will.

"God help me."

Sadness seeped into her soul.

She thought of Bryanna and wondered where she was.
What was it that had driven her away? Bryanna had been so
evasive about the real reason she was leaving but she'd been
adamant. There had been no stopping her.

"As headstrong as an ox," their mother, Lenore, had often
muttered under her breath. No amount of shaming or locking
away or forced prayers had dampened Bryanna's spirit or de-
stroyed her independence.

And so she'd ridden away before Morwenna could get
word to their brother Kelan of Penbrooke, before she'd been
able to persuade Bryanna to take a guard and a companion . . .
and . . . oh, for the love of Morrigu. 'Twas too late. Closing
her eyes and dropping to her knees on the cold stone floor, she
whispered a quick prayer for her sister's safety. Then, fighting
back the uncertainty that nagged at her, she rose, genuflected
at the cross mounted high on the chapel wall, and hastened
outside to the thickening mist.

He would be waiting.

Morwenna had never been one to doubt herself, but never
had she felt forced to lie to those closest to her.

She rounded the corner of the chapel quickly and gasped
at the sight of him leaning against the wall, one shoulder
propped against the smooth stones. How ironic, she thought,
that he chose to meet here in the shadow of the chapel, this
devil of a man.

They did not speak.

There was no need for words.

They'd said enough already.

She handed him her pouch, the coins jingling within the
worn leather. She was turning away, when, quick as an asp
striking, he reached forward and encircled her wrist with his
good hand. The other arm remained at his side, still stiff from

a wound he'd received while trying to track the killer who had terrorized Castle Calon.

"Will this then be enough?" he hissed. "If I am to do your bidding, will that mean that at last my debt to you has been paid?"

She thought for a second of all the lies, all the betrayal, all the anger and lives lost because of this man. Looking toward the shadows of the chapel, she knew his list of sins was long. He had beaten his own brother and left him at death's door, though he'd recovered since then, with Morwenna's care. Carrick's charms were so enthralling that he had even seduced Morwenna herself years ago, teasing her into a passion, then abandoning her before dawn.

Morwenna longed to end all ties with this blackheart. And yet, he was the only man with the strength and courage to assure her sister's safety. "Just do as promised." Keeping her voice low, she withdrew her hand and stepped backward, creating distance between them. "'Tis all I ask."

"For now."

"Forever."

His smile flashed in the darkness. A crooked slash of white that accused her of the lie. "You cannot trust me, any more than I can trust you."

"Go to hell," she spat.

"Is that not where I am already?"

She was unmoved. "Mayhap." Steeling herself, she stepped toward him and stared into his handsome, shadowed face. "But 'tis a hell of your own making, is it not?"

She turned again and hastened back to the keep. Silently praying and hoping beyond hope that her husband had not roused, she half ran through the garden and into the entrance near the kitchen. Already boys scurried about gathering firewood. Some of the cows were making noise, their udders full, their bellies empty as they waited for the milkmaids.

Morwenna hurried up the back staircase, knowing deep in her soul that she'd just made a deal with the devil.

*   *   *

Once again the woman appeared to him . . . and he wasn't aware of how much time had passed between her visits. Had it been minutes, or was it hours, mayhap even days. Each time Gavyn would try to call out to her, but it was no use, his voice failed him, and he was quiet, falling deeper into a wave of darkness after the deadly umbra that had been following her dragged him down.

Be wary, he thought, though he could not speak, and as the visions passed his sleep was light, thin as parchment. He was vaguely aware of whispered voices all around him, aware of the pain in his shoulder, as searing as a white-hot blade thrust into his flesh.

And then cool hands.

The woman of his dreams?

Gently she administered a salve that took away the fire and pressed something to his lips . . . a drink. He sipped the brew she offered, but it tasted so foul that he coughed and spat, then cringed as a pain like no other cut through his chest.

Was he alive or dead?

Or in a netherworld somewhere between?

At times he smelled the scent of sizzling meat, and hunger pangs would attack him. Other times he recognized the acrid odor of urine and thought it might be his own. Often he was aware of the scent of sweat, and as chills would come to him and be burned off by great black waves of heat, he thought that the scents might be his own. Once in a great while there was music, an off-key humming that buzzed through his brain.

Someone tending to him.

His thoughts were short and sharp, like shards of broken pottery, and as they passed behind his eyes he caught only glimpses of his life, tiny fragments that made no sense. He knew he was lying on a straw bed of sorts, and as the days passed and some of the darkness subsided, he tried to swim through the mire that was his brain, attempting to open his eyes. But then she would appear upon her white jennet and the pain would ease and he would succumb to the gentle embrace of darkness. . . .

"See, he lives," a woman's voice from somewhere far away whispered through the veiled darkness. "Did I not tell you?"

"Aye, 'tis healing powers ye have, Vala." This time the voice was that of a man, a big man by the sound of it. "'Tis why I brought him to ye when I found him in the woods."

"Ye say he fell from the ridge?"

"Aye, that he did. But he was lucky, he was. His fall was broken by saplings and brush."

"Lucky?" She snorted as a scraping noise began and somewhere nearby a cow lowed. "If bein' half dead and chased by Lord Deverill's men is luck, then, aye, this one, he's got all the luck in the world. Seems as if our lad here has killed himself Deverill's sheriff."

"Then I would think he should be knighted rather than hanged."

"Mmm," the woman said as the scraping continued. "Mayhap. But look at him. His face . . . by the saints, I doubt he will ever look himself. His nose is broke, one cheek shattered. His eye, there. If he can see out of it, 'twill be a miracle. He might've been handsome once, but will be no longer."

Good, Gavyn thought, for then he would never be recognized. Though the pain scraped down his muscles and bones, he risked raising an eyelid just a fraction, so that he was peering through the brush of his eyelashes. Although the light in the hut was dim, it still hurt his eyes, but he was determined to get a glimpse of his saviors or captors. Vala was right; his vision was blurred, but he could make out shadows and light. Concentrating hard, he took in a woman seated at a table of sorts, her back to him, long dark hair braided so that it snaked to her waist. Vala was a scrawny thing, her plain tunic sagging from her body.

A man sat across from her, his feet stretched out toward a glowing fire. Chickens scratched across the dirt floor, and from the sounds of heavy breathing, a cow was trapped on the far side of the room, behind him, though he dared not twist his head to see.

"There is talk that the sheriff's killer is to be ransomed," she said, and Gavyn saw from her actions that she was sharpening a blade.

The man pulled at the graying strands of his beard, scratching his chin. "I like not to do business with Lord Deverill. The less he knows of us, wife, the better."

"Money is money, whether it comes from a rich man or a pauper."

"Blood money," the man muttered.

"Money we need, Dougal, bloody though it may be. Money we need." Her narrow back stiffened, and though she was but half her husband's size, 'twas evident she was the one who ruled this home. Gavyn sensed that, if there were money involved, this woman would see him returned to his father.

"And so that's it, is it, Vala?" Dougal said. "'Tis money that keeps you at his bedside. All this while I thought it might be because he's a handsome devil." He was smiling, teasing her.

"'Tis no joke," she said, lifting the big knife and pointing it across the table to wiggle at her husband's nose. "Finding this murderer in the ravine was a sign from God, that it was. We are to do the right thing, Dougal, and return him to the baron's justice."

"Then why nurse him to health?" Dougal's smile had faded.

"Because any fool knows that a wanted man is worth far more alive than dead. This way, the lord can mete out his own punishment, make a display of him, show the people of his keep that he's just and fair but will accept no man's treachery, not even his own son's."

Dougal's gaze shot to Gavyn. "He's the baron's son?"

"Bastard," she said, a little glee in her voice over gossip of the highest order. "Born by a peasant woman from Tarth . . . some say a witch."

"Christ Jesus."

"And that's not all." Though Gavyn had no view of her face, he heard the smile of satisfaction in her words. "Rumor has it the boy's mother was murdered by Deverill's own men."

"What?"

"Aye. Seems the Lord of Agendor planted his bastard seed in the woman from Tarth, sending the Lady of Agendor into a jealous fury, barren that she is."

Gavyn didn't so much as breathe. How dared this wench spread such rot about his mother? His mother, a seamstress from the north, had been a good woman, far too loyal for her horrific fate.

"What do I care of a scandal in Tarth, far to the north?" Dougal sputtered. "And 'twould not surprise me if the woman was slain at Deverill's hands. Best steer clear of anything involving the Lord of Agendor."

"Too late for that, with his bastard son under our roof. Leave it to me. Deverill will pay dearly to have his troublesome son in hand."

"I don't know . . . ," the husband said nervously.

"Leave it to me. This one is a wanted man. I haven't been caring for him for naught. Before we let him go, he'll fetch us a few pieces of silver."

'Twas morning. From the darkness of his chamber at Chwarel, Hallyd heard the cock crow once, twice, thrice . . . and then silence. There was movement in the keep, the ordinary morning sounds of shuffling feet and murmurings, even the damned dogs barking. Soon the bells of morn would ring in the chapel—a hollow peal that he detested each dawn and dusk, for it reminded him of the days when he'd portrayed himself as a man of God, a believer in the holy faith. It had been a sham, of course, one of the many falsehoods of his life. In the past sixteen years, as he'd been kept an unchained prisoner in his own castle, Hallyd had moments of regret.

He threw on a tunic and laced up his breeches, refusing to wait for the servant who would soon appear at his door with an irritating cheeriness that was like a rash on his skin. Was the man a moron? Always talking of what a great day it was to be, how busy he was, how interesting was this castle.

'Twas rot, and nothing more, Hallyd thought as he tugged on his own boots and remembered all too clearly why he'd been so punished, nearly blinded.

He'd been young and his ardor had run hot and rash. Mistakenly he'd thought he could force a witch's hand. Now, he knew, he first had to use trickery to gain what he wanted. Magick . . . the dark seduction his father had mastered. Fortunately, Vannora, the old one, had taught him well over the years, and he'd slowly shed his facade of godliness in favor of a darker visage.

Vannora's arts were of the most sinister form, the power she bestowed upon him a gift for so willingly giving up his soul.

She had arrived at his keep soon after he'd lost his battle with Kambria, and it was Vannora who had advised him ever since. She had become his mentor, his guide, and though he followed her counsel, he did not completely trust her. No doubt, she held on to some secrets, the darkest spells and curses from the Otherworld.

But even Vannora with all her dark arts had not been able to lift Kambria's curse. Only she who now held the dagger would be able to free him.

As he cinched his belt, key ring and scabbard around his waist, the scents of sizzling fish, deer, and fowl reached his nostrils. So the cook was already working, the kitchen boys rotating the spit where the carcasses were turning over the flames. A sweeter scent, that of yeast for the rising bread, drifted upward with the smell of smoke and pork fat. Soon the meal would be served, and his stomach rumbled as he imagined thick chunks of eel, pike, venison, and pigeon dipped in a thick stew.

This morning he would take his food here in his darkened chamber, by the fire. The shutters were in place, only bits of gray morning light sifting through the cracks, not enough to bother him, just enough to tantalize.

On cloudy days he was able to look through the slats and view the workers in the keep. From behind the shutters, Hallyd had seen them all, the greedy lot of them. He'd spied upon the armorer cleaning chain mail in barrels of sand. Hallyd had witnessed the man winnow out a little of the steel for himself when he'd thought no one was watching. Hallyd had also watched as one of the comeliest of the milkmaids filched a bucket of cream. He'd even observed the captain of the guard pissing against the side of the stables because he and the stable master had come to blows over the miller's daughter, a dark-haired vixen who flirted with every man in the keep.

The simple truth was that he could trust no one.

His spies were no better than the rest of those who supposedly served him. Paid to be his eyes and ears, they were at the very least lazy oafs, at the worst liars and cheats. Even Cael, the one who was reporting back to him about the witch, was not trustworthy.

He considered riding out himself and finding her, this witch-woman who held the key to his future. But, so far, he'd reined in his ardor rather than risk making the same mistake he had made sixteen years earlier.

So if you trust no one, what of the old hag? Do you have faith in her? Could she not be lying to you as well? She appears an emaciated woman, but you know better, do you not?

"Bloody hell," he growled and picked up the jug of blood that had been left in his chamber.

He pushed open the door to stride quickly down the long corridor, where the few candles still burning amid lingering smoke were not bright enough to hurt his eyes. His boot heels rang loudly as he made his way to the south staircase, where the steps spiraled downward five full flights from his chamber on the third floor. Down he hurried, not stopping at the solar on the second floor, nor the great hall on the first, where he heard servants setting up the trestle tables.

Instead he continued downward to the levels belowground, past the dungeons and vaults to the lowest tier, where darkness reigned and, he was certain, madness dwelled. No light from above ever reached these shadowy chambers. Water dripped from the ceilings to run down the inside walls and smoke from the candles curled upward to blacken the walls and ceiling. The sounds of the castle above were muted, as if from a distant land.

'Twas fitting, he thought as he walked along a narrow hallway that wound through a dungeon and several crypts. He descended the short flight of stairs that led downward to the chamber he sought, one that was forbidden to most.

Withdrawing a key, he unlocked the door to a private room where no one else was allowed. Hence the key and dead bolt. 'Twas not to keep the inhabitant locked within, for that was an impossible, laughable task, but rather to keep anyone else out, the contents of this chamber secret and sealed.

The room was lit by a few candles. At the northern end of the chamber was a table that served as an altar. A circle had been painted with lime around the table, and upon the plank top were candles, a chalice, a bell, and a wooden knife with a blackened hilt.

"You come for answers," an old voice said, and he saw her then, lying upon her small cot on the far side of the room. She looked to be a hundred years old, mayhap even a hundred and twenty. Her tiny body appeared even more withered than the last time he'd seen her, but that, he supposed, was to be expected. Her skin was wrinkled and thin as parchment over the bones of her face. Yet she rejected living anywhere but this cavern she called home and refused any attention from the physician. When Hallyd had last suggested it, she'd laughed, exposing her few snags of teeth.

"Ha! Have that idiot Cedrik study my body as if he can see what disease I carry? Would you have him read my piss? Or stick his hungry leeches upon my skin? Or purge my body with figs so that my insides would cramp for days?"

She'd snorted in derision at the thought and wagged a bony finger at Hallyd's face. "The most that fool will do is pull at his beard and frown and suggest that I'm dying, which, of course, I am. For the love of Cerridwyn, even the woodcutter's half-wit of a son could see that my days are short! Humph. Nay, do not call the physician. *Ever*."

"You're wasting away," he'd protested.

"'Tis this body's time," she'd said without regret, and he'd wondered at her simple acceptance of her fate. Were he the one about to step over the threshold to the next world, he doubted he would go so willingly.

But then she had powers he did not.

She understood the separation of spirit and carcass.

She breathed and lived without the need of bones and flesh. Perhaps her time was not as near as she predicted, for, though she seemed dedicated to him, how much could he really trust her? Wasn't she, like so many of the others, using him for her own gain?

Mayhap even this vision of her desiccated body was a trick of the mind.

"Ah, there you go doubting me again," she said with far more clarity than he thought possible. From beneath the folds of skin that were her eyelids, her pale gaze followed his movements as he skirted the altar and approached her cot. "You are here to see the future," she said.

"Aye."

"Always." She lifted a frail hand. "You've never learned to accept your fate."

He didn't respond. 'Twas true.

"You know that she, the Light, is coming."

He nodded, and though the old crone was near blind, living in this cave by her own desire, he knew she could see him. Until her dying breath, and mayhap even afterward, she would see more than a hundred men combined. Oh, that he had her vision. Her power. Aye, it had dwindled over time, but it was still stronger than most.

"I have felt it, yes. The disturbance."

"Mmm. And yet, you're impatient." She levered up on one elbow, the bedding falling away to expose her emaciated body even more. Though she wore a chemise, the linen did little to conceal the shriveling of her flesh, the sunken breasts where his own grandmother had nursed.

"I've waited a long time, Vannora."

She cackled, her laughter dry. "Not nearly as long as I have, Hallyd. Nay. And you will wait some more. She is on her way. There is no hurrying her. She has much to learn before you meet."

"You talk in circles."

"Hmm." She didn't argue, just pinned him with her odd, whitish eyes. They had always made him wary, and he'd often wondered, if Kambria's curse wasn't lifted soon, would his own lenses turn the color of thin milk? Or again, was her appearance but a trick of the mind? He'd never seen her drink the blood, but thought she might find vitality within the cup.

"You must be patient, Hallyd, for no curse can be lifted before 'tis time. Yours is soon." She crumpled the edge of her coverlet in her fingers and glanced at the ceiling. "As is mine. Now, pour." A smile flitted across her lips, as if she were thinking about her youth.

He did as he was bid, walking to the altar and, without crossing the white line with his feet, pouring the goat's blood he'd brought her. The servants never asked why, when an animal was slaughtered, he insisted upon two cups of blood before the cook claimed it for pudding. And he always brought it here to this altar, where he poured it into the empty bowl. Aside from her daily bit of wastel bread and a gruel made from oats and honey, 'twas all she asked for. Pages were instructed to bring the gruel and water to her door each day, and to leave a clean bucket after removing the bucket of excrement.

Everyone in the keep thought she was a prisoner.

Only he knew the truth, that he was more of a captive than she.

"Aside from honing your patience, you must also be wary," she advised, as if she were, indeed, witnessing events that had not yet occurred. "There are others who are waiting for her, wanting her, following her. They are as eager as you are, and mayhap more determined and deadly."

He didn't believe her. No one could want her more than he. No one could have been as patient as he. No one had been as cursed as he.

Except for her.

CHAPTER FOUR

Bryanna sat at the edge of a stream. Twilight had nestled into the woods and the wind had died. For the past three nights, she'd slept on her own, with the forest and night surrounding her. And she'd waited.

For Isa.

For a vision.

For words of encouragement.

And she'd heard nothing but the soft sough of the wind rattling through brittle branches.

'Twas as if she'd made a horrendous mistake.

"Warts and wattle," she muttered. She leaned into the darkness and used the small net she'd brought along to forage for unsuspecting fish, frogs, and eels that she could gut and roast on a spit over the fire. Her stomach rumbled and she tried not to think of the cook's roast pheasant or custards or mincemeat on wastel bread thick with butter as she dragged her net through the dark, rippling waters.

She'd made no sense of the doeskin map for the past week, and yet she was certain if she were to figure it out, she would understand her mission.

But what of a child?

She managed to catch a couple of fat toads and a small trout. She killed them quickly, scraping out the innards and roasting them over the small fire. Alabaster stood nearby, a hind hoof cocked as she slept tethered to an old withered tree.

Tomorrow she would ride again.

But to where?

Bryanna stretched the map upon a smooth stone, turning it this way and that, trying to read the symbols upon the ragged deerskin as grease from the fish and frog legs sizzled against the hot coals.

Where was Calon on this pathetic map? None of the jagged lines resembled the place she'd lived with her sister for the past few months. What of her home at Penbrooke?

Where was Wybren, the keep not far from Calon, where a horrid fire had swept through the castle at night, taking the lives of the lord's family? Bryanna knew it well, for Morwenna had wed one lucky enough to have escaped the deadly flames that night, and yet she could not find it on this map.

Where was any other place she might recognize?

"'Tis a mystery," she said to Alabaster, though the horse didn't so much as twitch her gray tail in response. "Aye, not much do you care."

Still considering the etchings upon the piece of deer hide, she ate her fill, then walked out to the night again, pausing to take in the utter stillness. No breath of wind whooshing through the canyon, no flap of a night owl's wing.

The calm before the storm.

Bryanna shuddered as she thought of it.

"Do not trust the great tranquillity," Isa had said as she'd undone the knots of Bryanna's pathetic attempts at embroidery when she was but a child at Penbrooke. While her brothers were outside practicing their huntsmanship with targets set up against piles of straw, Bryanna was inside, forced to do embroidery or learn about healing herbs.

Her mother had been forever scolding Bryanna for her many transgressions. There was the time she'd been seen riding astride her brother's favorite steed with "a ruffian" of a stable boy. On another occasion she'd been caught stealing the tarts cook had set on the windowsill to cool. Once her older sister had discovered her hiding in the apothecary's hut, spying upon the man as he mixed his herbs. But mayhap her worst crime was when she'd donned the priest's robes and pretended to baptize her younger sister, Daylynn, which sent her mother to her bed and Father Barton into finding a multitude of ways for Bryanna to perform penance.

Bryanna knew her punishments could have been far worse. The stable boy had been whipped in front of her, taking lashes upon his bare back without so much as crying out. Bryanna had cried out for the stable master to halt, but he'd simply paused to glare at her while Morwenna tugged her arm and bade her be quiet.

After that Bryanna cringed with each crack of the man's snakelike whip. Red welts formed on the lad's muscular back, and, she noted, they were not the first. Other scars told of previous floggings. The miscreant, three years older than she, sent her a triumphant look as he'd been led away, his gray eyes red and shining, but no tears drizzling down a face still devoid of whiskers. He'd been banished from Penbrooke forever, sent away with nothing but the clothes upon his ravaged back.

Bryanna had felt a semblance of gratitude that she was not subjected to such severe punishments, though her mother always lamented that "willful Bryanna" needed to be reared with a strong hand. Already worried because of Bryanna's invisible friends, Lenore had been mortified at her daughter's unladylike actions.

Eventually, it was decided that the troublesome child would be relegated to Isa's care. This suited the old nursemaid well, for she was always telling Bryanna she was special, that someday her gift would be known. That is, if she quit flirting with boys of all stations, for Isa had been concerned that her young charge, soon to bud into a woman, was developing too keen an interest in the opposite sex.

At the time, Bryanna refused to believe her nursemaid. She stewed on the edge of her bed, watching in boredom as Isa's old hands worked relentlessly, cutting out the twists and pulling at the threads of her wretched and halfhearted attempt at embroidery.

"What's the great tranquillity?" she'd asked, pulling at the twists of wool appearing through the worn coverlet.

"The calm, 'tis but a ruse of Arawn, a way to set you at ease, make you forget your wariness." Isa had snapped the embroidery thread with her teeth, then turned away from her work to stare Bryanna straight in the eye. "'Tis the time when you should be most vigilant. Trust me."

Now, with Isa's words reverberating through her brain, Bryanna felt an icy cold deep as a winter snow seep into her soul. She walked to the stream and washed the grease from her hands. There in the darkness, with the water rippling beneath her fingers, she heard Isa's voice.

"He comes for you."

Bryanna looked up at the night sky. "Who, Isa? Who comes for me?"

"The father of your child."

"My child? But, Isa, I have borne no babe," Bryanna said, shaking her head. Why was Isa talking in such strange riddles? "You are mistaken."

"Be ever watchful," Isa said as clearly as if she were standing next to Bryanna.

"Of whom? Why?"

But Isa's voice said no more, and Bryanna felt as if ghostly fingers had played upon the back of her neck. She turned quickly, peering into the shadowy thickets where she sensed unseen eyes watching her, waiting in the dark.

'Tis nothing, she tried to tell herself. And yet, the dead woman's words had shaken her. Whether it was truly a voice or her own madness, from this point forward Bryanna would be looking over her shoulder.

Gavyn could continue the ruse no longer.

Too many times the woman, Vala, had nearly caught him watching her, watching and waiting for his moment to escape. And then there was the difficulty of lying so still his muscles ached and cramped all the more.

Nay, he had to escape this night, after the man and woman

had finished with their mating and were fast asleep. He could no longer chance that the couple would decide to cart him to his father's castle.

Escape would be difficult, as the woman was forever nearby. She never went far without leaving her husband in the hut as, Gavyn decided, some kind of guard. His ribs still ached as if a mule had kicked him hard in the side, but he felt the welts and bruises upon his body healing, just as the woman had said.

He heard the door of the hut open and close swiftly, with a thud that shook the rafters. The smell of rainwater and fresh earth mingled with the scents of burning wood and cow dung. Gavyn allowed his eyes to open the merest of slits to see what was happening.

Dougal was unwinding a scarf from his neck and walking across the packed dirt floor to the fire pit, where he warmed his hands. "'Tis time to get rid of him," he said without warning.

Vala, who'd spent part of the morning milking the cow and separating the cream while humming off-key, lost what remained of her good mood. Her voice was tight. "As I've been sayin' to ye, it won't be long now. . . . See how he's healing?" Vala went on, and he assumed she was pointing at him lying upon the straw. "Even with his beard, ye can see his face again, finally recognize him if ye know what ye're looking for. Aye, he be the baron's bastard. I supposed he looked jest like the old man before his face was mashed, and now that he's healing you can see a bit of resemblance. No wonder the baron lifted many a skirt in his youth. Look at him. He's ugly as sin now, but if ye imagine him healed, his nose straight, his cheek full, the scars running down his face and the bruising gone, he would be a handsome one."

"Handsome? Bah! Is that why ye keep him here, eh, Vala? Ye like the looks of him?" Dougal was standing at the fire, picking at his teeth with the tip of a knife. Across from him, Vala sat on a stool with the butter churn between her legs.

"Not the way he looks now." She laughed, a wicked

chortle. "But aye, if he looked like I think he did, I wouldn't mind him warmin' my bed. Eyes as gray as the king's silver, hair as black as a raven's wing . . . aye, he could slide between my sheets any time."

" 'Tis vulgar, ye are."

"Am I now? Well, if ye want to know the truth, I keep him because he's more valuable as the days wear on, now, isn't he? The baron, his men, have been looking for the body, scouring the weeds and thickets and creek beds. Over a week and they blame the canyon for swallowing him. Berth, she told me at the well just this morning that there's a price upon his head now, and that the soldiers who've been looking for the body not only think him dead, they believe that a pack of wolves or a wild boar or bear dragged off the carcass to gnaw on it. But Baron Deverill is not convinced. He keeps sending hunters and soldiers out there to search."

The paddles in the butter churn clacked loudly as the cow stirred behind him, breathing loudly. Gavyn had to strain to hear the conversation, but he recognized the smile in Vala's voice. She was proud of herself, thinking she had outwitted the Lord of Agendor.

Gavyn doubted she knew how ruthless his father could be. Having him here, hiding him, was not only dangerous but foolhardy.

"Then we should take him to the baron," Dougal said.

"Not until the price is higher. Just a wee bit higher." Vala chuckled again, already counting her silver.

"And what if the lord finds out we've been hiding him, eh? What then? What good will all the silver in Wales be when we're accused of treason? Hanging from the hangman's noose? Locked in the pillory? What then, Vala?"

"Shh . . . We just say that we did not recognize him. That a traveler dropped him on our door, claiming that the man was his wounded brother, then stole off into the night. We had naught to do but care for him, never thinking him to be the wanted man. We be but simple peasants, Dougal, remember that. And ye were never in Agendor's woods, do ye hear me? You were never hunting a stag or boar on the lord's property!"

"Ach! 'Tis bothering me."

"Oh, fer the love of God. Hold yer tongue a few more days. 'Tis all I ask, and don't ye be confessin' to Father Peter. I do not trust the man."

"He's a priest, for the love of God."

"And that be the problem. Methinks he loves himself more than the Holy Father."

There was a long silence when even the butter churn had stopped its clacking. "Do not tell me that you have already confessed your sins to him, Dougal. I know that he passed by here yesterday morn on his return to Agendor Castle."

More silence, and Gavyn imagined the husband worrying the edge of his cap.

"Oh, by the saints, Dougal, what have ye done?" Her harsh whisper was rising in pitch. "We'll be locked away in chains surely and—"

"Not if we turn him in to the guards at Agendor on the morrow. We could leave in the morn and be there by night-fall," Dougal said desperately. "I promised Father that we would turn in the man we thought might be Gavyn. Because 'tis true, Vala, we know not who he really is. And just now, as ye said, as his wounds have healed, we suspect that we've been lied to by a man who left him here." He was talking rapidly, his plan forming as he spoke, as if in so doing he could make things right with his wife.

"Ye're a fool, Dougal, and I don't know why I ever married ye in the first place." She began churning butter again, but the silence between husband and wife was deafening.

Gavyn worried that neither would sleep a wink.

It mattered not.

The dream had come to him again last night, the woman upon the white mare racing through the clouds. The darkness at her heels was closer to her now and gaining fast. He knew not what the dream meant, perhaps nothing more than the

results of the bitter concoction Vala forced down his throat
each evening, but he considered the dream an omen.

Tonight, no matter what the risk, he would attempt his escape.

"What is it that makes a marriage strong?" the Baron of
Calon asked his wife as she was unclasping her tunic.

They were alone in the chamber, the fire hissing, sleet
pounding at the battlements and shuttered windows. Cold air
caressed Morwenna's skin as she stepped out of her clothes,
hung them upon a peg, and slid into the bed next to the man
she loved.

"Love?" she replied around a yawn.

"Then what is it that makes love strong?"

She turned to him, propping her body upon one elbow, her
hair falling over one shoulder to brush his chest. "What is
this? Some kind of riddle? A word game?"

Playfully, she ran a finger down his breastbone, through
the mat of dark hair covering his chest. Her fingertip encountered scars, wounds that had healed not long ago when he'd
been here, in her keep, while he'd battled for his life. She
hadn't expected him to live, much less that she would fall in
love with him or marry him. Yet she was his bride. And now,
all the questions about love and marriage? 'Twas not like him.

"No game, Morwenna," he said, and she saw that he was
troubled, his blue eyes dark with concern. "I think that marriage is based on trust."

"Except when one is betrothed by one's parents," she said,
still trying to jolly him out of his foul mood.

"But that was not the case in our union," he said flatly,
without a trace of his usual affection.

"Of course."

"And so there would be no room for lies, would there?"

The first hint of anxiety slithered into her brain. "Of course
not."

"No need to sneak off behind each other's backs."

She realized then that he knew. Somehow he'd found out

about her clandestine meeting behind the chapel. Should she lie her way out of it? Even try to turn the tables and belittle him for doubting her? 'Twas not her way. But then, neither had been the deception.

The air between them seemed suddenly cold, as if they existed on opposite sides of a frigid river. "It would be best if there were never lies, even the smallest untruth between a man and woman," she said carefully. "But sometimes, so as not to worry the other, a man, or a woman, might be inclined to . . . protect the other."

"Protect?" He sneered the word and she cringed. Oh, this was not going well.

"I saw you the other night, Morwenna. With *him*."

She closed her eyes. "'Twas not what it seemed," she admitted, flopping down on the bed to stare upward at the canopy. Her fingers clenched into fists and she mentally kicked herself to hell and back again.

"It seemed as if you were meeting your lover."

"Nay! You, husband, are my true love."

"Then why lie, Morwenna? Why steal from the treasury? Why meet a man deep in the night and sneak back into our bed with hands and feet as cold as adultery."

"I would never betray you."

"You already have."

"I didn't lie to you."

"Avoiding the truth is the same."

His voice was hard, without emotion. There would be no talking her way out of it. "'Twas not about me," she admitted, "but Bryanna."

When the silence still stretched between them, she added, "I'm worried about her. She's alone. I—I wanted someone to look after her, to find her, to see that she is all right." Sighing, she took his hands and linked her fingers through his. "'Tis true, I paid him to look for her, but I've also sent a messenger to Kelan, at Penbrooke, to ask for my brother's help. I thought he, or Tadd, or someone there might search for her."

"You couldn't ask me?"

"I did ask," she reminded him gently. "And you said that it was Bryanna's choice to go alone, to find her way, to follow her destiny."

"Because that is what she told us she wanted."

"'Twas not what *I* wanted."

"You are not your sister's keeper," he said, and she felt the anger radiating from him.

"But you are mine?"

"Nay, Morwenna, but I am your husband and I expect you to be truthful with me."

"And to obey you?" she asked, and just saying the word rankled.

"To trust me," he said.

Grabbing the edge of the coverlet, she rolled over and turned her back to him. "That works two ways, husband. Trust must come from two like hearts." She seethed and closed her eyes, wanting to be angry and fight with him, but they both knew that she had, in fact, betrayed him by turning to his brother, Carrick. Morwenna had turned to the one man who shared a dark past with both of them. Carrick had been Morwenna's first lover, the first man she'd given herself to. He'd left her with nothing but anger and regret . . . and a babe she'd lost before its time. Aye, those were the sorrowful days of her youth.

And yet Carrick was her husband's brother. Could her husband not trust his own kin?

Granted, Carrick was the bad seed of his family. Until recently, many had believed him responsible for starting the fire that had killed his own family as they lay asleep within the walls of Castle Wybren. During their recent troubles here at Calon, Carrick had been somewhat vindicated. At least he was not guilty of setting his own family afire. And yet the black-hearted Carrick had committed a long list of transgressions: stealing his brother's own wife, leaving Morwenna pregnant, beating his own brother and abandoning him at death's door. Aye, Carrick was guilty of many a crime, though in this instance Morwenna suspected his intentions were more noble. Had she not sensed a new light in his blue eyes . . . a longing to be redeemed? Had she imagined it?

And what of Carrick's well-honed skills as a huntsman? Could her husband not see that there was no better man to track and protect her sister? In his ruthlessness, Carrick was strong and able; he would not abandon his mission until he had won.

And that was the sort of steely determination Morwenna needed to ensure her sister's well-being. Despite her husband's fury, Morwenna held fast to her conviction that she had done the right thing in hiring Carrick.

Clenching her fists beneath the coverlet, she stared into the darkness and imagined her sister's pale face and fiery red hair. "Godspeed, Bryanna," she whispered. "Godspeed."

CHAPTER FIVE

Bryanna had tried. Oh, by the gods, she'd tried. She had kept at her work, practicing her runes and spells at night, wondering if they worked, for she saw no evidence of magick at her hand. Each day she rode ever northward toward the mountains, looking for some landmark, for anything she would recognize on the bit of deer hide.

And all the while she'd felt that she was being followed.

As surely as if she'd seen a dark presence, she'd sensed someone watching her. She told herself that she was being silly, falling victim to her own worries of riding alone. And yet, she couldn't stop the hairs from rising on the back of her neck when she'd caught a glimpse of shadow on sunlight.

She'd come upon polecats, even surprised a fox chasing a hare through the bracken, but this was more than a simple forest creature on the hunt. Whatever it was that followed her was deeply malevolent, intrinsically evil; she felt the vibrations of sin deep in her heart when she sensed his presence.

'Tis Arawn, riding upon his pale horse with his white hounds accompanying him, she told herself. *He is coming for you, for your soul. Be wary.*

Now, as she sat at the fire, holding her cloak tight around herself, she felt not only hunger but despair. Her ears and eyes strained as she stared into the gloom, searching for a glimpse of the beast of darkness.

But she saw nothing.

"Think not on it," she whispered, trying to bolster her wavering confidence. Shivering, she rubbed her arms, then unsheathed the dagger. 'Twas not much of a weapon, but it would have to do.

She trained her eyes on the fire, where golden flames licked a mossy log and smoke rose to the heavens. Where was the enlightenment? The knowledge that would elevate her consciousness so that she could heal the sick, predict the future, or cast and lift curses?

She was torn, her faith stretched and thin. As a child she had been raised to believe in the Christ, the son of God. She'd spent hours upon her knees on the cold stones of the chapel. She'd learned to fear Satan, ready to tempt the most pious of souls.

But also Isa had taught her of another way, one that did not dismiss the Christ child, but did stray from the teachings of the church. Isa's faith was a wonderful blend of magick and spells, visions and healing. Her faith had room for all the gods and goddesses of the old ones. Morrigu, the Supreme Goddess of all, was always at Isa's side and she prayed to her.

As a child, Bryanna had melded the two, believing a bit of one and sewing it into the fabric of the other, learning from Father Barton at Penbrooke, and Isa, as well.

And now Bryanna feared that she had made a horrible mistake.

She could not possibly be a sorceress. Her faith was not strong enough. She was too weak. The old nursemaid had been wrong about her.

"Isa!" Bryanna railed in frustration, and from the stillness her voice echoed back at her, mocking her despair. "For the love of Morrigu, talk to me."

When she heard nothing, she stared at the crumpled piece of doeskin in her fist. This map, if that was what it was, made no sense whatsoever. She tossed down the doeskin and nearly spat upon it. What did it matter what the map said if she couldn't read it?

*　　*　　*

"And you know this how?" the Lord of Agendor asked the pathetic priest standing before him. He was tired and ready for bed when Father Peter, named after Christ's most trusted disciple, had imposed upon him.

'Twas odd.

But then so was the priest.

Not trustworthy.

Father Peter was a fleshy man with a hooked nose, weak chin, and absolutely no spine whatsoever. His piety was questionable, his loyalty always in doubt. Yet here he was, in the great hall of Agendor, as if he had some pressing news to impart, or his own conscience to clear.

Deverill waved him into the other chair, one with shorter legs to ensure that no one ever sat taller than the baron.

The priest took the seat gratefully and eyed a platter of cheese, dried prunes, and jellied eggs as hungrily as did the castle dogs who lay near the fire, watching each bite that went into the lord's mouth.

"A cup for the priest," Deverill said to a page who had refilled his goblet with wine. He noticed the tiniest of smiles upon the thin lips of this supposed man of God. "Now tell me, Father, in great detail, what it is you think you know."

And the priest did. As he gulped wine and stuffed himself with cheese, bread, and eggs, Father Peter explained that he'd spoken to a man—not during confession, of course—about a wounded man who'd shown up at Dougal the farmer's hut nearly a fortnight hence. The man was near dead, to hear Dougal tell it, and without the nursing of his wife, Vala, would not have lived.

"She be a witch, then?" Deverill stated.

"Oh, nay, nay, a pious, God-fearing woman is Vala." The priest shook his head and swiped at a few crumbs that had fallen onto his cassock.

The three dogs were on their paws in an instant, growling at each other, the largest bitch grabbing the morsel.

"Sit!" Deverill ordered, and the mongrels, snarling just a bit, their silvery-black hackles still stiff, returned to their place by the fire. "Miserable curs," he said, though in truth he loved the dogs, mayhap more than he did his most recent and decidedly barren wife.

"Vala has a talent, a gift from God in aiding the sick, but I assure you, m'lord, she does not practice the dark arts, nor dabble in the ways of the old ones."

"Then let us visit her."

"Now?" the priest said.

"If 'tis true and she's hiding the traitor, then we shall arrest him." Deverill snapped his fingers at a page. "Tell the stable master to prepare my horse and alert the captain of the guard that I need five men to ride with me."

"But, m'lord," the priest protested, obviously distraught, "I was given this information in confidence, and Dougal promised to surrender his . . . prisoner on the morn."

"No need to wait then, is there? You said yourself, you did not tell me of another man's confession. So there is naught to fear, for you've broken none of your vows."

The priest blanched.

Serves the pious liar right, Deverill thought, already on his feet. Sensing his excitement, the dogs swarmed around him as he ordered the servants to fetch his mantle, sword, and boots. A thrill of excitement sizzled through his blood. If the priest were telling the truth and Dougal had not just been bragging, then, at last, here was a chance to bring Gavyn to justice.

His back teeth clenched hard as he considered his bastard son, the result of many a night spent with a comely seamstress who lived on the outskirts of Agendor. True, as a young man he'd planted his seed wherever he saw fit. 'Twas his grave misfortune that the one bastard child he knew of, the only fruit of his loins, would prove to be a defiant scallywag.

Even as a youth, Gavyn had been a thorn in his side. The boy had resisted Deverill's help, refusing to catch a few coins tossed his way, never meeting Deverill's eye. Were his mother not so engaging, Deverill would have flogged the boy himself, more than once. But Ravynne with her ebony hair and silver eyes . . . how they'd rutted through many a night.

Deverill's lust for the boy's mother had roiled for years. At times, he thought it might be the death of him, as Ravynne had taken her son far from Agendor, forcing Deverill to ride north to Tarth or off to Penbrooke to quench his voracious need for her.

Aye, it had all ended badly, with his fair but barren wife, Marden, interceding. Recognizing Deverill's keen lust for the seamstress, Marden had gone behind his back and ordered Ravynne dead. And that fool Craddock had carried out her wishes.

Damn them all! Ravynne's death had riled the boy beyond reason. 'Twas nearly two years ago and now Gavyn, a man of twenty years, had wrought a vengeance most violent on the sheriff of Agendor. With Craddock's murder, Gavyn had forced his hand, leaving Deverill no choice but to punish the murderer. Now, at last, Gavyn would be caught, finally brought to justice. His mockery of Deverill would be put to rest.

Over the priest's weak protests, Deverill yanked on his gloves and strapped on his scabbard, then slid his favorite sword into its sheath. Once his boots were pulled over his leggings, he was out the door, stepping into the brisk wintry night. Most of the huts were dark. Only the coals at the farrier's forge burned red in the night. His boots crunched through puddles that had already iced over as he strode along the path.

Hunting had always been his favorite pastime, and he loved it best when the quarry proved a challenge.

His bastard son had shown himself to be more than a worthy opponent.

Through the fog, her lover came to Bryanna. Dressed as a hunter and riding upon a dark horse, he appeared through the mist. He was tall, his shoulders wide, his face obscured in the darkness, and yet she knew he was the one for whom she'd been waiting all her life.

"You have the dagger."

It was not a question, but she answered anyway. "Aye, 'tis mine."

"And the jewels?"

"I've yet to find them."

"You are traveling north." He dismounted, but try as she might to view the features of his face, she saw nothing but shadows from his hood and the ever-thickening fog. "For the opal."

"Yes." Of course.

"And once you find it, you'll go east?"

"East?" she repeated, but as she said the single word, she understood a new meaning to the ancient riddle:

An opal for the northern point,
An emerald for the east,
A topaz for the southern tip,
And a ruby for the west. . . .

All the while she'd thought the mention of points on a map indicated the placement of the missing jewels in the hilt of the dagger, for surely there were holes where they had once been inset. Now, she had a new perspective, a new path to follow.

"Yes," she said as she realized he was waiting for her to speak. "First I'll travel north, then east. . . ."

"So you do understand." He advanced upon her, this huntsman, his face still obscured. Though she could not recognize him and knew not his name, she felt no fear of him, even welcomed him to this, her small camp in the woods.

Before she could look into his eyes, strong arms surrounded her. She didn't protest, didn't fight. Her own arms circled his neck, her fingers finding the strident cords at the back of his neck as the wind seemed to rise, swirling through the canyon. He leaned over, bending her back, her hair nearly brushing the barren ground.

Cold, eager lips found hers and he kissed her so hard she could barely find her breath. She heard only the wildly pulsing beat of her own heart, felt the first warm yearnings of desire curl through her blood.

His tongue slid between her teeth, gently teasing as his hands moved against her back, kneading and holding her close. He buried his face in the cleavage of her breasts and her blood ran hot with a newfound desire. She wanted more of him and her fingers dug into the muscles of his back as his hot, wet breath brushed against her bare skin.

"I want you," he whispered, and his lips caressed the top of a breast.

The wind began to whine and the first stars of the night were visible through the cold wintry haze.

By the gods, she ached for him.

As if understanding her need, he stripped down her bodice, exposing her skin. Goose bumps rose on her flesh. Her nipples puckered in the icy night air. But inside she was heating, warming to the touch of his body, the smell of his musk.

She knew there was no turning back.

This man of the shadows, a familiar stranger, unlaced her tunic, pulling it to the ground. Then, kissing her, he untied her chemise to let it puddle around her.

"Who are you?" she asked, as he untied his breeches and over the moan of the wind, so soft it was barely discernible, she heard the cry of a babe.

"You know."

Of course she did, but she couldn't call up his name as he turned her, and the infant's muted cry again reached her ears.

"Wait," she said as his hands surrounded her, holding her breasts. But the crying stopped and he pressed hard against her from the rear, parting her legs. Bracing himself against the bole of a tree, he drove, drove deep into the most feminine part of her.

She gasped.

He thrust again.

Oh, by the saints, her mind was spinning. Surely that was not a child crying, surely her mind was playing tricks upon . . . Oh God, he slid out only to push hard again.

She melted against him, hot and malleable and breathing with difficulty as he moved back and forth, in and out, his rhythm and breathing slow and hard at first, then faster and faster, to a frantic pace as the forest and sky began to spin around her.

"Oh, sweet Morrigu," she cried, feeling as if she might collapse. With a final thrust, he let out a yell that pierced the night. Her body jerked in release, and as she panted in his arms, jewels rained from the starlit sky.

Opals, shimmering with the color of the moon.

Emeralds verdant as a forest.

Topaz as bright and sparkling as the sun.

And finally rubies, dark and deep, the color of blood, pouring to her feet, the sharp edges cutting her skin as her lover scraped aside her hair and pressed a sharp gem into the tender skin of her neck.

Bryanna's eyes flew open. She lay inside the cleft in the rock, a small recess that was not much of a cave. The fire was still burning, the embers bright in the night, the flames low and hissing against the charred wood. Her heart was still knocking wildly, her skin moist with sweat, though now that she was fully awake she shivered.

The dream had been so real, so vivid. Lying against the smooth leather of her saddle, Bryanna rubbed her arms and searched the darkness, seeing only Alabaster, a ghostly mare tied to a nearby tree. Nothing was out of place. Nothing was disturbed.

And yet the dream lingered. Who was the huntsman who had been her lover? Why had she trusted him? How had he known about the jewels and her dagger? Had she really heard a baby crying over their cries of passion? Why had she so eagerly given herself to a faceless man, who, in the end, had turned on her? She touched the back of her neck and withdrew her hand. Upon her fingers was the slightest trace of blood.

Hers?

She cringed as she remembered the dream. . . .

Swallowing hard, she told herself that she had, no doubt, scratched herself in her sleep. That was all. Mayhap she'd dozed against a spot where a rock's edge was sharp, or a tiny branch from one of the trees had blown against her neck.

Why then had her hair not protected her from the cut?

"Bother and broomsticks," she whispered, feeling as if the timberland were truly closing in on her. It was then she realized she was holding her dagger, as she did each night as she fell asleep. Turning the blade over in her hand, she wondered who had crafted it so long ago and what had happened to its precious stones. Were they cast to the four winds as the dream, nay, the *prophecy* had foretold?

Sweet Mother, was that what the dream had been? An omen? A vision into the future? *Her* future?

Bitter dread gripped her heart.

What, in the name of Morrigu, had she gotten herself into?

"Trust in yourself." Isa's voice rang through the woods and echoed in her mind. *"'Tis almost time. You've learned much, daughter. By nightfall two days hence, you will come to a keep. 'Tis the castle of your mother."*

"My mother?" Bryanna repeated, disgusted. "Nay, Isa, I've been traveling far from where my mother was born."

But Isa's voice was still again, and Bryanna glanced behind her, certain that she was being watched.

By the spirit of her old nursemaid?

Or by someone else?

Some*thing* else.

She swallowed hard as the wind turned before ebbing to nothing. 'Twas as if a demon's cold breath had whispered over her skin.

The sounds of the night were suddenly still.

The frogs had stopped their croaking, the wind had ceased to rattle the bare branches, and the insects were no longer singing their night songs. Even the brook, rushing nearby, sounded muted and quiet, as if afraid to ripple over its stones.

Morrigu, be with me.

The flesh on the back of her scalp crinkled in warning.

As she whispered a spell for protection, she fingered the amulet she wore around her neck, a bloodred stone worn smooth from Isa's old fingers rubbing it for years.

Something evil was out there in the darkness.

Watching.

Waiting.

Ready to strike.

Her insides turned to ice and she reached for her dagger, though she knew in her heart that this foe was more than a mere mortal; a simple knife could not stop whatever it was that had the power to quiet the forest.

Nor, she feared, could she.

He waited until the rustling of the straw mattress had abated and the husband's snoring was even and steady. Gavyn chanced opening one eye. The fire had all but died and 'twas nearly dark within the long room, the tiniest hint of red embers giving him enough sight to ease off the bed. In a flash he was across the room, reaching for his tattered clothes hanging on a peg near the door. One of the chickens clucked loudly and he froze, hand on the latch.

The snoring stopped, interrupted. Gavyn didn't so much as breathe and quietly counted his own heartbeats. There was a snuffling sound as the man snorted noisily, then the rustle of straw as he changed position. Gavyn waited, slowly letting out his breath, hoping the damned hen had settled onto her roost in the rafters again and that the woman hadn't awakened. As he did, he heard another noise, the sound of hoofbeats fast approaching. In the dark of the night?

Why?

For you. They are coming for you.

All the spit dried in his mouth.

He could no longer hide.

Quickly, he stole the man's hunting knife and sheath, always left on the table, along with the quiver, arrows, and bow that hung by the door. Quietly, he opened the latch. He grabbed the shovel without a sound and, closing the door behind him, slid into the shadow of the night. His legs weren't steady, for the few times he'd been able to walk around the hut when no one was inside hadn't prepared his muscles and bones for this. The air was clear, no cover of fog to hide him.

Time and safety were quickly running out.

The horsemen were closer, the thunder of hooves shaking the ground.

Flattening himself against the exterior wall at the side of the hut, his fingers gripping the handle of the shovel, he heard the hoofbeats slow. Horses snorted, leather creaked, and bridles jingled in the night.

He raised the shovel, ready to use it as a club.

"You, Reece! Stand guard." A man's muffled voice cut through the night. Gavyn recognized it. 'Twas the Baron of Agendor.

His father.

Guts twisting, he waited.

"The rest of you, with me . . . and aye, that means you, Father," Deverill instructed.

"But, m'lord, nay. 'Tis not my duty—" His thin voice began to whine.

"Hush! 'Twas you who brought the news to me that my son was hiding here, was it not, Father Peter? Let's find out just how much truth there be in it."

Gavyn's jaw clenched. Was there no escape?

Ears straining, he heard the men dismount, then the sharp pounding of a fist upon the door.

"Dougal, open up," the gruff voice of one of the guards yelled through the thick panels of the door. " 'Tis the Lord of Agendor."

No response.

"Dougal! Open up or I'll break down yer door, I will. The baron, he's come to talk with ye."

"Wha—" A groggy man's voice from within.

"Oh, by the saints." The woman sounded fully awake. And frightened out of her mind.

Gavyn heard more anxious whispers that he couldn't understand. More rustling and a gasp. No doubt they'd discovered him missing. He slung the quiver and bow over one shoulder.

"What do ye want?" Dougal asked.

"Shhh," the woman whispered, distress evident in her voice. Gavyn eased closer to the front of the hut.

"Dougal, do you not hear me?" the soldier tried again. "Open the—"

"Hell!" His father's voice again.

"Oh, dear God . . . ," Vala wailed.

Crash!

The latch of the door broke free. Heavy footsteps pounded into the tiny cottage.

"Where's your prisoner?" Deverill's voice now. Gavyn edged to the front of the hut. The door hung open, horses stirring nearby.

"Me what?" Dougal repeated. "A prisoner, ye say? As ye can plainly see, there's no one here but me and me wife. I've no—"

Crash!

Something, mayhap a stool, was flung hard against the wall. Vala screamed.

Gavyn risked peering around the edge of the building. The one guard left outside was astride a tall steed, leaning toward the open door to observe the confrontation inside. The other animals shuffled restlessly but remained close.

"Where the hell is he?" the baron hissed as chickens clucked and the woman began to mewl. Gavyn didn't want to consider what kind of force his father and the men might use to get to the truth as he eased from his hiding space and slipped between two of the horses in the darkness. The animals were nervous, but the guard didn't notice as Gavyn loosened first one cinch, then another.

"Ye need some help, Lord Deverill?" the guard called as the scuffle inside escalated. Gavyn slunk away from the horses, far enough that he had room to swing, and just as the guard turned . . . "Hey—what the devil?"

Gavyn struck. Rounding, he swung the shovel hard and bashed the guard across the midsection.

"Oof!" The soldier grabbed wildly. "M'lord!" he cried. The horse squealed, rearing, and Deverill's guard toppled to the ground, hitting hard. "Hey!" he cried, but Gavyn had already swung into the saddle of his father's dark steed. "Thief!" he yelled at the top of his lungs. "Nay! Halt! Oh, bloody Christ! Lord Deverill!"

Men shouted and boots thudded as Deverill and his company filed out of the hut. But the sounds were already fading as Gavyn leaned over the big stallion's neck, pushing the horse forward.

Gavyn urged the stallion into a gallop. The beast responded with a quick surge of speed, long legs bunching, then straightening, neck extended as he ran full out, his strides smooth and steady. Leaning into the whistling wind, Gavyn squinted into the darkness, the air cold and frigid. He felt the power of the animal, his father's favorite mount, as they thundered north along the road, using moonlight as a guide.

Certainly a few of the men would follow, but the others—his father without a horse, and the two who would have to tighten the cinches of their saddles—would be left far behind.

They would never make up the distance.

He had no doubt that stealing the horse had just added insult to injury, but so be it. He had sealed his own damned fate and knew the names by which he would forevermore be branded.

Traitor.

Murderer.

And now horse thief.

The irony was not lost on Gavyn as he rode upon his stolen steed: the once unwanted child was now a very wanted man.

CHAPTER SIX

Upon his bed, Hallyd dared not move. His eyes, if he had any left in his head, burned so painfully he thought he would never see again.

'Twas as if all the embers of hell had been stuffed into the sockets of his skull to sear away the flesh and scorch his pupils. No amount of cold water or compresses or poultices from the physician alleviated the pain. And he could release no tears. The witch had seen to that. 'Twas part of his curse, and this searing sensation would be with him for hours, until dusk had given way and the shadowy night, forever his companion, returned.

So he had to trust in others.

Those who had their own gnawing hungers.

"I know not how to treat your condition," the physician said, frowning. Cedrik had taken some of Hallyd's urine to check it, but frowned at what he found—as if there were a vial of piss somewhere that would actually make the stern man smile. 'Twas all nonsense. Just as Vannora had said. If only he'd listened to her and held on to his unraveling patience, he would not have gone riding and risked the dawn. Now 'twas too late to second-guess himself. The damage was done, and no doubt the old hag in the basement would berate him for his foolishness.

Through the haze of pain, Hallyd caught a glimpse of the perpetually scowling Cedrik. Short of stature and slightly built, the physician had little hair upon his pate. What was left was gray and matched his thick beard. Cedrik's nose wrinkled when he was deep in thought, as if he were forever coming upon a bad smell. "Leeches might help." He scratched at his chin thoughtfully and his scowl deepened as he studied his patient.

Hallyd lay upon his bed and tried to ignore the agony screaming through his skull. "Bleeding? Nay." Closing his eyes, he held a cold compress to his face and bit down hard. The pain would eventually go away. It always did. He'd been foolish, drawn into the woods before day had broken, hoping to find her, but the dark clouds had given way to sunlight and he'd had to trust his horse to take him back to the keep. No amount of shading from his hood could protect his vision. In the end he'd ended up here in his chamber, lying upon his bed, hoping blessed darkness would arrive and he would find comfort once again.

At the thought of his crippled state, bile rose in the back of his throat. Silently he berated himself.

You became too anxious, were not willing to be patient. You've waited sixteen years and you cannot wait a few more days? She is coming; you feel it.

"Bloodletting is known to cure some ailments. I would place the leeches carefully in the areas of the body that affect the eyes," the physician said, his voice holding the merest trace of superiority.

'Twas like salt in his wounds.

"I said no bleeding," Hallyd ordered. "Did you not hear me? And the same goes for purging. God's eyes, I'll not be in the latrine all day."

The physician sighed as if the weight of the castle had fallen upon his already overly burdened shoulders. Cedrik did not pander to anyone, let alone a stubborn, ill-advised patient. "Then I can do nothing for your vision."

Of course you can't. 'Tis part of Kambria's damned curse, Hallyd thought, though he held his tongue. Cedrik's craft was of little use; he needed a witch to raise this curse. Only those closest to him knew of the dagger, of Kambria, and of the curse she cast upon him before she died. Those who had kept his secret were still in his company, though his trust in them had faded with time. Already some who had gossiped of that day on the ridge had died.

Quickly.

Hallyd accepted no excuses.

He held the compress over his eyes and ground his back teeth together. Eventually, the night would come and the excruciating pain pounding through his body would subside to a dull throb deep in his skull, behind his owlish eyes of mixed color. He could endure it. He had in the past. And then he would wait, just as Vannora had instructed, because, he knew, within a fortnight Bryanna would arrive.

Gavyn's breath fogged the air as his horse slowed. Every bone in his body ached, but he pushed onward, determined to put as much distance between himself and his father's soldiers as he could.

For two days Gavyn rode northward, passing through sleepy villages, where he bartered the prey he'd managed to kill. A duck or pheasant or hare could be traded for a hot meal and a measure of grain, even a cup or two of beer. He always ate in a dark corner of an inn, keeping to himself. He was always looking over his shoulder to make certain he wasn't followed.

He guided his horse along roads seldom used, past millponds and through streams, urging the stallion ever deeper into the mountains. Though he had no evidence that his father was giving chase, Gavyn knew it was only a matter of time before he heard the anxious baying of the castle dogs mingled with the excited shouts of soldiers as they tracked him, their quarry.

The Lord of Agendor would not rest until he'd hunted his bastard down. Deverill would watch without emotion as Gavyn was led to the gallows. Only when Gavyn's spine had snapped would his father be satisfied, glad at the sight of

Gavyn's corpse swinging from creaking timbers, relieved that the thorn in his side whom he'd sired would no longer disobey or embarrass him. His father would delight in seeing Gavyn's irreverence punished.

Unless he could outfox the old man.

Which was exactly what he intended.

There was still time.

Gavyn wasn't dead yet.

So he rode the big black steed as if Satan himself were breathing down his neck. Ignoring the pain in his shoulder and the fever that sometimes swept over him, he rode on, his bones jarred by each long stride the stallion took.

If he were clever, he supposed, he would sell the steed for a good price, then buy a smaller, less visible mount and some different clothes. On a more modest horse, he could play the role of a pauper, using flour to gray his beard and hair, attiring himself in plain peasant garb.

But he wasn't about to sell the black destrier.

Not only did he admire the sleek stallion, but the fact that Rhi was his father's pride and joy only made it that much more satisfying to ride him.

So he risked recognition and felt that the farther he was from Agendor, the less likely anyone would take note of the black horse with the peculiar long-tailed star upon his forehead and the irregular white stocking.

Near twilight on the third day of his trek, fine flakes of snow coated his shoulders as he searched for a campsite. In no time at all, a light dusting of snow covered the ground and undergrowth, and icy patches glistened under the darkening sky.

From the corner of his eye, he caught movement—a silvergray shadow that darted into a thicket. His horse snorted and minced, ears flicking nervously.

"Shh, boy, 'tis all right," Gavyn said, though the hairs on the back of his neck had lifted and he felt an icy warning in his veins. "Hold on, Rhi."

Too late!

His mount shied and reared suddenly, his sturdy legs pawing the night air.

Gavyn started to slide backward.

Quickly, he grabbed the pommel of his saddle with his free hand and sheathed his knife in one quick movement.

Pain shot up his arm and ripped through his shoulder.

The steed's front legs hit the ground again. With a frightened whinny, Rhi lunged forward. Bit in his teeth, he tore through the woods, hooves kicking up dirt and striking rocks. Clenching his teeth, Gavyn leaned over the frightened stallion's neck, pulling back on the reins, riding low to avoid the branches that swiped and scraped at him.

He felt the black's muscles bunch, then release as he sailed over a fallen log to land hard on the other side. Pain screamed through Gavyn's rib cage. Wrapping the reins around his fists, Gavyn fought to control the big beast, pulling hard on the reins, all to no avail. Lather appeared on the horse's wet coat as Rhi galloped wildly through the trees, somehow avoiding tree trunks and briars and badger holes.

"Come on, come on, slow down," he said, feeling the big horse tiring at last.

The ground rose slowly. Rhi, nostrils distended, charged up the hill, but finally began to slow, his long strides becoming shorter, his breath coming hard.

"That's it," Gavyn whispered. "That's a boy."

Still nervous, Rhi eased into a trot that rattled every bone in Gavyn's body before finally the horse slowed into a steady walk.

"See there, not so bad, is it?" Gavyn asked.

Gavyn glanced over his shoulder. Through the undergrowth, lingering a stone's throw behind them, was the silvery gray fur of a wolf.

No wonder the horse had shied.

Gavyn kept a wary eye on the beast, but the shadowy creature hung back, visible occasionally, but never too close. As he rode, Gavyn searched for a glimpse of other snarling wolves. Where there was one, there was sure to be more—the rest of the pack, ready to circle and attack or waiting for the slightest sign of the flagging or faltering of the quarry.

But no other wolves showed themselves on this night.

This one appeared to be alone and slightly crippled, for though she was fast, her gait was uneven and she limped.

On the third night since his escape from the hut of Dougal and Vala, Gavyn chose to camp by a stream. The wolf lay just out of the circle of light of the campfire, her eyes glowing in the darkness, reflecting the flames. She was a shaggy beast, silver with a fringe of black fur around her neck. Gavyn wondered where the rest of the pack was and thought that this one may have been cast out, perhaps for attacking the leader and losing.

Not so unlike his own fate.

"So why are you following me?" Gavyn asked, speaking for the first time to the animal as it settled against a fallen log, its gaze unwavering as Gavyn roasted an unlucky rabbit and squirrel on a makeshift spit. "Where're all of your friends, eh?" he asked, as if the animal could respond. Fat dripped onto the embers of the fire, sizzling loudly and sending black smoke curling upward through the trees.

Gavyn sat on a flat rock, knife in hand, scraping the inside of the rabbit's pelt. He'd already cleaned that of the squirrel and added them to the few he'd collected over the past couple of days. He hoped to sell the sleek hides to a peddler or tailor in the next town, though rabbit, squirrel, and polecat were plentiful and worth very little.

The wolf's silvery-gray coat would fetch more money.

He eyed the beast as hungrily as it stared at him.

'Twas not a large animal, not compared to some of the wolves he'd seen, but not scrawny either. He rotated the meat over the fire, finished cleaning the pelt, then removed the spit and gingerly placed the hot charred carcasses on a rock.

All the while, the wolf's eyes never stopped watching him.

"Hungry, are you?" Gavyn sliced up the squirrel and pulled the small carcass apart. Though he did not trust the wolf, he wondered why it had strayed from its pack. Perhaps it had been in a fight with another wolf or a boar or other wild creature. Or the cur could have been wounded in a trap.

Though he was probably encouraging the beast, which was just plain stupid, Gavyn tossed half the squirrel into the woods and the shaggy creature pounced upon the charred delicacy as if she truly were starving.

" 'Tis all I can spare," Gavyn said as he finished the smaller rodent, then tore into the rabbit. The succulent meat was heaven, and he tried not to notice that the damned wild wolf had edged closer to the fire, head raised, gaze fastened to Gavyn as he took each bite. "You'll have to kill your own damn food." He tore off another bit of seared flesh and chewed while the wolf stared hungrily. "I said no more."

Why had he fed the beast to begin with? 'Twas only asking for trouble. He sucked on a bone and the wolf lay down, paws outstretched, head lying on her front legs. "Don't you consider it for a second. I could kill you. Turn in your tail for a reward, or maybe tan your hide so that your fur could trim a lady's winter mantle, eh?"

So now you're talking to a wild animal? First the ridiculous dreams and now speaking to a wolf? Christ Jesus, Gavyn, you've gone round the bend!

Disgusted with himself, he picked off a good portion of meat from the roasted rabbit, then tossed the remains to the wolf, which barely chewed the small bones before swallowing as much as possible.

"That's it. There is no more," Gavyn said, then silently told himself he was *not* like the beast, wandering the forest alone, cast out by his own family. That was not his true fate.

Wiping his hands, he tucked his mantle around him and lay on the horse blanket. He stayed close to the fire, his stallion's reins knotted around one hand, his knife in the other. If the steed was the least bit disturbed, either by beast or human, Gavyn would feel it.

He planned on sleeping but a few hours and then riding northward, to the realm of his mother. He had lived in Tarth with his mother, moving north when he was twelve. At the time he'd thought his mother was trying to escape Deverill; later he'd learned that it was Deverill's wife, Marden, who was the real problem. Her voracious jealousy had sent Gavyn's mother scurrying all over the countryside, from Agendor to Penbrooke to Tarth. He had not visited his mother's last home since her death, and if Deverill decided to search that area, well, then, so be it.

The Lord of Agendor could bloody well come find his bastard.

He drifted off but slept fitfully, only to awaken at dawn to find his campfire nothing more than the blackened remains of sticks and ash. The black horse stood relaxed at his side, stirring only as Gavyn arose and stretched, his eyes searching the surrounding trees and ferns for any sign of the wolf.

The beast appeared to be missing, which was just as well, Gavyn thought. He relieved himself against the rough bark of an oak, then worked his muscles. His side still ached and the arm that had been wounded hurt like bloody hell. His fever had passed for the moment, but his ribs ached and it would take some time to regain his strength. Not that it mattered. He was free now, at least for the moment.

Swinging into the saddle, he winced as he pulled on the reins and left his small camp. He'd ridden nearly a mile when he noticed the wolf again, a slinking shadow keeping its distance, but never far out of sight. "Not so lucky as to be rid of you, eh?" Gavyn said, but he decided the furry creature was no threat and would probably tire of following along.

When he took the main road, the wolf disappeared and Gavyn was certain the creature had turned back. After trading his pelts for an ill-fitting pair of breeches and a mantle from a rotund peddler on his way to Wybren, Gavyn once again rode northward. Soon, through the rising mist heralding dusk, he spied the silvery cur once more.

Smiling to himself, Gavyn headed deep into the mountains, and without fail the shaggy wolf with its hungry eyes and uneven gait followed.

CHAPTER SEVEN

Perhaps his luck had changed.

Through the trees, the shifting light of a campfire danced in this night that was blacker than black, the sky heavy with thick clouds promising rain or worse. Tired, the pain in his shoulder throbbing, Gavyn turned toward the distinct glow. Time to move in on an easy mark.

As silent as a water snake gliding through the ripples, he slid from his saddle and tied the reins of his horse's bridle to the low hanging branch of the nearest pine.

His bones ached from hours in the saddle, his head pounded, his mouth was dry and foul tasting. Each time his horse had taken a step, the pain in his ribs had reminded him that they had not healed. Worse yet, the wound on his shoulder felt hot to the touch and had started to ooze.

Which was too damned bad.

Soon enough he would arrive in Tarth, the land that had once been home to his mother. Surely he would find a friend, a healer there to help him.

For now, though, he would deal with whatever unsuspecting camper had made the mistake of settling here for the night. Unsheathing his knife, he approached with caution, his boots making not the slightest noise as he crept beneath branches and over needles littering the forest floor.

Then he spied her.

Not a band of robbers or cutthroats or a company of soldiers, but a lone woman.

The very woman of his dreams.

He froze. For the love of Christ, could it be? The same damned woman he'd seen upon the white horse night after night?

Nay! 'Twas impossible. Disbelief and rational thought told him he was, yet again, creating a vision in his mind, bending what was real so that he could see what he wanted. And yet . . .

There she was.

Standing at the fire.

Holy Mother Mary.

From a habit of his youth, he made the sign of the cross over his chest, though he'd lost faith years before. 'Twas his fever, that was it. He had to be seeing an image that didn't exist; whatever illness he'd been fighting was causing these visions.

Yet he was certain this woman in the woods was she. Her hair was the same red bronze, falling down her back in thick, curling waves. Her features were even, her chin strong, and though he wasn't close enough to see for certain, he expected there was the merest smattering of freckles upon her short, straight nose.

His jaw tightened and the dull, nagging ache in his shoulder subsided. How in the name of the devil had he imagined her, this woman he'd never seen before? How had his mind conjured her image?

You've been cursed, he heard his mother say as clearly as if she were standing just behind him. But he didn't believe in magickal spells or hexes. Glancing about the small campsite, where the scents of burned fish still lingered, he saw her horse, the very same mare that raced through his dreams, causing stars to shoot from her hooves. 'Twas dog dung. Mind rot. And yet he was staring at the very same white jennet with her gray muzzle and stockings and bits of gray and black in her mane and tail as well.

He blinked, as if to dispel the vision, but the image remained the same and the woman stood at the fire, holding a ragged piece of something—leather?—in one hand.

In his dreams, she'd always been clad in a white dress embroidered with gold thread, the gown diaphanous and airy, her arms bare, her breasts and nipples visible through the sheer fabric, the strength of her calves and thighs obvious as they clenched the mare. He'd even caught a glimpse of the flatness of her abdomen and the soft red thatch of curls at the juncture of her legs when her filmy skirts had billowed around her.

This night, when he viewed her in the flesh, the gauzy white gown was replaced with heavy warm clothes. A black velvet mantle trimmed with rabbit fur and silver studs fell to her ankles, and though she was not wearing it, a hood was visible beneath her hair. As she paced to and fro near the fire, the hem of the mantle parted, the skirts beneath flashing a deep crimson color.

The dress of a noblewoman.

Riding alone?

Barely breathing, he studied her.

Who was she? Aside from the woman he'd conjured in his dreams, he knew nothing of her.

Why was she here in the middle of the woods?

Again he swept his gaze over the grounds around the campfire, where stones surrounded the fire pit and twigs and small logs burned brightly. Again he saw no one, but surely she was not camped out in the forest by herself. Someone had to be with her, either her husband or a guard or some kind of companion. Someone who was either relieving himself in the woods or was hunting for food.

But as the minutes slid by and the moon rose in the sky, no companion appeared from the surrounding darkness.

She seemed to be by herself.

And she was angry.

She was talking to herself, holding the leather scrap in her fist as she shook it toward the heavens. As if she were a raving lunatic, railing at the gods. Though her words were unclear, she was definitely vexed, her pretty features twisted in rage, her body fairly shivering in fury.

Throwing both her hands into the air, she shook her head, her long, wild hair moving against her back and reflecting the fire's light. "Please!" she yelled, and the word echoed through the trees of this lonely canyon. "Isa, come to me!"

Isa? The name rang a distant bell in his memory. So she wasn't by herself, after all. She had a woman companion with her. Someone who was hiding from her? Playing games with her? Or someone who had left her?

"Can you hear me? Isa! I beg you, come to me, now! I need you."

And yet the woman to whom she called remained silent and concealed in the darkness.

Finally, she gave up. Her arms fell to her sides. "Fine! So be it," she cried and slowly opened her palm, unrolling the piece of leather. "I shall do this for myself." Frowning, she used one finger of her free hand to trace upon the deer hide, as if deciphering the contour of the leather.

"Isa," she said again, more quietly. The name came to him on the smallest of breezes, calling up a faint, near-forgotten memory. He'd heard the name somewhere in the distant past, he was certain of it. But how? And when?

Calmer now, the woman plopped onto a large stump by the fire, then smoothed the scrap of hide onto a flat stone. Reaching into the cow's horn strapped at her waist, she sprinkled some kind of powder upon the burning wood. The flames reacted, turning blue and snapping, sparks streaming upward as the woman chanted softly.

God in heaven, did this woman, this *beautiful* woman, think she was a witch? 'Twas nonsense. 'Tattle. Aye, he believed some women knew how to heal and care for the wounded, better than any physician in many cases. But the calling up of spirits and casting of spells and laying on of curses was surely no more than horse dung.

But she flung dust into the fire and turned it blue.

So what else was she carrying in the horns and pouches

tied to her belt? Aside from powders and mayhap potions and scraps of leather, did she carry anything of value with her? Money? If so, why was she here, in the forest, alone? Was she foolish enough to think her spells would keep her safe from the criminals who banded together and haunted these woods? Was the woman, Isa, truly with her? Or had she abandoned this would-be sorceress? Perhaps because she was truly mad? Or was it possible Isa did not exist?

Again he wondered what valuables she had tucked inside the folds of her mantle.

He felt only the tiniest bit of guilt, for though he would not harm her, the thought of stealing from her still wasn't far from his mind. He could use whatever bit of silver or gold she was carrying or wearing. There were no rings upon her hands and her collar was too high for him to catch a glimpse of any sparkling strands of gold or jewels around her neck, but just because nothing was visible didn't mean she wasn't wearing a necklace or brooch that he could pocket and sell.

If he could really steal from her.

Suddenly, in that instant, she became silent. Her head snapped up. Her eyes—blue with the greenish luster of dappled leaves in the forest—stared directly at him, at his hiding place. As if she'd heard his thoughts and knew he was concealed in the darkness. He didn't move a muscle, didn't so much as blink, but his heart knocked wildly within his chest and he wondered if she could hear it, could see him somehow.

By the Christ, she was beautiful. Now that she was looking at him, the firelight warm against her skin, he saw the even features of her face. She was indeed the woman of his dreams. With high, sculpted cheekbones, finely arched dark eyebrows, and full lips around a small mouth now pursed in vexation, she glared at him.

"Damn you," she said clearly. "Come to me!"

Who? Damn who? His heart nearly stilled. Was she speaking to Isa again? Or directly to him? Could she see him in the darkness? Did his eyes reflect the firelight?

"Show yourself, cur!"

He heard a noise beside him, a rustle of leaves.

Someone else was in these woods?

Isa?

Or another thief scouting out his prey?

A murderer?

Someone intent upon attacking her, robbing and raping her, then killing her, this woman who had come to him in his mind?

Was that a bit of movement in the darkness . . . or just the play of firelight? He shifted into a crouch, ready to spring, every sense heightened as he searched the darkness.

Gripping his knife more tightly, he studied the shadows, now unmoving and still.

Two gold, unblinking eyes appeared.

Holy Christ.

The damned wolf.

The hungry beast was staring at the horse as if it were her next meal.

"You there!" the woman called. Her furious turquoise eyes cut through the night to bore into his soul. "Yes, you, son of Satan," she clarified, and he knew she'd somehow seen him. "Show yourself."

In the second he'd taken his eyes off her, she'd retrieved her knife and was standing in front of her horse, wielding the blade as if she intended to defend herself. "I know you're there, coward. If you do not come out of the darkness, I swear I will curse you with a spell that will cause your mind to rot so that you will have fewer brains than the village idiot." Her eyes narrowed in seething fury. "And that's not all. Once you are brainless, I will cast a hex upon you that will cause your cock to shrivel and dry like a dying worm in the sun, then crumble into tiny pieces before falling off completely, making you no longer a man."

She let her words sink in and one side of her mouth lifted into a satisfied smile.

If he believed in such nonsense, he might have felt a shred

of fear. Instead, he let her rant and found himself amused at her conviction.

"Do you hear me? From this night and forever the maids in every town you visit will titter and laugh and point as they whisper between themselves, calling you eunuch. If you don't step into the light at this very instant, I will ruin your life with a snap of my fingers."

What rot!

Bryanna glared into the night.

Someone or something was out there. She felt whatever it was watching her. With her free hand she touched her protection necklace, a red string upon which a strip of black snakeroot was tied.

Whoever concealed himself in the shadows was not an assassin, for no arrow had been shot at her heart, no mace swung at her head, no sword lunged through her body. If the presence she felt had wanted to kill her, she already would have left this mortal life.

Alabaster suddenly lifted her head to the wind, her gaze focused on the edge of the wood, her ears forward in attention.

"What is it, girl?" Bryanna asked, still searching the dark undergrowth, her gaze following that of the mare. She clenched her knife more tightly and suddenly wished it was much, much larger. In an instant she saw a flicker of light, the reflection of the fire. Her heart stopped.

From deep in the shadows, gold eyes narrowed upon her.

Man?

Beast?

Or something else? Something somewhere in between?

Fear turned her blood to ice. Her mind swam with thoughts of boars and wildcats, of robbers who would easily slit a throat, or worse yet, of demons from an underworld where evil reigned in wicked souls who could easily turn from human form to ghost.

Be with me. Give me strength, she silently prayed as a

damp breeze crawled across her skin. Her heart knocked against her ribs and her blood pounded in her ears.

Alabaster moved and snorted, gaze fixed on that one terrifying spot in the darkness.

"Shah," Bryanna said and whispered a prayer for protection.

The eyes followed her every move just as the castle dogs had when she was eating from her trencher and picking at a succulent roast boar or goose. 'Twas as if their gaze was fastened to her. So these eyes, out in the forest, a stray cur?

Nay, more likely a wolf.

Her heart nearly stilled. She swallowed hard. *Morrigu, help me.* All of the spells she'd learned for protection—the red string she'd tied, the lavender, and eye of newt and ivy she'd pulverized and spread around her, the black snakeroot in which she'd rinsed her clothes—none of these seemed strong enough to go against a beast as clever and deadly as a wolf.

Alabaster let out a frightened whinny as the wind gusted and plucked at her hair. Suddenly Isa's voice came to her as clearly as the tolling of a church bell in the night: *"There is more evil here than you know,"* the dead woman's voice confided. *"The wolf is not the beast of the night you should fear. She is your protection. . . . Do you not remember her? When you were a child, she was with you."*

"This is no time for riddles," she hissed, but she sensed Isa's words were not a lie. 'Twas almost as if she smelled the beast. She felt her presence over the threat of sleet in the air. There was another force beyond that of the wolf—a dark, soulless predator haunting the forest.

By the Great Goddess, how had she gotten herself into such a predicament?

Her gaze scoured the shadows.

Mayhap the wolf was not an animal at all but a being capable of taking another shape, a demon who could appear in human or animal form, a beast like no other.

Morrigu, be with me now.

She stared the brute straight in her evil eyes. She held her free hand toward the beast, all five fingers spread, their mag-ick untested. "What devil are you, cur?" she demanded, and the wind picked up, pushing her hair from her face, whisper-ing through the dry leaves, keening through the canyon. "Did you not hear me that I will destroy your life?"

She braced herself, ready for the monster to lunge.

"Why not just kill me?"

Bryanna nearly jumped out of her skin at the sound of a deep male voice.

"If you're so powerful, why bother with addling brains and shrinking cocks?"

"What?" Surely the wolf was not speaking to her! By all that was holy, she was going out of her mind. That was it. Finally she was certain that she was mad.

"I said, why not just kill me now and be done with it? 'Twould save us both a lot of trouble."

By the gods, was he serious? "Who are you?" she de-manded, her heart beating faster than a hummingbird's wings. Where was the voice coming from . . . surely not the wolf. Nay, it came from a spot near the downed tree, a fair distance from the crouching canine. "Why do you not show yourself? Are you afraid? A coward? Or hideous to the eyes?"

He laughed then, a deep, disgusted sound that rippled through the canyon. "Aye," he answered, this hidden man or beast. "You *are* a sorceress, as you've divined not only that I am so afraid as to be unable to move, but that I'm ugly as well. So horribly disfigured that you would cringe at the sight of me."

"Oh, for the love of Rhiannon." How dared the man or whatever he was bait her? Irritated and keeping one eye on the doglike brute still crouching formidably just beyond the fire's glow, she said, "Have you any idea that you are standing only a few yards from a wolf?"

"She's with me."

"*With* you?"

"Aye." He actually chuckled, as if he were amused at her

vexation. Well, then, let him be eaten alive! "She will not harm you."

"How do you know this? Is she . . . what? Your bloody pet?" What the devil was going on here? To whom did this voice with its deep timbre and easy amusement belong?

He laughed again, further riling her. "Pet? Nay. A stray who follows me."

"And wants to rip out your heart."

"I think not. If she wanted to kill me, she already would have tried. She's been with me for the better part of a week."

"She may still be waiting. And who the devil are you?"

"She's an animal," he said, ignoring her question about himself. "She takes what she wants when she wants it."

"And stalks her prey until it is either tired, weak, or lets down its guard." *Just as you are*, she told herself. *Be wary. Remember Isa's warning.* "Enough of this! Whoever you are, quit hiding," she ordered. Before the words had passed over her lips, a man emerged from the shadows.

At the sight of him, she nearly took a step backward, but somehow she held her ground.

He was tall, his shoulders broad. His body had long, muscular lines, though he seemed gaunt and emaciated. Wearing leather breeches and a worn brown mantle that hung on his skin and bones, he stopped on the far side of the campfire. By the gods, he was horribly marred. His face was discolored, his nose obviously broken, purple and green smudges beneath deep-set eyes. One eyelid still drooped a bit and flesh was healing where his skin had been scraped raw from his cheek.

She was surprised he was still standing. *This* was the warrior, the dark force she was supposed to fear? There had to be some mistake, for though he probably had been a strong, vital, muscular man at one time, he now appeared to have been beaten to the brink of his life.

"What happened to you? Was it the wolf?" Nervously she glanced to the spot where the creature still lurked, though the man's wounds did not look to be the result of a mauling by an animal. No bite wounds were visible.

White teeth flashed within the man's dark beard. "Nay."

"You said that she's . . . with you?"

"She followed me."

"And you're not worried that she'll attack?"

"She has not yet."

The man was daft—that was it. The wolf would strike only when the man was so weak that he was unable to fend off the attack, which from the looks of him would be soon. "So what happened to you?"

"I fell."

"You fell? From where? The top of a castle battlement? The side of a mountain?"

"From grace," he said, and beneath his dark beard his lips twisted wryly. "Let's leave it at that."

No doubt the tumble had rattled his brain.

As he stepped closer she saw that blood lingered in the whites of his eyes and his hands and cheeks were coated with scabs. Was he dangerous? She couldn't tell, but she decided not to drop her knife.

"Where is Isa?" he asked.

"What?" He knew that she talked to her dead nursemaid?

"I heard you calling to her."

"Oh." So he didn't realize she was traveling alone. Good. She saw no reason to let him think otherwise. "She, uh, went ahead for supplies, but should return. I expect her and . . . mayhap her husband at any moment."

"She's married?" He seemed skeptical.

"Aye, for many years." Her mind raced with the lie. "Her husband, um, Parnell, he is a strong man. A warrior."

"Who left you alone."

She forced a smile. "The two are inseparable," she said, lying glibly now, caught up in her fantasy. He would never know otherwise, so what did it matter?

"You sounded angry."

"I am," she said quickly, and that much, at least, wasn't a lie, even if she were furious with herself. But she didn't dare tell this battered man who traveled with a wolf the truth. Not yet. "They were supposed to be back by nightfall."

"Mayhap something happened to delay them." He stepped closer and she pointed her knife at his throat.

"Aye, but they will be here," she said. "Now who the devil are you?"

"Mayhap your bodyguard."

She nearly laughed. How absurd! The man was half dead already. "Are you serious? Look at you. You cannot take care of yourself, let alone another person." She lowered her knife a bit. "Surely you have a name."

"Aye. I'm Cain of Agendor," he said without hesitation, though he watched her as if she might react. As if she'd heard the name before. "And you? What's your name?"

She doubted she should trust him, and yet there seemed no reason to lie. "Bryanna."

She saw a flicker of something in his gaze. "Bryanna?"

"Aye."

"And you're traveling from where?"

"Calon," she admitted, though she wanted to give him only the barest of information about herself.

"Calon." His eyebrows slammed together. "Far to the south?"

She nodded, glancing back at the woods to be sure the wolf was not circling to attack. The shaggy gray beast sat poised, as if at rest. Although Bryanna was loath to admit it, this wolf resembled the animal she'd conjured in her youth. Aye, even the markings were the same, a black scruff against silver fur.

"Where are you going so far from Calon?"

Of course she didn't know, nor would she have confided in him if she did. "North. What about you? Where are you from?"

"Here and there," he said, lifting a shoulder. His gaze drifted downward to the stone where Isa's vexing piece of leather was visible. "Is this a map?" he asked, picking up the scrap of deer hide and holding it outward so that the light from the fire backlit the skin.

"A poor one." She snorted, disgusted with the torn piece of hide.

"Hmm." Frowning, he turned the smooth leather over, then upside down. "I thought so." Nodding to himself, he glanced at her. "Where's the rest of it?"

"There's more?" she asked, perplexed. She'd found this torn bit of doeskin in Isa's hut and it was all there had been.

"There should be." He turned a little so that Bryanna could see the markings through the hide. "See there, those mounds? One might think they were hills, but they are really the three rocks."

"Three rocks?" she repeated skeptically.

" 'Tis what it's called, as you pass by the cliffs, here—" He indicated the three big mounds on the map. "You see three immense rocks, one on the west and two to the east. From there"—he drew upward with his finger—"you travel but half a day to the village and keep. Only someone who has lived in Tarth or traveled there often would know what they are called."

"And you do?" she asked, a little confused. "Do you live there?"

He shook his head. "Once, long ago. 'Tis the home of my mother and grandmother, but it's been years since I was there." He flashed the hint of a smile, his teeth gleaming white against his black beard. For a split second there was something about him that called up an old memory—a fleeting feeling that he was somehow familiar—but it passed quickly. "Lucky for you that I'm heading to Tarth. 'Tis a few days' ride north and west. On the second day, we'll come to the main road, as you have been following a path that is nearly forgotten." He traced a wavy line upon the leather with his finger, then slid the same finger over to a spot on the map that had not been etched. "The main road, which should appear about here"—he pressed his fingernail into the blank spot on the soft doe hide—"travels in the same general direction as the path you've taken, running north and south, but it is straighter, wider, and takes less time to get from one town to the next. However, it is well traveled."

"Which I don't want?" she guessed from the tone of his voice.

"Which *I* don't. But worry not. I'll show you the way."

"I'm not worried. I can get there. On my own. You need not think you have to ride with me."

"It only makes sense. If we are going to the same destination, we should ride together."

"Ride? On what?" Surely he didn't expect her to share her mount. The very thought of him seated behind her, pressed against her back, his arms surrounding her . . . nay, that would never do and 'twould be too hard on her horse.

As if reading her thoughts and being amused by them, he grinned widely. "I have a steed."

"Here?" She glanced around. There was no horse that she could see, and from the looks of him any animal he would be riding would never be able to keep up with Alabaster. "This steed, is he a phantom?"

"A flesh-and-blood horse, I assure you."

"So where is he?"

"Nearby. Fear not."

Good advice, though I don't think I can take it from you.

"Nearby?"

He slapped the map into her free hand. "You could use a bodyguard."

She almost laughed as she stared into his battered face. "So could you."

Despite his paleness, his smile grew to wicked proportions.

"Mayhap I should become your bodyguard," she suggested, "rather than the other way around."

"And protect me with your spells?" he asked, unable to hide his skepticism.

With his face so bruised his own mother wouldn't recognize him and his skin scraped raw, she suspected he could use a little protection. From the way he carried himself and winced, she suspected that he had a few broken ribs to boot. Then there was the matter of a darkening stain on the shoulder of his tunic—indication of a bleeding wound.

"I don't think I could do any worse than you have, Cain. It looks to me as if you could use a spell or two."

"Spoken as if you are truly a witch."

"Sorceress. And aye, I am."

He snorted. "Trying to keep me safe might be dangerous."

"Obviously."

"We could help each other," he suggested, then drew in a quick breath as if he were in pain.

"I don't even know you," she pointed out. "You say you're riding to Tarth, but only after pretending to study this." She held up the map again and gave it a shake. "And then, after supposedly reading it within seconds, this map that I've yet to understand, you tell me that I, too, am heading to the same destination. How convenient." He started to interrupt her, but she said quickly, "Then you mention you have a horse, an animal you've left to fend for himself in the forest. For all I know this is a bald lie and you really intend to steal mine. A wolf accompanies you and yet you tell me to fear her not, while you, battered and beaten, offer to be my bodyguard." She lowered her knife but didn't bridge the distance between them. "I think I'll take my chances with my spells."

"Wait here."

As if she were going anywhere.

Without another word, he strode quickly out of the circle of illumination and vanished into the forest again. The wolf, however, didn't so much as move. Within seconds, Cain returned, leading a tall black destrier with a big barrel chest and white markings. The horse was well fed, muscular, and, Bryanna guessed, worth a fortune—a nobleman's mount, or mayhap the horse of a decorated soldier, though the animal had no visible scars from battle. Nay, he was sleek, as if groomed for a lord. Resisting the lead, pulling against the bridle and prancing nervously, the stallion was agitated, the rims of his dark eyes white. He tossed his head, his ears flicking this way and that as he snorted his unease.

" 'Tis all right, Rhi," Cain said, rubbing a soothing hand over the steed's neck. In a low steady voice he spoke softly to the big animal and the stallion slowly calmed.

From her tethering point, Alabaster snorted, then nickered. After measuring the value of the steed in her mind, Bryanna again took in Cain's state of dress, as a peasant. For all she knew, he could have been beaten while stealing the animal.

"This is your stallion?" she asked, not hiding her disbelief. Cain had a way with horses, that much was obvious, and it didn't surprise her. Again the sensation that something about him was familiar swept over her.

"Aye, 'twas my father's." Was there a hint of irony in his voice?

"Who is a very rich man," she observed.

"A gambling man."

As if he'd won a prized animal in a game of dice. She didn't believe it. This horse was as valuable as any in the stable at Penbrooke or Calon. "How do I know you didn't steal him?" she asked.

"You don't."

"And yet you expect me to hire you as a bodyguard."

"Only until your companions return. Isa and her husband, what was his name? Parnell."

"Yes," she said quickly.

"I'll stay with you."

"I don't think so."

"A woman should not be traveling alone."

"I told you, I'm not alone. Isa and Parnell will be back soon."

He shook his head. "You know, Bryanna," he said with a glint in his eye that warned her she wouldn't like what he was about to say, "you may be a witch of some sort. Or at least think you are." With one finger, he motioned to the amulets and pouches and horns she had tucked near the stump. "And you're a beautiful woman, probably the daughter of a lord.

Anyone would guess that, looking at your clothes and your manner. The way you address me, as if you're used to ordering people about." He nodded, agreeing with himself and rankling her that he could discern so much about her when she knew so little of him. "But there's one thing you are not, and that is a good liar. In fact, you're pretty damned miserable at it."

"And how would you know?" she demanded, irritated.

His smile, somewhere between sinister and sexy, crawled across his unshaven jaw. "Because, my lady, I'm the best damn liar you'll ever have the displeasure to meet."

CHAPTER EIGHT

B other and bog's worts!

Was she doomed to become this strange man's companion? Bryanna had tried to decline any offer of help, protection, or conversation, and yet the man remained.

Worse yet, the oddly marked silver wolf had stayed as well.

She'd tried to pry information from the man, but to no avail. When she'd asked a few questions about his past, he'd been vague and clever, dancing away from the truth. Which was just as well, she supposed, as anything he did tell her was probably a lie. She wasn't even certain that Cain was his name, nor that the horse he rode belonged to his father. Once or twice when the fire cast light on his face, she felt certain she'd seen him somewhere before. Then shadows flickered and again he resembled a bedraggled stranger.

'Twas a stroke of misfortune to have met him and the wolf, who skulked through the thin trees, her shadow causing Bryanna's heart to throb anxiously and Alabaster to nicker and pull on her lead. She did not feel safe traveling with this man, certainly not sleeping in such close proximity to him. And yet, he had brought her insight into the meaning of Isa's map. What had he called the terrain? The three rocks. If his interpretation was right, the information at least gave Bryanna a direction to travel in—though she would have preferred traveling alone. By the gods, who knew what this . . . this lying, perhaps horse-stealing peasant might do!

Now, with the man slumbering on the other side of the small campfire, Bryanna didn't think she could sleep a wink. After allowing his horse to drink from the nearby stream, he'd removed the stallion's saddle, wrapped the reins around his palm, then curled up against the saddle and used his mantle as a blanket. Before she could argue or protest that he couldn't stay in her camp, he was softly snoring. All this before she'd picked up her pouches and amulets or braided her hair for the night. He'd fallen asleep so quickly she suspected he might be pretending slumber, but as she stared at him he barely moved.

Her eyes remained on the stranger as she gathered her things and used the horn comb she'd brought with her from Calon to plait her curly tresses. As she worked, she watched for any sign that he was feigning sleep. But as the moon rose in the dark sky, she witnessed no indication that he was acting, and she realized that if he truly wasn't awake, he could do her no harm.

Well, so be it, she thought, sending up a prayer to the Great Mother and walking to the stream to rinse her hands and face. The water was cold as ice and she shivered, only to look up and see the wolf on the other side of the creek. The creature moved toward the water as if to drink, but paused and stared at Bryanna, her reflection ominous in the moonlight.

"Go away," she said. "Leave!"

The wolf lifted her head and Bryanna felt something stir in the night air. In the reflection on the water, where the wolf's image should have swirled, was that of a woman—a beautiful woman with creamy white skin, sea green eyes like her own, and a ring of bruises at her neck.

A low growl rumbled deep in the animal's throat, and the image disappeared.

Alarmed, Bryanna turned to stone, not daring to move a muscle. But she quickly realized that the wolf was not about to attack her. The animal was looking past her, deeper into the forest. Her skin crawled as she looked over her shoulder quickly. Did she see a glimpse of something in the trees, a figure darker and more frightening than the beast on the other side of the water?

"Get back," she whispered.

The wolf lunged into the stream.

Bryanna braced herself, her knife ready. She'd plunge the dagger deep into the beast's shaggy side.

Water sprayed as the wolf leapt through ripples. Growling and snarling, she raced by, her coat nearly brushing Bryanna's legs as she vanished into the darkness.

"Dear God," Bryanna whispered, her heart hammering. What had frightened the animal? What was she chasing?

Alabaster snorted and tossed her head, her eyes rimmed with fear as Bryanna hurried back to the camp. Cain's big black stallion also snorted and reared, the reins yanking Cain's arm, awakening him.

"For the love of Christ, what's happening?" Cain demanded, instantly alert. The horse backed up and Cain was on his feet, trying to quiet the stallion.

"The wild wolf." Bryanna went to Alabaster and tried to soothe the frightened mare. "There you are . . . good girl."

"What about the wolf?" Cain asked as he tried to ease his own horse's anxiety. "That's it . . . you're okay," he said to the stallion, his tone low but firm.

Bryanna, in control of the frightened mare, said, "The wolf was drinking on the other side of the stream when I approached. She . . . she stared at me for a bit, then started growling, her fur all on end. I thought she was going to attack me!"

"But she didn't."

"She missed by the breadth of a thread."

"If she'd meant to harm you, she would have."

Though Cain's words made sense, they didn't slow her racing heart. "She ran right by me, nearly knocking me over as she took off into the woods." Bryanna was holding the mare's reins in one hand, her dagger in the other. She pointed the knife toward a spot beyond the firelight where the wolf had been swallowed by darkness. "She ran through there, past the tree with the split trunk."

"But she didn't harm you."

"Nay, but—"

"You're just scared. Like the horses." Satisfied that she wasn't hurt, he turned his attention back to his frightened stallion. "Whoa, Rhi . . . you're all right," Cain said softly, though the black horse still sidestepped and tossed his head. Nervous sweat had broken out on the steed's sleek black coat and he pulled hard on the bit, yanking on Cain's arm again.

Cain sucked his breath in through his teeth, then swore, all the while trying to steady the horse. "By the gods," he said, then, "Shah . . . boy, there now . . . that's better." Slowly the animal calmed. "See . . . nothing to worry about." He rubbed Rhi's muscular neck, glancing over his shoulder to the dagger still clutched in Bryanna's hand. "You didn't need that."

"I was defending myself against a wolf. She's a wolf, Cain. Remember?" she said and noticed that he seemed to have paled beneath his bruises, that he appeared weaker as he led his horse in a small circle. "The horses and I . . . we know that. You seem to think the beast is just some friendly castle dog, ready to be patted on the head and scratched behind the ears. 'Tis foolish."

"You weren't hurt," he pointed out.

"But you were."

"I'm fine."

"And you call yourself a good liar," she mocked.

"The wolf didn't harm me."

"She scared the horse, who reared and yanked you out of sleep, mayhap opening your wound again."

"I said I'm fine. Leave it."

She held her tongue for the moment but noticed that he favored his right arm, transferring Rhi's reins to his left hand.

She knew all about men and their false pride. While she was growing up, her brothers had taught her about the silent prowess of men in dealing with pain or discomfort or embarrassment, how they preferred to hold their tongues and pretend not to suffer while the women would cackle and cluck about any little thing. And so it was with Cain. She knew she should tread carefully with him, but she found it impossible, because he irritated the hell out of her.

"Why did the wolf run off?" he asked her.

"Because she's a wild wolf," she said, exasperated. She threw the hand holding her dagger toward the sky. " 'Tis not as if she's a rational being."

"Did you hear or see anything that would have caused her to run into the woods?"

"Besides my heart pounding harder than an armorer's hammer? No," she said quickly, but then added, "Well, I did . . . I did have the sense that there was something—or someone—watching me. But 'twas most likely just the beast. The wolf was right across the stream from me."

Frowning, he glared into the dark, silent forest and slapped Rhi's reins into her hand. "We'll see," he said, unconvinced. "Stay here with the horses."

"What?" she cried, her fingers curling over the leather straps as he slipped his quiver and bow over his back, then headed into the forest. "You're not going after her?"

"I'll be back soon."

"Cain, do not leave," she insisted, but her words fell upon deaf ears as he jogged off, vanishing into the gloomy, night-dark thicket. She stared after him. "Fool of a man," she muttered under her breath. She hadn't wanted his company, had not invited him to stay with her, but now that he'd run off, she felt a sudden odd sense of loss.

She tended to the horses, stoked the fire, and scratched out a rune for his protection, drawing three overlapping circles in the earth. Then she said a quiet prayer for both the man and beast. In truth, Cain was right. The shaggy wild wolf had done nothing to harm them.

Watching the moon rise, she huddled against the bite of the wind and the whir of bat wings overhead as the fire's flames crackled over moss and pitch. When he didn't return immediately, she tried not to worry, her eyes wandering to his saddle and the leather bag. Glancing over her shoulder as if she thought he might be watching, she ventured over to the place where he'd been sleeping and opened his pouch. Maybe she could find something in his personal belongings that would reveal more about him.

She opened the pouch and withdrew its meager contents: a small whittling knife, tips for arrows, a whetstone for sharpening his weapons, and nothing more. Nothing personal. 'Twas as if she were looking in a soldier's pack.

"Find what you were looking for?" His voice rang from the darkness on the other side of the fire. She dropped the pouch and felt heat climb up the back of her neck.

"Aye, you carry a whetstone with you. My knife is dull."

"You could have asked." He walked out of the woods, his gaze stern.

"You were not here and I wanted to stay awake to wait for you. The wolf?"

He shook his head. "Missing."

"Mayhap gone back to her pack."

"I think not." He pushed the hair from his eyes and frowned. "What's that?" He pointed to the earth where she'd scraped her rune into the dirt. His lips twitched in amusement. "Practicing your magick again?"

"'Tis for protection and it worked," she said. "You returned."

One side of his mouth lifted as the campfire popped and sparks rose into the air.

Oh, he was a pain in the backside and, aye, she didn't need him about, but there was something a little endearing about him. As she tilted her head to look at him again, she was certain she'd met him somewhere before. The feeling, though fleeting, was bittersweet, a little pleasure mixed with a little pain. It didn't last long enough so that she could examine it and truly remember him, but it was there, that feeling of recognition.

"You care?"

What was he asking? The night seemed suddenly close. "About your safety? Yes."

"And why is that?"

Her gaze found his and for a second her breath was lost, her mind wandering into dangerous territory. "I don't know."

"You're attracted to me."

She almost laughed. "Ah, that is it," she said, shaking her head. "Have you any idea what you look like?"

"It matters not."

"Of course it does."

His gleaming eyes accused her of the lie. "Aye. Of course it does." He walked to his horse and once again wrapped Rhi's reins around his palm. This time, though, he tethered the horse to his left hand, and as he settled back against his saddle again, he grimaced.

"Your shoulder," she said. "It bothers you. You're in pain."

"*You* bother me," he retorted, closing his eyes. "Good night, Bryanna."

As if she could sleep! With the wild wolf roaming the woods and the eerie sense of a dark presence nearby, she felt certain sleep would elude her.

She settled on the ground by her own saddle and wrapped her mantle about her to ward off the cold of the night, but her restlessness made the night sounds seem exaggerated. The frogs were croaking again and an owl gave off a lonely hoot over the hiss of dying flames.

Her mind teased her with thoughts of the warmth of Calon until she chastised herself by recalling the reasons she'd left. She glanced over at Cain, who was already sleeping, and somehow the sight of this strange man eased her guilt about Morwenna's husband.

Cain was wrong, of course. She was *not* attracted to a self-proclaimed liar who looked as if he'd been trampled by an army. She wouldn't think twice about the man if he hadn't of-fered up information about her quest.

That mysterious quest, elusive even to her.

Oh, Isa, what is this quest I'm on?

'Twas folly, she thought, sliding lower on the saddle as weariness took hold of her muscles. She closed her eyes and heard him moan, his first small cry of pain.

Well, too bloody bad.

She hadn't invited him to be a part of her camp and she certainly didn't want a wolf skulking in the shadows on the other side of the fire. She didn't know much about this man who called himself Cain, but she was fairly certain he brought trouble with him.

As if she didn't have enough of her own.

He moaned again, more loudly this time, and she tried to close her ears to it. She reasoned that the pain couldn't be that bad if he could manage to sleep through it.

Again, he let out a miserable groan.

She couldn't stand it a second longer. She rose to her feet and circled the fire, moving close to him. His face in repose was still strained, as if he were in agony. God's teeth, he was battered and suffering.

There was a chance she could alleviate some of the pain.

With deft fingers, she sorted through her pouches and horns, finding some powder that Isa had used. She filled Isa's iron cup in the stream, then placed it on a flat rock that jutted over the embers of the fire. As the water warmed she sorted through her dried herbs and seeds, deciding on willow bark, flax, and Saint-John's-wort. Once the water was steaming, she tossed in her powder and waited until the herbs had steeped.

She worked in silence but for his continual laments of pain, and she couldn't help but feel empathy for the man. Using the hem of her mantle to protect her hands, she carried the steaming potion to the spot where he lay.

"Cain," she whispered. "Cain, wake up."

He didn't move.

"Cain . . . ," she said more loudly as she knelt beside him. When he didn't rouse, she touched him gently on the shoulder.

Still nothing.

She moved her hand to his neck and there her fingers brushed against the spot where she could feel his pulse, the lifeblood pounding through him.

The instant her fingertips touched his bare skin, she saw an image, a brief, vibrant portrait of a boy on the verge of becoming a man whose hair was dark with sweat, his head twisted to look over his bare shoulder as he braced himself. Two faceless men held him steady.

And then she saw a black whip snake forward and bite into his tanned flesh.

His body jerked.

A red welt appeared as the whip slid backward over the dry grass. The sky above was dark as death, the clouds parting and roiling over the scene, the barebacked boy taking his punishment from the Penbrooke stable master.

"Gavyn," she whispered.

The whip snapped again. Hissing through the air, it slashed into his back.

"Gavyn," she cried.

The image of the beaten boy disappeared and she was in the forest again, her fingers upon a stranger's throat. No, not a stranger. Gavyn.

His eye opened groggily, the light within alert and knowing.

"Holy Mother," she whispered, pulling back her hand as if she'd been burned.

How had she not recognized him, this man who had once been her friend?

His dark gray eyes focused hard on her and she felt tears gather at the back of her throat as she recalled the brutal punishment he had endured.

"I wondered if you'd remember," he said.

"By the saints, why did you not tell me?"

Frowning, he pushed himself upright, leaned forward, and draped his arms over his bent knees. He watched her thoughtfully and shook his head. " 'Twould be better if you did not realize who I am."

"Why?"

"Because there is much you don't know about me, Bryanna," he admitted, rubbing his chin. "Some things you're better off not knowing."

"Nay."

"Aye." He nodded, staring into the fire. Somewhere far off, a night bird called, his song nearly drowned out by the rush and gurgle of the stream.

"You should have told me," she insisted.

He cocked his head, as if considering all the implications and consequences of revealing the truth. "Mayhap, but what would have changed?"

I might not have lied. Mayhap I would have trusted you.

She didn't utter the words aloud.

"Hmmm. See?" he said, his gaze unnerving as he glanced back at her again. "Nothing. So . . . 'tis your turn for the truth. What is the spoiled daughter of a baron doing alone in the wilderness casting spells, calling to a woman who isn't there?"

She wasn't about to answer, realizing that the truth would have made her sound crazy. Could she tell him that Isa had been killed, yet the dead woman still spoke to Bryanna? Could she admit that she was on this quest to save some child she'd never met? Could she acknowledge that she'd stolen amulets from a dead woman and escaped Calon for fear she was in love with her sister's husband?

Of course not. "There's truly nothing to tell," she said, "and I was never spoiled."

"Aye, your father's favorite."

Oh, for the love of the saints, now she knew he was a half-wit. "My father's favorite was my brother Kelan."

He snorted and shook his head. "While your older sister tried to outdo her brothers, you had but to smile at your father and he would allow you anything."

" 'Tis true," she admitted. Their eyes connected and something in his quicksilver gaze sparked the memory of another time, when she was but a child riding across a dusky meadow, her little brown jennet struggling to keep up with the rangy dun-colored gelding and the boy astride the taller beast. The boy had turned in the saddle, flashed a gorgeous smile, slapped at his horse's withers, and then bolted off on his dun. Leaping ahead, the horse had scattered grasshoppers and butterflies and even pheasants as he raced across the tall grass at sunset.

"Gavyn of Agendor," she said, shaking her head as he dropped his hand. How had she not seen it? Not recognized him?

Three years older than she, he'd had long and lean muscles starting to show sinew as he worked with the horses. His hair had been dark but streaked with red in the late summer. She'd watched him as he leaned against the reins of a particularly headstrong black colt, the sweat running down his neck, the muscles bunching in his shoulders and arms, his hair nearly curling into black ringlets.

She'd felt the first stirring of womanhood looking at him, the odd swelling feeling deep inside that had made her flush and babble whenever he was near. She'd found that her mouth was often dry, her tongue wetting her lips as she watched him work.

And then they'd begun to talk and laugh. She'd often made excuses to wander to the stables or be around the horses. She'd readily agreed to sneak the horses out and ride in the twilight. Of course, when they returned and the stable master realized what had happened, Gavyn had been blamed.

Gavyn was the boy from whom the stable master's whip had drawn blood. Gavyn was the boy who had been banished from Penbrooke forever.

Because of her.

She swallowed hard, nearly dropping the hot cup. God in heaven, could it truly be him?

His mouth twisted in a smile without a trace of humor. "So you remember."

"Aye," she whispered, though she had trouble believing it. This broken, battered, bullheaded man was the boy with whom she'd stolen honey from the beekeeper? The lad who had dared her to pick up an asp? The freckled-faced youth who had taught her to skip stones on the millpond and challenged her to scale the walls of the abandoned ruins of a crumbling cathedral? The very same boy who had ridden over the fields with her and been flogged for it, right before her terrified, guilt-ridden face. "Why . . . why did you not say who you were?" she asked, seeing him with new eyes. And old eyes. Her vision split between that of the boy she'd known and the man before her.

"I thought it would make a hard situation more difficult."

"And lying would be easier?"

"Aye." He yawned and stretched, then grimaced. "Now," he said, "was there a reason you woke me?"

"Oh. Yes. Drink this." She held out the cup.

He looked at her as if she'd gone mad.

"You were moaning in pain. In your sleep. This will help." She handed him the cup and pushed it upward toward his lips. "Careful. It's hot."

Watching her over the rim, he took a sip, then scowled and tried to hand the cup back to her.

"Good?" she asked.

"It tastes like boar piss."

"Which you've drunk?" she asked, pushing the cup back to his lips.

"I've smelled."

"But this brew will help. I promise," she said, coaxing him to drink.

"Did you ever drink it?"

"Many times," she lied. "I think it tastes like Berthild's, the alewife's, mead. You remember her?"

"Aye, the big woman with red hair and . . ."

"Huge breasts. I know."

"I was going to say freckles."

"Of course you were," she said, disbelieving.

"Well, if her beer tasted like this concoction you created,

trust me, there would be no sots at Penbrooke Keep, and
Berthild would be drawn and quartered."

"Drink it and stop complaining."

Scowling, he tossed back the foul-smelling concoction
and emptied the rest of the cup. When finished, he handed the
iron vessel back to her and wiped his mouth with his sleeve.
"The least you could do, *sorceress*, is chant or pray or cast a
spell to sweeten that foul-tasting brew."

"I promise, you'll feel better in the morning."

"I'll hold you to it," he said, and smiled at her.

Stupidly, she felt a warmth steal through her blood just as
she had all those years ago when they were little more than
children. As if he read her thoughts, he looked away.

'Twas all she could do for him for the time being.
Tomorrow, she'd tend to his wounds, if he'd let her, and
then . . . sweet Mother, they would ride together to Tarth,
she supposed. Although she suspected Gavyn had a cache
of secrets.

*Did he not create a false name for himself? Aye, he was
Gavyn, 'twas true. And once he was your friend. But did he
not take your beating for you? If you feel guilt, and you do,
what do you think he feels? Anger? Resentment? Rage?
Remember, Isa told you to be wary and this man lied to you.
Even when he recognized you, he kept up his falsehoods.*

She was too tired to think about it now. She picked up her
amulets, horns, and pouches of herbs, then returned to her
place by the fire. Exhausted, she lay against her saddle, intending not to sleep but to rest her eyes while her ears
strained to hear anything out of the ordinary. As Gavyn did,
she wrapped her horse's reins through the fingers of her right
hand, as in her left, her strong hand, she held Isa's dagger.
Even though she now knew that the man lying a few feet
from her was a friend from her youth, she still wasn't certain
she could trust him.

Soon his worrisome moans eased into a gentle snore, and
Bryanna concentrated instead on the sounds of the night—
the flap of bats' wings, the rush of water in the creek, the gen-

tle breathing of their horses. Overhead the clouds oozed their way across the sky, obliterating the stars and moon.

Trust him not, she told herself. *He is not the boy you knew. He is a grown man and, most likely, a dangerous one.*

CHAPTER NINE

In the great hall of Chwarel, Hallyd's keep, the spy counted his coins, clinking them together as if he hoped the rubbing of silver would somehow create more.

"Tell me," Hallyd said impatiently. It was late. They were seated before the dying coals of the fire, the castle dogs curled up and sleeping, the bitch letting out soft little yelps as she dreamed. One guard stood at attention near the main door. The others, Hallyd suspected, were dozing at their posts.

The scrawny little man with his large hooked nose and bulbous eyes glanced up, though his fingers still rubbed the coins greedily, as if touching them fed some insatiable need deep within him. 'Twas as if he were mentally calculating how far he could push Hallyd, how much more money he would be able to extort if he said the right words.

"You have drunk more than a cup of my wine and have been paid for your work, which may have been a mistake, as you have yet to tell me what you learned."

"I was attacked," Cael grumbled, rubbing his leg. "By a wolf. This witch . . . she must've trained the wild dog to do her bidding. A huge creature she was, bigger than a horse, I tell ye, wilder and fiercer than any natural creature that walks this earth. She had glowing red eyes, she did, a shaggy mane 'bout her devil of a face, and fangs yea long." He held up his gnarled hand, his thumb and forefinger spaced three inches apart. "Blood and spittle rained from her mouth, and her roar was unlike any bestial cry I'd ever heard before. 'Twas the dog of the devil, I tell ye. Nearly had me down, she did, that beast from hell." He held up his leg and, sure enough, his breeches were torn and slashed, blood evident on the tattered edges.

"So how did you escape?"

"Me courage, that's how! I looked the beast square in the face, I did, and swore at her. Then I tried to slide through her ribs to her black heart with me knife, but she was too quick for me, she was. Grabbed me by the leg and shook me about and I was able to slice at her snout."

"And she ran off?"

"Aye."

"Must've been the swearing at her."

"Do not mock me, m'lord. The wolf, she was a terrible, fearsome creature. I'm lucky to have escaped with me life. These coins, they are hardly enough for me to sacrifice me life, now, are they?"

"You survived," Hallyd said dryly, irritated that the man was obviously trying to collect more money than what they'd agreed upon. Hallyd hated the fact that he had to rely on fools, charlatans, and imbeciles to do his work during daylight hours. How he'd love to ride after her himself. He would if she weren't three days' ride from here—a torturous journey for one who could not bear the light of day.

"I'm wounded, I tell ye," the spy went on. "Perhaps crippled fer the rest of me days. I'll be lucky if I don't have to use a walking stick."

"Then you're saying you cannot go out and follow her again?" Hallyd lifted his eyebrows in question and fingered the pouch in his hands. The coins within jingled, and Cael nearly salivated as his eyes slid to Hallyd's purse. "You have told me nothing, except about an attack by a wolf."

"Not just any wolf, m'lord, but—"

"Get on with it." Hallyd was tired of the pathetic spy's excuses and stories. "What did you learn?"

"The girl . . . she is not only with a beast from the fires of hell, but she's traveling with a man."

"A man?" His head snapped up and sudden rage roared through his veins. "*What* man?" Did this rodent of a spy need to have every word prodded from him?

"He called himself Cain of Agendor, and he looked like he'd been beaten by ten men. His face . . . I saw it in the fire-light and—"

"Let me guess. 'Twas the face of a devil?"

"Aye, a demon, with red eyes."

"And you saw him with Bryanna?"

"Aye." The weasel nodded his little head rapidly.

"They are traveling together?"

"To Tarth," he said, and that, Hallyd thought, was the first valuable nugget in the spy's tale. Had he not seen it himself? Had Vannora not foretold that Bryanna would be drawn to the very place where the curse had been born?

"Do you know anything else about him?" Hallyd asked, ir-ritated at the thought of any man with her.

"Only that he called himself Cain, and he rode a black steed that was as big and strong as any of your own horses. A prize stallion, I be thinkin'."

"A beaten man with a destrier? A horse thief, this Cain of Agendor?" The name was unfamiliar, but he would find out the truth about the man, his wolf, and warhorse.

"I . . . I know not. He claimed the horse was once his fa-ther's."

"An easy lie," Hallyd said, tenting his hands and leaning back in his chair. Who was this interloper? Why had Vannora not spoken of him? He didn't like the sound of it and sensed there was a falsehood within the tale. From the spy? From this Cain? 'Twas easy enough to find out. He read the hesitation in the spy's worried expression. He was holding back, not saying everything that he knew. Now why was that?

Hallyd decided to test the vile little man. "I might be will-ing to pay for further information," he suggested, watching Cael's reactions carefully. Was it possible he was turned? Paid more by one of Hallyd's enemies and was, in fact, here gathering information rather than reporting it? Hallyd thought not; the man was just not that clever. "If you'd like to earn more," Hallyd said, "you shall ride to Agendor and talk to the peasants and servants who work for Deverill. Find out what they know of a black stallion, and a man beaten within an inch of his life."

"Agendor is a long ride," the weasel said, already sharpening his bargaining skills. "And me leg . . ."

"If you cannot do it, then send up Frydd. I'm certain he would be glad to earn a few coins for an easy task."

"Frydd! Oh, fer the love of God, m'lord. What are ye thinkin'? Frydd is too big, too loud, his red beard far too noticeable. Now, me, I blend in. I can sneak through cracks, listen at doors, disappear into a crowd and no one notices. Frydd!" He twisted his face into a knot of disgust and snorted. "Nay."

"Then don't argue with me. If you want the job, then you shall have it and I will pay you the usual fee. Take it or leave it."

"Well, because I feel such loyalty, of course I'll ride, if I'm able."

The spy's pledges of dedication were nearly as sickening as his complaints. "Have the physician look at your wound and stitch it, then be off. I'll expect you to report back to me from Agendor within the fortnight." He leaned forward again. "Now, tell me, was there anyone else with Bryanna, aside from the devil himself and his demon dog?"

Cael caught his cynicism and was not amused. He defended himself quickly. "I am not lying, Lord Hallyd. 'Twas just as I said."

"But there is more, isn't there?"

Cael chewed on his thin lower lip, as if he were afraid to reveal something. Which was rot. Hallyd had paid for all knowledge.

"Was there?"

"I . . . I know not, m'lord," he admitted, and suddenly there was no guile in his big features. " 'Twas an eerie night. Cold. But without a breath of wind and I felt . . . I mean, I saw no one else, but 'twas as if there were a presence, a dark spirit within the forest. Something that could not be seen nor heard, only sensed."

"So you're telling me that a man, nay, mayhap Satan himself was traveling with the witch? And with him was a demon wolf."

The spy was nodding.

"But beyond all that, there was also a dark spirit lurking within the forest."

"Aye," Cael whispered and made the sign of the cross over his birdlike chest. He swallowed hard and glanced up at Hallyd. " 'Twas the very force of evil, I swear."

The man believed it to his very soul.

As did Hallyd.

Bryanna wasn't certain how it happened, how she gave herself up to slumber, but sometime during the morning hours she dozed. When she awoke and glanced over to the spot where Gavyn had been sleeping, she found both him and his steed missing. Her mare, however, was still leashed to Bryanna's hand.

Stretching in the cold of the gray dawn, she wondered about the events of the night before. A wolf? A black horse? A boy, now a man, from her past? Bryanna had nearly convinced herself that she'd dreamed it all, that her imagination had run wild.

And yet, she hadn't. Boot, hoof, and paw print were etched into the mud around the campfire, telling her differently. The cup she'd used to brew her potion was where she'd left it on a rock near the fire, which now burned brightly. Late last night the campfire had dwindled to the barest of red embers, so she had to assume that Cain—nay, Gavyn—had found firewood and stoked the dying coals to new life before he'd left.

Why? To make her more comfortable? Then why leave without waking her?

A horrid thought struck her. Had the liar stolen off with her possessions? Her heart clutched in fear, as she searched frantically for her talismans, amulets, herbs, and money. Surely he would not have stolen from her? Then again, he might think it some form of twisted justice for the punishment he'd endured.

A quick search allayed her fears; she found everything where she'd left it, including the dagger still clutched in her hand. She let out her breath. How long had she slept? How deeply? Though she'd thought she had barely closed her eyes, it appeared that she had been near dead to the world for some time as the wintry morning sky was light.

And now, Gavyn was gone.

After he'd been so insistent that he stay with her and accompany her to Tarth.

If that was where she was supposed to go.

She checked her things again and found the map—a lot of good it would do her now.

Well, if she was heading to Tarth, so be it. It seemed from the map, if Gavyn had been telling the truth, that she should keep following the old overgrown road that ran ever northward.

But why to Tarth? Just because Gavyn had interpreted the map a certain way? For all she knew, he could have been lying once more. He may not have had any idea what the etchings on the piece of doeskin meant.

Stretching, feeling her cramped muscles loosen in the cold morning, she stared up at the sky. The clouds overhead were gray and ominous, their great underbellies swollen. 'Twas only a matter of time before rain or sleet or snow would fall from the heavens.

Shaking her hair loose of the braid, she walked to the stream. On the bank, she twisted her hair behind her back, knelt on a flat stone, and searched the depths of a pool for a fish. Her stomach rumbled with hunger. She'd gotten quick enough with her dagger to impale a trout or eel if she was lucky, though it usually took more patience than she possessed this morning. She'd also learned how to block a part of the stream and create a dam with sticks that trapped fish in a smaller pool. The temporary dam had been useful in snagging trout, pike, and eel—enough to last her several meals.

Today, she saw no flash of silver scales, nor did she spy an unlucky toad near the stream for her breakfast. She'd have to wait until she reached the next village, where she would use some of her rapidly dwindling money to buy food for both herself and her horse. She had a fleeting thought of Gavyn. Aye, she almost missed the miserable lying son of a cur, but that feeling was just plain foolish. He'd left, and good riddance. The last thing she needed was a man, nay, a patient who needed tending.

She thought again of the boy he'd once been, so near manhood with his long muscles, taut skin, and first bit of dark hair sprinkling his chest and abdomen. She'd spied upon him whilst he swam and chopped wood, and one day by the stables she'd come upon him working with a horse. She could still see him leaning hard against the lead rope of that unruly colt, muscles straining in the sunlight, sweat staining his hair and running down his face to where beard shadow dared touch his jaw.

"Silly woman," she muttered to herself as she splashed water upon her face, then checked the far bank of the creek where the wolf had crouched last night, eye to eye with her. Although the silver beast had ample opportunity, she had not harmed her. She had probably just gone off chasing something in the brush. A roe deer? Or had it been something worse? Something shrouded in the dark night?

Shivering, she told herself to forget whatever she'd thought had been watching her. 'Twas only her imagination, fed by Isa's warning and the wolf's actions. Had she heard the animal snarl and fight some other beast? Nay, she'd disappeared into utter silence. Even now, just thinking about it made the flesh of her arms tingle eerily.

"Forget it," she ordered herself. She dried her face on the

hem of her mantle, then considered leaving this morn and riding for hours, stopping only to feed herself and the horse.

Tonight, if she reached Tarth, she would pay for a room for herself and a stable and feed for the mare. If it took one night, so be it, but before she scoured the village in search of . . . what? A child? Before she went about her quest, she would eat plum pudding or eel pye or roast goose or baked apples with cinnamon. Her stomach rumbled at the thought, but even over its hungry growl, she heard the sound of hooves pounding against the ground. She looked up sharply and squinted through the oak and fern.

She almost smiled as she caught a glimpse of a tall rider upon a big black stallion.

Gavyn!

So he'd come back. He hadn't stolen away in the night and left her. Foolishly, her silly heart leapt at the sight of him, bruised and battered though he was.

Though she should have cursed his return, she felt a lifting of her spirits, a sense of relief and, mayhap, something more. Something she didn't want to examine too closely. She half expected the wolf to be with him, but the wild cur was nowhere to be seen.

As Gavyn rode into the clearing and dropped onto the ground, she noticed two squirrels, a hare, a stoat, and a pheasant strung upon a thin pole and lashed to the back of his saddle.

"You killed all these this morning?"

"'Tis the best time, if you know what you're doing."

"So you're a huntsman, Gavyn of Agendor."

"When I have to be."

Bryanna remembered that about him, how the boy who was so good with the horses was just as agile with a bow and arrow. Often he'd joined the hunters and had always returned with a fat goose, boar, or stag.

"And you're feeling better?"

He nodded. "No doubt it was that foul-tasting potion you insisted I drink."

"No doubt."

At the stream, he gutted and skinned his kills as she stoked the fire. Two crows appeared, landing on high branches, cawing loudly and greedily staring at the dead animals. Other birds appeared, fighting and twittering, hoping for scraps of forgotten carrion.

Bryanna plucked the feathers from the pheasant, then singed the shorter hair feathers and rubbed the bird with bits of rosemary she'd picked a week earlier. She helped Gavyn roast the carcasses upon a wooden spit supported by two forked sticks. The livers, heart, and pheasant's stomach were cooked upon the same flat rock she had used to heat water.

She turned the meat often while he scraped any remaining flesh from the skins, which he told her he hoped to sell. Gavyn saved most of the pheasant's feathers to repair his arrows.

She had hoped that Gavyn would look heartier than he had the night before, but 'twas not to be. With the daylight, his wounds were all the more visible, his skin discoloration more distinct. The whites of his eyes, no longer softened by the night shadows, looked raw and red. Then there was the bloody patch showing on his tunic. It seemed larger than it had been the night before, as if his injury were bleeding again. Had she not touched him the night before and caught a glimpse of a vision, she would not yet recognize him.

Once the meat had cooked and they were eating, she said, "Your wounds need tending."

"They'll heal."

"I could help."

"How? Another cup of boar piss?" One dark eyebrow arched, almost daring her to try and make him swallow so much as a drop of the potion.

"You admitted it helped."

"Mayhap." He sucked on a small bone from the pheasant.

"You felt good enough to go out riding and hunting, and it seems your aim was true."

"Due to the potion?"

"Nay. Of course not." She took a final bite from the coney's leg. " 'Twas only your good eye, strong bow arm, and perfect aim that saw you through."

"You're making jest of my skills?" he asked, one dark brow rising as he tore off one of the pheasant's legs and bit into the crispy meat.

"Oh, nay, Gavyn, I would not."

He skewered her with a disbelieving glare.

"It's just that I know of herbs and medicines and—"

"And runes and witchcraft. No, thank you."

Frowning, she tossed her clean-picked bone into the fire and licked her fingers. "You expect me to ride with you, to accept you as my bodyguard, when you're half dead as it is."

"I'll be fine."

She didn't believe it for a second.

"So where are Isa and her husband. . . . What was his name? Payton?" he asked, obviously trying to change the subject.

"Parnell," she corrected quickly. Had he not listened to her lie? Had he forgotten? Or was he testing her? Should she trust him with the truth? . . . Nay, not yet. For she was certain he had not been completely honest with her. If she had not called him Gavyn, he would still allow her to think that his name was Cain.

She used some of the hot water in the cup to clean the grease from her fingers. "As you can see, they did not return, so I'd best be off soon to search for them."

One side of his mouth twitched as he tore off a pheasant wing and bit off the morsel of meat beneath crisp skin. "You'd best," he agreed, chewing and trying to hide his grin. "What if you don't find them?"

"Then we'll meet up in Tarth."

"That was your plan?"

"Yes."

"Even though you didn't know where you were going? Had no idea where Tarth was?"

She bristled a bit and suddenly recalled that even as a

youth he had nettled her, gotten under her skin. "We all were heading northward and a little to the west. We had agreed that if anything happened, we would find each other in the town."

"Of Tarth?"

"Yes, though I knew not its name."

"Do they?" he asked, wiggling the wing bone at her. "Isa and Parnell. Do they know where they're going? Do they, too, have some kind of pathetic drawing guiding them?"

Oh, dear Lord, this lie was getting more difficult by the minute.

" 'Tis Isa who gave me mine."

"Does she have the rest of it?" When Bryanna didn't respond, he added, " 'Tis obviously only part of a larger map. Where is the rest of it? Who has it?"

"I don't know," she admitted.

The breeze picked up, rustling the dry leaves.

Gavyn looked up sharply, then stood. He dropped the pheasant bone and grabbed his knife. His eyes grew narrow as he stared into the surrounding brush. Bryanna's own gaze followed Gavyn's to the brambles, moving with a flash of silver and black.

The wolf had returned.

"I wondered when you would show up again," Gavyn said, relaxing a bit. He took what was left of the squirrel carcass and tossed it into the woods. The wolf pounced on the treat and crunched it in her jaws.

For some strange reason, Bryanna was glad to see the furry cur. "I was hoping she was gone for good," she lied.

"Unlikely. I feed her."

"Dangerous."

"So far, not." He started to hurl another morsel into the underbrush, but as he drew his arm back, he sucked in his breath and dropped the meat at his feet. "Holy Christ," he muttered between clenched teeth.

"You are hurt!"

He sat down and let out his breath. " 'Tis just a twinge."

She tossed back her hair and shook her head. "A twinge? I

think not. Now lie down and let me look at your bloody shoulder. There is no nobility in suffering."

"Is that an order, m'lady?"

"That's right, so let's get to it. By the gods, you were a stubborn boy and now you're a headstrong man." She frowned. "You should not have gone out hunting."

"Then you'd be hungry."

"I can manage, thank you. Next time . . . oh, there will not be a next time. Lie down."

Grudgingly, he did as he was bid, stretching out on the ground, his long legs in front of him, his back propped up against the trunk of a sapling.

Bryanna washed her hands in the creek and, as she'd seen Isa do a hundred times before, examined the wounded man while her small cup heated water over the fire.

The whites of his eyes were turning from red to pink—an improvement—and his eye color, a rich, dark gray, was evident now. Whatever swelling had surrounded them had disappeared and most of the bruises on his skin were healing, turning from purple and green to a sickly yellow. Only a few were still the deep purple brown of a fresh wound. He allowed her to touch him, and she did so gingerly, her fingertips barely skating across his skin as she scrutinized each cut and scrape, all of which were healing. Some of the scabs were falling away and showing new, pink skin. Good signs.

There was a chance that when he'd finally healed, he wouldn't be hideous at all, but a fair-enough-looking man with somewhat straight teeth, a strong jaw, and high cheekbones. Of course, now one side of his face was a bit sunken and a scar slit the skin from temple to chin. Fortunately much of that slice was hidden in his beard. His nose was broken crooked, and she thought he'd forever have a bump upon it, but even so, he might pass for better than ugly. Once he was healed, she suspected that no woman would turn her head away when this man passed by.

Nay, all in all, he would not be disfigured, she decided,

though certainly he was no longer the handsome man his youth had promised.

"That bad?" he asked as she examined a particularly nasty scrape beneath one ear.

"Worse."

He laughed, and she couldn't help but smile. She glanced back at his eyes and found him staring at her—so close—barely an inch separating the tip of his broken nose from hers. The intensity of his gaze made her uncomfortable, even nervous. She'd tended the ill before, but always under Isa's tutelage and never with the patient scrutinizing her.

She swallowed hard and tried to ignore the sudden rush of her own blood in her ears.

His gaze shifted to her lips and she felt as if the entire forest hushed. For a second she thought he might kiss her, and something deep inside her crackled with wanting and fear. Kissing this man would be a mistake of monstrous proportions; she knew it as well as she knew her own name. She couldn't trust him. She wouldn't.

Biting her lower lip, she pressed on. "I . . . I need to look at your eye," she said.

"So look."

Oh, God.

Her hand was actually trembling. She flexed her fingers quickly and reminded herself that Gavyn was little more than a liar who had been kind enough to bring her breakfast. There was nothing more to it, no room for any romantic fantasies, for the love of St. Peter!

Gently, she lifted one eyelid and peered at the top of his eyeball.

"What do you see?"

"You mean other than a stubborn, wounded man?"

His mouth twitched. "You see that much, do you? So 'tis true. You really are a sorceress."

She smothered a smile and said with mock severity, "Oh, well, there's more to it than that. I see a stubborn, *foolish* man who doesn't know when it's wise to keep his mouth shut." She dropped the eyelid and sat back on her heels, then traced a scar along the side of his face with a finger. "I'm afraid this may linger," she said. "The skin is not healing perfectly."

"So cast a spell and make me handsome."

"I'm a sorceress, Gavyn, not God."

He laughed again.

"Now take off your tunic."

He lifted a dark brow, and even with his battered face, it was an intrinsically sexual expression. "You want me to undress?"

"If I am to examine your wounds, then I'll need to see them."

"You take it off," he suggested.

She had not time for this. "Me?" She shook her head and refused to flirt with him. As it was, her pulse was already pounding. "For the love of Rhiannon, Gavyn, just pull it off and be quick about it."

When he didn't move, she blew out her breath in disgust. "So be it." She leaned closer so that she could tug at the hem, lifting it upward, exposing the bare skin and hard muscles of his abdomen.

Bunching the fabric, she tried to pull the tunic upward over his arms and shoulders so that the dark hair on his chest became visible.

"Careful," he said, gingerly lifting his shoulder. Swearing roundly, he yanked the tunic over his head, tossed it away from his body, and leaned back against the tree.

She blanched at the sight of his chest and the gaping wound that was oozing blood and pus. Any thought of teasing him further died.

"Bad?" he asked.

She met his gaze and nodded.

"Just don't tell me you want to put leeches on it."

"Nay . . . but what has to be done will be painful."

He lifted his opposing shoulder. " 'Tis painful already."

For the first time since meeting him, she believed him. She would need a bandage, and since there were no cloths or towels, she would have to resort to using her chemise. "Wait," she instructed as she walked to a spot behind a copse of trees and stripped off her clothes. Cold air teased her skin as she removed her chemise, then tossed on her tunic and mantle. Using Isa's dagger to cut into the fabric, she tore the chemise into strips and returned to the clearing with an armful of bandages.

"You didn't have to hide to undress," he said, and she shot him a look.

"You are too sick to want to watch a woman take off her clothes."

"Never," he replied as she carefully picked up the cup of water steaming near the fire, then bent down to tend to him.

Using one of the torn strips, she dabbed at the wound on his chest, cleaning it gently. Though he tried not to react, she noticed his muscles flex and his jaw tighten as he gritted his teeth.

"Aren't you going to whisper any spells or toss some of your herbs in a circle around me? Mayhap even draw a few more figures in the dirt?" he asked as sweat beaded on his brow despite the cold morning air.

She slid him a glance. "Mayhap later. Though, considering what I might want to do to you, 'twould be best if you didn't hear the spell."

"You've already threatened to addle my brain and shrivel my cock. What could be worse?"

"Trust me, Gavyn, you don't want to know. I've a special one for those who lie to me."

"Do you?" He managed the barest of smiles.

Leaning closer to him, her fingers grazing the tender reddish flesh surrounding the wound, she felt the muscles of his chest tighten even more. A tiny thrill swept through her blood and for the briefest of seconds her breath caught in the back of her throat. Despite his injuries, he was strong. And male. Though he was bruised and beaten, his face mottled with color, there was something intense and sensual about him—

his broad bare shoulders and hard, sinewy chest—something that reached past all of her defenses and scraped her very soul.

She swallowed with difficulty, then wrapped the strips of cloth around his torso. As she smoothed the bandage over his back, her fingers encountered ridges upon the smooth muscles—scars from the whipping so long ago.

Oh, dear God.

She looked up and found him staring at her. Her heart beat a suddenly erratic tattoo, and all of her consciousness centered on that spot where her fingers touched his skin.

"Bryanna," he said, and she reacted, pulling her hand back, breaking the touch.

She wasn't fast enough.

Quick as lightning, he grabbed her wrist, callused fingers encircling her fragile bones. "Tell me," he said, his voice a raspy whisper. "What are you, Bryanna of Calon?" His skin was drawn taut over his cheekbones, his thick eyebrows knotted together in vexation, his silver eyes sparkling. "Woman?" he demanded. "Or witch?"

"Mayhap a little of both." She couldn't think, and though they were the only two travelers in this huge plot of forest, the clearing seemed to shrink around them.

"Is that so?" His fingers moved slightly, their warm pads touching the sensitive skin at the back of her wrist, where her pulse was pounding out of control. "Mayhap we should find out." His face was but a hairbreadth from hers, his eyes on her mouth.

Oh, by the Fates, he was going to kiss her. She knew it, wanted it, though the prospect scared her to death.

Her heart pounded wildly and the sounds of the forest faded as her blood rushed in her ears. His lips pressed against hers, warm, firm, causing her blood to heat as he drew her close. Oh, by the gods, she could barely breathe. But she closed her eyes and felt the heady pressure of his mouth against hers, the feel of his lips and tongue as it urged her mouth open.

She tingled inside and kissed him back, lost in a fever.

Hungrily, her body screamed for more. He shifted, still holding her wrist, forcing her hands over her head as his body slid over hers and her pulse pounded so fast she was certain her heart would burst. *More,* she thought as his free hand tangled in her hair. *More!*

Through her clothes, she felt his hardness, heard his own ragged breathing. His hand trailed downward, the warm tips of his fingers brushing the pulse pounding at her throat.

In a split second, she felt his own rapidly beating heart and a vision passed behind her eyes.

Vivid.

Visceral.

As clearly as if she had been at Gavyn's side, she saw a struggle, a violent fight that smelled of blood, sweat, and piss. The sky was scarlet, rain falling in bloodlike tears. . . .

On the ground lay a man, a man of the law with a clipped white beard and sightless brown eyes that stared upward from a bloodied face. His neck was broken, his head twisted at an ungodly angle.

Dead.

Killed by Gavyn of Agendor.

"Liar! Thief! Murderer!"

His lips found hers.

Hot.

Eager.

Filled with the hunger of a starving man.

And her traitorous body responded, his warmth invading her body. Her heart pounded in eager expectation as her mind filled with images of him holding her in his arms, pulling her tunic over her head, filling his callused hands with her breasts and letting his lips and tongue stray from her mouth, along the column of her throat, and ever downward. . . .

"Nay!" She pulled back and yanked her hand away from his grip. Her heart was beating crazily, her breath impossible to find. Was it because of a vision of death that ran like quicksilver through her brain?

Or from the wanting of this man, this murderer?

She swallowed back her passion and wiped her lips, cleansing where his mouth had pressed so urgently to hers.

His gaze found hers and locked.

He knew.

Her stomach dropped like a stone in a bottomless pond and she fought the desperation that tore at her with needle-sharp claws.

She couldn't believe her misfortune because, no matter how she looked at it, the truth was that she was falling in love with a murderer.

CHAPTER TEN

"Who was it you killed?" Bryanna demanded, backing away from him as if she'd just peered into the darkest depths of his soul.

"What?" Gavyn felt as if the spinning earth had suddenly ground to a brutal halt.

"I saw a vision and you . . . you were standing over a man whose neck was broken, his skull all bloodied . . . and, oh, sweet Morrigu, that's why you're running."

She turned away from him and began packing all of her things into the leather saddle pouch.

There was no longer any reason to protect her from the truth. "'Tis only part of the reason," he admitted as he grabbed his tunic and struggled into it. The bandages were tight, but already the poultice felt good against his skin.

"There's more?" she asked, looking at the heavens as the first drops of rain fell from the dark sky. "Mother of the earth, what more do you have to hide?"

"The horse. 'Twas not a gift."

"You stole it?"

"From my father."

"A murderer, a horse thief, a liar. Is there anything else I should know about you?" She tossed the water from her cup over the remains of the fire, wiped it dry with the hem of her skirt, and packed a few herb pouches inside. Then she placed the cup, her horns, and some amulets into the bag.

"You already know I'm a bastard."

"In more ways than one," she said angrily as she tied the lace of her saddle back, then lashed it to the saddle. "Who was this man you killed?" she asked, and when he made an attempt to help her place the saddle upon her mare's back, she shot him a glare that would turn a man's blood to ice. "I can do it. Who did you kill?"

"Craddock. The sheriff."

"The sheriff?" She threw her hands up in disbelief. "God's teeth, this just gets better and better! Was there a reason for killing the sheriff or are you just plain addled?"

" 'Twas a simple matter of him or me. I thought I should live."

She stiffened a minute, her back to him as she let the words sink in. Then she adjusted the saddle blanket before pulling on the cinch one final time. Turning, she skewered him with a glare and asked, "And why was the sheriff trying to kill you?"

"He thought it would be easier than arresting me." Gavyn settled the saddle rug over Rhi's broad back, then picked up his saddle with his good hand and swung it into place. "He was wrong."

"And why did he want to arrest you?"

"To keep me quiet." He threaded the leather cinch through the buckle as the rain began to fall in earnest. "Because I know too much."

"And what is it you know?"

As if weighing just how much he should tell her, he pulled the buckle tight. "Many things, none of them good."

"Such as?"

Kicking dirt over the remains of the fire, he said, "The less you know, the safer you'll be."

"What a load of goat dung! What kind of answer is that?" Her face was flushed, her lips pressed hard together as she strode back to him, approaching him for the first time since he'd kissed her. "Do not talk to me in riddles, Gavyn." Her sea-green eyes snapped fire and her hands were planted firmly on her slim hips as rain began to run down her cheeks and dampen her hair. "If you are riding with me"—swiftly she held up a finger—"and I haven't said that you are, but if you intend to, then by the gods you must tell me the truth. No more lies. No more half-truths, and no more talking in circles. What is it you know?" she demanded, her fury and the rain only adding to her allure. "Well?"

"That my father had my mother killed."

"He . . . what?" she gasped, one hand flying to her chest.

"She died outside her cottage. It appeared as if she fell from a woodpile while she was chopping kindling, that she tripped over a rolling piece of yew and somehow cut herself with a hatchet."

"And you don't believe it?" she asked.

He saw that she was clinging to the hope that he was wrong, that no man who had conceived a child with a woman would take the woman's life.

"I saw his hired killer riding away from the scene of her death." His jaw hardened at the memory. "By the time I got to her, she was already dead, a bloody ax in her hand." He remembered rounding the corner of the path that led to the hut where his mother, a seamstress, lived alone. When the house loomed before him, he heard nothing—no sound aside from his own wild breathing and the blood pounding in his ears. Everything—the hut, the small garden, even the few chickens near the front door, picking at bugs—seemed skewed, out of kilter. Gavyn had been winded, his legs screaming in pain, but he ran forward, calling to her. "Ma!" he yelled. "Ma!" He threw open the door to see the fire still burning, a blackened pot boiling wildly. He spun, still yelling, but knowing the truth deep in his heart. Outside again, he rounded the corner of the hut to the woodpile, where he saw her and the blood . . . blood everywhere. . . .

He blinked, felt the cold rain running down his back, found himself staring into Bryanna's concerned gaze. "The way she died, the position of the wounds on her body, 'twas obvious that she'd been . . ." He winced. "She was murdered, left to die."

"Could she not have fallen upon the blade?"

"A fall would cut once. 'Twould not account for the many wounds she suffered."

"And who did this? Who was the man you saw riding away?"

He secured his bow and arrows, lashing them to the saddle. "Craddock, my father's sheriff. Journeyed all the way from Agendor to do my father's bidding."

All the color drained from Bryanna's face and a deep sadness settled into her features. She blinked rapidly. From the rain? Or tears? "I'm sorry," she whispered and touched his shoulder, the first contact she'd made with him since their kiss. "I guess I just don't understand why. Why would a man order to have his lover killed? She did him no harm."

" 'Twas simple enough. Half of Tarth knew my mother had won the baron's favor, and Deverill made no secret of his illicit coupling. She was an embarrassment to his new wife, the Lady of Agendor."

"Over jealousy?" She shook her head in disbelief.

The rage that had been with him since those days burned bright. "Aye, men have killed for less," he whispered, trying to push aside the image that had been seared into his brain that day, the vivid picture of the one person he trusted in the world lying still, her eyes wide open, and blood everywhere. Her skin stained crimson, and the deeper, darker stain that discolored her skirt and pooled around her. He'd dropped to his knees, listened for any heartbeat, any breath, but her skin was already chilled. Dead.

He remembered hearing the mocking cry of a solitary crow sitting upon the top of the woodpile, black feathers shining in the intense summer sun.

"Her name was Ravynne." He cleared his throat and looked down at Bryanna standing in the rain. " 'Twas nary three years ago," he said.

"But you've not forgotten."

"Nay."

"And you've spent those years being a burr under your father's saddle, always reminding him."

"Short of killing the son of a cur, what better way to punish him?"

"Kill the sheriff," she said as easily as if it were the most natural thing in the world. "That certainly sends a message."

Gavyn smiled coldly. "I hope so." He glanced at the threatening sky. "I hope it's a message that's never forgotten."

"You have found nothing? No trace of him?" Deverill paced angrily from one side of the room to the other while the captain of the guard laid his weapons on the thick oak table.

"Not yet." A tall barrel-chested man with a thick beard beginning to gray, Aaron had been a soldier all of his adult life. As he yanked off his gloves and shook his head, Deverill's eyes fell on the captain's old injury. Half of one of his ears was missing, the result of a battle in his youth.

"It's been nearly a week." Deverill was vexed. How had the bastard escaped again? On Deverill's steed, no less.

"Aye, that it has." Aaron slapped the gloves into a waiting page's hands, then began to peel off his chain mail, the metal suit rattling as he undressed, then handed each piece to a waiting page. Once all the heavy pieces of the chain mail were in his hands, the lad carried them on wobbly legs to the armory, where they, along with the captain's weapons, would be inspected, repaired if necessary, and cleaned.

"By the Christ, how is that possible? Are your men imbeciles?"

"They are *your* men, Lord Deverill," the armorer reminded him, obviously tired and hungry and not concerned about the baron's foul mood.

Deverill wasn't about to be put in his place by the burly captain. "I authorized you to increase the reward."

"Aye, and we have. But no one has stepped forward claiming to have seen him. Nor the steed." The page returned, this time with a jug and two mazers. With a nod from Deverill, the pock-faced boy poured them each a cup, then offered the first to the baron.

Deverill took a long swallow, but he barely tasted the wine. Would that he could just forget his bastard son. Would that he could act as if the boy had never been born, that Deverill had never sought comfort in Ravynne's bed and rutted with her to the morning hours. But she, of all the women in his life, had been the one he had craved. Bedding the seamstress had been more than an act of sex; there had been power in it, a lifting of the spirit, a brief sating of an unquenchable hunger. And once the deed was accomplished, his appetite had only increased.

Ravynne had been as insatiable as he, eager and ready, her tight womanhood like warm honey as he'd thrust inside her, her mouth opening in a gasp of delight, her arms wrapped around his neck, her legs surrounding his waist as he'd taken her upon the straw mattress, or up against the wall, or upon the table where she'd mended ripped seams. Oh, what a sweet, hot slit she'd had. Unlike his wife's barren, cold crevice, where penetrating her was difficult as sticking a knife through hard, cold butter. Even once he had finally thrust deep into her, she lay like stone beneath him. Cold as marble and not as soft. No moisture. No heat. No passion.

Not like Ravynne.

'Twas no wonder his wife had insisted he get rid of her. It certainly didn't help matters that Ravynne was so fertile; his seed planted so easily and eagerly as to quickly take root and produce a bastard while his wife, Marden, remained childless no matter how frequent the coupling.

Deverill had no legitimate heirs. No legal issue. Perhaps that was why he felt driven to control his only known son.

And in turn Gavyn was intent on humiliating him with his wild defiance.

Aaron walked to the fire to warm the backs of his legs. "We have searched for miles, scouring forests, hills, and villages, even offending the monks at St. Michael's Monastery near Castle Gaeaf. You will probably be hearing from the bishop."

Deverill pinched the bridge of his nose. How could one man, his own damned son, make so much trouble? Mayhap the best thing to do was to let him disappear. So he'd made Deverill a laughingstock. So he'd stolen his horse. At least he was gone and that, Deverill hoped, would bring him some peace.

"Keep looking," he said without any enthusiasm, "and when you find him, do not kill him. 'Twill do us no good if he is thought of as some kind of hero or martyr. He needs to be brought in front of the court."

"Which is you.

"Aye. Gavyn needs to face me and my justice."

The captain of the guard stared at Deverill for a second, and though there was a question in the soldier's mind, an obvious query about justice, Aaron had the good sense to keep his mouth shut.

"Find him," Deverill ordered. "And, as I said, bring him back alive."

"You must travel to Tarth alone, Bryanna. Do you hear me? Alone."

Isa's voice was clear as the nearby hawk's screech on this quiet night. The wind and rain of the day had stopped with nightfall, when she and Gavyn had made camp.

"So now you tell me the name of the town," Bryanna whispered as she glanced over at Gavyn sleeping close to the fire, his hand forever wrapped in the reins of his horse. He was snoring softly, but his moans of pain had ceased. His wound was healing, and after the long day, Bryanna was starting to feel comfortable with him again.

Aye, he was a killer and a thief and a liar and the gods only knew what else, but at least she was no longer alone. Not only was he company, but she supposed as he healed he would be able to provide more and more protection.

Unless he is just biding his time before he steals away from you. 'Twas her own voice warning her this time, not Isa's.

She snorted and drew a rune in the dirt with a dry stick. *Isa.* The old nursemaid was so often silent, but tonight the dead woman had decided to tell her to find a way of ridding herself of Gavyn, and acknowledged that she was, indeed, supposed to ride to Tarth. Just as Gavyn had said.

"Why Tarth?" Bryanna whispered, hoping Isa would answer. She was tired to the back teeth of these conversations being one-sided and at Isa's whim.

Maybe you're just going mad.

"Oh, bother. Mad people don't know they aren't sane." Angrily, she dug the stick deeper into the soft mud. For nearly a day she and Gavyn had battled the steady drip of the rain, but finally the clouds had parted, allowing silvery shafts of moonlight to filter through the branches and giving Bryanna some hope that spring would eventually arrive.

And when the first flowers bloom and sun shows signs of warmth, where will you be?

She rocked back on her heels and thought about her future. What would it be? Would she still be on this quest? Would she ever meet this child she was supposed to save? Find the jewels for the enchanted dagger . . . if that was what she was really fated to do?

Fate?

Did she even believe in it?

And what of the lover she was supposed to meet? The father of her child, wasn't that what Isa had told her? She looked at Gavyn again and bit her lip. Was he to be her lover or the enemy? Isa had said there was danger. Even in death, the old nursemaid was still frightened for her.

Frowning, Bryanna tried to engage the dead woman again. "Why should I ride alone?" she demanded, her voice hushed so as not to wake Gavyn, though she knew that after he'd drunk the healing potion at nightfall, he would sleep for hours. "Why did you not tell me this earlier?" she whispered harshly. "What is the significance of Tarth, the home of

Gavyn's mother?" Her stick split and she tossed down the piece of dry wood that remained in her hand. "Is there another piece of the map? Where is it?" She glanced over at Gavyn again, sleeping so soundly. Her heartbeat quickened at the sight of him. His bruises, though still visible, were receding.

So rarely did he smile at her during their ride, but when he did and she caught a glimpse of the boy he'd once been, her heart had beat a little faster, her hands had gotten sweaty on the reins, and she'd felt somewhat lightheaded and giddy.

Don't even think that way, her own voice in her head—not Isa's—advised. *Do not allow yourself to be attracted to him. Remember the last man you found masculine and handsome, eh? The husband of your sister! One of the reasons you left Calon.* Her cheeks warmed as she thought of her misguided interest in a man who was forbidden. *You only want what you cannot have, Bryanna, the men who are challenges and dangerous. 'Tis foolish!*

Since the night when she'd first cleaned Gavyn's wounds and bound his chest, there had been no more visions.

No more kisses that caused her blood to heat and her heart to pound so wildly.

Just a steady ride northward through villages, fields, and forest.

They had stopped in one town by a river, where Gavyn had managed to sell two stoat and three rabbit skins to a tailor. Afterward Gavyn had insisted they take shelter from the driving rain and have a hot meal and beer in a local inn while the horses were fed, watered, and groomed. He'd managed to barter the rest of his hides for a little silver, as well as a few dried pieces of meat and beans from a farmer.

Later, at the edge of the village, upon spying a woman close to Bryanna's size, Gavyn had bought the chemise off her body. The woman, carrying a covered basket, had blushed to the roots of her dark hair and shaken her head. But her husband, a practical stonemason, had urged her to take the offered coin. In the end the wife had hurried into her small hut, where she'd managed to remove her underwear and quickly redress in her russet gown and apron. Still blushing, she'd emerged and handed the plain chemise to Bryanna.

The purchase had been awkward and embarrassing, but Gavyn had insisted he owed her the chemise, and Bryanna had not argued. Her own tunic had rubbed painfully against her skin during the hours of riding. At the first opportunity, when they were once again in the woods, she'd left Gavyn to tend to the horses while she changed. Ducking into a dark thicket, she'd undressed quickly, rain sliding down her spine and the back of her neck. She'd been forced to hang her mantle and tunic upon a branch so they wouldn't get muddy while she slid into the soft linen chemise. Quickly she'd flung her outer clothes over her body, replacing her tunic quickly and striding back to the spot where Gavyn, upon his steed, was trying and failing to hide a smile.

"What?" she'd asked as she'd climbed upon her mare again. Had she put something on backward? Was there a smudge of mud upon her face? Was her hair sticking out wildly? "What?"

From the vantage point atop her saddled horse, she'd turned and caught a glimpse of the thicket where she'd taken cover to dress. "Oh, no," she'd whispered, realizing that there was a definite parting of the branches, a spot where they were barer than the rest, a window into the copse. Her mouth had fallen open and she'd quickly snapped it shut. She'd turned and shot a glare up at him. On his taller horse he'd probably had an even better view of her as she'd changed. "For the love of Morrigu, did you watch me?" she asked, taking up the reins and feeling warmth steal into her cheeks. "Did you, Gavyn of Agendor, see me without my clothes?"

As if on cue, a squirrel high in the branches of an oak tree began to scold her.

Gavyn lifted his good shoulder. "I was just waiting for you."

"Liar! Sweet Mother Mary," she'd said, lapsing into the words of the faith in which she'd been raised. "Can I not trust you to do something as simple as avert your eyes when a lady is dressing?"

One of his eyebrows had risen, but he'd said nothing.

"There are names for men like you," she'd told him, embarrassed to the depths of her soul as she'd considered what a sight she'd been without a stitch on. All too easily he could have viewed her breasts, even her buttocks. And when she'd bent over to adjust her hem, her back had been to him and oh, by the saints, she wouldn't even consider *that* sight.

Feeling vulnerable and oddly stirred, Bryanna had pulled her cowl more tightly over her head and urged Alabaster through the trees toward the path. God in heaven, how had she ended up with this . . . this . . . sick spy! To further her dilemma, as she'd ridden, hearing the hoofbeats of Gavyn's mount at her heels, she'd spied the wild wolf slinking through the trees.

The wild cur never accompanied them into the villages but always reappeared when they were in the forest again. She had followed them to this spot, a protected area of a ravine, where thick trees offered some concealment. Now, having devoured some of the remains of a hare and duck that Gavyn had killed and roasted, the beast lay a few feet from the circle of light cast by the campfire. As ever, the wolf studied her with interested gold eyes and she wondered, not for the first time, what it was that had frightened her. What had sent the wolf lunging into the darkness?

Something she'd been unable to see. An unseen evil?

'Twas odd.

And frightening.

The incident had altered Bryanna's opinion of the wolf and she felt more comfortable around her, though, as she reminded herself, the wolf was still a wild animal, for the love of St. Peter!

Bryanna dusted her hands and was about to lie upon her horse rug near the fire when Isa's voice again rang through her brain. *"Leave, Bryanna. Leave now. Ride to Tarth and get thee inside the castle walls. You'll be there by morn, before Gavyn has awoken. You must go alone!"*

"Now?" she repeated. In the middle of the night?

"Aye. If you ride now, you will be at Tarth before he stirs. Listen to me, child. Leave now."

"Why is it you always tell me to do what I don't want to do?" she grumbled, again glancing at Gavyn.

"This is your quest, Bryanna."

Bryanna rolled her eyes to the clear heavens and sighed. She considered disobeying, but could not. Even if she were truly losing her mind, she felt obliged to follow this journey through. What choice did she have, with a child's life at stake?

She took another quick look at Gavyn, rolled inside his mantle and horse blanket, sleeping soundly. She remembered his quick smiles, intense gaze, and the moment when they'd kissed. A murderer, liar, and thief, he'd insisted she have warm food, safety, even the chemise she now wore. Could she really leave him? Steal off into the night? Her heart cracked a little and she blinked against an unexpected rush of tears.

Oh, how stupid was she?

She swiped the tears from her eyes and gave herself a quick mental kick. The worst thing she could do was fall in love with him further.

"Go, child! Go now! Do not tarry," Isa instructed. *"'Tis your fate to reach Tarth by dawn!"*

Wonderful, Bryanna thought sarcastically. Here she was exhausted and giving up not only a night's sleep but Gavyn's company and protection. 'Twas idiocy to leave, and yet Isa's guidance had gotten her this far.

"By the saints, Isa, you try me," Bryanna said crossly, though she gathered her rug and laid it gently across Alabaster's back. "And please, do not mention my fate again. My twisted fate is a pain in the arse."

CHAPTER ELEVEN

Atop a high cliff Castle Tarth rose through the late-morning mist like a great stone serpent appearing from the depths of the sea. Spirelike towers knifed into the gray sky of dawn and wide wall walks were protected by massive crenels built of the same tan stone as the rest of the keep. The main gate yawned open, the portcullis raised. But as Bryanna rode nearer to the giant keep, she saw that the towers were crumbling, pieces of the curtain wall missing, the entire castle looking as if it were on the brink of decay.

Bryanna had memorized the few marks on the map and remembered Gavyn's description of the area. In the first morning's light she'd reached the three rocks and the cliffs on either side of the old road. After passing through the narrow pathway that rarely saw the sun, she had ridden across the icy river that rushed beneath Alabaster's belly. Bryanna had lifted her feet, but her boots and the hem of her mantle had gotten wet before she made it to the main road, a wide dirt cart path that bore the footprints, hoof marks, and wheel ruts of hundreds of visitors.

She'd joined the slow traffic, riding past an oxcart filled with woven sacks of flour. A spotted team struggled to pull the heavy cart toward the town as mud collected on the creaking wheels and the driver cursed his luck. Two huntsmen were returning, a dressed stag flung across the back of one horse, and a string of quail, geese, and ducks across the other.

Tired and aching, Bryanna rode into the town and tried to imagine what she was to do here. The shops were already open. An innkeeper's wife sweeping the stone steps to her establishment caught Bryanna's eye.

What would it hurt to pay for a hot meal and a few hours' rest in a bed? Bryanna didn't think twice.

Since Isa had not seen fit to tell her what to expect in this town, she ignored the heavy wife's raised eyebrows at a woman traveling alone. She paid for a hot meal, warm bath, and private room for herself and a grooming and fodder for her horse. Before she actually took over the room, she walked through the town and found a seamstress shop, where an elderly woman was patching the sleeves of a pale green mantle. There were a few clothes for sale—tunics, breeches, mantles, shawls, and hats that, for one reason or another, had been left in the shop. Bryanna found a periwinkle shift that was a little large for her and a belt to cinch the waist tight. She also purchased another chemise, and a bag in which to keep her extra clothes. A few other pieces of apparel caught her eye, though they were far too costly. Still, she couldn't help but imagine how smooth and warm the purple fabric of a long velvet dress would feel against her skin, how the woolen mantle trimmed in black fur would warm her.

"I could make you a bargain on the dress," the old woman said from her stool. "'Tis like no other in all of Tarth. I was commissioned to sew it for a noblewoman who was staying at the keep, but she was ill and took a turn for the worse. When she died, her husband refused to buy it." She frowned, the wrinkles in her face deepening. "I tell you, this is the most beautiful dress you'll find. Oh, you can visit the tailor at his shop on the next street, but, Wallyn, he drinks more than his share and you can see it in his work. His stitches are often long and uneven." She climbed off her stool and pointed a gnarled finger at the lovely embroidered velvet. "I did this myself. See that silver thread?" She ran a broken nail along the perfect stitches. "Is it not exquisite?"

"Beautiful," Bryanna agreed, and she wasn't lying. In her

mind's eye she saw herself in the dress, walking down the long staircase at Calon, or dancing in the great hall.

The old seamstress slid a glance at Bryanna. "You know, this gown, it looks as if I made it just for you. It would be much lovelier on you than the fine lady whot commissioned it, with her hair the color of a rat's fur and teeth too big for her mouth. Not that I mean to speak ill of the dead, mind you. But you, now, you would look like a true lady in so fine a gown."

Bryanna fingered the fabric and thought of all the beautiful clothes she'd left behind, hung upon pegs in her room at Calon. She would *love* this dress, but 'twas impractical. She could not be burdened by anything but absolute necessities on her journey. Sadly, she shook her head. "Not today. Sorry. Just these things here." She held up the practical tunic, belt, and chemise.

The old woman clucked her tongue. "Sorry? Aye, 'tis sorry you'll be when some fine lady buys it out from under you."

Bryanna remained firm and, after paying for her purchases, walked onto the street, where a drizzle had begun again. She hurried past children chasing each other, and carts and horsemen on the street. Dodging puddles, scurrying rats, and piles of dung, she made her way to the inn, where she was shown to her room.

'Twas heaven!

Two men brought up the tub, and a boy, the innkeeper's eldest son, lugged up buckets of warm water, then lit the fire. A girl lined the wooden tub with towels and offered soap. Once she'd left, Bryanna stripped off her clothes and sank gratefully into the warm water. She removed the plait from her hair then slid below the surface. Her muscles relaxed, the strain of riding for days and sleeping on the cold ground melting as she lifted her hair, washed it, then scrubbed her body. Using a pitcher of warm water left by the girl, she rinsed herself as best she could.

Once she'd finished washing, she leaned back in the tub and closed her eyes. Of course, her thoughts returned to Gavyn. She'd not ridden a hundred feet away from the camp before she'd begun to miss him. "Stupid girl," she whispered aloud, just as she had all night long. But his image had lingered in her mind and she'd thought more than once that she'd made a horrible mistake in leaving him.

All because of a dead woman's words. She wondered where he was at this moment. Surely he'd awoken by now. Oh, she knew he'd be furious with her, and that thought brought a smile to her lips.

Sighing, she tried not to remember his quicksilver eyes or how they'd sparked with amusement or sometimes a smoky desire when she argued with him. Nor did she want to think too much about the way she'd felt when he'd kissed her. Nor would she even consider the jokes they'd shared or the way his dark hair fell over his forehead or any bloody thing about him.

Would she see him again?

"Aye," she said aloud. Of course. She just didn't know when. There was a chance that he would follow her here; then again, he might be angry enough to head in the opposite direction. If that were the case, then someday, after this wretched quest was finished, she would track him down.

The warmth of the water oozed through her muscles to her bones. By the gods, she was tired. . . .

Bryanna was riding, faster and faster, leaning over the white mare's withers, hearing her labored breathing. "Run, Tempest, run," she yelled, urging the flagging horse upward along the rocky spine of the snow-covered ridge. Wind whistled eerily as the horse pounded up the incline, breathing hard.

Bryanna glanced over her shoulder and through the thin, brittle saplings she saw men in dark robes, their faces hidden. From atop their strong and fleet steeds, they chased after her, determined to run her to the ground.

Dear God, what was this?

Where was she? What mountains were these where the trees were sparse, the air thin, and the threat of evil lurking behind every outcropping of stone?

Her heart was racing a million beats a minute. Fear spurted through her bloodstream and it was difficult to draw a breath. 'Twas as if her windpipe were closing.

She leaned down, her nose nearly in the mare's coarse mane, her hands wrapped in the reins. "Hurry!" she cried, her throat so tight it ached. "Hurry. Faster!"

She heard shouts behind her.

Who were these determined men on their dark horses?

Why . . . oh, God, why were they racing behind her relentlessly? The clamor of the horses' hooves thundered in her ears. Bryanna felt the snap of their excitement. She sensed the bloodlust in their souls.

"Gavyn," she cried.

Where was he? Had he not been with her but a second earlier? Sleeping beside her by the campfire, reaching out to kiss her and . . .

Her horse stumbled, nearly pitching Bryanna to the ground, and her gaze dipped downward to the bottomless chasm with its sheer stone walls. *Oh, sweet Mother Mary!*

"No!" she cried, pulling on the reins so hard that the frozen leather snapped in her hands. The horse suddenly broke free, galloping faster and faster, ever upward into the whiteness of a blizzard that screamed around her.

From behind, she heard the sharp shouts of her hunters, and from the depths of the dark canyon below the howl of a wolf rose on the shrieking wind.

Bryanna scrabbled for the torn reins as she saw the pinnacle of the ridge and beyond it nothing but blowing snow and open air. "Tempest!" she cried to her horse. "No . . ."

But it was too late. The horse raced at a breakneck pace, upward. Faster and faster until the ledge was beneath them. Every muscle in the mare's body bunched. Bryanna gasped as the horse sprang over the edge of the sheer cliffs, flying through the air and into empty space.

Holy God, help me!

Bryanna clung to the mare's mane and hardly dared

breathe. Cold . . . so cold . . . and the breeze seemed to whisper her name. "Bryanna . . ."

She looked up.

Through the swirling flakes she spied a rosary falling ever downward, the sharp beads glistening, green, red, gold, and white. She tried to grasp it but the slippery holy loop eluded her fingers and fell over her head just as her horse began to fall into the dark nothingness.

Where was Isa when she needed her?

Where was Gavyn?

The rosary circled her throat and began to close around her like a garrote being pulled ever tighter by an unseen hand. She coughed. Gasped. Tried to scream, but her throat was closed, the sharp-beaded drawstring strangling her, cutting off her air as she fell. The world was turning black! She clawed at her throat, clenched her hand around the garrote and pulled with all her strength.

The rosary broke.

Jewellike beads rained around her. . . .

An opal for the northern point,
An emerald for the east,
A topaz for the southern tip,
A ruby for the west.

Downward through the blizzard she fell, the horse disappearing from beneath her as she plummeted into the deep crevice where there was no light. . . .

"Bryanna!" Isa's voice came to her at last. *"Bryanna, awaken. There is no time to tarry. You must find the first stone. Look for the woman, Gleda. Trust her. Do as she says."*

Her eyes flew open.

Bryanna found herself still in the tepid water, a crick in her neck from resting against the rim of the tub. Goose bumps rose on her flesh and her teeth chattered, but most of the chill was the result of the lingering nightmare.

It had seemed so real. And now she felt as if she'd seen that ridge before, ridden upon the horse she called Tempest. 'Twas insanity. She knew of no such mare, and she'd never climbed high into the mountains of such a barren, snow-covered land. She had no rosary made of the stones of the old riddle. She touched her throat where the rosary had choked her; she still found it difficult to breathe.

The water in the tub was cooling by the second. She rubbed her arms, stood, and tried to dispel the horrid images as she dried herself by the fire.

"Isa?" she said, shivering as she threw on her new clothes. "Isa, are you here? Who is Gleda? Why should I trust her?" As she picked up her new belt, there was a soft rap upon the door. Half expecting the old nursemaid to appear, she called, "Come in," as she finished cinching the belt around her waist.

The innkeeper's daughter arrived with a platter of hard bread, cheese, and a bowl of lentil and onion soup. Seeing that she'd interrupted Bryanna's dressing, the girl blushed and appeared frightened as a doe suddenly facing an archer. "Excuse me, but you said to bring it up in an hour."

"Yes, thank you." Bryanna's stomach rumbled in expectation at the scent of the food. "Just put it here on the hearth, where it will stay warm."

The girl settled the platter near the warm coals. As she straightened she asked, "Would you like me to have Henry come up and retrieve the tub?"

"Not just yet," Bryanna said. "Don't worry about it. I'll let someone know when I'm done with it."

When the girl left, Bryanna tossed her dirty clothes into the tub of cooling water and set to work rubbing soap into the fabric. In truth, she had little experience with such a chore, but she'd seen the washerwomen at their task at both Penbrooke and Calon, so she did the best she could, scrubbing her chemise and tunic. Once she'd rung them of most of the moisture, she draped the clothes over a bench near the fire, then sat on a corner of the bed to eat. Dunking pieces of hard bread and cheese into the warm stew, she ate every last drop.

She was still tired and her vivid dream hadn't quite disappeared, but at least she had an immediate task: to find this Gleda woman. She couldn't imagine what she'd say to her when she met her.

Hello, I'm Bryanna of Calon. Yes, the daughter of a baron, and I've traveled many, many miles to meet you upon the orders of a dead woman.

No, that wouldn't work.

Well, hello there, Gleda. I'm Bryanna and Isa sent me to find you. I don't know why, and oh, by the way, Isa's dead.

Not much better.

"Fie and fiddlesticks," she grumbled. Using her comb, she eased the tangles from her hair. She longed to let her hair dry as she sat by the fire, but, of course, it would take too long. Hadn't Isa told her to move? She had to find this Gleda before Gavyn showed up.

Assuming that Gavyn actually made the journey to Tarth, she knew that once he arrived he would be mad as all the dogs in Hades.

Quickly she plaited her damp hair. Donning her mantle and boots, she hurried down the stairs and through the hallway to the doorway, then stopped and turned when she spied the innkeeper's wife hovering near the door to the kitchen. Perhaps she would know of Gleda.

Bryanna retraced her steps and approached the hefty woman. Obviously she had been close to the fire, probably cooking. Her round face was red as a winter apple and sweat was rolling down fleshy cheeks, where bits of flour indicated she'd been baking. "Do you know a woman named Gleda?" Bryanna asked.

"Gleda?" The wife frowned as if she'd heard incorrectly, all the while dabbing at her chin with the hem of her apron. A striped cat, slinking in from the kitchen, wound itself through the woman's thick ankles. "The beekeeper, ye mean? Ye're asking about her?"

Bryanna had no idea, but nodded. "Yes, the beekeeper."

"Gleda, she's an odd one, she is." The woman's eyebrows

became one line and her nostrils flared as if she were smelling rotten fish. "Why would you want to see her?"

Why, indeed? "'Tis personal, a message I need to deliver," Bryanna said with a smile. "Where could I find her?"

Rebuffed that she wasn't going to learn a little gossip, the woman lifted a disgruntled shoulder. "She lives on the east side of the village, not far from the river." The wife waved a pudgy hand in disgust. "Her husband, he raises goats and pigs on the other side of the creek. Ye can't miss the place. It reeks to high heaven." She turned back to the kitchen, where the fire was burning brightly. Pyes were baking and a cauldron hung from a metal chain, its contents boiling rapidly and the scents of savory meats seeping into the hallway.

Bryanna wasted no time and hurried out the back door to the stables. Alabaster had been fed and groomed, and though tired, greeted Bryanna with a gentle head butt. "That's a girl," Bryanna whispered into the mare's ear as she scratched her neck.

"'Tis a fine horse ye 'ave 'ere, m'lady," the lanky man said as he saddled the mare. "Docile, yet she has a bit of fire in her, yes?"

"A bit," Bryanna admitted, and allowed the man to help her into the saddle.

"That's good. Too much and ye've always got yer 'ands full, ye do, but not enough and 'tis as if they're 'alf dead—no amount of whippin' will do ye anna good."

"Do you know Gleda?" she asked.

"Liam's wife? Aye." He nodded, scratching his head. "What would ye want with her?"

"They live near?"

"On the farm, east of town, just across Butler Creek." He worried his lip a bit. "But, m'lady, you donna look as if ye be in need of honey or a midwife, so I don't know why ye'd want to be anywhere near Gleda."

"Is there something wrong with her?" Bryanna asked.

"Nay, oh, nay," he said quickly, but she noticed as she took the reins that he turned away to make a quick sign of the cross over his chest.

"Thank you." Whoever Gleda was, the townspeople avoided her.

Yet Bryanna had no time to be discerning. With a quest to fulfill, she would have to take her chances.

She pulled on the reins and guided Alabaster through the narrow streets littered with the carts of peddlers, merchants, and farmers. Peasant women and children picked through the pottery, baked goods, cheese, and sacks of grain.

She found her way to the main road that ran along the river and turned Alabaster east.

To whatever lay ahead.

CHAPTER TWELVE

The witch's daughter was near.

Hallyd closed his eyes and shut out the noises of the keep as he stood at his window. His eyeballs ached, but the clouds were dark enough that the pain was bearable, and he'd been drawn to the window of his daylight prison by her impending approach. His nostrils flared and he caught her scent, closer than before. His hands clenched into fists upon the sill and he felt a rush of blood through his veins, his manhood swelling as he imagined her lying beneath him.

In his mind, he saw her lying upon his bed, her eyes turning from blue to black as anticipation and fear dilated her pupils. She knew he would take her and that their rutting would be violent and harsh. She would welcome him with a semblance of terror, all of her senses heightened as the wanting and the fear collided, making her tremble with female lust. He would kiss her, taste her, and run his tongue over her hard little nipples until she quivered with need, writhing and bucking beneath him, and then, oh, then he would thrust into her with all the fury of sixteen years of denial.

And she would give him the dagger, soon replete with magick stones, possessing the power to lift the curse, the power to elevate him to an indomitable ruler.

The woman and the dagger.

The time was near. So near.

He rubbed his fingers together expectantly and his mouth

was dry with the wanting. He forced himself away from the window, snagging his black mantle on a hook near the door to his chamber. Damn, the darkness that confined him! He tugged it free, then hurried into a hallway dimly lit by sconces, smoke curling to the ceiling. He hastened down the stairway, his boots clanging loudly, spurring him onward to the chamber far below. Today he carried no cup of goat's blood, no bit of gruel to appease her, but simply flew down the steps and half ran down the hallways until he reached her door, unlocked it, and strode into the dark cavern.

A few candles were lit, burning low, their tallow pooling and dripping down the sides of the altar. Steam rose from the small bowl upon the altar cloth. He glanced around the large bare chamber. Her cot was empty, the sheeting thrown back, and for a second he thought Vannora was gone.

Then he spied her.

Small and gaunt, aye, but upright. Vannora's cloudy eyes seemed brighter than usual, a swatch of color in her bony face. She emerged from the darkness to stand behind the altar, her bare feet within the circle drawn upon the floor, her long black tunic pooled at her ankles. Gold and silver embroidery decorated the bodice and sleeves of this gown, one he'd never seen before, but then it didn't surprise him. Nothing about Vannora did. Though she'd never admitted it, he knew she did not stay in this dark chamber night and day.

She prowled.

He'd felt her move, slipping through the keep like a cold, invisible wind. He'd felt her presence outside, though of course he'd never seen her leave this dungeon.

He'd thought about it over the years and decided she had the power to not only change her shape but to manifest herself as others wanted to see her.

And that frightened him.

Was she actually an old crone about to die? A bygone sorceress herself, ready to pass into another realm?

Or was she stronger than he imagined and, using him for her purposes, feigning the limits of her power?

"You know she is near," Vannora said in her raspy voice. Her hair was no longer white but streaked with gray, and she managed the thinnest of smiles upon lips that were starkly red, as if she'd feasted on something raw. "'Tis time. The witch's daughter is at Tarth. But you know this already, don't you?" she said, her hair darkening in the feeble light. "You already caught her scent."

He nodded.

Her smile stretched a little wider, a bit crueler. She glanced into the bowl of water with its steamy surface, though no fire heated the liquid. Her eyebrows flicked together for a brief second, as if she'd seen something that surprised her, an image that shouldn't have appeared. "You must ride at dusk," she said as water ran down the walls in slow drips, puddling upon the floor outside the white circle.

When he didn't reply, her eyes narrowed. "What is it? There is something bothering you."

"The witch's daughter is not alone."

One eyebrow arched. "And this troubles you?"

"She rides with a man."

"Ahhh . . . and you are threatened?" She nodded, those milky orbs gleaming with interest.

Hallyd's jaw tightened. "Concerned. I'm concerned, not threatened. I've heard that he may be the bastard son of Deverill, Lord of Agendor."

To his irritation her lips curved in satisfaction. "A bastard? Of a nobleman?"

"If the rumors be true."

"Much like you," she mused.

He felt hate rise in him. "My mother and father were married."

"After you were born, though, wasn't it? After that sweet little mother of yours killed your father's wife? What was it now? A potion of hemlock? Or nightshade?" Her smile faded. "If the *other* bastard threatens you and ah, ah, ah—" She raised a single finger in front of his face to stop his protests.

"If he threatens you, treat him as you would any enemy. Dispatch him."

Hallyd's hands closed into fists. He felt his blood grow hot and a twitch develop above one eye. When he spoke, his voice was strained to the point of snapping. "In sixteen long years, Vannora, there was never mention of a man. *Never.*"

"Worry not."

"This is no oversight," he said. "You knew of this and yet you decided not to tell me."

"Trust in yourself. You can deal with the man. In fact, 'twill be good for you." Her expression was pure cunning as she stepped closer to him, her toes not quite touching the edge of the ring drawn so carefully around the altar.

Was it a trick of light, or was she becoming more vital with each breath? She seemed younger than when he'd first walked into the room, her flesh smoother and plumper.

"And you must also remain patient, for though the time has come for the mating, you must not be overeager. I know your fantasies, Hallyd, that you will take the woman as your own for as long as you want, make her yours, brand her with your demon seed. For it is not just the lust you must quench but the burning revenge against the one who bore her. Still . . . you must not harm her yet." Her face was pure determination and in it he saw the pulse of his own life. "Only she can find the stones. Only she can renew the power of the dagger. Only she can set you free of the curse."

He felt the muscles between his shoulders bunch. "I've waited so long. To consider more time as a prisoner to a witch's spell is unimaginable."

"Nine months is but a small price to pay for your sight, for your freedom, for your power." He was about to argue with her again, but she stopped him cold. "I have helped you, Hallyd, and I will continue to do so, but only if you promise to obey what I tell you. Only then will the curse be lifted."

"I am truly damned."

"Aye," she agreed, but again a smile touched her lips, "but not forever. Now, we can begin. If you agree."

He nodded, though he gritted his back teeth until they ached.

"Good. The prophecy will be fulfilled."

"The prophecy?" His strong fingers clenched into fists. "What is this you speak of?"

"The ancient legend of the Chosen One. Do you know it?" she asked lightly, as if she were toying with a babe.

Since he had abandoned his father's dark arts and the cloaks of Christianity, Hallyd put no stock in prophecies. "Yes, of course I know it." Drivel. Why should it matter to him?

Vannora was already chanting quietly, like a child savoring a favorite rhyme. "Sired by Darkness, born of Light, protected by the Sacred Dagger, a ruler of all men, all beasts, all beings. It is he who shall be born on the Eve of Samhain. . . ."

"Another ridiculous forecast. We know where the Sacred Dagger is. There is no Chosen One."

"Not yet," she whispered, a secret smile on her shiny lips.

"What's that supposed to mean?"

"You shall see, in time. For now, we must set it all in motion."

She held out her hands, her palms faced toward him so that they were directly above the white circle. He placed his palms against hers and felt a coldness so sharp and icy he had to summon all his strength to press his flesh to hers. "With this power I bestow upon you, you shall be able to seek her out, to touch her, to fool her. She will be given a potion to make her pliant and submissive. A wanton vixen."

"If you can do this, why not just lift my curse?"

"Ah, Hallyd, if only I could. But the curse must be lifted by the blood of Kambria. You know this. Only through Kambria's daughter."

"You could have given me this power before now," he charged.

"But you were not ready; the time was not right." Her cloudy gaze stared deep into his and began to glow with an eerie, inhuman light that bored straight to his heart.

Her voice lowered to the timbre of a beast. "Speak no more," she ordered, and linked her fingers through his. She smiled with a malice as evil as hell itself, revealing the snags of her yellow teeth. Before his eyes those jagged teeth appeared to straighten and whiten. Lengthen. Sharpen.

Within the room he felt a wind blow hard and fierce through his body and into his soul. Her flesh, once as cold as the sea, suddenly heated and he felt her pulse, her lifeblood, beating in his own body.

Stronger.

Faster.

Her fingers tightened their grip, until he imagined they were great talons, piercing his skin.

She uttered words in a strange language, one he didn't understand, without moving her lips.

A fierce wind rushed through his body, threatening to crush his bones and pulverize his organs. Pain screamed through every inch of him. He let out a scream that never reached his ears and still she clung with a ferocity and strength he would never have believed. Blood flowed from his hands, red drops falling to hit the white circle, where they sizzled and hissed.

And the circle moved.

Shifting.

Spinning.

The room seemed to fade and he saw a vision of the dagger, shiny and bright, the stones intact. Someone was raising it to the heavens, higher, higher. The blade ignited. Fire rained and, with a deafening, rumbling roar, the earth cracked.

He looked into her eyes, saw into the vortex of her soul. She was suddenly more beautiful than he could have imagined, her hair long and black, her smile seductive, her eyes clear and beguiling. Yet beneath it all was the lure of pure, pulsing, perfect evil.

He knew not if Vannora actually changed, or if it was a trick of light. Was she just playing with his mind?

It didn't matter.

The dice had been cast, his fate determined. His nerves were singing, his blood rushing hot through his veins.

"There will be a child born of this mating," Vannora said, "and then the curse laid upon you will be lifted. You will rise again and rule again, not just here at Chwarel but over other baronies as well. But first you must destroy all of your enemies, any who would thwart you. Do these things and you will be powerful, Hallyd. So it is written."

She dropped his hands.

He glanced up quickly, caught a glimmer of something in her suddenly clear eyes. "What?" she asked, the spark in her eyes quickly extinguished. "Is this not what you want?"

"What about you, Vannora? What is it you are waiting for? Why is this so important to you?"

She smiled enigmatically. "'Tis my mission to right the wrongs that have occurred because of the loss of the dagger. Kambria's actions have upset the balance between the worlds. My entrance to the Otherworld relies upon that babe . . . the Chosen One. As the prophecy makes clear, he will be born on the Eve of Samhain, the only night when the veil between the worlds lifts for passage. Just as you need the dagger, I need the child."

So this was the reason she had appeared to him soon after the dagger was lost and the curse was cast upon him. He had wondered why a dark witch would choose to live here, aligning herself with a near-blind, cursed man.

Now 'twas clear. She needed the babe . . . a special child.

"You want my son."

"The child you would never want. The child who, if he ever found the dagger, would have the power to rule all of Wales, including you."

"So why should I beget this threat?"

"Ahh," she said, smiling as if she understood his very soul, "because the creation of the babe I need, 'twill be a glorious task for you—mating with Kambria's daughter. Your demon seed with a sorceress of Light. Yes, the fulfillment of your lust will bring me the power I need to enter the Otherworld. And fear not. Without the dagger, the Chosen One will be helpless. You, Hallyd, will be the true ruler of all Wales."

He felt the wanting swell deep within at the mention of his imminent reign . . . and Kambria's daughter.

"Patience," she warned. "Don't let this chance slip through your fingers as Kambria did."

His jaw clenched and pain flared in his temples at the mention of the witch. The memory of the hot, stirring wanting and her cold rebuffs still resounded with the pain behind his eyes. How he'd ached to spill his lineage of darkness within that fiery temptress. . . .

"You will have your chance with Kambria's daughter," Vannora said, reading his thoughts. "For now, you must let the sorceress find the gemstones. Only she can do this. Take care not to thwart her on her quest, or all will be lost."

Hallyd didn't argue. He had always suspected that she was using him, just as he was using her. His gaze skimmed her renewed body. "You seem to be getting younger, to have somehow recaptured your youth."

"Is that so?" she said with a laugh, and for a second she appeared no more than twenty. Her face was full of vigor, her hair shimmering, her eyes bright as amethysts, the color of twilight. " 'Tis an illusion, Hallyd, for I, on this earth, am old as the moon."

He snorted in disbelief. "And young as the stars."

"Mayhap," she admitted. "But when the sun sets, you must leave. Tonight is just the beginning."

A shudder passed through Bryanna's body.

As if something bitter and cold had slid through her soul.

'Twas lunacy, of course, and yet she glanced over her shoulder as she rode. "Stop it," she ordered and wrapped her hands more firmly in the reins as she rode away from the village, toward the fresh smell of the river. Who did she think was chasing her?

Faceless men wearing dark cassocks?

Like the dream.

Or are you hoping to find Gavyn riding like a wild man, desperate to catch up to you?

The question irritated her. She leaned over the mare's withers and urged Alabaster onward, ever faster. She didn't want to admit that the dream had scared her, nor did she like the idea that a part of her was hoping for a glimpse of Gavyn, furious though he might be for her abrupt departure.

"How foolish is that?" she wondered aloud as the first rays of sunlight slanted through the mist that had clung to the sky until late afternoon.

Concentrating on the road ahead, she felt the sun on her back as she passed several huts and told herself to ignore the reactions of the innkeeper's wife and groomsman. So they thought Gleda a little odd; people at Calon and Penbrooke had thought the same of Isa.

And yourself . . . when you were a girl and saw playmates no one else could.

Still, she could not help but feel a bit of trepidation as she crossed a narrow rushing creek that snaked through the valley, then spied a flat wooden structure with a thatched roof, a goat pen attached to it, and a row of bee skeps made of straw not far from the living quarters. Smoke rose from a chimney of stone while pigs were rutting in a copse of oak trees, their snorts audible over the occasional bleat of a goat. Bryanna decided she must be at Gleda's home.

She dismounted and walked to the front door, where a man was seated upon an upended oak log, sharpening his scythe. As she approached he spit upon his whetstone and ran it, screeching, along the tool's curved blade.

"Excuse me," Bryanna said when the farmer, so interested in his work, didn't look up as she approached. "Sir?"

As her shadow reached him, his head snapped up. He stared at her from beneath the brim of his cap, his deep-set eyes looking her over before he glanced at her horse. "Eh?"

"I'm looking for Gleda," she said as he blinked beneath the brim of his cap. "Does she live here?"

"Gleda, y'say?" he repeated, shouting so loudly one of the goats lifted his bearded head.

The door swung open and a woman, looking frail as a newborn bird, crossed the threshold. "You don't have to yell, Liam," she reprimanded as she wiped her hands on her apron. "For the love of God, we're not all as deaf as you are—oh . . . my . . . by the stars! Kambria?" she whispered, turning white as a swan's feathers.

"I'm sorry. My name is Bryanna."

"Nay . . . oh, lass . . . you look just like . . ." The woman swallowed hard, her hazel eyes rounding and her right hand moving deftly, making the sign of the cross over her small chest.

This little spry thing was the person two people in the town feared?

"Come in . . . come in," she insisted, ushering Bryanna inside and leaning back to say, "Have you no manners, Liam? See to the lady's jennet. By the stars!" she said, shaking her head as she closed the door behind them.

A fire burned in the hearth, casting red and gold shadows on the whitewashed walls and warming a pot of stew that hung from chains over the flames. Chickens clucked and roosted on crossbeams, and a cat, spying Bryanna, slunk deeper into the room, away from the large plank table where a distaff, teasels, and a pile of goats' wool had been left.

"That man! Sometimes I wonder if he has any manners at all. Now, please"—she waved Bryanna onto one of the benches—"sit down and rest a bit. You look like you've ridden a long way. Where have you come from?"

As Gleda pushed her spinning items to one end of the table and sat on the far side, Bryanna slid onto a bench facing her. Absently she rubbed at a sore spot on her throat as she gave the older woman a shortened description of her journey. Rather than admit that she was being guided by the voice of a dead woman, or that she'd spent time with a murderer, she said only that before Isa's unfortunate death, the nursemaid had entrusted Bryanna with some of her personal things, one of which was a dagger, another the map. She removed both items from a pouch and placed them on the table before Gleda.

" 'Tis a miracle you found me," Gleda whispered, tears shining in her eyes as she fingered the dagger and smoothed the map upon the tabletop. "I thought Isa may have had these, but I was not certain. She never admitted as much." She smiled despite the sadness evident in her features. "Isa . . . dear God," she said, her voice husky. " 'Tis horrible that she was slain."

Worse than you know, Bryanna thought, but did not say the words. "Her murderer was found out. Justice was served."

"Good, good," she said, but seemed distracted and far away for a few seconds. Finally she cleared her throat and asked, "So . . . now you are here because of your mother?"

"Nay, 'twas Isa who sent me."

"Oh, yes, I know. But you seek me out because of your mother and the curse."

"My mother was cursed?" Bryanna asked, shaking her head as the fire hissed and a cat with mottled fur slid beneath a stool by the hearth. Cursed? What was this farmer's wife talking about? "She didn't tell me."

"Of course not. She couldn't." Gleda laid a wrinkled hand upon Bryanna's, and the lines around her lips tightened. "She died shortly after you were born."

"What? Nay! My mother died but a few years back at Penbrooke. I was there." She drew her hand away and stood quickly, knocking against the bench and startling the cat. It hissed and slipped quickly away to hide behind a small cupboard.

What was this heresy? She knew her mother, was raised by her. Bryanna remembered all too sadly how she'd stood at Lenore's bedside and seen her unmoving body, just as she'd witnessed Isa's.

"Who was your mother?" Gleda asked softly.

"Lenore. Lady Lenore of Penbrooke."

"Ah. Then 'tis true." The older woman was still seated, but

she shook her head sadly. "As I thought. Lenore was not your true mother, not the woman who conceived you, child."

"Nay!" Why had she bothered to come here? Nearly stumbling over her bench, Bryanna took a few steps backward, toward the door, but the old woman's voice stopped her from departing.

"This map"—Gleda pointed a knotty finger at the bit of deerskin laid upon the scarred planks of the table—"is your mother's. And that dagger." She crooked a finger at the weapon still in Bryanna's hand. "The Sacred Dagger was hers as well."

"Sacred Dagger?" Bryanna scoffed.

"Aye, before the stones were pulled from it, before it lost all its magick. The magick of Llewellyn."

"What?" The woman was talking nonsense, and yet she knew of the jewels. "Llewellyn?" Bryanna said, repeating the name of the great Welsh warrior.

"Isa knew."

Bryanna's heart turned cold as stone.

"Knew what?"

"What had happened to Kambria's girl child. The babe that was missing."

"And you think that this missing baby is me."

"Are you not sixteen? Born in the winter?"

Bryanna nodded slowly in disbelief, not wanting to hear the words coming from the old crone. So what? The beekeeper was daft, an old storyteller spinning legend. Her tale meant nothing.

And yet Bryanna felt every nerve in her body tighten as wariness, like the premonition of evil, crinkled the back side of her scalp.

"Do you have siblings?" Gleda asked. "A sister or two?"

"Y-yes."

"Do they look like you?"

"Yes!" she said so loudly a rooster who'd been sleeping in the rafters crowed loudly and ruffled his feathers at being disturbed.

Gleda's old eyebrows lifted in question. "You all resemble one another?"

"Aye!" Bryanna insisted, though she knew it was a lie. Swallowing hard, she watched a solitary coppery feather drift from the ceiling. Is this what she had ridden so long to hear? Lies about her mother? Lies about her birth?

But as she counted out the heartbeats pounding in her ears, all the old doubts assailed her. 'Twas true, she was the fairest of all her siblings. She was the only sibling who used her left hand, the only child whose eyes were not the same deep blue as Lenore's. Her hair was curlier and redder than any of the others' and . . . Oh, dear God, she thought she might be sick.

What was this woman saying? That all of her life had been a lie? That she didn't even know her own mother?

"You know I speak the truth," the woman said sadly. "And because you are here, I know without question that Isa is dead, may she finally rest in peace." She blinked against a sudden spate of tears but sniffed them back and placed an old hand upon Bryanna's shoulder. "You, child, are Kambria of Tarth's daughter. There is no doubt. You're the one we've been waiting for. You, as foretold, are the sorceress. And with you comes the darkness."

CHAPTER THIRTEEN

His head pounded and his bladder was stretched to the point of bursting.

Gavyn opened one eye and winced as daylight pierced into his brain, not the gray of dawn, but a higher mist with sunlight reaching through the branches overhead. He rubbed his aching head and blinked to push the sleep from his brain. By the gods, he felt as if he'd drunk too many cups of mead the night before, when all he'd had was that miserable-tasting potion that the beautiful witch had concocted.

He glanced over to the area where Bryanna had been sleeping.

It was empty, the log where she'd propped her saddle now bare. "What?" he whispered, disbelieving. He rolled over, his gaze, now clear, searching the surrounding area. Maybe she'd moved away from the fire. . . .

But there was no sign of her.

Nothing.

"Bryanna?" he called, the sound echoing in his chest, for he knew she'd disappeared, felt the emptiness. Yet he couldn't stop himself. "Bryanna, where are you?"

He sat up quickly, yanking on the reins, and Rhi snorted at the disturbance.

The camp was empty.

She was gone.

As was her horse.

And all her things . . . the dagger, pouch, map, amulets, and horns of herbs, too, were missing. All that remained was the damned wolf, sitting up near a mossy oak tree, looking at him expectantly.

"And where were you, eh?" Gavyn asked the wolf. "Could you not warn me?" Determined not to think about the headache thundering in his skull, he climbed to his feet and quickly searched the camp for any sign of her. There was none. For a second he thought something might have happened to her, but there was no sign of a struggle, no blood upon the ground, and he was certain her cries would have awoken him from his deep sleep. Since neither his own stallion nor the damned wolf had let out so much as the smallest of sounds, he assumed no foul play had occurred. Nay, she had left of her own volition.

Without so much as saying good-bye.

"Damn fool woman," he growled, kicking a charred stone from its place by the fire and sending it flying into the woods, where it slammed against a tree trunk, then ricocheted to hit another sapling.

Why had she left him? It wasn't thievery. She'd not taken any of his few pathetic belongings. No, she'd just stolen off into the night.

Well, she was an odd one now, wasn't she? With her spells and potions and curses . . . a damned witch. And a beautiful one at that.

His head felt as if a steel-shod destrier was trampling his brains. Most likely she'd mixed a strange herb into that foul piss-tasting brew she was always forcing down his throat.

Furious at himself for trusting her, for caring what the hell happened to her, he walked to the nearest tree and relieved his overloaded bladder. He had slept far longer than usual, as evidenced by how thick and long was his stream, as well as the position of the sun, which, though shrouded in mist, was obviously high in the sky. Lacing up his breeches, he cursed again.

At the creek, he splashed water upon his face and raked it

through his hair to clear his thick head and cool his temper. Still furious, he packed his few things quickly and considered changing direction. Why follow her?

Because you cannot resist.

Because she is the woman of your dreams.

Because you're a complete and utter idiot.

"Christ Jesus," he said as he saddled his stallion and climbed astride. It had been his intention to ride to Tarth before stumbling upon her; he shouldn't change his plan just because of the whim of some bloody woman.

As he lifted the reins, he glanced back at the wolf, still sitting and staring at him. Probably hoping for some breakfast. Too late, for either of them.

"Well?" he said to the wild dog as he kneed his stallion and took to an overgrown path leading to the road. "Are you coming?"

As if she understood, the wolf scuttled under a fern, leapt over a fallen log, and started following the horse, always trailing ten or twenty yards away, running in the shadows of the trees, just as she always did.

When he reached the road, Gavyn didn't think twice. He turned toward Tarth. He'd not yet reached the three rocks, but they were nearby, so, if he was lucky, he'd reach the village before nightfall.

He'd been blinded by her beauty, and aye, by her quick tongue, but it might have all been a trick of his mind. She had, after all, left him. And could he blame her? Nay. He touched his wound, where now there was little pain. His headache was also fading. Truly, the woman had the healing touch, and though he'd nearly stupidly lost his heart to her, he did feel clearheaded again. He'd seen her dagger often enough and wondered if it was the magickal, legendary knife, the Sacred Dagger of Tarth. His mother had spoken often enough of it, and as a youth he had dismissed it as an old woman's tale, a puff of smoke. But she'd told him of the intricately carved hilt, and Bryanna's blade had been just as his mother had described it.

According to legend, the Sacred Dagger was once owned by a powerful witch. Its magick was strong enough to cause storms to rise, the sea to roll back, or the earth to crack. Men had killed for the dagger and wars had been waged. Fearing it would get into the wrong hands, the witch had dismantled it, removing the magick stones from the hilt and scattering them to the four winds.

Though he hadn't believed in the tale, why would a noble-woman, riding alone, have such a blade? Devoid of stones, the knife was worth no more than a huntsman's weapon. But, if the jewels could be found, the damned dagger would be worth a king's ransom. Valuable enough to buy his innocence or, mayhap, bring his father to his arrogant knees.

If he believed in the legend.

Which he did not!

He felt a jab of conscience, but not for the old man. Nay, Deverill's soul could rot in the hot embers of hell for all eternity. But Bryanna had been kind enough to him and helped him heal, and he could not lie about how his blood ran hot at the sight of her.

Though she had lied from the beginning. He knew not why he'd caught her scolding and calling for Isa, but he didn't believe for a second that the woman and her husband would be patiently waiting for Bryanna at Tarth. Nay, 'twas a bold untruth said quickly to convince him she was not really alone. But as the hours had passed, she had never once admitted the truth.

'Twas a mystery.

Did you not lie to her? His conscience was such a nag! He'd been forced to avoid the truth for most of his life, and yet he felt more than a tad of regret that he had not been completely honest with her.

He imagined her now, riding alone on some kind of mission, on her way to Tarth. He missed her. As irritating and bossy and headstrong as she was, he'd gotten used to her and had spent many an hour dreaming of what he might do with her were their trip together to continue.

Angry with himself, he spat into the bushes.

Aye, 'twas a curse to be attracted to her, even care for her. "Damn you, woman," he muttered, as if she were nearby. Her face flashed in his memory, her laughter trilled in his ears and her fury, when she'd been angry with him, was still nearly palpable. He'd been half in love with her before he was a man at Penbrooke, and those old feelings were surprisingly rekindled. There had been other women in his life, but none who had left such a searing impression on his brain.

And just these nights past, it had been all he could do not to kiss her. She had felt it, too. He was certain of it. Had he not witnessed the fire in her gaze when she'd touched him? Had he not felt a thrill slide down his spine, a tightening in his groin? Had he not imagined making love to her long into the night and groaned when his cock had become rock hard, a stiff shaft aching for release?

Now, *that* was a curse.

He reined Rhi past the carcass of a dead boar, flesh rotting. Its predator was nowhere to be seen, though crows cawed overhead in anticipation of a meal.

So was it true? Could Bryanna of Penbrooke, that spoiled, fearless child who had confided that she had friends no one else could see, truly be a witch? Could that bit of map be some kind of ancient chart that would lead her to . . . what? A spot where the hidden stones were buried or locked away? Where were the other pieces of the map? He'd memorized the etchings and they made little sense. Mayhap only a true witch could read the old piece of deer hide.

"Bah!" He didn't believe in hags with cauldrons, magickal potions, and curses and spells. He urged Rhi northward. He would ride to Tarth and find Bryanna if she was still there. If not, he'd track her down.

Why? he wondered. *Why follow her? Why not just leave her be? She left and you can wash your hands of her. Aye, she's beautiful and aye, she does seem to have some healing powers, but so what? There are many women who profess to heal or know magick. So what if they are not the woman you dreamed about? Leave her and be done with it. She's trouble, Gavyn. As are the dagger and map.*

And therein lay the problem.

If there was one thing Gavyn could not ignore, it was trouble. For the first time that afternoon, his lips twisted into a determined smile.

Like it or not, he was going to catch up with her.

" 'Tis a lie!" Bryanna could not believe the untruths of this little woman she'd traveled so far to meet. But all the doubts, all the questions, everything that had made her think she was different from the rest of her family rushed through her mind. The noise became a dull roar, like that of the sea crashing inside a cavern on a cliff face. In an unsteady voice she asserted, "I am the daughter of Lenore of Penbrooke." She hooked a thumb at her chest and suddenly doubted everything she'd held true for all of her sixteen years.

"Are you certain?" Gleda asked. "Because, I swear to the stars above, you're the spitting image of Kambria." Gleda turned to the door and latched the lock. " 'Tis my husband," she said in a whisper. "Though he's deaf as a stone, 'tis surprising what he sometimes hears."

She walked to the fire, stirred the stew with a long spoon, then ladled some of the soup into a cup and brought it to the table. After setting the mazer in front of Bryanna, she took her seat across from the younger woman again and leaned over the planks. Her voice was little more than a whisper when she said, "Now listen to me, Bryanna, for this is the story of your birth. You can tell me you do not believe me when I've finished. You can call me a lying wench, if you see fit. But trust me, what I'm about to tell you is the truth and I swear it upon my poor son's grave."

Bryanna wanted to disagree, to tell this goat farmer's wife that she'd made a horrible, stupid mistake. Instead, she swallowed back her protests, placed both her hands upon the mazer to warm them, and nodded for the old woman to continue.

"You are the sorceress, here to light the way for the Chosen One. Nay, do not argue—" Gleda held up a quick hand, palm out, to silence the protest she saw forming upon Bryanna's lips. "Just listen. I know you think that Lady Lenore of Penbrooke is your mother, and that's as it should be, for she herself knew no differently."

"What? Nay! 'Tis impossi—"

"Shh," Gleda scolded. "Hold your tongue until I'm finished." She glanced toward the door, then, satisfied that her husband wasn't listening at a crack in the wood, continued.

" 'Tis true enough that you're the Lord of Penbrooke's daughter. Lord Alwynn, a handsome man was he, and lusty, too. He spread his seed near and far from Penbrooke."

"I want not to hear this about my own father." Bryanna felt her face warm as she stared down into the mazer she held in a death grip.

"Yes, you do, Bryanna. Elsewise why would you have traveled all this far? You are Alwynn's daughter, aye, but your mother was an apothecary's daughter. Her name was—"

"Let me guess," Bryanna said mockingly. "Kambria." She didn't believe a word this old crone said, except, mayhap, that she knew of Isa and her father.

"Yes." Gleda's thin lips pursed. "Kambria was a small woman, but strong, with flaming red hair and eyes as green as the emeralds in her dagger."

Bryanna froze, her gaze rising from her cup to stare at the woman.

"So you know of that, do you? I did not know if you were aware of the missing jewels. Without the gems, the knife, as you see," she said, lifting the ugly dagger, "has no power."

Bryanna didn't answer and Gleda, apparently satisfied that she was convincing the younger woman, placed the blade onto the table near the map again. "Like you, Kambria had a flare to her dogteeth and used her left hand more often than her right."

How did this woman know so much about her? How could

Gleda know that while all of Bryanna's siblings had straight teeth and favored their right hands, she did not?

"Oh, Kambria was smitten with your father, and 'twas her undoing. But who could blame her? Alwynn, he was a handsome devil." She sighed and, though she was staring at Bryanna, in her mind's eye Bryanna guessed Gleda was envisioning her father as a young man. "He was a tall, strapping baron, with a twinkle in his eye and an easy laugh. He'd caught a glimpse of the apothecary's daughter in the village and had been enchanted."

"Her being a witch and all."

"Shh," Gleda reprimanded sharply. From the other side of the door a goat bleated, its bell ringing as it walked. Gleda ignored the noise and continued. "Lord Alwynn, he had come to Tarth in search of recruits and mercenaries, but with one look at Kambria, he set his mind on having her."

"But he was married. . . ."

Gleda narrowed her gaze upon Bryanna, as if to convey a wisdom shared only by women. "Aye, that he was, though a marriage vow hasn't stopped some men from lifting the skirts of someone other than their wives. And, mayhap Kambria knew of his wife but didn't care. She was as rebellious as I think you might be, and couldn't or wouldn't resist his advances. It matters not now. The result was the same. Theirs was a short, albeit passionate time together, but it lasted long enough that you were conceived."

"Nay! My mother is—"

"Yes, yes, I know. Lenore." She sighed. "I'm getting to her."

Bryanna wasn't certain she wanted to hear the rest of the old woman's tale, no matter how false it might be. It seemed a sacrilege, even heresy to hear lies about her parents, both now dead and unable to defend themselves. Cringing inside, Bryanna braced herself with ever-increasing dread.

"As the Fates would have it, Lady Lenore, too, was with child. Alwynn had planted his seed with both of the women he loved within two weeks of each other."

"I doubt that—"

" 'Tis the truth I tell you, Bryanna," Gleda insisted as she plucked a bit of goat's hair that had caught on a nail in the table. She rubbed it between her fingers, twisting it into a fine string. "When nearly half a year had passed from his visit, after summer had faded and the leaves on the trees had started to curl and turned brown around the winter apples, it became apparent that Kambria was with child. No longer could she cover her swollen belly with clothes that hid her shape. The local priest at the time was Hallyd, who now is the Baron of Chwarel, which is less than a day's ride from here, to the east."

"A priest?"

"No longer. His brother, who was baron, befell a horrible accident. Within hours of the death, Hallyd quickly gave up his holy cassocks for the barony. Truth to tell, he was anything but holy or God-fearing. But as a young man, he was power hungry. He had heard of Kambria and was obsessed with her, the dagger, and her magick. Upon learning that she was with child he became enraged. Proclaimed her both a whore and a witch. It was ugly, I tell you. Hallyd railed against her and threatened her with her life if she did not tell him the whereabouts of the dagger.

"She refused, but Hallyd was relentless in his persecution of her and he was determined to bring about her ruin. 'Twas thought that he had wanted her, and it infuriated him to learn she'd given herself to another and carried his child. In the end, Hallyd would be satisfied with nothing but death for her and the babe."

Bryanna protested no more.

"Foreseeing his vengeance, Kambria stole away one dark winter's night. She headed south and east. To Penbrooke."

Bryanna's stomach cramped. "No," she murmured. "Oh, no . . ."

Gleda was nodding, her fingers working the wool. " 'Tis true. Within days, Lady Lenore's time had come, but the birth was not easy and lasted far too long. When the babe finally arrived, the cord wrapped around her tiny neck, she was blue and could not breathe. Lenore, too, struggled, bleeding and nearly dying herself. Had the babe survived, most likely she would have been severely addled, a half-wit, but it was not to be."

"The child died?" Bryanna whispered.

"So it is said."

Bryanna shivered. She had never heard this story, never known that she'd had another sister. . . .

"When Kambria appeared at Penbrooke, Alwynn, fearing his wife would not survive knowing she had lost a babe, made a bargain with his lover." Her old eyes found Bryanna's and she no longer rubbed the thread of goat's wool. "He agreed to place Kambria's daughter to Lenore's breast."

"You're saying that was me," Bryanna said, disbelieving. Oh, this was wrong, so very wrong!

"Lady Lenore, so near the brink of death herself, did not notice the difference. 'Tis said that when the babe took her teat in her mouth and suckled, Lenore began to grow stronger."

"Oh, that is such rot!"

Bryanna shook her head so violently that the cup within her hands sloshed, splashing hot broth onto the table and her hands. As if she'd expected the reaction, Gleda dropped her piece of twisted thread and quickly mopped the hot liquid with a rag from a pocket of her apron.

" 'Tis the truth I speak, child," Gleda said.

"Then how do you know of it?"

"The only person who witnessed what happened, other than Lord Alwynn, was the woman who cared for Lady Lenore's children."

"Isa," Bryanna whispered, stunned.

"Aye, not even her servant Hildy guessed the truth," Gleda said, mentioning Lenore's most loyal servant.

Bryanna was shaken by the truth in the old woman's tale. The notion that she was not Lenore's flesh and blood explained so many things. Had not she been different from her siblings? Had not Gavyn pointed out her father treated her differently than he did her sisters and brothers? Bryanna took a sip from the broth while her mind raced in a dozen different directions. Morwenna and Daylynn were but her half sisters? Tadd and Kelan not her full-blood brothers? Oh, sweet mother of the earth, was that why she was so different, why she was chosen for spells and visions and curses and charms. . . ?

"Aye, 'twas Isa," Gleda answered, sniffing and swiping at her cheeks with the back of her sleeve. "She was sworn to secrecy."

"What then happened to Kambria?" Bryanna asked, feeling a chill that ran the length of her body. Though a part of her wanted to hear the rest of Gleda's tale, another part warned her that she wouldn't like what she was about to learn.

Again the older woman sighed. " 'Twas a tragedy. She returned here to Tarth, and Hallyd, he was waiting. Demanded the dagger, he did, and when she wouldn't give it to him, he and the men closest to him chased her high into the mountains. 'Twas winter, everything covered with snow and ice. She could not escape. Killed for her witchcraft, she was. And when her body was found, strange markings were found upon her throat, much the same as the bruises upon yours."

"What? On mine?" Bryanna touched her throat.

"Aye." Gleda brought her a mirror of polished metal and held a candle to Bryanna's face. She saw her image, her tousled red hair, eyes that appeared more green than blue, the pupils huge. Circling her throat was a ring of tiny bruises.

"The rosary," she whispered and thought of her dream. Fear curdled the contents of her stomach. What was this? How could something she only conjured in her mind bring a physical impression upon her? She pressed a finger to the small bruises and winced in pain.

"They are real," Gleda told her solemnly. "They are identical to the marks upon Kambria's neck when her body was discovered. Bruises and cuts, as if she'd been strangled by something . . . aye, a rosary would do it. Some say she was strangled, but rumor has it Hallyd and his men stoned her."

"Dear God," Bryanna whispered, thinking of her dream. Could any of this be true? Fear, like smoke oozing under a doorway, crawled up her back.

"You know 'tis true. Dreams that are grounded in truth leave a mark. Your dream came to you to reveal your mother. I suspect you felt her tragic destiny quite deeply."

"It seemed so real."

"'Twas only a dream," Gleda said, but she seemed saddened, as if she knew something she didn't dare confide. "You, Bryanna, are the only sorceress who can protect the Chosen One. Only you can piece the dagger together. It's important, you see, for you will need the Sacred Dagger to save the life of the child. You must keep it with you always."

"This child . . ." Bryanna shook her head. "I know not of a babe."

Her eyes grew wide as Gleda slowly repeated the old prophecy. "Sired by Darkness. Born of Light. Protected by the Sacred Dagger. A ruler of all men, all beasts, all beings. It is he who is born on the Eve of Samhain. 'Tis your destiny, Bryanna, to save the child."

"From what?"

"All that is evil."

"Who is he?"

"Your own child, Bryanna. For you are the Light the prophecy mentions."

"What? No!" She couldn't think about this nonsense.

"'Tis the truth I speak."

Bryanna's mind ran in circles. Certainly this couldn't be true. "Then what . . . then who is the Darkness?" she demanded, her heart racing. "If I'm the Light, then who is the bloody Darkness?"

When Gleda didn't answer, Bryanna said, "I do not have a child. This . . . this is all the musings and gossip of . . . of old women. A bunch of lies, that's what it is. Lies!" She gathered in a deep breath as the older woman stared at her.

"'Tis the truth I speak."

"Then prove it. Where is she? Kambria. Where is she buried?"

Gleda snorted. "Your mother is in a pauper's grave outside the village walls, far from the sanctity of the church's cemetery. 'Tis nearly a day's journey from here."

"So all who were a part of this are dead, yet you know of this, how?" She studied Gleda, who was suddenly overcome with a deep sadness. "From Isa?" she guessed.

The elderly woman went over to the fire and picked up the metal prod. Jabbing at the burning logs, she adjusted the wood so that the flames crackled and burned bright. "Aye. Isa was my sister," she said.

Was that true? Isa had never spoken of her family.

"Waylynn, Kambria's father, was our brother. He was your grandfather. An apothecary."

"Is he yet alive?" Bryanna asked, though she guessed the truth.

"Oh, nay. He died years ago. Far away, crossing the River Towy." Her mouth puckered as a veil of sadness came over her. "So you see, child, you are of my blood. Of Isa's blood. Kambria was our niece, mine and Isa's. And we're all descendants of Llewellyn."

"The great one?" Bryanna said. "Is—is that why people in the village fear you?"

Gleda nodded and sighed, as if she found the whole ordeal tiring. " 'Tis natural, I suppose. And then there are rumors that it's not just Llewellyn, but Rhiannon as well, that she had a child sired by him."

"The great witch? You're saying that you and I . . . and Isa and this Waylynn are all descendants of an affair between . . ."

"Mortal and immortal, aye."

"That's impossible." Bryanna wasn't going to swallow this fish of a lie. 'Twas insanity.

"So you're one of them? A disbeliever, eh? Don't you know that all people fear that which they do not understand?"

"Then I would be afraid all the time because I understand nothing! Nothing!" Dead women talking to her, sacred daggers, now this . . . this heresy that she was . . . not even completely human. 'Twas an old woman's folly. But an old woman who believed every word she breathed. Bryanna saw it in her eyes. "All right," she said, catching her breath and trying to think clearly. "Do you have the stone?"

A whitish eyebrow rose.

"The first stone," Bryanna said. "If all of this . . . belly rot is true, then you can prove it, right? By coming up with the first stone. So do you have it?"

"You mean a jewel for the dagger?"

"I . . . I don't . . ." In truth, Bryanna wasn't certain, but Isa had definitely mentioned a first stone. "Yes, the jewel," she said emphatically, for then the little woman might tell her more, at least a portion of the truth. "Where is it?"

"Nay, 'tis something you must find."

"I must find it? But I'm here. If you have the bloody gem, then—"

"I don't."

Bryanna was flabbergasted. This was crazy. "Then why did I come all this way?" she asked, trying to make sense of this. "So . . . so . . . *how* am I supposed to find it?"

"You'll find a way. I'll help."

"You will?" She stared at the tiny bit of a woman. How could she possibly help? "So, now, let me understand this," she said, trying to think while a hen clucked softly overhead. "You . . . you are a witch as well? You draw runes and cast spells and pray to the Great Mother?"

"A witch? Nay. Not really. What I feel is not nearly as strong as what Isa sensed." She shook her head. " 'Tis true that I have seen visions at times. I foretold my own son's death, I did. But I've learned to keep them to myself. When I saw that one of the potter's daughters would drown in the river, or that the innkeeper's wife would bear no sons, people got angry and afraid." Her thin lips drew downward. "You see, they don't understand." She glanced around the interior of her home again. "Now, come. We have but a few hours of daylight left and much to do."

"Just a minute." Bryanna was still struggling to make sense of it all. "If you and Isa and I . . . and Waylynn are all of the same blood, why was not Isa, or you or any of the progeny of Waylynn, the child of Light? Why *me*?"

" 'Tis written."

"Where?" Bryanna demanded. "Written *where*?"

"Here." Gleda tapped the piece of doeskin with her finger, then picked it up. "This"—she wagged the leather under Bryanna's nose—"is only a piece of it. 'Tis your quest to find the rest." Turning her back on Bryanna, she carefully wrapped the dagger in the deer hide, then tied it together securely with the twine she'd twisted from the goat hair.

"My quest?" Bryanna repeated, tired to the back teeth of riddles and circles and half-truths and especially quests or journeys or missions of any kind. "I thought my 'quest' had to do with a child. And the bloody jewels and dagger."

Gleda smiled and handed the wrapped knife to Bryanna. "Keep this with you, always. Do not let anyone see it."

Bryanna nodded and didn't mention that already Gavyn had seen the map, that it was he who had pointed her in the direction of Tarth. Nay, from the serious expression in the birdlike woman's face, Bryanna had best keep that information to herself.

"We'd best be off," Gleda said, watching as Bryanna tucked the dagger and doeskin into a pouch on her belt.

As the woman rose from the bench, Bryanna experienced a chill. Was it possible Gleda could read her thoughts? She claimed she had some powers, that she had foretold events before they'd happened, but . . . nay, certainly not. The old woman crossed the packed floor and snagged a worn brown cloak from a hook near the door. "Your journey does involve a child, Bryanna." There was a glimmer of sadness in her eyes as she tossed the mantle around her thin shoulders. "Now let's find out what that is."

"And how are 'we' going to do that?" she asked.

"By entering Tarth Castle."

Bryanna remembered the castle upon the hill. "Why?"

"You need the protection of the castle gates, the guards and the castle walls."

"From whom? Hallyd?" she asked, and without thinking about what she was doing, she touched the bruises at her throat. "The man who killed the woman you presume was my mother?"

"Aye." She adjusted her cowl, drawing the string tight around her face. "You need protection from Hallyd. But there are others as well."

"Others? Oh, no. Isn't he enough?" Oh, this was crazy! *Trust Gleda*, Isa had told her. *Do as she says.*

"Many know of the dagger and its power. There have been legends and tales and lies spun for years, exaggerations."

"So its power is limited?"

"Aye," Gleda said, reaching for the handle of the door. "It depends upon the person who holds it in her hand. The Sacred Dagger derives much of its strength from she who holds it. Nonetheless, many would kill for it."

"How comforting." Bryanna didn't bother hiding her sarcasm as Gleda opened the door and a rush of fresh air caused the fire to brighten.

"Oh, child," Gleda said with a knowing smile as she stepped outside, "nobody said setting upon a quest would be easy now, did they?"

CHAPTER FOURTEEN

Sleet pounded upon the roof of the inn as the mercenary sipped his ale in a dark corner of the establishment. Carrick of Wybren had finally heard something that might lead him to the woman he sought—Bryanna, with her dark red hair, quick smile, and dancing eyes. She was as beautiful as her sister, Morwenna, the ebony-haired beauty he'd plundered so many years ago.

He felt a twinge of conscience at the thought of Morwenna. What odd twist of fate had led her into the arms of his own brother, to become his brother's wife? He'd been a fool not to take her as his own, but then, how could he be expected to keep it in his breeches with so many fair wenches to chase? 'Twas best to ignore his conscience, just as he had for so many years. Ignore the regrets and enjoy the weight of the coins in his pocket, savor the game of tracking, the thrill of hunting.

Carrick took another swig and leaned over his mazer, the wound in his upper arm aching slightly. It had begun to heal over the past weeks, though it still felt raw at night. Ironic that the wound had been inflicted by the red-haired woman he was now pursuing. Not that he blamed Bryanna. At the time tension had been high in the keep at Calon, a killer on the loose. Still, it seemed odd that he was trying to save the same woman who'd damned him to this pain.

"Another cup would ye like?" the comely serving girl

asked as she breezed past. With a tiny nose, pouty lips, and
pillowy breasts, she was pretty and she knew it, using her
flirtatious nature to her advantage. "Or more pye can I get
fer ye?"

"No, thanks." He'd already pushed the remains of his food
aside. Though the crust had been flaky and sweet, the mixture
of fish, onions, and lentils had been dry and tasteless. No
amount of chives nor parsley could disguise the fact that the
fish had been on its way to becoming inedible before it was
cooked.

He drained his mazer, paid for the meal, and armed with
his newfound knowledge, slipped into the night, where the
sleet still slanted from the nearly dark sky and the mud on the
streets was thick enough to stop several carts. Oxen struggled,
trying to slog onward, and drivers cursed, their whips useless
in the bog, their clothes drenched and covered in mud as they
tried to inch their cart wheels forward.

Turning his collar over his neck, Carrick glanced up at the
sky and silently cursed the weather as he climbed astride his
steed. He had considered staying in the town. He could afford
to pay for a room and a woman for one night, but he'd ignored
the temptation. It was best to keep moving, continue tracking.

Though he'd not yet located Bryanna, the gossiping girl at
the tavern had sworn she'd served a woman who looked like
the one he described. "Aye, red hair and fair complected she
was," the serving girl had said. "Dressed like a noblewoman,
but her gown was dirty and . . . Oh, by the Fates, I remember
now. How could I forget? She wasn't alone."

His head had snapped up at this information.

"Nay. She was with a man, and a good-looking one he was.
Dark hair and eyes, but from the looks of him he'd been in a
spot of trouble. He'd had a horrible beating, still bearing the
bruises he was. Even so, you could tell he was handsome
enough and a hunter, I think. I heard he traded his furs for
goods—including the chemise of the mason's wife!" Eyes
gleaming, she'd leaned over the table, giving him a closer
view of the tops of her breasts as she added, "The hunter, he

insisted upon having the chemise. I tell ye, the poor woman barely had time to get into her house so she could undress with a little privacy. He practically ripped it off her body."

Was this so? Or simply the imaginings of this chattering ninny?

"What did he want with the chemise?"

" 'Twas for the noblewoman he was riding with, of course," she'd said with a wink. "No doubt he ripped the other off as he bedded her. He looked the kind, I'm tellin' ye."

"So you know that kind, do you?"

She'd licked her full lips so that they glistened. "That I do."

He'd ignored the obvious invitation, an offer of a warm bed and sex long into the night. But now, riding into the coming night with sleet running in icy rivulets down the back of his neck, he knew he was a fool.

Tarth Castle appeared more eerie and decrepit at twilight than it had in the daylight hours. Though torches and sconces burned brightly, the bits of illumination did little to make the crumbling stone walls and dangerous spires look more welcoming. As she rode toward the town, Bryanna shuddered at the sinister appearance of the keep, rising up on the hill, the sky darkening ominously over the surrounding mountains.

Not for the first time she wished that Gavyn and his powerful black horse were with her, for though he was still recovering from wounds, surely he was more reliable than this sparrow of a woman astride the ancient, nearly lame horse Liam had not wanted out of his sight. Bryanna wondered where Gavyn was this moment. He would have awoken hours ago, and there was a chance he was riding to Tarth, approaching the village gates this very minute. Her heart beat a little faster and she told herself she was a romantic ninny, but she couldn't help but look for him or the black steed with its white markings.

Silently she cursed Isa for insisting that Bryanna leave him.

"Ride to Tarth and get thee inside the castle walls! You must go alone!"

Riding up to the fortress, Bryanna was glad to have Gleda at her side, if only for company. The old woman had insisted that Bryanna collect her meager belongings at the inn, though Bryanna had a fair share of misgivings about staying in this decrepit castle, even if hospitality were to be offered.

As they approached the main gate of the castle, a guard wielding a long quarterstaff stepped out from the shadows and blocked their path.

"Halt, there," he ordered in a bellowing voice. "State your name and business."

"'Tis I, Quigg. Gleda. So hush. There is no reason to yell at me," she said, as if her feathers had been ruffled.

"The gates are to be closed."

"Oh, fie, Quigg. Enough of this. Send for Father Patrick and be quick about it."

"'Tis my job."

"I've known you from a boy. Now send for the priest or let us pass."

Grumbling, Quigg conferred with another man whom Bryanna thought might be the captain of the guard. Gleda inched her horse closer to Alabaster and leaned near enough to Bryanna to whisper, "Quigg knew my son. Fought with him in the battle where he died. He's a good man, just . . . narrow-minded. Now the priest is in charge of the keep, but that is only temporary because Baron Romney followed his wife to the grave, the result of a sickness that killed so many here just after the Christmas Revels. His son, Lord Mabon, is now the baron, but he's still returning from a battle far to the east. He and my son fought side by side," she added sadly. "'Twas Mabon who brought me the news of Frey's death. He's a good man and no one at Tarth will want to anger him. Not even Father Patrick, the priest who is serving as baron until Mabon's return." She smiled, though Bryanna noticed her teeth were clenched and her lips barely moved as she spoke.

"Excuse me," the soldier, Quigg, said. "Would you please state your business?"

"Of course," Gleda said as a few drops of rain began to fall and splatter on the ground near the castle walls. Gleda motioned to Bryanna with a gloved hand. "This is Lady Bryanna. Her sister is Morwenna of Calon and her brother is Lord Kelan, the Baron of Penbrooke. 'Twould be a shame if Sir Mabon returned to Tarth and found out that during his absence the daughter of an ally wasn't offered hospitality but was turned away, would it not?"

The guard shot a dubious glance at his superior, a huge man with eyes set deep in his skull and a complexion that had been ravaged in his youth.

"I'll see that Father Patrick knows you are here," the captain said. He barked an order at a page standing by, shivering in the rain, and the boy took off at a dead run. The captain introduced himself as Sir Giles. As he chatted with Gleda, Bryanna waited under the cover of the yawning gatehouse with the portcullis raised above them, smoke from night fires drifting to her nostrils. The cold of the coming night seeped through her mantle, and she wondered, not for the first time, if coming to Tarth had been a mistake. From astride Alabaster she was able to view the bailey, where a few leafless fruit trees grew and a single well was visible, its bucket creaking as it moved with the shifting of the wind. Alabaster's head was up, nostrils flared, and she sidestepped nervously, as if she, too, sensed something evil within.

'Twas idiocy to be here, she told herself. Bryanna wanted to argue again that she'd paid for a perfectly good room at the inn and could stay there, but that protest had already fallen upon Gleda's deaf ears. "You need the security of a fortress," the older woman had told her. "Gates and guards and castle walls."

What had Isa told her? *Get thee inside the castle walls!*

When Bryanna had asked why the older woman had stared at her long and hard, Gleda had looked over her shoulder suspiciously before answering.

"Have you not felt it? The evil that stalks you? Surely you've sensed it ever nearer."

Bryanna had not been able to protest, for the older woman's words were true. She'd never been able to shake the blood-chilling certainty that she was being watched and followed.

By whom or what, she knew not.

Nonetheless, she doubted Tarth would keep her safe within its crumbling walls, its rumors of spirits haunting the barbicans and towers. Staring up at the interior of the dark fortress, Bryanna felt as if dozens of unseen eyes were watching her from the dark windows, crenels, and arrow loops.

She was ready to insist that they leave when she saw something in the older woman's eyes, a shadow of worry.

"There's something you're not telling me," she said, suspicion curling inside her. "Something you hide from me. What is it?"

"Nothing that can be changed," Gleda said, her eyes haunted by great sadness.

Before Bryanna could insist she explain herself, the page splashed through the puddles in the bailey, running as if the devil himself were chasing him. Breathless, the boy with strawlike hair nodded at Bryanna. "Father Patrick invites the guests inside, to warm themselves and stay the night. He says he'll see you both now."

"Good of him," Gleda whispered sarcastically.

They rode to the stables, left their horses with a groom, and accompanied Sir Giles inside the castle. The big man said a word to a guard standing at the entrance of the great hall as the door was opened, and Gleda whispered to Bryanna, "Do not let this pretender to the lordship bother you."

The women followed the page into a cavernous area where faded tapestries hung over walls that needed another coat of whitewash. The trestle tables had been turned against the walls and a priest stood near the fire, his vestments as clean and stiffly pressed as the rest of the keep was dirty and shabby. Bryanna couldn't help but notice the rings glittering on his fingers. He was dwarfed by a hearth so massive that the priest, of short stature, could easily have walked into the fiery pit. Massive logs burned upon iron dogs holding them in place, the fire's flames casting an eerie light on the priest's beatific smile and his pink face, as clean shaven as a babe's.

"You must be Alwynn of Penbrooke's daughter," he said, his gaze upon Bryanna. He squeezed her fingers, his hands soft, plump, and clammy.

"Aye, Father," she said with a forced smile as she shifted uncomfortably under his scrutiny. It seemed to Bryanna that he held himself with a pride and fastidiousness that bordered on arrogance, as if he were not only the baron here, but king of all Wales.

"Lady Bryanna has ridden from Castle Calon, where her sister, Lady Morwenna, rules with her husband. As Lady Bryanna's father, Baron Alwynn, was an ally of Lord Romney, she expected Lord Mabon would eagerly extend his hospitality. 'Tis a shame poor Romney and his wife were stricken." She made the sign of the cross over her breast and with a quick glance at Bryanna conveyed that the younger woman should also show some piety and grief. As Bryanna made the sign of the cross, Gleda added, "Please express my condolences to Baron Romney's family as well as everyone who lives here in the keep." She sighed loudly.

"It is not for us to understand God's ways," the priest intoned.

"But I am certain both Lord Romney and his son would insist the lady be their guest."

"Undoubtedly," the priest said, not hiding his irritation.

Standing near to the beekeeper, Bryanna felt awkward and unwanted, almost as if she were a piece of goods that Gleda was intent on selling to the priest. She wished she could turn and depart, but then Isa's words rang through her mind once more, reminding her to follow Gleda's instructions.

"Please, have a seat here near the fire. You must be exhausted from your travels." He motioned to two small benches positioned near the hearth. Sinking onto one of the stools, Bryanna felt the weariness of the day deep in her bones. She managed to smother a yawn but noticed tantalizing aromas rising from the kitchen. The scents of sizzling pork and tangy onions mingling with cloves and cinnamon wafted into the great hall, making Bryanna's stomach rumble hungrily. Perhaps with the prospect of a warm bed, mouthwatering fare, and servants to bring her wine and warm water, it wouldn't be so difficult to spend a night in this gloomy, inhospitable keep.

"Is it not true that Sir Mabon is returning soon? Aye, but he is sorely missed," Gleda persisted, making her point as there was an almost imperceptible tightening of the priest's mouth. "And isn't Sir Mabon well acquainted with Lord Kelan of Penbrooke?" Eyeing the rafters as she rubbed her chin, she nodded confidently. "Aye, I think they were pages together at Braddock Keep and fought side by side in some battles. Yes, my sister Isa mentioned it to me on more than one occasion, and she was the nursemaid for all of Baron Alwynn's children."

Bryanna wanted to kick Gleda. 'Twas embarrassing. Father Patrick had already given them entrance. The priest was cornered and he knew it. He managed a thin smile, as if it had been his idea to host the lone woman from Calon all along.

He turned to the page, snapped his bejeweled fingers, and ordered, "Geoffrey! Bring Lord Mabon's guests some wine and a platter of meat and cheese." As the boy turned toward the kitchen, Father Patrick added, "And this time, do not sample the fare. Now"—he clapped his hands rapidly—"be quick about it."

The page seemed to take forever to return, but finally he reappeared with a jug of wine and three mazers. Another boy carried a platter of succulent boar, venison, and salmon along with a brick of cheese and mincemeat tarts. Whatever ill had befallen the castle, the malaise hadn't extended to the kitchens.

Bryanna ate and drank as if she hadn't had a meal in a

month. The wine was the sweetest she'd ever tasted, and each time she took a sip a page promptly refilled her mazer. She tried to maintain society, but the priest's conversation bored her. Father Patrick kept discussing how he had all the powers of a baron, along with the blessing of the church. Feigning interest, Bryanna took another sip. Though the room spun a bit, she couldn't help but indulge in this delicious wine after such a long drought.

Gleda argued with Father Patrick while Bryanna, more than sated, tried with all her might to stay awake. Finally, Gleda pushed her chair back and, promising to return in the morning, stood to take her leave.

"You cannot leave," Bryanna said, her mind spinning. She had assumed the older woman would stay at the keep as well.

"Oh, I must get back to Liam," Gleda insisted, rising from the table. "What would he do without me? Thank you for the hospitality, Father Patrick."

"'Tis not me you should thank, but the Lord." Father Patrick's expression held no warmth as he nodded curtly and took his leave.

"But . . . but, 'tis late," Bryanna argued, trying hard to make her words come out without a slur. The wine was catching up with her, making her tongue thick, her legs wobbly. How much had she drunk? No more than usual. Was she ill, then?

"All the more reason I need to get home. No telling how worried Liam will be." Gleda's old eyes twinkled as she adjusted her mantle. "More about the horse than his wife, I'm afraid."

"Please, Gleda. Do not leave me here alone." Bryanna rose but found herself clutching the table for balance. Why did the room spin so? She kept her voice low, though there was no one about. Even the guard at the door was deep in conversation with another soldier.

"I'll be back tomorrow," the old woman said, her voice the barest of whispers. "We'll visit your mother."

"At her grave?" Bryanna asked, aghast. "Nay!"

"I think you two should meet."

"But . . . she's dead," Bryanna said, stepping backward. Though her mind was a little muddled from the wine, she did know that Kambria wasn't alive.

"Even so, she has something you need. You'll need to look inside her coffin."

"Are you mad?" Bryanna shook her head. "By the saints, Gleda, this is lunacy."

"And it must be at night."

"What? You can't be serious," Bryanna said on a gasp.

But the old woman's face was set. Determined. "You can use the moonlight as your guide."

"Nay, Gleda, I'm *not* about to go digging up coffins." Panic stormed through Bryanna. This was beyond lunacy. The woman had truly gone round the bend.

"And be wary of the dark warrior."

"*What* dark warrior?"

"The one who plans to do you harm, of course."

"Are you daft?" Though she was whispering, the words seemed to ricochet through the keep. "'Tis nothing more than nonsense you speak of."

"Shh!" Gleda glanced over her shoulder. "I can say no more." She touched Bryanna's arm, a consoling gesture. "Go up to bed. Sleep. You look exhausted, and we have much to do on the morrow."

"But—" Before Bryanna could protest further, Gleda was out the door, only a cold gust of wind left in her wake.

"Dear God," Bryanna whispered, leaning against the wall as a sallow-skinned woman carrying towels and a bucket of water appeared, almost as if she'd been standing on the other side of the staircase, listening to their conversation. 'Twas not right, this swirling storm in her head.

"M'lady," the serving woman said, "I'm Hettie and I'll be showin' ye to yer room now."

Great, Bryanna thought, annoyed with Gleda for leaving her. A shiver slithered down her spine like a sleek snake. What did that cryptic comment about meeting her mother mean?

Was Kambria a ghost? Could a witch rise from the dead? Or was it all a lie?

Dear God in heaven, what had she gotten herself into?

"Drat and dog fleas," she muttered.

"Pardon?" Hettie asked, and Bryanna shook her head.

"'Tis nothing," she said, thinking she must've misheard Gleda. The wine . . . that was it. Surely there had been no suggestion of digging through a paupers' cemetery. Nay! She pushed the horrid thoughts of decomposing bodies, pits looming in the damp, dank earth, and vermin crawling through deep, dark places out of her mind, at least for the moment.

She had to clear her head of this nonsense.

It wasn't easy.

More than a little tipsy, Bryanna followed the dour-faced Hettie up three flights of stairs that seemed to shift a little as she climbed them to the guest chamber. The cold, dark room on the third floor was furnished with a large bed draped with crimson silk, a stand for a basin, a bench, and a folded wooden screen to be used for privacy while dressing. Her head spinning, Bryanna nearly stumbled into the room, only righting herself by grabbing hold of a bedpost.

Hettie's lips had tightened in disapproval. "The latrine is that way, around the corner," she'd said, pointing down a dim hallway away from the main stairs. Without so much as cracking a smile, Hettie lit the fire and a candle, then pointed to the stack of extra wood near the grate.

Only after the dour maid had departed did Bryanna slip out of her clothes, blow out the candle, and slide between the cold linen sheets of the canopied bed, which seemed to spin every time she closed her eyes. The fire cracked, hissed and popped, sparks floating upward, flames casting a dancing golden light upon stone walls that hadn't been whitewashed in decades. The sheets felt rough against her bare skin and the feathers of the mattress probably hadn't been fluffed or cleaned in months, but Bryanna was too tired to care. She'd been awake for a day and a half, and now her head felt heavy.

She closed her eyes and wondered how many nights she

could stand residing in this decrepit castle. Yes, she had received food, drink, and forced hospitality. Aye, there were soldiers and battlements and gates that locked, so being here insured her some kind of protection. But she had no plan to idle. If she was to be on a quest, then so be it. She didn't want to spend an extra minute at Tarth.

"Oh, Isa," she whispered. "Why do you not give me instruction? Why do you always talk in half-truths and send me to people who have no more answers than I myself?" God's teeth, it was frustrating.

But for one night, she would sleep.

Weariness was already dragging her into slumber. In the morning, she would try to speak to the dead woman again . . . *And what about Gavyn?*

Ever since she'd left him, he was never far from her thoughts. She thought of him constantly, wondered where he was and, yes, she wished he was with her.

She reached one arm across the expanse of bedding, where no one lay beside her, and imagined him there. Sighing and pounding her pillow to plump it, she considered his hard muscles, his quick smile, his quicksilver eyes.

Silly girl.

She thought of their one brief, heart-pounding kiss, and how she'd looked into his soul and seen that he'd killed a man.

Did it matter?

If he was telling the truth, then he'd killed to save himself and to avenge his mother's murder.

Then again, he was a liar . . . a bald-faced, self-proclaimed liar. Had he not said so himself? She let out her breath slowly as sleep pulled her under. Her last thought was that she was surely and steadily falling in love with him.

Could there be any worse fate?

The night was cold as demon's piss, but the drizzling rain had finally stopped and the clouds parted to show a bit of moon. Gavyn rode unerringly past the three rocks, along the water, until he reached Tarth, a village that held bitter memories for him.

The village had grown in the years he'd been gone, but he recognized some of the shops and streets and guided his steed to the one inn with its stable attached. He had friends and relatives here who would give him shelter, but he wanted, at least for one night, to keep to himself. He paid for his horse to be cared for and stabled, then bought a room for the night and found a place at a corner table downstairs where he could sip ale and watch the locals. He listened to the gossip floating from one table to the next while men drank mead or wine, flirted with the innkeeper's daughter, or played dice.

Gavyn had to ask a few questions to get the conversation rolling, but no one recognized him, perhaps because of his bruises, or more likely because he'd been away awhile. The conversations he overheard entailed little more than cursing about the weather that was damaging crops, or worry about Lord Romney's son not being able to run the castle as well as his father. The girl who filled his cup, however, was all too willing to gossip in more detail about how a priest was running the keep until the baron returned, and, aye, that she had seen a noblewoman traveling alone, a woman with red hair, dirty clothes, and a white horse.

"Paid for a room she did," the girl said as she poured another stream of ale into his mazer, "then visited the seamstress before bathing and riding off. We expected her back, but when she came, she had the old woman Gleda with her. Gleda, she's the goat farmer's wife. She keeps bees herself and sells honey here and to the cook at the keep."

Gleda. He turned the name over in his head but it meant nothing to him.

"So the red-haired girl left to stay with Gleda?"

"Could be." She lifted a shoulder. "I know not."

He smiled. "Do you know where Gleda lives?"

"Aye, about a mile outside of town to the east, mayhap less." She caught her mother's critical eye. "Oh, I'd best be off taking care of the other customers," she said hurriedly, her cheeks instantly flaming.

'Twas odd, he thought. Why would Bryanna pay for a room and then vacate it? What had she learned from the farmer's wife? What was so damned important that the woman returned with her and helped her move out?

He drummed his fingers upon the table, then decided that if he was to find Bryanna, he would have to find the bee-keeper. For some reason Bryanna had sought the woman out. He had little doubt it had to do with the map and the dagger. But what?

He lingered a bit longer, listening for anything else that was of interest, then paid for his ale and walked into the night. He glanced up at the castle rising high on the hill, a dark, fore-boding keep.

It, too, had been pictured upon Bryanna's map. A rudimen-tary square with towers pointing upward.

He walked along the well-trod road leading to the main gate, where puddles and dung and mud had collected in the deep ruts. When he was near the keep, he heard voices from within, then the groan of metal and the grinding of ancient gears as the portcullis was winched upward.

Backlit by a few torches, a lone rider appeared upon a small dark horse. A woman. Strange that a woman would be leaving the castle alone, this late at night.

His heart beat a little faster at the thought it might be Bryanna. As she rode beneath the rattling grating, he ducked deeper into the shadows and squinted, but he knew instinc-tively this little, hunched-over woman was not her. He'd spent hours with Bryanna and knew every inch of her silhouette upon her horse. Nay, 'twas not her . . . and the broken-down animal the woman was riding was not Bryanna's white jennet.

With darkness as his cover, he followed the woman, keep-ing to the shadows. When she turned her horse toward the river, then eastward along its banks, he wondered if this woman could be Gleda, the beekeeper and farmer's wife, the woman Bryanna had been with. At the tavern Gleda had been described as an old woman living on a downtrodden farm.

More voices reached him. Male and deep, approaching from the short road leading to the gatehouse. Gavyn hung back in the shadows behind the corner of the stable and caught bits of the conversation as two foot soldiers passed.

". . . not happy about having an unannounced guest."

"Hell, the father, 'e's not 'appy about nothin' these days. Not lookin' forward to the return of Sir Mabon, if ye ask me."

"*Lord* Mabon. 'E's the baron now and ye'd best be remembering it. And ye're right, Father Patrick will have to get used to living like a priest again instead of a lord."

The two men chuckled as they reached the inn, where lights burned bright and conversation spilled into the night.

"I wonder if she'll still be there," one of the soldiers said. "What do ye make of it, a woman riding alone?"

"She had a companion."

"Who left her there."

"With the good priest."

Again the men laughed and Gavyn's jaw tightened. He was certain that the guards were talking about Bryanna. Slinking through the shadows, he was determined to find her.

It shouldn't prove too difficult, for he'd lived in Tarth as a youth and had returned here after being banished from Penbrooke. He knew which doors in the town were locked and which were open. He'd spent enough time in the castle to know how to enter and leave without being noticed.

It would be simple enough to sneak inside and find Bryanna.

Gavyn only had to bide his time.

The storm worsened unexpectedly.

And became terrifying.

Urging the lazy gelding through the pouring rain, Gleda wondered if she'd made a mistake. Mayhap she should have taken advantage of Father Patrick's hospitality, even though it had been offered without enthusiasm. Holier-than-thou, sanctimonious, and downright mean-spirited, the priest ruffled her feathers more than most men, and whenever she was around him, she wanted to take him down a peg, give him a dose of his own supercilious disdain.

"Fool," she muttered, and as the rain ran down the front of her cowl she wondered if she were talking about herself or the bloody priest.

"Hurry on there, Harry," she said to the horse, clucking her tongue as the wind picked at the hem of her dripping mantle. She didn't have far to ride, just half a mile. Once she crossed the creek she'd be home and she could toss off her wet mantle, shake the rain from her hair, and warm herself by the fire, where Liam was probably sitting now, refitting the shafts of his arrows with feathers or steel tips.

Oh, to be warm and dry again.

Her old bones felt soaked through.

And Harry, with his uneven gait, was not a comfortable horse on which to ride. He'd been hurt as a foal and ever since favored one leg, though he never seemed to be in pain.

She spied the creek, a dark snake of water that cut through the earth and wound across the valley. The rain had swollen the creek to a rushing stream, and Harry balked at the prospect of stepping through. "Oh, for the love of St. Peter, ye've done it a thousand times before, you stubborn nag. Come on now." She gave him a little kick, just enough to show him she meant business, and still he refused, backing up and nearly rearing.

Her house was in sight just on the other side of the water. She saw the fire burning through spaces in the closed shutters, smelled the scent of burning wood.

"Come on, damn ye," she said. "What in the name of the Holy Mother is wrong with you. . . ?" But as she said the words, she saw something in the dark, swirling depths. 'Twas a body floating in the creek, caught on a shelf of rocks.

"Oh no." Without a thought she climbed off her horse and stepped into the swirling eddies. Ice-cold water caught on her skirts and filled her boots, dragging her down as she made her way in the shallows to the place where the man lay, face-down. He was certain to be dead, no doubt a traveler who had stumbled when he tried to cross the stream. She reached him in the knee-deep water and pulled on his shirt. Though it was dark, there was something familiar about him, about his size.

"Liam?" she whispered, her old heart clutching in her chest. Surely not her husband. He was a cautious man, a care-ful farmer who would not endanger his life even to save his own livestock. "Liam!" She leaned over and, using all her strength, rolled the dead weight of the man over, exposing his pale face.

Pain and despair cut her to the bottom of her soul.

Her husband, dead and cold, stared sightlessly upward.

"No!" she wailed in anguish. "No! Oh, God, no!" She sobbed and clung to him, cold water soaking through every-where. "Please, Liam, for once in your stubborn life, fight!" she cried, pounding on his chest. How dared he leave her? What foolish notion had enticed him to emerge from the warmth of their hut? Had one of the goats escaped? Had a boar taken off into the woodland? Or . . . had he come look-ing for her?

Guilt clawed at her and she refused to let her thoughts wander in that direction. She couldn't, wouldn't think that he'd lost his life because he was worried about her. She'd told him she would be long . . . oh, sweet Jesus! Sobbing, she pulled upon his heavy body, trying to drag him to the bank. Her boots slipped in the mud and her teeth chattered in her head as the water slapped her ever downward.

"Here, boy!" she yelled, calling to the horse. "Come, Harry. That's a boy." If she could rap the reins around Liam's cold hands and then force the horse to back up and drag him from the creek, then maybe, just maybe, she could save him.

He's gone, Gleda. Liam is dead as a stone.

She wouldn't listen to the reason in her head and called to the horse over the wind and rain. "Come on, Harry. . . ."

Snorting, the horse took one step in her direction before stopping and rearing. "Harry!" she shouted in frustration.

Pounding hoofbeats resounded in the wind. She turned and saw a dark rider approaching from the other side of the creek. "Help!" she yelled, blinking against the rain. "Please help me! It's me husband—" But her voice was dulled by the wind.

Frantically she waved at him, and the rider splashed through the shallows, his big destrier cutting through the water. He had seen her! He was coming this way. Her hands relaxed on the hem of Liam's wet shirt, and she felt a moment's relief.

Please, she silently prayed to any deity who was listening. *Let Liam live. Let me get him home to safety, let—*

She gasped as she saw the rider's arm swing high in the air. Something in his hand?

A sword? A dagger? No, something round and—

Quick as lightning, he hurled it directly at her.

She tried to duck, to throw up a hand, but she was too slow. A rock with edges honed knife-thin crashed into her forehead.

Pain exploded in her skull. Flashing bursts of light . . . and then darkness.

She stumbled backward, twisted, then fell facedown into the icy water.

CHAPTER FIFTEEN

He came to her in a dream in the dark of the night.

Rain had begun to splash upon the roof tiles so noisily that Bryanna groggily woke, barely aware of the gurgle of water coursing through the gutters. She glanced up briefly, confused at the swirling bloodred silk overhead. 'Twas just the sleeping chamber at Tarth Castle. Bryanna turned over beneath the coverlet and wandered back into the dark unknowing, caught somewhere between wakefulness and deep sleep.

Facedown upon the pillow, she fell into a chaotic, distorted dream that took place within this very bedchamber of Tarth Castle.

The details of the hand-hewn bedposts and crimson silk hangings were vivid, as was the touch of the man.

Her lover, it seemed.

For though she couldn't see his face, she sensed he was there, hidden in the shadows and moving soundlessly to the bed. She tried to roll over to face him but was pinned to the mattress. Strong hands covered her shoulders, forcing her to lie prone, upon her stomach so that he could come to her from behind.

"Wait," she whispered, but her breath died in her throat as he pushed her hair aside and kissed the back of her neck, his breath warm and sensual. Her veins tingled and her blood began to heat. Desire curled deep inside her as his lips trailed along the slope of her shoulder. She wanted him.

"Who are you?" she asked, her voice husky and unfamiliar, muffled by the pillow. "Why are you here?"

"For you." Strong arms surrounded her, slipping around her waist, fingers inching up her rib cage. Hard. Hot. Determined as they found her breasts and began to knead, pulling her to her knees upon the mattress though she was still facing away from him. His fingers summoned fires within her unlike any desire she'd ever known. He knelt behind her, never releasing her, always touching. Body pressed to body. Male and female. Poised to mate.

Her mind swirled and she told herself this was a dream, a sensual dream, sweet and thick as honey. She knew no lover, and yet he was with her. In the bed. In the dark. In this nether land of primal desire and hot flesh.

"Bryanna," he whispered. "Wanton witch."

Hard fingers scraped her nipples, teasing them, toying with them.

"Mmm . . ." She growled like a tigress as he pinched one nipple lightly, causing a needle-sharp sensation to pierce her consciousness—sweet, deep, and overpowering.

What is this? The question floated above her, and yet it didn't seem to matter as desire thrummed deep inside, her body responding and eager as he held her tight against him. His chest rubbed over her naked back and a thickness pressed hard into her buttocks, smooth and slick, rubbing . . . rubbing . . . moving against her. How she loved the feel of him . . . hot, hard, so smooth.

Who is this man with his honed muscles, skilled hands, and insistent pressure?

A lover?

A friend?

An enemy?

But she had slept with no man. . . . Who would she allow to be so intimate with her, so sexual?

Gavyn.

Her heart leapt when she realized he'd found her.

He'd known where she was going; it was he who had first deciphered the map.

Of course.

She smiled in the darkness.

He is teasing me. Tormenting me. He will only reveal himself to me once I have given myself to him.

Aye . . . then he shall have me.

She sighed and leaned back against him, giving herself over to the waves of pleasure, the throbbing deep inside as he kissed her bare shoulder. Reaching one hand upward and back to sink her fingers into his hair, she stretched languorously. He growled deep in his throat, one hand splaying over her breasts, the other lower, toying with her as she smelled his deep, musky odor.

"I know who you are," she said, and though she was facing away from him, she reached back behind him, her fingers skimming the strong, smooth muscles of his back.

"Of course you do." Wet lips trailed along her spine and she gasped as he began to spread her legs with his fingers and touch her intimately. She shivered, not from the cold but from a want, primeval and deep. As he pressed her downward into the mattress, she lifted her hips and writhed, eager for release.

His hardness pressed intimately along her backside, searching for entry.

"Gavyn," she whispered. "Please."

The ministrations stopped. "What?" he asked.

"I said, please," she murmured. *"Please."*

"You called me Gavyn."

"Yes, yes," she said, pressing her hips to him. She could not bear the thought of his hands dropping from her hot, moist skin, his body moving away from hers.

"I'm not Gavyn," he whispered in a heart-stopping instant.

Part of her could not make sense of his words. What could that mean? 'Twas nonsensical. A mere laugh in this swarming roar of sensation. All confusion melted in the blistering heat of his body over hers. One knee slid her legs apart and strong fingers slid between her legs, bringing a wild frenzy to the recesses of her being.

"Now, witch," he said, " 'tis time to fulfill your destiny."

A wall of pressure from behind pushed her face down into the pillow as he thrust deep. Hard.

A cry escaped her throat at the rending of flesh. Her maidenhood gone. But her voice quickly quieted to murmurs of pleasure as he pulled back and plunged into her again . . . and again and again.

How she loved the slow sultry rhythm of mating! She had never been with a man before and yet her body seemed to know what to do. She felt herself opening to him as her hips writhed in time with his, eager to meet him, to receive him, to feel him deep inside her.

She felt his excitement in the slick sweat that melded his body to hers, smelled it in the deep odor of musk, heard it in his panting. His ardor stoked the flames that curled within her, hot and crackling, dancing and leaping skyward. His passion became her passion, his lust her lust.

Her fingernails dug into the sheets as the warm honey began to soak through her body, thick and sweet, hotter and hotter as he moved faster and faster. But the dense nectar in her veins slowed her passion and dulled her senses like a dark potion until she felt her spirit floating aloft, separate from this man moving over her.

With a final deep stab, he growled and collapsed over her, their bodies enmeshed in feverish heat and sweat.

"Daughter of Kambria, you are mine," he said in an animal voice that seemed to come from a distant chamber. "Forever bound."

The keep had changed since his last visit. Gavyn, who had slipped unnoticed beneath the gates when the foot soldiers had returned, walked through the wet bailey, just as he had years earlier. He'd been a groom then, tending to the horses, learning his skills from Neddym, the stable master.

Unerringly he made his way through the darkness, across

the bailey and beneath the pentice near the kitchen. He looked up at the keep and wondered which of the windows would open to her room. Not that he could hope to scale the sheer walls, and yet, being so near her, knowing she was close, he felt a glimmer of life return to him, like a returning hawk. He was still mad as hell that she'd left him, though in truth he couldn't deny his fascination with her.

He'd told himself that he was chasing her down because of the map and the dagger, to satisfy his curiosity and, mayhap, even to rob her of the jewels, should she locate them. Aye, that would serve her right for leaving him.

But, truth to tell, he suspected it was something more that drove him to be near her, something just as unsettling. He couldn't get her out of his damned mind. From the moment he'd seen her in the forest railing at the wind, yelling at the mythical Isa, he'd been unable to get her out of his mind. The fact that she was the woman in his dreams and the girl he'd been smitten with as a youth had only added to her allure, her intrigue.

Then there was the keen sense that she was in danger, the darkness that followed her whenever he saw her in his sleep.

Damn the woman to hell, he thought, scanning the dark windows cut into the walls of the keep. A few had faint light, as if from dying fires. He assumed she was inside one of those rooms, safely asleep.

And yet . . .

He glanced toward the moonless sky and sensed that same malevolence he'd felt in his dreams.

He only hoped the fortress that was Castle Tarth would keep whatever depravity he perceived at bay. Compelled to find her, he slipped inside the kitchen door. He knew how to steal into the castle, how to slip through the corridors like a ghost, for though the rules and the faces of the guards may have changed, the routine would not have been altered. It would be the same as it had been when he was a boy stealing salt pork and tarts from the kitchen or wine from the buttery, right beneath the steward's nose.

Lord Romney was nothing if not a rigid man, one who did not change his mind or habits easily. And as his son Sir Mabon had not yet returned to take over his duties as the baron, no one would have changed where the guards kept the key rings, nor meddled with security within the castle. Gavyn knew which doors would be locked and which were allowed to remain unlatched, just as he knew every twist of the dimly lit castle corridors.

Like a wraith, he climbed to the third floor and moved silently along the hallway. The lord's room was in one direction, attached to the solar, and down the other way were empty chambers, rooms for guests or children.

Although the keep was quiet, he knew guards were about, most likely playing dice or drinking mead or dozing at their posts. Stealthily he moved down the corridor past candles that had long burned out. He tested the first door, pushed it open, and found an empty chamber that smelled of must and mildew, a room once occupied by Mabon and his brother. Softly he shut the door, then walked to the next chamber. When he pushed against the door, it didn't budge, and he knew she was inside. Locked away. Safe.

He felt momentary relief, then walked along the corridor past the latrine to a staircase and window that looked out to the bailey. He paused, staring out at the rain slanting from the sky in a shifting silver curtain, pounding on the roof.

Something moved behind him and he whirled, hand upon the hilt of his knife as he ducked into the window's alcove. Tense, ready to lunge, he expected to hear a guard's deep voice accost him.

Instead, he saw nothing.

And yet he felt a disturbance in the corridor. A palpable evil, swirling in a maelstrom of darkness. Cold as death, it swept past him, though he saw nothing, heard no footsteps.

Tarth Keep is haunted, Gavyn. Remember it always, his mother had told him, though he'd always suspected it to be a rumor, a way for her to keep him from making his nocturnal forays into the great hall, which he was forbidden to enter. *Do not cross the threshold where the dead roam.* Her warnings, though dire, had only added allure to an already daring challenge.

Never once had he encountered a ghost or specter or demon.

Until this moment.

He thought again of Bryanna and hurried back to the locked door. Without a second's hesitation, he pushed upon it again and it opened easily. Noiselessly.

He stepped inside, where a fire barely glowed but gave off enough light to see her tousled curls upon the bed.

He paused, taking in the sweet sound of her soft breathing. She moved, rustling the sheets, then lifted her head for a second, almost as if she were looking straight at him. God's eyes, she was beautiful. Though it was shadowy in the chamber, he could still make out her features, her straight nose, wide eyes, and full mouth. Her hair was tangled and wild, falling about her shoulders in tumbled disarray.

"Gavyn," he thought she whispered, though her lips barely moved. Mayhap it was a trick of thin light from the shadow. Their eyes met and his heart thumped wildly. Her eyebrows drew together and her eyes closed sadly. "Why?" she asked, her voice cracking. "Why would you do this?"

"Do what? 'Tis you who left me," he said, stepping closer.

"I only did what was foretold."

He stepped closer to her.

"Do not be angry," she murmured, though he wasn't certain she was completely awake. "Please."

His heart melted at the sight of her, uncharacteristically vulnerable. Usually sharp-tongued and headstrong, usually quick to tease and taunt him, she now appeared confused. Mayhap she wasn't quite awake.

"Sleep," he said, his anger melting. "I just wanted to see that you were safe."

"Is that what you call it?" she said and laughed, almost in relief. "I thought . . . why did you not say so? Why did you not kiss me on my lips?"

Was she teasing?

"I did." He thought of the one kiss they'd shared in the forest, how it had ricocheted through his body.

"Nay . . ." She shook her head drowsily, her eyes half closed.

"Sleep well," he said.

"You're not going to kiss me good night?"

He couldn't believe what she was saying. She'd left him in the middle of the night, snuck away like a thief, as if she were angry with him or trying to run away from him. So now that he'd stolen into her bedchamber, why was she suddenly so warm and inviting?

He should leave.

Now.

If he had even one bit of sanity, he would slip through the door and pretend that he'd never stepped into this shadowed room with its dying fire.

"Good night, Bryanna." He took a step toward the door.

"Do not leave," she whispered. "Please, Gavyn, do not leave me like this."

"Like what?" he asked, turning back to her.

"Alone. Not after what we shared." Her voice was drowsy and filled with sleep.

Although he felt sure she must be dreaming, he couldn't deny the lust that ran through his body as he gazed down at her thick red lips and tossed red curls. "We have shared little," he said.

"Little? By the gods, Gavyn, you're a cur." She spat the words and he couldn't help but smile. This was the woman he knew, the woman he fantasized about, the woman he thought he might, if he allowed himself, fall in love with.

"I wouldn't think you a coward, Gavyn, to sneak away in the night."

"Christ Jesus, woman, what do you want of me?"

"A kiss good night," she said groggily.

He thought of what they'd shared, the days in the forest, riding, hunting, tending to the horses. The nights around the fire with a wolf lurking in the shadows. Her warm hands as she'd tended to his wounds and scolded him for not taking better care of himself. And then there was the kiss. A heart-stopping, blood-firing kiss that he'd wished would never end, a kiss he now wanted desperately to forget.

"After what we shared, is one kiss too much to ask?"

"Mayhap," he said, fighting the urge to fall into the bed with her, to kiss her on her lips, her eyes, her neck, her breasts. God in heaven, it had been a long time since he'd been with a woman, and never had he wanted one more than Bryanna. Still, something was amiss here. . . . She was not herself. Talking clearly one second, and not making sense the next.

Don't do this, his mind warned him. *Wait. There is no harm in waiting.*

She reached upward then, her hand finding his, the sheets slipping downward, one bare breast exposed. He swallowed against a suddenly dry mouth as, even in the shadows, he noticed the rosy tip of her breast, a hard, tempting disk.

"Love me, Gavyn. But this time, kiss me on the lips, let me see your face."

This time?

She ran her free hand up the length of his leg, past his knee and upward, to his thigh.

His manhood, in expectation, thickened and swelled, straining at the laces of his breeches. Sweat broke out along his back as images of making love to her flashed behind his eyes. He saw their sweaty bodies entwined, her breathing hurried, her face flushed, her arms surrounding him as she eased herself lower on the mattress, kissing him, running her tongue over his abdomen and lower. . . .

Groaning, he tried to step away but couldn't.

"Bryanna," he said, his voice raw. "This isn't a good idea."

"You say that *now*?" she asked, an edge of anger in her voice.

He closed his eyes to her, the muscles of his legs tense where she touched him. "It's just that—"

"That *what*? You cannot love a woman face-to-face?" Her

fingers tightened over the muscles in his thigh and he fought every urge in his body not to fall into the bed with her.

"Is that what you want?"

"Am I not asking?" She seemed awake now and rose to her knees, the sheeting falling away from her naked body, inviting. Though it was dark, he could see her, smell her, sense the wanting. Her head was even with his chest, and as she spoke her breath seemed to permeate his tunic and mantle. "Do you not want me now?" She tilted her head up, causing her hair to spill over one shoulder. Her exposed throat glowed white in the night. "You're finished with me?"

"Oh, lady," he groaned, knowing that was the furthest thing from the truth. Her hands slipped upward beneath the hem of his tunic, her warm fingertips skimming his skin. His blood pounded through his veins, his heart pumping crazily as need and desire overtook him.

He stepped out of his breeches and dropped to his own knees on the bed. She peeled off his tunic, her fingers as eager as his own. Pressing his bare chest to her full round breasts, he gathered her small body into his arms and kissed her, his mouth fastening over hers, his breathing ragged and rough.

This is wrong!

Don't do it!

Stop now before it's too late.

She is acting strangely . . . oh, sweet Jesus . . .

He pressed his tongue to her teeth and she opened to him, easily, hungrily, her own tongue playing with his. Her chest began to rise and fall rapidly as her breaths came in short bursts. His hungry hands scaled her ribs, and she gasped in expectation as his thumbs found her nipples and toyed with them until they became hard and her breasts swelled in his hands.

She was hot.

He felt the warmth radiating from her.

Knew that deep inside she was melting, readying herself.

He imagined thrusting into that warmth to feel her wetness cling to him.

"Oooh," she cried, closing her eyes and letting her head loll to one side as he leaned over to kiss her sweet, curved throat. So white. So vulnerable. So damned sensual.

Don't do this, Gavyn. Stop while you still can. A few more seconds and there will be no turning back.

He kissed her throat.

Hard.

His lips sucking.

"Gavyn," she cried.

His blood was singing in his ears as he rolled onto his back and pulled her atop him, his hands embracing her small nip of a waist, his fingers splaying over her spine and that glorious indentation just above her perfect little rump.

"Oh, oh, God," she murmured as he filled his mouth with her.

The room melted away as he felt her moving over him, rocking with a primal desire.

His fingers dug into her buttocks and she arched upward, her back bowing as his tongue and teeth scraped over her nipple. Her hands dug into his hair and she held him to her as he suckled, hard and fast, his fingers kneading her, readying her, dipping lower, beyond the cleft to that special spot.

She cried out, bucking as he entered her with a finger, feeling that moist sweet spot.

"Please," she whispered, her voice hoarse with sweet agony. "Gavyn, please . . ."

"God forgive me," he whispered and pulled her atop him, his stiffness piercing her hard, sliding deep into her hot, moist womanhood.

She moved above him and he helped her, his hands upon her waist, his hips rising as she came down on him. Over and over again. Hard. Fast. Hot. Oh, God, so hot. He was sweating, holding back, watching her move above him. Her firm, erect breasts trembled with the motion of their lovemaking.

Her back was arched, her mouth open as she gasped.

Her ardor fueled the flames in his blood. His mind swam in exquisite sensation, and it was all he could do not to spill himself inside her. Instead he clenched his teeth and drove harder and faster.

Just as she cried out, her body jerking in a violent spasm, he thrust as far as he could, lifted his shoulders and grasped her tight in his arms. He kissed her breast again, filling his mouth with her. The pressure started deep within, building, faster, hotter, his mind splintering as his entire body jerked.

His release was complete.

As was his guilt.

CHAPTER SIXTEEN

"*Don't leave.*"

Bryanna's words seemed to echo in the dark chamber and clatter through his damned heart. Although she was sleeping now, during the night she had begged him not to leave, and he had succumbed. Now Gavyn kicked himself for staying as long as he had, making love to her into the early-morning hours while the fire had burned out completely and the rain had increased, pounding on the roof above.

Much as he wanted to stay with her, it would be dawn soon enough. The castle would begin to stir as men and women went about their tasks, and Gavyn could not risk being discovered.

He was still a wanted man, and there was a chance that word of his crime had traveled here to Tarth, where some villagers might recognize him. He had to be careful, at least until he'd spoken with former acquaintances, people who'd been friends with his mother.

He'd spent enough time in Bryanna's bed as it was. He'd dozed after making love to her the first time, and then, upon waking, had drawn her sleeping body to his and made love to her again, discovering anew the wonder and magick of her body.

Sorceress? Nay. He didn't believe she had any magic, other than to bewitch and beguile him.

Woman? Aye. Like no other.

Temptress? No bloody doubt.

As she'd slept, he'd extricated himself from her arms, slipped out of the bed, and gotten dressed in the dark.

The last thing he wanted to do was leave.

But staying would be just plain foolish.

When she let out a soft sigh and turned her cheek on the pillow, it was nearly his undoing. Why not slide back between the covers for a little longer? Could he not hide out here in this chamber? He imagined what it would be like to watch her awaken and find him in her bed. He considered her reaction, the surprise, then the pleasure in her turquoise eyes. How he would love to kiss her and make love to her in broad daylight. 'Twould be exquisite to stare into her eyes, watch her body move, witness her wonder and delight and pure pleasure as he made love to her. He thought of kissing her, seeing her lips, and then later, during the act, observing her kissing him, trailing her lips down his abdomen and lower. He grew hard as he thought of what she would do, how her eyes would look up at him in naughty amusement, how her tongue would flicker and taste him, how her mouth, oh, God, that wonderful, sensual, full-lipped mouth would work its magick upon him.

He nearly slid back into the bed but he heard a noise—the scrape of leather against stone—a boot or shoe in the hall outside the door.

He tensed. His fantasy shriveled along with the thickening of his cock.

His heart flew to his throat.

He strained to hear, but only the sounds of the rain on the roof and wind whipping around the keep met his ears.

For the love of God, he couldn't forget they were not alone. Nor could he take the chance of being discovered, worse yet caught in the lady's room and trapped here. He had much to discover about Tarth—how safe it was for him and for her—before he showed his face.

He unsheathed his knife and, after listening at the door, eased himself into the hallway. Bootheels ringing on the stairs told him it was time for the changing of the guard, so he headed in the opposite direction, away from the main stairs.

Before starting down and possibly running into another sentry, he ducked into the windowed alcove where he'd hidden before and listened. Whoever had been climbing the main stairs had not followed. He let out his breath and stepped toward the staircase.

"Hey, you there!" a deep-voiced guard yelled from the bailey far below.

Gavyn didn't move a muscle.

Someone had seen him in the window!

Damn! Blast his luck! What were the chances that a guard outside the great hall would see him? Gavyn's fingers tightened over the hilt of his knife.

"Boy!" The sentry's deep voice shouted again.

Boy?

"John, is it? The tanner's son? What the bloody hell are ye doin' out tonight in this blasted rain? Get along now, away from the kennels and back to yer father's hut. If he knows ye sneaked out, he'll be tannin' yer own hide rather than that of the huntsmen's stags, now, won't he? Now, git, before I flay ye meself."

Gavyn let out his breath and looked through the window, but the rain was too thick to see much. After he was certain the altercation between the boy and soldier had been resolved, Gavyn hurried down the staircase and stepped outside and into the last remaining hours of night. Rain peppered the ground and splashed the surface of puddles. Gavyn slipped along the darkest part of the bailey, cutting past the armorer and thatcher's huts and nearly tripping over a wet surprised cat that hissed and shot out from beneath a hayrick to slink behind a pile of wood.

Flattening his body along the side of the curtain wall, he moved stealthily to the stables, with which he was most familiar. He knew a spot in the hayloft where, as a lad, he'd taken many a nap undetected.

With one last glance upward to the window on the third

floor of the keep—Bryanna's chamber—he stole through the doorway and entered a familiar realm smelling of leather, oil, manure, hay, and urine. Easing through the stalls, he hit his knee on a bench that stuck out and bit back a curse.

Horses neighed and snorted and he held his breath, hoping not to disturb any of the grooms sleeping nearby.

"Shh," one man muttered, then immediately began snoring again.

Stealthily as a cat, Gavyn slipped through the shadows and up an ancient ladder to the hayloft. He hoped to high heaven no one else had taken over his spot, his small nook below the rafters. But no one had; the nook was empty. He curled up and pulled loose hay over him. Come the morning, if Neddym was still the stable master, he'd take the older man into his confidence.

If not? If Neddym had passed on?

Hell, he was just too bloody tired to think of it.

With the cock's crow, he would come up with a plan.

"Gavyn?" Bryanna whispered, reaching across the cold bed. . . . Wait a minute. He'd been with her, right? Her head thundered, pain pounding behind her eyes. When she sat up, the world still spun a bit.

She lay back on the pillows and thought.

Had she really made love to Gavyn? Had she spent hours in his arms, moving in and out of ecstasy in the dancing light of the fire?

She stretched in bed as the memories, thin and gauzy as spiderwebs, breezed in, then out of, her mind. The sweet wine of last night had soured on her tongue. Perhaps it was spoiled. Tainted?

Had she been dreaming?

Closing her eyes, she tried to concentrate, to remember, but it was all so dreamlike, her mind so detached. "Oh, Holy Mother of God."

Where in the world was Isa?

Why had her voice suddenly stilled?

Bryanna remembered bits of the night before. The way she'd been so wanton and voracious, so unlike her. Granted, she'd been so tired, drunk far too much, and part of the night was a blur. . . .

She opened a cautious eye and her head pounded with pain.

The fire had died, and though the room was cold, Bryanna's body was drenched in sweat. No doubt because of the dream, part nightmare, part fantasy. Sweet Rhiannon, it had seemed so real!

As her flushed skin cooled, Bryanna pulled the covers to her neck. The gray light of dawn was filtering through the shutters and the rain, finally, had stopped.

She heard people stirring within the keep. Boots clomped by her doorway and muted voices filtered through the oak door. She was still exhausted; her slumber, though deep, had been restless. Her bones and muscles were not relaxed, nor refreshed, and she wondered if she were ailing.

She forced herself from the bed.

And winced in pain from the tender area between her legs. Of course, he'd taken her virginity.

Images from the night before flashed behind her eyes. Flesh, sweat, and pain. Desire so intense she'd begged him to take her. Then passion and pleasure. She flung open the sheets and saw the small stain: blood, dark red turning to brown. 'Twas not her time of the month, so . . . it must be because . . . because the dream was real. . . .

Aye, he had loved her so completely that she felt a thrill at the thought of it.

Thoughts running amok, she tossed on the chemise she didn't remember taking off . . . or did she? "Oh, for the love of God," she whispered, remembering how wantonly she'd bared herself to him, how she'd been atop him, his member hard and stiff inside her.

Could it have been?

Had she made wild love to him nearly all of the night?

Did she remember him leaving in the predawn hours?

Everything was such a blur, a blending of truth and fantasies.

Her head throbbing, she walked to the basin on a small table and tossed cold water onto her face. Another splash of cold water dampened not only her face but a few strands of her hair. She grabbed the linen towel left at the basin and looked at the piece of polished metal that had been hung on the wall. In the reflection she saw her face, white as death, and near her throat the ring of tiny bruises.

From another dream. Physical evidence of a nightmare that had torn through her brain while she slept. Could not the blood on the sheets, the burning between her legs, be the same? If so, could she not be already with child? A babe conceived of a dream lover? Though it seemed unthinkable, she was not so naive as to believe pregnancy was impossible.

Anything, it seemed, was possible.

Biting her lip, trying to deny the turn of her thoughts, she looked into the mirror again. Haunted blue-green eyes stared back at her. "Oh, Morrigu, no," she whispered, ashamed to the depths of her soul. It could not be. It had to be a dream . . . but as she glanced down at herself, she remembered the weight of the man who had stolen into her room. She glanced at her image again and there, over one shoulder, lurking in the shadows behind her and staring at her reflection, was the image of a man, a dark warrior whose features were blurred by the metal.

Someone insidious and evil.

Her heart stopped.

She remembered that first spate of rutting, for to call it lovemaking would have been a falsehood. She'd not seen her lover's face, only felt his hot body against hers, his steamy breath and sharp teeth scraping against the nape of her neck.

And what had he said? *"I'm not Gavyn."*

Hugging herself, she stared into the looking-glass as if it could surrender the secret. "Who was that man?" she whispered aloud.

In the mirror was a glimpse of his face, eyes that were almost black, the tiniest bit of color around huge pupils. One brown, the other blue. Both shining intently. Malevolently.

She twirled, ready to lunge at the demon, to claw out his eyes, but the room was empty.

Still.

She found herself alone in the cold dim chamber, her breasts rising and falling with each breath, her heart hammering, vengeance firing her blood.

Her skin prickled in apprehension just before a deep voice filled her head:

"Bryanna of Tarth,
Daughter of Kambria,
Granddaughter of Waylynn,
Descendant of Llewellyn
And the Great Witch Goddess, Rhiannon.
Yours is a world unknown, a world of darkness.
A world where untamed beasts and demons, the hated and the feared, rule.
Only you, of mixed blood, can enter the realm."

The voice faded and she stood, stunned, her eyes wide, her mind screaming disbelief. "What realm?" she whispered, her voice hoarse. This was the voice she'd heard last night, the voice of the man who had taken her by force. By the gods, was she going mad?

"Show yourself, demon," she insisted, walking barefoot to the spot where she'd thought the image had stood. She felt a disturbance, a chill in the air, a bitter fury. Her skin prickled, the marrow of her bones turning to ice. "Coward, appear to me!" Her breath fogged in the air. "By all that is holy, show yourself!"

She thought of all the spells she knew, the runes and chants for protection that had failed her. Even this castle with its barricaded gates, guarded towers, and thick curtain walls had not saved her. Gleda had insisted she seek shelter here, for her protection.

Or had Gleda harbored another motive?

Mayhap the woman who claimed to be Isa's sister was just

another liar, an enemy hidden in the guise of a beekeeper. And what of Gavyn? Had he really come to her last night, or was he, too, just an image imbedded in her mind, nothing more than a manifestation of her wishes?

Oh, she'd been such a fool.

So trusting.

Of some vexing voice only she could hear.

The bitterly cold air of the room faded in an instant.

"Isa, where are you?" she demanded, needing to know that her mind was not addled completely. Voices without bodies, strangers in mirrors, bold, unwanted warriors appearing in her bed. Why? Because of some old prophecy? A curse? A stupid doeskin map and useless dagger? Not just any dagger, mind you, but a Sacred Dagger.

She should have stayed with Gavyn in the forest instead of wishing him into her bed and dreaming so intimately of him.

Why had she left him? Because of Isa? What kind of idiot was she?

"Isa, please, if you can hear me—"

Just then, soft knuckles tapped at her door. "M'lady?" a woman called through the thick panels.

Startled, shaken out of her reverie, Bryanna quickly found her tunic and tossed it over her head.

"Just a minute." Hurriedly, the bodice still unlaced, she walked to the door and held it open just a crack.

A slight serving girl stood in the hallway, a bucket of steaming water hanging from one fist. Her eyes were gold as a morning sunrise, her face spattered with tiny freckles, her eyebrows thin and red as her hair. She dipped her head in a half curtsy.

"I'm Daisy," she said shyly. "Garnock—he's the steward here—he asked me to see to you," she said in explanation, then seemed to take in the disheveled state of Bryanna's clothing and hair. "But . . . I, um, don't want to bother you. If you'd like to sleep some more, please do so. . . . Otherwise, mayhap I can help you dress?"

Grateful that she'd been sent any servant other than the

cross, sallow-faced Hettie, Bryanna said, "Yes . . . please, come in." She pushed the door open wide enough for Daisy to pass.

The girl hurried inside. She poured the cold water from the washbasin into the empty bucket before refilling the basin with warm water and leaving a fresh cake of lavender-scented soap on the table. "Garnock said to tell you that breakfast will be within the hour," Daisy said.

Bryanna stepped behind a screen and scrubbed herself, including the tender area between her legs. Afterward, Daisy, warming to her new charge and chattering on about the scandalous behavior of the wright's eldest daughter, helped her finish dressing. Daisy's stories continued on as she combed and plaited Bryanna's hair.

Bryanna was glad to let Daisy chatter on, as her head ached and she couldn't escape the feeling that last night had been more than a nightmare, much more than a sensual dream. While Daisy prattled, Bryanna's thoughts strayed to the night before.

Once the girl was gone, she thought about everything she'd learned in the past day. Could it be true? Could she be the daughter of Kambria and Alwynn, and thereby an ancestor of Llewellyn and Rhiannon?

It seemed highly unlikely.

She touched her neck where the chain of bruises ringed her throat and thought of Gavyn. Why, even in her dreams, would their initial mating have been so harsh, so loveless, so brutal? Why would he not have turned her to face him? Kissed her on the lips as he had before? Why would he have made the act so vile, so malicious?

And then, why would he come to her a second time as a passionate yet caring lover?

Because he's angry with you for leaving him alone in the forest. He's punishing you. He's a violent man. He's robbed and killed. He murdered that sheriff. You infuriated him; he got his revenge.

Mayhap he didn't intend to attack you. He might have

stolen into the keep intending only to rob you. Remember how he looked at the dagger? How intent he was upon reading the doeskin map?

She couldn't think about it another second or else she truly would go mad. She had to do something—*anything*. Without wasting a second, she bundled her things together: her extra dress, her herbs, candles, amulets, and the leather map, still wrapped around the dagger, the knot Gleda had tied still tight.

She slipped it into her pouch just as Daisy knocked on the door to announce that breakfast was ready. Bryanna walked down the two stone flights of stairs and inquired about a monk or a scribe, someone who could pen a letter to her sister at Calon. She was hoping that Father Patrick would agree to send the letter by messenger.

On the main level, they walked through a short arched hallway that opened into a great hall, where the trestle tables had been placed and candles burned brightly. At the far end of the enormous room, upon a raised step, the lord's table had been covered in a fine cloth and Father Patrick was already seated next to several men she didn't recognize, possibly members of Lord Mabon's family.

She took a stool near his. "Good morning, Father."

He offered her a beatific grin, but rebuked, "You were not at the chapel this morn."

"I'm sorry, Father, I overslept."

"'Tis not an excuse, daughter." As a page filled his cup with wine, he added, "No matter how weary we are, we must find time to give praise and penance to the Holy Father and his Son."

"Of course, Father Patrick."

"I hope you've not let Gleda influence you, Lady Bryanna, for she is . . . well, I wouldn't say she's a heathen, but let's just say she sometimes strays. Her allegiance to God is often in question."

"Is that so?" Bryanna said, nettled. "I found her to be a woman of uncommon faith."

"Then, I fear, you're mistaken," he said as three pages with platters entered the room and approached the lord's table. Smoked trout and cheese on one wide platter, wastel bread and roast boar with onions on the next, and jellied eggs with fig and milk pudding smelling of cinnamon on the third.

"Ahh, I see the cook has outdone himself," the priest said. He offered up a long prayer once the savory food had been served upon thick trenchers.

Once the long prayer was over, Bryanna ate hungrily. She avoided most conversation except to ask for help in sending a missive to her sister, which the priest, though seeming a bit annoyed, agreed to do.

When she'd nearly finished eating and the castle hounds were stirring, staring hungrily at the gravy-sodden trenchers and bones, a soldier strode into the keep. Grim-faced, he wended his way through the trestle tables filled with castle workers and soldiers. At the lord's table, he leaned down and whispered gravely to the ruddy-faced constable, who listened, frowned, then brushed off his fingers. "Don't move them. I'll be right there," he said. Then, as the soldier made his way back through the tables, the constable turned to speak to the priest in low tones. The only word Bryanna was able to hear was "Gleda."

She'd been dipping a piece of bread in gravy, but she put down the food as she turned to the priest. "What is it?" she demanded, for the expression on the constable's face was dire.

Father Patrick made the sign of the cross over his chest. "They are in the guardhouse?" he asked. The constable nodded as he pushed aside his trencher and stood. "I'll be there soon."

As the tall man left, Father Patrick turned to face Bryanna again. "I'm afraid there is bad news," he said with more kindness than she would have expected.

Bryanna's stomach dropped. "What?" she asked, though she wasn't certain she wanted to know.

"It's Gleda. Both she and her husband, Liam, were found this morning by hunters."

She thought she might faint. "What?"

"They were both dead, apparently drowned in the creek."

"No!" Bryanna shot to her feet, nearly knocking over her stool. "But she was here last night. You and I, Father, we . . . we talked with her. She was alive and well and . . . this I can't believe." Tears filled her eyes, but she dashed them away with the backs of her hands.

"There is no reason for my men to lie," he said.

"I want to see her."

"What? Oh, child, I don't think that—"

"I want to see her and I want to see her now," she insisted, her voice rising enough that several soldiers at a nearby table looked her way.

"Perhaps we should pray," he said in that melodious, self-important voice she was quickly learning to detest.

"I just want to see her. Now. Take me to her. We can pray over her body." Bryanna was already heading for the door. Not bothering with a mantle, she rushed through the crowded great hall, ignored the guard, and pushed open the door. The air was thick and moist from the recent storm, tinged with the scent of wood smoke.

Following a pathway muddied by a trickle of water running downhill, she headed across the bailey to the guardhouse. Already some girls were gathering eggs while two boys, red-haired twins by the looks of them, were strewing oyster shells and seeds for the clucking, pecking chickens. Dyers were at their vats, swirling spun cloth with wooden paddles in their open-air huts, and the potter's wheel was whirling as he shaped mazers and ewers and jugs. A thatcher was on the farrier's hut, fixing the roof, and the clang of a stonemason's hammer and chisel rang through the bailey.

Bryanna found her feet flying over the earth, passing the kennels, where hounds were barking, and the stables, where horses whinnied and nickered as they were being fed.

Gleda? Dead. No, no, no! It couldn't be!

She brushed past a man who was standing in the shade of a hayrick and stopped dead in her tracks when she realized he might be Gavyn. She turned quickly to seek him out, but in a matter of a heartbeat he was gone, probably just a figment of her imagination. Her wild imagination . . . hearing voices and following a mysterious quest.

Breathlessly, she hurried onward, her shoes slipping in the mud, her mind still caught in a web of thoughts of Gavyn.

Forget him. He left you.

Concentrate on Gleda and what happened to her.

Bryanna's heart sank as she swept past the guard at the door of the gatehouse and forced her way inside.

"Wait, m'lady," he cried, and she recognized him as Quigg, the flat-nosed soldier she'd met the night before, the sentry Gleda had known since he was a boy. "Please, 'tis not a good idea—"

Ignoring his protests, she pushed her way past other men standing around a table. A fire burned, candle flames flickered, and weapons of all sizes and shapes—knives, swords, quarterstaffs, maces, and broadaxes—were mounted on the walls. But she paid little attention to anything but the two bodies lying upon a wide plank table.

"Oh, sweet Jesus," she whispered, her hand flying to her mouth as she recognized Gleda and her husband, Liam. They lay side by side, the pallor of their faces a dismal gray, their clothes still clinging and wet, water dripping onto a puddle on the stone floor. "No," she whispered, shaking her head as if she could dispel the image by denying it. Gleda looked so small and frail. Bryanna couldn't believe that just yesterday the feisty little woman had told her about Kambria, the woman who was supposedly her mother. "How . . . how could this have happened?"

"An accident," the captain of the guard said, his face sober. "M'lady, I don't think it's a good idea for you to be here. Mayhap you should wait at the keep for—"

"What kind of accident?" she demanded, ignoring his suggestion.

"She and her husband drowned in the creek, not far from their home," he said. "Two hunters on their way out this morning found them and brought them back to the keep."

"Why did they drown?" she demanded.

"Who knows?" The captain shook his head. "The sheriff, he's on his way to look at the creek, but probably Liam here came looking for his wife, who had been late coming home from the keep. 'Twas a bad storm. Mayhap the horse shied and she fell, striking her head on a rock. . . . There is a mark upon her forehead. But who knows? 'Tis a tragedy."

Bryanna wanted to collapse, to fall to her knees and scream at Isa or God or anyone who would listen. Instead she gritted her teeth. "You are certain this is an accident?" she demanded, feeling the eyes of all the soldiers in the room boring into her.

"Aye. As far as we can tell, nothing was taken. Their horse was wandering nearby, still saddled and bridled. There were coins in Liam's pocket, and their house seemed undisturbed."

Bryanna found it impossible to believe that on the very day Gleda had spilled a secret she'd held for sixteen years, both she and her husband would die, not just one, in his or her sleep, or after a long illness, but together and suddenly. It seemed too coincidental.

And yet why would someone kill both Gleda and her husband? To what end?

She heard the priest huffing and puffing as he picked his way along the wet bent grass and mud. "Oh, dear," he said, viewing the bodies.

Before he could suggest that everyone pray over Gleda and Liam, Bryanna slipped outside into the fresh air. Bile rose in her throat, and she feared she would lose all of her breakfast. Leaning back against the wet stones of the gatehouse, she tried to stave off tears by staring at the ominous clouds scudding across the sky.

What had happened to Gleda?

To Liam?

An accident?

Or, she feared, something darker and much more sinister.

CHAPTER SEVENTEEN

S he couldn't stay here.

Sniffing back her tears, Bryanna hurried to the keep. Though she knew the priest would want her to stay and pray for Gleda's soul, the very soul he'd dismissed so easily at breakfast, she had no stomach for it. She needed to get away. To escape.

To find Gavyn, the voice within her mind demanded as she chased a waddling goose up the path and sidestepped the spots where others from the flock had defecated.

Word of Gleda's death had already whispered through the castle walls, and children were huddled near the door of the gatehouse while laundresses, eyeing the steely sky, carried baskets toward a huge open-air shed to dry their recently scrubbed linens. Gossip floated on the air. . . .

"Drowned, fer sure, but coulda hit her head. . . ."

"Both of 'em, ye say? 'Tis a shame." The heavier of the two women clucked her tongue and shook her scarf-wrapped head as she set her tub onto the ground.

"A shame or a sign from God," the other laundress said. "Old Gleda, some people say she was a witch. . . . Well, if not her, then at least her niece, the one who died a while back."

Two boys raced past, their noses running and hair flying. Gleefully they chased three dogs heading toward the gatehouse.

"Hey! You, there! James Miller! Get those pups back to the

kennel master, right now! You, too, Jones! Now!" She turned
back to the thinner woman, adding, "The witch's name was
Kambria, if I remember right."

"Aye." Folding the linens over a strung robe, her heavy
friend nodded. "'Twas the one. Must have been some sixteen
years ago, mayhap more, but a horrible stoning."

"If you ask me," the laundress muttered under her breath,
"nothing's too horrible for a witch."

Bryanna tried to dismiss their gossip as she walked briskly
past the tongue-clucking laundry workers and flew into the
castle. She took the stairs two at a time and strode into her
bedchamber, where a fire had been lit, the rushes cleaned.
Without thinking twice, she gathered her things and began
packing them into the leather bag she'd carried all the way
from Calon. As she checked to be sure she was tucking away
the dagger wrapped in the map, the crimson silk bed hanging
touched her cheek, causing her to venture one last glance at
the bed.

She bit her lip. How drunk had she been to have acted so
wanton, so willing, so demanding? Hadn't she nearly begged
Gavyn to stay with her? She blushed and swore under her
breath. Had he really come to her last night? If so, where was
he now? Where did he go when he left her?

What was it Gleda had said? That she had to meet her
mother, dig up a grave and . . . and . . . what?

Open the coffin. That was it.

"Sweet Jesus," she whispered and made the sign of the
cross quickly over her chest. It seemed crazy, but then everything did, from talking to dead women to visitations from
phantom lovers. *Not a ghost, Bryanna. Gavyn was real. You
only have to look at the sheets again or feel the soreness between your legs to know that last night happened. Gavyn
came to your bed . . . while Gleda and her husband died.*

"God in heaven." She looked down at the pouch in her
hand. The damned dagger. "*Sacred* Dagger," she reminded
herself. What twiddle! And now it was not only tied with a
thin leather string, but also the twine of goat's hair that Gleda

had twisted. For the first time since Gleda had handed the pouch to her, she studied it.

Something was different. Or was it?

Though she felt an urgency to leave, she took the time to untie the bindings and flatten the map out. The dagger looked the same, but now instead of one scrap of doeskin, there were two, one layered upon the other.

"What?" She slid the knife to one side and laid the two pieces side by side on the bed. Her heart knocking, she rotated the second piece until it obviously meshed with the first and the map was suddenly twice its original size. Now, not only was Tarth visible, but another village was revealed. She suspected that the squiggly lines represented water, a river, and there were other scrapings—runes and symbols—upon both pieces of doeskin. Where the two maps joined, there seemed to be part of a hieroglyphic message, one she didn't understand.

But she did see one small drawing that was clear as a mountain stream: a simple drawing of a cross and casket.

No doubt the place Kambria was buried.

So why had Gleda slipped this piece of the map to her without saying anything? Had she experienced a premonition that she might die? Did she realize her hours were short? Then why not warn Bryanna? Or had the old woman simply wrapped the folds of deer hide together, intending to explain about it later?

Except there was no "later."

Gleda and poor deaf Liam were dead.

As was Isa, who had also owned a portion of the map.

Was Bryanna, too, only a step ahead of the messenger of death? Her heart thudded in fear at the prospect.

What did it all mean?

She couldn't stop for even a second to think about it; nay, she had to keep moving, stay one step ahead of whoever or whatever was chasing her.

She found Isa's amulet, the one she always wore for protection, and slid the leather thong over her head. The smooth stone fit naturally below the hollow of her throat. There. She needed all the help she could get.

She said a quick prayer to Morrigu, the Great Mother, and then, as a precaution, one to the Christian God, invoking his Son's name. No time for runes or spells or mass this morning. She grabbed her satchel and mantle and hurried down the stairs. Father Patrick would be detained until the afternoon. There was the matter of the two dead villagers, and at breakfast he had mentioned his long list of duties to maintain peace in the keep. This morning he would be listening to the farmers' squabbles as well as making certain all the taxes and fees had been paid for using Lord Mabon's lands for grazing and hunting.

Glad for an excuse not to see the tedious priest, Bryanna found the steward on his way into the great hall. "Please give Father Patrick my best wishes and thank him for his hospitality."

"You're leaving?"

"Aye, I must be on my way," she said, then lied through her teeth as effortlessly as if she had been doing so all of her life. "I have family awaiting me and I need to leave soon so that I can arrive before nightfall." With that, she headed straight for the stables.

As she walked through the bailey, she saw that more people had gathered near the gatehouse and many of the workers had interrupted their daily tasks to huddle together and discuss the disquieting deaths of the beekeeper and her husband. Moving quickly toward the stables, Bryanna passed a thatcher working on the roof of a new structure where two other men were weaving wattle for the walls. There was some discussion about the placement of a window, and they seemed the only two people in the keep who weren't consumed by the deaths of Liam and Gleda.

Bryanna passed them and cut through a pathway past the armorer's hut. For a fleeting second she thought she recognized Gavyn and stopped dead in her tracks. When the man looked up from his work pounding chain mail, she realized how mistaken she was. Though the armorer, too, suffered from a bruise upon his face, his features were softer and flatter than Gavyn's, the lines on his face suggesting another ten years.

'Twas just another trick of the mind.

One of far too many.

At the stables she was met by a burly man with a short neck and a red nose. The hair sticking out beneath his cap was gray and curling like lamb's wool. As he wound a rope between his arm and the vee between his thumb and forefinger, he regarded her from beneath the folds of drooping eyelids.

"I'm Lady Bryanna," she said, her eyes adjusting to the darkened interior, where horses' heads were thrust over empty mangers and the smells of leather, dung, and oil were thick. One reddish destrier snorted and tossed up his head, then stomped a heavy hoof.

"Quiet there, Rosemont," the man said to the roan, then took the time to rub the nervous horse's long nose. "There ya be." With a smile showing a few missing teeth, he turned to Bryanna. "'Tis Neddym, I am, stable master for Lord Romney, er, Mabon. Sorry. I can't quite get used to the change yet. Lord Romney, he was a good man. Fair. I'm thinkin' his son, when he gits back, will be the same." He hung the coiled rope upon a peg jutting from a post. "What can I do fer ye?"

"I'd like my horse," she said, pointing to Alabaster. "I left her here last night and it's time I left."

He frowned. "Usually the lord, er, in this case Father Patrick, he sends word."

"He's busy."

The big man shrugged. "Makes no matter to me. I'll see that the white one, she's saddled and ready in a few minutes."

"Thank you." Bryanna eased out of the dark interior and waited beneath an overhang that offered some protection for a boy seated upon a stump and repairing the bit of a bridle. She rubbed her arms and glanced at the gatehouse, again thinking of Gleda. The crowd was dispersing, soldiers ordering people back to work. She recognized the constable and

Quigg and . . . Her heart leapt as her eyes narrowed on a man who was of the same size and build as Gavyn, a man hanging back from the rest of the throng, one who cast a quick glance in her direction before walking behind a cart filled with stones for repairing the castle walls.

She stared after him, her pulse racing, and the man, dressed in clothes similar to those Gavyn had worn, again glanced in her direction, only to disappear around the corner of the stables.

It had to be Gavyn!

Had to.

She took a step in his direction and started to call out to him, then thought better of it. She was imagining things again, that was all. Just as she had as a child with the friends only she could see. Her mind sometimes created images that just weren't there.

'Twas almost as if last night was nothing but a dream, an erotic, sexual fantasy, as well as a dark nightmare.

"Here ye go, m'lady," Neddym said from somewhere behind her.

She spun to find the big man leading Alabaster from the stables.

"Oh, thank you." She strapped her bag to the saddle, then climbed onto the horse and adjusted her hood. Though it wasn't raining and the clouds were breaking apart, allowing glimpses of blue sky and sunlight, the day was still cold. She rode through the castle gates and headed to the river and Gleda's house. Although the old woman wasn't going to be with her, Bryanna would need some tools if she were intent on digging up a coffin that had been buried for sixteen years . . . her mother's coffin. She shivered at the thought, but pressed onward, trying not to think about the dull ache between her legs.

"Let us not allow this to come between us," Morwenna said. She'd found her husband on the watchtower, alone, standing under the flagpole where the standard of Castle

Calon snapped in the wind. His hands were planted on the ledge, his shoulders bunched as he gazed across the bailey and outer defenses toward Wybren, land of his birth, only a day's ride from here. Although the fire damage of more than a year ago had been repaired, Morwenna suspected the horrors still burned on in his mind.

Or was it longing she saw in his sky blue eyes? Did her husband think often of returning to Wybren, a fortress twice the size of Calon with perfectly rounded turrets mounted high on the castle walls? In truth, Wybren was in need of a ruler. The steward was doing his best to maintain order in the keep, but in order to prosper a castle needed a ruler.

The sun had risen and already hammers were ringing, saws growling, hounds baying in the nearby woods. A hawk swooped from the sky and disappeared from view as two boys carried buckets of sloshing milk into the kitchen.

"You did not think you could confide in me?" He turned to face her, his dark hair glistening in the sunlight. The shadow of suspicion in his blue eyes broke her heart.

"I . . . I was wrong." Oh, those words were hard to say. "I should have talked to you first."

His lips tightened. He waited for her to go on.

"I was afraid that you would stop me and I was so fearful for my sister, so certain that . . . that she needed me. I'm sorry."

A muscle worked near his temple and he glanced away from her, his teeth grinding a bit. " 'Tis my fault as well," he admitted. "I should not have moved into your keep. You were used to doing things your own way, without anyone interfering. You consider Calon yours."

"Nay," she argued, but when he raised a questioning eyebrow, she could say nothing further.

"We should move, spend time at Wybren, not just here."

She felt a new panic. "Who would run Calon while we were away? The constable? The steward?" She thought of Alfrydd, the scarecrow of a steward, and shook her head. Nay, she could not trust her keep to either man. And yet she could

understand her husband's desire to return to Wybren. Was he
not the only survivor of the dreadful fire there who was now
fit to rule Wybren Castle?

"You could trust Alexander, the captain of the guard. Or
mayhap your brother Tadd."

She rolled her eyes. "He's much too busy lifting skirts and
rolling dice and drinking ale to run a keep." She paced from
one side of the tower to the other. "Nay, none of them will do."

"That's the trouble now, isn't it? No one will do. Not even
your husband."

"No!" she said, and then realized there was a grain of truth
in his brutal words. She glanced to the bailey. Far below, she
heard a squeal, then watched as two boys chased the escaping
piglet along a path near the candlemaker's hut.

"Morwenna." His voice was soft seduction. He stepped
closer, his hands surrounding her upper arms. "I know you
spent many years trying to prove to everyone that you were
just as strong and smart as Kelan, and I know you have had
your share of . . . disappointments. But, Morwenna, I am your
husband and you need to trust me."

That much she understood. "You would not have allowed
anyone to follow Bryanna."

"Is that what you think? 'Tis not true, but I would have
liked to have had a voice in the matter. I would have preferred
to discuss it with you rather than having you sneak around
like a stray cat in the night, purloining from the treasury." His
hands tightened over her arms for a second; then he released
her. "But you are not completely mistaken," he admitted. "I
would not have allowed *him* to go after her." Any warmth in
his expression was now gone. "You knew this, and yet you
went behind my back."

"I said I'm sorry," she said, and she truly regretted her decision to act without consulting her husband. 'Twas a mistake
to hire his brother, an excellent tracker, aye, but a man whose
reputation had been blemished time and again by his own
selfishness and poor judgment. Had his improprieties not
scandalized all of Wybren? Had he not ambushed his own

brother and left him for dead? Had he not stolen Morwenna's heart and abandoned her when she was with child? 'Twas all in the past, and yet Morwenna could see how it still made her husband's heart heavy to think of his brother. "There's nothing more I can do now."

"You could call him back. Send some of the soldiers. They could track him down."

"But Bryanna," she protested.

"We could send someone else to find her. Alexander would do anything you asked."

Her head lifted sharply and she saw the truth in her husband's gaze. So he knew how the burly soldier felt about her. Unrequited love. Always a mess. "You would let the captain of the guard leave his post?"

"To find your sister?" He leaned his hips against the wall of the keep. "Of course."

"Your brother is the best," she insisted. "Better than Alexander."

Her husband's eyes narrowed, a white line of irritation appearing near his brow. "He's also a mercenary. A criminal."

"I know, I know . . . but he will not hurt Bryanna."

Her husband snorted and shook his head. Pushing himself from the wall, he walked to the stairway. "How can you be so certain, wife? He has a history of hurting women, does he not? If anyone should know of this, it should be you." With that he left her alone on the watchtower, her heart nearly crumbling.

He doubted her love.

Just when she realized she was with child.

"I don't like this, not one little bit." Pitchfork in hand, Neddym frowned at Gavyn as they stood in the darkened stables.

After little sleep the night before, Gavyn had woken and searched out Neddym. The stable master was glad to see his old charge, though spooked by the horrible fate of Gleda and her husband. Upon hearing the news, Gavyn had gone to the gatehouse to see for himself and nearly run into Bryanna. She'd been hurrying to the stables, a woman on a mission, her full lips set, her eyes scanning the bailey, her mantle billowing behind her in the cold air.

He couldn't risk having a confrontation with her or allowing anyone other than Neddym to know that he was here, so he'd avoided her. But not for long.

"Ye come in here like a bloody thief in the night," Neddym said, forking hay from a pile he'd pushed down from the mow, "on the very night two people are found dead, and ye yerself're wanted fer murder. I should be turnin' ye in, I should, instead of harborin' ye." He tossed hay into the manger, then ran a sleeve under his nose and sniffed. "If it weren't that I promised yer mother I'd take care of ye, I'd be collectin' me reward and buyin' meself a pint or two."

"I didn't kill the beekeeper and her husband."

"Then where were ye? Up to no good, I'm thinkin'."

"Is it a crime to wager a few coins on a roll of the dice?"

"Humph. I'm better off not knowin', I am."

That much was true, Gavyn thought as he recalled his night with Bryanna. God in heaven! If he let his thoughts wander back to the hours he'd spent in her bed, his damned cock would grow hard again.

"Then don't be asking questions that are none of your business. Trust me when I say I didn't kill the two people lying on the table in the gatehouse."

"And what about Craddock, eh? The sheriff of Agendor?" When Gavyn didn't answer, the bigger man shook his head and returned to scattering hay along the deep trough separating them from the horses. "Agin, I'm better off knowin' naught of it. Fergit I asked. So . . . because of yer sweet mother, may she rest in peace—" He jabbed the pitchfork into the ground, spat, then made a quick devout sign of the cross over his chest. "I packed some food fer the horse and yerself." He scowled as he pointed Gavyn toward a sack by the door. "Now git outta here, and do na let anyone see yer lyin' hide, or I'll lose me job and either end up banished, drawn and quartered, or forced to be the dung farmer, cleaning out the bloody latrines."

With the sack of grain slung over his shoulder, Gavyn left the stables and slipped into the traffic of peddlers, farmers, castle workers, and peasants milling about the bailey. Some still gossiped about the death of Liam and his wife, others went about their business, still others were leaving and arriving. Young children played tag and raced through the pathways, while older boys carried firewood or hauled buckets of water. Oxen dragged carts filled with stones and wheat, girls fed chickens, and the kennel master was busily trying to herd nine dogs on leashes toward the main gate. At times, the noises of the bailey blended into one great cacophony: banging hammers, creaking wheels, neighing horses, and boisterously shouting men. Thanks to all the huntsmen and soldiers riding beneath the portcullis, it was easy enough for Gavyn to blend in and ease through the main gate. Once he left the castle walls he walked quickly into the town, where he'd stabled Rhi for the night.

The horse had already been fed and groomed when he arrived. While a stable boy saddled Rhi, Gavyn made a few inquiries about a certain red-haired woman traveling alone. He quickly learned that Bryanna had headed east, along the river.

He followed the road, a little-traveled route that led away from the bustle of the village. A flash of movement in the woods on the other side of the river drew his attention, and he smiled. Though he only caught glimpses of a shadow darting between the bare trees, he saw enough of a silvery hide to know that the furry creature was traveling with him.

The wolf had found him again.

Blood thundered through his brain, pounding in his ears. Every muscle in his body taut, ready for battle, Hallyd burst through Vannora's door. "You thwarted me!" he accused, his anger burning white-hot, his need for vengeance running so deep it charred his soul.

His gaze scraped the cavernous room and he found her

lying on the cot, spent, an old woman again, too frail to lift her head.

He glanced at the altar, but it was dark, no steam rising from the cauldron, no candles dripping tallow. The white circle on the floor appeared to have turned gray.

"I didn't thwart you, Hallyd," she said evenly, her voice a cold whisper. "I saved you."

"Saved me? From what?" He strode closer, ready to crush her bones in his bare hands. How deep was her betrayal? How insidious were her plans? "You lied," he said, spit flying from his lips. "To me!" Outraged, he hooked a thumb at his chest.

She sighed upon the bed, her bones apparent beneath her shriveled flesh. Her patience was obviously thin as cook's pudding. "I saved you from destroying yourself."

"What heresy is this?"

"If you would just take control of yourself, you might understand." She managed to lever herself up on one bony elbow, though the effort seemed to cost her dearly.

"First, you picked a poor time to carry out your bloodlust," she hissed. "What were you thinking? Do you realize you could have ruined all of our plans by revealing yourself in the act of killing those powerless mongrels?"

He flexed his fingers, the strong grip that wielded a sword with craft and art. "The woman had to die. She was from Kambria's line."

"It matters not," Vannora said sharply. She looked ready to collapse, her small, brittle bones ready to snap, but there was a steely strength in her voice. "We will do this as I say. Without me, you will fail. Why do you think the guard was distracted when you sought entrance to Tarth? How do you explain the gate being lifted? And what of your lover's eagerness to accept a stranger in her bed?"

"You were there?" he asked, off balance. He'd thought his spy within the castle had been the reason he'd gained entry so easily.

"Trouble yourself not with questions you can't answer,"

she advised, and the hairs on the back of his neck lifted at the thought that she could see into his mind.

She let out a low, disgusted laugh. "You are safe, Hallyd. We are of the same mind, the same lineage."

"Lineage? Related by blood?" he asked. He knew not what she was, but he wanted no part of it. Except, of course, for her power. *That* he could use.

Her amusement was evident in the gleeful sparkle in her old, cloudy eyes, the gaping twist of her nearly lipless mouth.

"You think we are related?" He shook his head, knowing that she was tricking him. "I have no relatives who are yet living."

"Ah, yes, you saw to that now, didn't you?" Vannora's eyebrows lifted, and beneath the mask of age, he caught a glimpse of a child, a dark-haired girl of seven. The girl was submerged beneath the surface of the creek, her eyes staring sightlessly upward. Bubbles from her lips erupted on the clear rushing surface as she struggled against the current, against the tumbling water, against the strength of his hands around her neck. His hands.

He recoiled.

Nay, this could not be.

His younger sister was long dead.

Buried.

"Ah, Hallyd, so you remember?" Vannora said.

"You . . . you are not Leigh," he said.

The image passed as if he'd banished it. Yet he was shaken to his core. Who was this woman who had appeared to him not long after Kambria's death and had sworn to help him find the dagger? *What* was she? He stumbled backward. Suddenly he felt dry, his mouth and throat void of spit.

"Aye, I am not your sister, and yet I am a creature born of the same Otherworld that fathered you. Sired by Darkness, you and I."

His heart grew cold as death at the thought.

"There was a reason you came to visit me," she said, her voice cracking, as if even whispering was an effort.

But that reason had melted in the heated uneasiness of dealing with Vannora in this spiteful state, a viper about to strike. She was far more powerful than even he imagined, and yet she lay on the dirty old cot like a woman about to leave this earth, her bones ready to turn to dust.

"What was it?" she asked, a chilling gleam in those milky orbs.

Suddenly, his grievance resurfaced in his mind. "There was another," he bit out. His rage, though tempered slightly, still burned. "A man!"

"What do you care? Did you not bed her? Have your way with her?" Her lips twisted into a wicked grin that suggested this was not news to her, that she'd known. "Was it not what you expected, a night you had waited so long for? Did you not mount her, feel her writhe beneath you?" She threw up a dismissive hand. "You got what you wanted."

"Not near enough. I should have ignored what you told me and brought her here."

"Ignore me?" she repeated, her voice instantly clear. "Do not even consider it. If you go against me, Hallyd, if you do not obey me, then all will be for naught. You and I, disgusting though it may be, we need each other. Never forget it. Never *ignore* me. 'Twould be a grievous mistake. One I would never forgive, one you would forever rue."

"'Twould be easier if she were here."

"Easier for you to bed her. Easier for you to punish her for being the daughter of Kambria."

"It is because of her that I am cursed!"

"It is because of her mother, Hallyd," she clarified, and for a blistering, heart-stopping second, he saw Kambria in the crone's opaque orbs. Her face was red, the rosary around her neck squeezed tight.

He froze.

What trick of magick was this?

"Now listen to me. You will do as I say," Vannora hissed, Kambria's image fading. "If you brought Bryanna here"—she

motioned to the keep above her—"how would you ever find
the jewels to complete the dagger and lift the curse?"

"I would force her to tell me."

"By beating her? Degrading her? It would not work. Have
you learned nothing in all these years? Even if she did know
where the jewels were, she wouldn't tell you."

"There are ways—"

"Oh, for the love of Pwyll! Did those ways work on
Kambria? Did you force her to tell you where she hid her
daughter? No," she said, and he saw her truth. "Besides, no
one, not even Bryanna, knows where the stones are hidden.
Kambria made certain of that." There was a bit of fire behind
her opaque eyes, a flash of fury.

Again he wondered if she could change her shape at will.

"Is your lust as blinding as the sun to you? Is your desire
so feverish that you cannot think sanely? I thought one night
with her might sate you, but it seems to have made your impatience worse." She sank back on the cot. "This conversation
tires me." She waved a gaunt hand toward the door. "Leave
me now."

"*He* was with her."

"The bastard of Agendor?" Her voice held a little more interest.

"Yes." So Vannora knew. His skin itched at the thought. He
sensed an unspoken betrayal in the air.

"And this bothers you, why?"

"She is mine, Vannora. Mine."

She closed her eyes. "Aye, Hallyd, she is yours, but mayhap not yours alone."

He couldn't believe what he was hearing. "You don't
care?"

"Why should I?"

"The child. What if a babe is conceived and I am not the
sire? What if *he* takes her to his bed and gets her with child?"

"Worry not." She rubbed a gnarled finger over her forehead. "Just make certain you know where she is. Have your

men follow her and report back to you. Then you can ride in the night and catch up to her if need be."

He didn't like the plan. Not at all. This time, he was certain that the old crone was wrong. And after all, *he* was the baron. He damned well intended to do things his way.

She shifted on the cot and fingered the linen sheet, gazing thoughtfully into the distance. Lost in a vision only she could see. "Do not fight me, Hallyd, for you will lose." Lifting a thin eyebrow, she stared up at him. "Whoever gets the dagger will be the true ruler of Wales." This time when she smiled, her spiked little teeth gleamed in the dull flicker of light. "'Tis as simple as that."

CHAPTER EIGHTEEN

So now she was a thief.

The thought was more than a little disturbing.

Bryanna could not imagine that her quest would lead her to such depths as to steal from a dead woman, but here she was in Gleda's house, expecting someone from the castle to show up at any second and catch her in the act of stealing.

With the eerie feeling that she was stepping upon the dead woman's soul, she moved through the simple hut, where the fire had long since gone cold. The chickens clucked as if expecting food, a cat glared at her from behind the butter churn. Outside, goats bleated, expecting to be milked, and Gleda's horse had returned. It broke Bryanna's heart to see the bewildered creature half dozing, one foot cocked near the back door. Bryanna had taken the time to scatter some hay in a rick onto the ground for him. "Looks like you'll be going on a quest too, Harry," she told him consolingly as he nosed the hay.

She'd ridden to this little house with a deep sadness, and when she'd crossed the creek, the scene she encountered overwhelmed her. The trampled prints of a horse's hooves along the creek bank and the bloodstains upon a rock hinted at the chaos that had transpired here. But knowing that Gleda had lost her life in those rocky shallows made the violent images that much worse. She'd nearly thrown up.

Somehow, she felt responsible.

If not for her, Gleda would not have been out late at night, nor would Liam have been out searching for her.

Guilt had torn through her soul as she'd crossed the rushing water of the gurgling stream, urging Alabaster onward.

And now, searching through the empty house, she felt Gleda's presence so vividly. She imagined Gleda happily spinning wool from the fleece of her goats, or churning butter or making cheese, or tending to her bee skeps and collecting honey. A lump grew hard in Bryanna's throat when she considered old Liam, stoking the fire or whittling.

"Peace be with them," she whispered, not knowing if she was talking to Morrigu or the Christian God.

She knelt near the cold ashes of the hearth and drew a quick rune upon the grate, a rune for peace. She whispered a prayer for Gleda and Liam's souls, wherever they were now.

"May you have eternal rest," she said as she stood.

She could tarry no longer. 'Twas only a matter of time, she knew, before the soldiers from the castle would arrive. If no relative came forward to claim the property, it would be taken over by the baron. The animals would be cared for, either by livestock thieves, concerned neighbors, or Mabon's men. The pigs, goats, and chickens, and aye, even the cat, for its mousing abilities, were far too valuable to be abandoned.

While the cat watched and the rooster stretched his neck to crow, she fitted the two pieces of the map together once more and committed the etchings to memory. Afterward, she wrapped the pieces together over the dagger and turned to Gleda's larder.

What was she searching for? She wasn't sure. Tools, certainly, if she was going to be digging up a grave as Gleda had instructed.

Some things were obvious: the shovel and ax, Liam's weapons, a few candles, feed for the animals, a sewing pouch, beeswax, and some of the salted meat and fish. The worn leather bags hanging near the front door. As rapidly as possible, she filled the bags, then loaded them up onto Gleda's horse, Harry, whom she'd use as a pack animal.

Then, without a look back at the scene of so much tragedy, she headed off, whispering, "Morrigu, help me."

Bryanna traveled along the river until it came to a rutted path leading away from the main road. Holding on to the reins with one hand and the lead with the other, she twisted to look back periodically and assure herself that Harry, with his uneven gait, was not strained.

She also checked to see if she was being followed.

There is no one there. No one is following you. Who would trail after a woman without an ounce of good sense? her conscience nagged at her.

"Shush!" she said out loud. Behind her, Harry flung up his head in fright, his reins nearly pulling her arm from its socket. "Oh . . . sorry," she apologized to the horse. "Come along, boy."

With a disgruntled snort, the gelding calmed and resumed his trot.

Heading north, Bryanna passed few travelers along the way as the sun moved across the sky and morning bled into afternoon. She stopped once at a creek, allowing the horses to drink while she ate a piece of salted fish that she'd taken from Gleda's home. No one would blink an eye at the supplies she'd taken from Gleda's larder. The horse, however, as well as the weapons and tools, would no doubt be looked upon as stolen property.

So now you're no better than Gavyn, her mind taunted her. Though it was far from the truth. She hadn't killed anyone.

Yet.

"Stop it," she muttered, angry at her nagging conscience. She leaned over the creek to wash her face and hands. Sitting back, she saw her reflection in the eddies.

"Do not be downhearted." Isa's voice was clear as a clarion's call echoing through her mind. *"Continue onward, to the spot where Kambria rests. You will find two items that will aid in your quest."*

"I want nothing more to do with this bloody quest," she said aloud.

At that moment she glimpsed Isa's face in the swirling waters. Skin gray and distorted, eyes full of woe.

And just as suddenly the face disintegrated, foaming over the stones with the gentle current.

"But the child . . . ," Isa's voice protested.

"Oh, gods and gadflies, what child, Isa? Who is this child you keep speaking of?"

And then she saw him. A smiling toddler with bright eyes and plump cheeks and curling red-blond hair that caught in the wind. He giggled, revealing tiny teeth.

Bryanna gasped and he was gone, his image washing downstream with the tumbling water.

She scrambled away from the creek. 'Twas a trick of the light, a prank within her fertile mind. She saw no real boy child, no innocent babe!

"Nay?" Isa's voice mocked.

"Oh, sweet Jesus." She swallowed back the fear that rose as her mind raced to consider what it all could mean. Was that boy's future dependent upon her? Surely not. Oh, dear God.

"Go, Bryanna. Ride on. Find Kambria's grave. . . ."

Unwilling to believe what she'd seen in the water, Bryanna climbed astride Alabaster and patted the mare's neck, as much to touch something warm and living as to calm the horse. Then, with a determination that belied the shaky feeling inside, she gathered up the reins again and rode steadily toward a cleft in the hills, the point she'd seen upon the map.

She traveled the entire day, passing a few farms and several fields of stubble. Around nightfall, she reached a spot where the trail cut between the two hills. The sun was rapidly dipping toward the horizon, the moon rising in a purple twilight sky. Spying a rocky outcrop at the edge of the forest, she rode onward to a spot where the ground was loamy again, moss mingling with weeds and grass.

If Gleda remembered correctly, 'twas here that her mother had been laid to rest. There were no wooden crosses to show the burial plots, no tombs, no pile of stones.

Just the body of a dead woman below the crust of dirt and

grass. "Oh, Morrigu, help me," Bryanna whispered as night descended and she heard the whir of bats' wings and the soft hoot of an owl.

The isolation of the desolate woods pressed in around her, and the thought of digging up sixteen-year-old bones made her skin crawl. She cursed her quest, the mysterious mission that had her poised to dig up a woman's bones under cover of darkness. A lonely quest. She thought of Gavyn and the apparition of the night before. Where had he gone? Had he even been with her?

She found enough sticks in the surrounding woods to build a small fire, but as the flames crackled and snapped, she felt no warmth. Her thoughts turned to the nights she'd spent in the forest with Gavyn, staring at the coals, watching meat roast upon a spit. How she'd wanted to trust the man who moaned in pain by night and made her laugh by day.

"Snake dung," she muttered, breaking a few more twigs and tossing them into the fire.

Feeling more alone than she'd ever felt in her life, she gazed up at the stars and drew in several calming breaths. As serenity surrounded her she began to chant, her voice soft and low but full of passion. She spoke to the night and its creatures, to the dark wind and midnight hour, to the deep forest and damp earth, the words tumbling off her lips easily.

Her chant gave way to the sounds of the forest as she waited for the moon to rise. She felt the movement of the wide luminescent disk as it swam above the trees, offering a silvery ethereal light. Under the glow she found one large flat stone that peeked out of the grass—a stone she'd seen on the map. Using the stars as guidance, she walked ten paces north. Then, murmuring a prayer under her breath, she drove Liam's shovel into the soft wet earth.

"Isa," she said aloud as she dug, tossing shovelfuls of earth to one side, "I hope to Morrigu that you have not misled me."

She half expected the dead woman to respond in this chilly night.

But of course Isa's voice was still.

Instead she heard a deep male voice reverberate through the surrounding hills. "For the love of God, Bryanna! What in the hell do you think you're doing?"

Startled, Bryanna jerked the shovel closer.

She was alone in this desolate clearing.

She glanced sharply in the direction from whence the voice had come.

Gavyn?

Or her imagination?

Oh, please! Please!

Never in her life had she missed someone more.

And yet, what were the chances?

Most likely it was the voice of a robber or . . . but he knew her name.

She swung her shovel over her shoulder as if she intended to use it as a weapon and stared through the mottled moonlight. "Show yourself!" Her heart was in her throat, her nerves stretched, her breath fogging in the cold night air.

He emerged from the umbra, a dark figure upon his black horse, like a soldier returning home.

Gleda's warning raced across her mind: *Be wary of the dark warrior.*

"Gavyn?" Her shovel was still poised, as if she intended to whack the rider from his steed.

"Christ Jesus, Bryanna," he said, "what have you got against old Rhi, here? You look as if you're ready to bash his head."

"The horse? Nay, I would never hurt Rhi!" Relief washed over her and tears threatened her eyes again, but she willed them back. What was wrong with her? She'd never, *never* been one of those teary-eyed women.

"Oh, so it's me you're planning to knock senseless." He rode closer to the fire and her eyes glided gratefully over his figure upon the black horse with its white stockings.

Gavyn.

Her silly heart squeezed at the sight of him. Thank God! She didn't care about Gleda's warnings or even Isa's. She dropped her shovel and threw herself at him as he dismounted. Never in her life had she been so glad to see a person. His arms surrounded her and it was all she could do not to break down and sob against his chest. She'd been so alone on this quest . . . and now, if only for a few moments, she was with someone she trusted.

"Miss me?" He chuckled.

"Never!" she lied, laughing as he kissed the crook of her neck. Then, holding her face in his callused hands, he kissed her lips. He tasted of the night, of cool wind and wood smoke and moonlight. Her blood heated instantly as a wave of memories seared through her, memories of the night before and the lovemaking that had taken them deep into the night. Hot. Thick with wanting. His body pressed so intimately to hers. . . .

"Wait!" She pushed back, feeling an immediate chill of separation. "Just wait." Shoving her hair from her face, she took a step backward and drew in a long, calming breath. She tried not to notice that she was trembling inside. Relief? Desire? Probably a mixture of both. "You . . . you left me," she accused.

"*You* left me." He shook his head and walked to the fire. "Don't try and turn this around. I was sleeping in the forest, remember? Recovering? And you snuck away in the middle of the night, without a word." He squatted, warming his hands beside her small fire.

She couldn't deny it, though she desperately wanted to explain.

"You know, had it not been for the wolf, I think you would have taken my horse as well."

"Nay! And where . . . where is that wild animal? The wolf?"

"Bane?"

"Bane? As in wolfsbane?" The herb was used by farmers to kill animals. She'd heard of covering a piece of meat with the deadly herb, hoping that marauding wolves would eat the

poisoned meat and die before they attacked the farmer's livestock.

"She needed a name. I couldn't just call her Wolf."

"For the love of God, why not? I can't believe you actually
named her." A blast of icy wind keened over the hill. The gust
tugged at her hair, pressed her mantle tight to her body and
caused the fire to bend and shiver, flames flickering madly.
"You named the wild beast as you would a pet. Isn't that just
a little bit daft?"

"Not half as crazy as talking to people who aren't there,
Bryanna."

Grudgingly, she thought he'd made a good point. Didn't
she doubt herself and what she'd heard? Well, the proof would
be found out tonight, would it not? If there was indeed the
body of a woman buried in these hills, in an unmarked grave,
found only because of a map torn into pieces, then she could
quiet her own doubts.

Still considering the wolf, she pulled her mantle tighter
around her and cast a quick glance to the surrounding area,
just out of the fire's light. She searched the undergrowth for a
familiar pair of gold eyes.

"She'll show up." Gavyn stood up and closed the distance
between them.

"You've seen her?"

Gavyn laughed with amused affection. "That lazy cur
knows that I've always got an easy meal for her."

"She could attack the horses."

"Not alone. Nay." Offering up one of his irreverent and
much too sexy grins, he looked around her camp, his gaze
landing on the dozing Harry, who was tethered to the same
branch as Alabaster. "So you do have another horse. One not
as fine as Rhi, but good enough for a pack animal. I guess you
had to settle for someone else's when you couldn't steal
mine."

"I didn't steal . . ." She let that thought drift away. "Listen,
Gavyn, I would *not* have taken your horse and ridden away
that night in the forest. I would never have left you stranded."

Blood surged through her veins as he held her gaze. His eyes were healing well, the red almost completely gone, and the bruises on his face were faded to dull shadows.

"But last night," she whispered, afraid that he might deny it. "You were with me and . . . then you left."

"I could not take the chance that I would be caught. There is still a price upon my head."

"But why . . ." She didn't finish the question. Her memory was fuzzy. Mixed with flashes of pleasure, pain, fear, and desire all jumbled together in a nonsensical twist.

But now she knew her time with Gavyn was true, not a dream. Parts of it cut through her brain and she remembered the brutal way he first took her, how angry he'd been. "Why, Gavyn, were you so vicious with me?"

"Vicious? But I wasn't—"

"I was a virgin, Gavyn. 'Twas my first time."

He was staring at her as if she were mad.

"Could you not tell?"

"Christ Jesus, Bryanna, I . . ." He seemed ultimately vexed. "I had no intention of . . . of making love with you last night. I sneaked into the great hall to make certain that you were alive and safe and—" He lifted his hands to the sky as if in disbelief. "I . . . ah, well, 'tis over now. If . . . if I hurt you or was rough with you or offended you, then . . . I am sorry."

Her heart cracked as he seemed so sincere, so disbelieving, so inwardly disgusted with himself. He shoved his hair from his eyes and muttered a curse under his breath before adding, "I thought . . . I mean, it seemed as if you were enjoying it, too."

Again she felt her cheeks grow warm and silently prayed that the darkness would mask her embarrassment.

"Were you not?" he asked, glancing up at her. "Enjoying yourself?"

Oh, God, yes. "In the end, yes . . . mayhap it was my mistake. I just didn't understand how it would feel, what it was between a man and a woman. . . ." But the woozy memories flashed behind her eyes and she sensed something was very wrong.

And what of the image she'd seen in the mirror? A trick of her mind? The voice claiming she was "forever bound." Not Gavyn's voice, but one she couldn't explain.

"'Tis no use," she said as the wind began howling again. "No way to explain. . . ." She was so sick of thinking about it, studying it, dissecting what had happened. "Enough has been said of it."

He scratched at his beard, his dark silver eyes full of questions.

"I mean it, Gavyn. Let's not speak of it again. Why don't you tell me how you found me."

"'Twas simple. I followed you."

"But I was careful, watching over my shoulder to the empty road. No one was behind me."

"You stole a lame gelding, Bryanna. I've worked with horses all my life and I'm a hunter. 'Twas simple enough in the mud to follow an animal's track, especially one favoring a leg. And, as you said, there were not many travelers on the road. Which only made tracking that much easier."

He crossed the distance between them, his boots sinking into the wet grass as he motioned toward the shovel she still held in one hand.

"So why don't you tell me, Bryanna, what are you doing here in the middle of the night, digging into the ground? And what is it you plan to bury?"

Cael was trying to think of ways to bilk a few more coins from Lord Hallyd, when he spied the soldiers riding through the small village. Their uniforms were dirty and mud-spattered, their horses appearing weary, but they wore the colors of Agendor. Scarlet and gold, dirty but true.

Could his luck have turned on this night lit by the full moon?

He'd been in the saddle for days. His rump was sore, his leg aching from the bloody wolf's attack. Though he was loath to admit it, he might just have to track down a physician. The wound, though healing, was ugly and hot to the touch.

He'd just stopped for a pint and was tying up his horse when the soldiers arrived and filed inside the inn.

He followed a little distance behind, scaring a beady-eyed rat that was lurking in the shadows but quickly scurried away, his long tail following his body into a hole on the porch. Cael walked into the raucous establishment and slid onto a stool in the corner. The small room was crowded and warm, smelling of body odor, sour ale, and mayhap even vomit. He ordered his mead and watched as the men settled onto benches and stools. They paid for pints and flirted with the serving girl as she brought them leather cups filled with ale.

Good girl, Cael thought, and though he was thirsty and would like nothing more than to bury his own nose in his cup, drink it down and have another, he contented himself with sipping the strong beer slowly and watching.

It didn't take long for their collective bad mood to lift, and there were jokes and jabs among the men, their voices rising. Altogether there were five soldiers, a small but effective hunting party, Cael guessed. After talk of battles and hunts and bedding the most willing women in the barony, one of the men said, "But we dinna find the bastard, now, did we? Nary a sign."

Cael smiled and held his cup to his lips, his ears straining to hear the conversation above the loud wagers, exclamations, and rattling of the bettors' dice cup at a table near the fire.

"We'll find 'im, we will."

"And how'll we do that, now, Seamus? His trail has gone cold as a dead man's cock."

Several of the other soldiers laughed and grunted their approval while the dice rattled noisily.

"Someone will see him. Recognize him. Or catch sight of the horse." Seamus wasn't about to be the butt of a joke. "We 'ave to find him, Aaron. We must to avenge Craddock."

"Craddock was a dung sucker," the big one, Aaron, said,

turning to look at the serving girl. As he did, Cael saw that the big soldier was missing part of one ear. "He deserved to die."

"So now ye're defendin' the murderin' bastard," Seamus charged. He looked ready for a fight, his face turning as red as the color of Agendor's crest. Seamus's muscles bunched, as if he wanted to throw a punch or go for his sword. 'Twas obvious to Cael he wasn't as smart as the others. Indeed, he'd often been the butt of a joke and was itching for a fight.

"Whoa, there, Seamus," the one with the bad ear said. "Calm down. I was jest sayin' what we all think. Now, we'll find Gavyn, aye, and we'll bring him back to Lord Deverill's justice. 'Tis our duty. But I'm tellin' ya that the bastard could have done a worse thing than killin' Craddock."

A roar went up at the dice table next to the spy. Men laughed and cursed.

Cael strained to hear more of the conversation, but the soldiers shifted, huddled over their drinks, and lowered their voices.

It mattered not.

He'd learned what he needed to know.

He considered approaching the soldiers himself, but then thought better of it. Let them return to Agendor. Let them admit that they couldn't find the murdering horse thief. Let them incur Deverill's wrath.

Only then would Cael demand an audience with the baron. Only then would he barter for the information he had. For surely the price upon the bastard's head would increase.

He smiled into his cup.

Indeed, his luck had changed.

Bryanna leaned against her shovel in the silvery moonlight. "Nay, Gavyn," she assured him. "I'm not burying anything tonight."

He looked at the hole in the earth. "Then—?"

"I'm digging up something already buried." Before he could ask what, she added, "Supposedly this is the burial place of Kambria of Tarth, and if Gleda, rest her soul, is to be believed, not only is Kambria buried here, she was also a witch. And, as it turns out, me old dear mum."

"What? Wait . . . your mother? I thought Lenore of Penbrooke was your mother. I saw you with her when I worked in the stables. I was there."

"Aye, I know. But according to Gleda, the story of my birth was a lie. She insisted that I was born to Kambria and was switched with Lenore's sickly babe. My father knew of it."

"Your father?"

"Yes, Lord Alwynn," she said, snorting her disgust. "Another man who apparently could not keep his breeches laced."

"He had a child with Kambria about the same time as he had one with Lenore?"

"Aye. So Gleda said. It's written."

"Where? On what?"

"That, I can't tell you, except that now I have not one scrap of a doe hide map but two that apparently fit together, like pieces of a puzzle."

"The map you had was not whole." He nodded.

"So now you can help. Here!" She tossed him the shovel, as her muscles were already sore. As long as he was here, he may as well work. "You start digging." She indicated the spot where she'd started making a hole in the earth. "And I'll tell you what I learned."

"Just like that?" he asked, driving the shovel deep into the soil. "You're going to tell me everything? After leaving me in the forest?" Clearly he disbelieved her, and she didn't blame him. But she'd been keeping too many secrets. Bryanna could stand it no more. Isa's warning be damned; it was time she trusted someone, even a murderer and a thief.

She pulled her mantle tighter around her to ward off the cold. "I'm sick to my back teeth of lying and half-truths and riddles, and so I want you to be honest with me and so I shall be with you. Unless of course Isa tells me not to."

"She's here with you?" he asked skeptically. He tossed a shovelful of dirt to one side, then slammed the blade of

Liam's shovel into the ground again, slicing more dark wet loam. "She and her husband, Parnell was it?"

"Of course she's not here, and no, she was never married, *Cain*," she replied, emphasizing the false name he'd given her when they'd first met.

He snorted a laugh. "Fine, fine, so I admit it, I lied when we met, too. We're even."

"Doubtful," she said dryly, and he chuckled again.

"So, Isa, is she meeting you?"

"Maybe. I don't know." Shrugging her shoulders, she looked away and cleared her throat. She wanted to be completely honest with him but found it difficult. Could she really admit that she was listening to a dead woman?

"So where is she?"

"Well . . ." She hesitated while he continued to dig. How exactly could she admit that Isa was talking to her from the grave? Nervously, she touched the amulet at her throat, the one she'd retrieved from Isa.

"I thought this was the time for the truth."

"It's kind of hard to believe," she admitted, watching the mound of discarded earth grow.

"Try me."

"Isa's dead."

He stopped shoveling. "Dead?"

"Oh, yes."

Leaning against the handle of the shovel, he said, "You know, before I dig any more, why don't you tell me exactly what it is you're talking about?"

"I intend to. But don't stop. You keep at it." She motioned to the ever-deepening hole. "I'll explain."

"Then talk."

And she did. From the beginning. As he threw shovelful after shovelful of soft loam onto the mossy grass and the pile grew, she told him of Isa's death and of the strange conversations they'd shared. She explained about taking Isa's things and setting out on her quest, of learning spells and chants and how to dig, dry, and use herbs. As he drove the shovel deeper into the earth, Bryanna reminded him of how they'd met and, later, about how Isa's voice insisted she leave him in the forest. She told about the quest to save some child she'd never met, of the dagger and stones, of using the leather map and riding to Tarth, where she'd met Gleda.

Bryanna caught her breath and looked up at the glowing full moon as she relayed how Gleda had shared with her the secrets of her birth.

". . . that is, if I can believe what Gleda said," Bryanna confided as she walked closer to the fire. She picked up a dry, brittle stick, then banged it over her knee, the wood splintering and cracking.

"You don't believe her?" Gavyn asked.

"I'm here, aren't I?" She shook her head at the events that had brought her here to this place, with this man. "I find it difficult to think everything she said was true."

"And do you not think it's strange that she and her husband died on the very night that you met? A coincidence?"

"Worse than that, I think she might have known she might die." She tossed the pieces of wood into the fire. Hungry flames crackled and burned around the new fuel and golden shadows danced against the rough bark of the surrounding trees.

"A premonition? That she would have an accident?" he asked, throwing his shoulders into his task.

"Or that someone would kill her."

"Kill her? You mean on purpose? Murder her and her husband?" He flipped a thick scoop of dirt onto the ever-growing mound.

"Why else would she have left the second part of the map with me?"

"That's how you got the second piece?" he asked, looking up.

"Yes, I was getting to that." She added twigs to the fire and continued with her story as the flames grew ever brighter. "And so I stole the horse and some things from her home, then followed the map to here."

Gavyn stopped digging to mop his brow with the back of his hand.

" 'Tis quite a tale, Bryanna," he admitted. "Some people would think you were daft."

"And you?"

He smiled, a slash of white in the darkness. "No, I don't think you're mad, but it seems almost as if I'm in one of the old ghost stories that we shared as children. 'Twas always a challenge to come up with something darker and scarier, a tale that would frighten your friends, especially the littler ones. All this digging up coffins by the light of the moon." He motioned to the starry sky. " 'Tis a little dramatic, don't you think, like the old woman did it just to scare you?"

"I know not why this all had to happen at night."

"Near midnight, right?" he asked, and she nodded. " 'Tis nothing more than sheep's dung, a ghost tale." He shrugged, "But, 'tis fine. Here we are. Why not dig for dead witches?" He looked up at her, his sarcastic grin needling her. "I guess we can be thankful 'tis a moonlit night."

"Just dig."

His smile widened. "I will, but not forever. Not just to prove you right. Soon, I should come upon a coffin. If I do, then we'll know if Gleda was telling the truth."

"And if you don't?"

"Then I doubt, lady, that you are truly the new sorceress of Tarth."

Bryanna didn't know what to hope for.

Either her entire life had been a lie and she was the daughter of a witch or she was, indeed, mad, listening to dead women and old crones who wove legends with truth. She rubbed her arms. "If you would like a rest, I'll dig for a while."

"I think not." Gavyn drove the shovel deep.

And hit something hard, which made a loud, clunking sound.

Bryanna's head snapped up.

Her heart turned stone-cold.

"Got something," Gavyn said, and gone was any trace of cockiness, his smile fading.

As Bryanna walked closer to the deep hole in the earth, he leaned into his task, digging the shovelfuls faster, his blade striking something solid time and time again. Each time she heard that thunk, Bryanna stiffened.

She peered into the dark hole, where Gavyn scraped away the remaining dirt with the side of the shovel. "'Tis a box, all right," he said.

He was right. In the pale moonlight she saw the outline of a long wooden box, probably a rotting pine coffin. Out of habit, she sketched the sign of the cross over her bosom, while quivering to her very soul.

"Dear God," Bryanna whispered as she stared at the casket. The wind rushed around her as a solitary cloud, gauzy and fine, drifted across the moon.

"Looks like Gleda was right," Gavyn said, and without waiting for any word from Bryanna, he reached into the hole and swiped off the remaining dirt with a hand. "Do you want to do the honors?" he asked once the broken, rotting pine box was exposed.

She shook her head. "Go ahead. Open it."

"All right then." He positioned the blade of the shovel to lever off the lid of the coffin, and the soft decomposing wood gave way easily.

Bryanna, her mouth dry as sand, braced herself as she lay on the wet ground and leaned over the edge of the grave, her arms dangling into the wet hole. She wrapped her fingers around the soft wood, and as Gavyn leaned on the handle of the shovel, helped him pry the cover off the casket.

With a loud, unworldly groan, the wood gave way.

The lid fell to one side.

The casket and its contents were exposed.

What Bryanna saw caused her heart to stop and a scream to die on her lips.

Lying in the box, black eye sockets gaping, was a skeleton,

the bones of Kambria of Tarth, the barest scraps of rotting cloth visible.

But the dead woman wasn't alone.

Cradled in her fleshless arms was a tiny separate set of bones, the perfectly formed skeleton of a baby.

CHAPTER NINETEEN

" 'Tis my sister," Bryanna said, certain the baby cradled so carefully in the dead woman's arms had to be Lenore's missing child, the infant that had been switched.

"Lenore and Alwynn's child."

"Yes," she whispered, a lump in her throat so large she could barely breathe.

"So the legacy, Gleda's tale, is true. Or parts of it."

"Mayhap all of it." She sat back on her heels and looked up at the moon riding high in the sky, its watery illumination shining over the land.

"There is something more."

"More?" she asked.

Gavyn was staring at the woman and child. "See there? Look." The serious tone of his voice gave her pause. New trepidation assailed her as she eased over the rim of the hole again and peered into the darkness.

She saw the smallest glitter, like a bit of glass catching light, within the casket, about midway inside, between the dead woman's hip bones.

The back of her scalp crinkled in revulsion. "What is it?" she asked, but in her heart she knew. It was a stone. One of the gems for the dagger. Shimmering pearlescent and bright.

Part of the legend ran through her mind.

An opal for the northern point . . .

" 'Tis the opal, is it not?"

"Let's see."

Bryanna felt her legs go weak as he reached between the bones. She looked away, fearing she might be sick. "Someone hid it in the casket with her," she said, as if that were a plausible excuse.

"I don't think so."

Oh, God! He was right. Why would someone hide it there rather than steal it? And its position . . .

Again bile climbed up her throat as she thought of what Kambria had endured, what she had done to save her child, to save Bryanna. Her voice was a whisper when she said, "Isa . . . Isa said that there were two items. . . . One would be the stone, and the other must be the child. . . ."

"We'll see . . . ," he said and reached farther into the casket, his fingers pushing aside the bones to retrieve the small stone.

Bryanna cringed, feeling that Kambria and the infant were being violated all over again. She knew the disturbance was necessary. For the love of God, that was why she'd come here, to locate the first gem to place inside the dagger. And yet, it still seemed wrong.

The moon rose even higher, giving off more light, until the night seemed a blue, filmy day. Bryanna held her breath as Gavyn rose from the grave holding the shining opal and handed the gem to her. Oval-shaped, it looked perfect in the silvery light, a smaller, elongated version of the moon itself.

"There is something else," he said, and again disappeared into the pit. Still feeling ill, Bryanna poised at the graveside and peered in with ever more trepidation.

She knew where his fingers were burrowing and gagged as he retrieved what looked like a dark twig.

"Morrigu, Mother Goddess," she whispered as the truth was evident to them both. "The stone and this . . . These items were not intentionally buried with her," she said. "No friend or ally left them with her."

He looked up at her and shook his head.

"They were hidden within her. Deep in her body." Bryanna

shuddered as she realized that Kambria was so desperate to keep her secret that she had hidden the jewel and the twiggish thing inside her, pressing them deep within her womb.

"Aye," he agreed solemnly. "She must have known she would die soon."

"So what is that? What did you find with the stone?" She motioned to the item in his hand.

"It looks like a piece of rolled leather."

"Another part of the map." Bryanna met his eyes in the moonlight. "The two things Isa told me about. The opal and the map."

She glanced down at the skeletal mother and the bones of a baby who'd been born by another woman. Buried together. *Forever bound.* She felt herself pale. This could not be the babe Isa had mentioned. "Isa never mentioned that we'd find the baby here."

"Maybe she didn't know. Let's see if there is anything else." As Bryanna fingered the stone and bit of rolled leather, he searched the rest of the coffin, carefully examining around and beneath and inside the bones. Finally, he shook his head and straightened, his eyes just inches below hers. "There is nothing more here."

"Then we must bury her again, along with the child." Bryanna whispered a quick prayer. "Now they can finally rest in peace."

"I would hope."

Together they replaced the lid on the coffin. As Gavyn shoveled earth over the casket, Bryanna said another prayer to any god or goddess that would listen.

The opal winked knowingly in the moonlight, while the brittle piece of leather was lifeless and drawn. She walked to the fire, opened her pouch, and removed some of the beeswax. She worked the wax into the old stiff leather, softening it, massaging it, making it more pliable. Bryanna didn't want to think about Kambria's despair or her fear. What would it take to force this piece of leather up inside the very essence of one's womanhood, to hide it there with a valuable stone? And the baby. Gleda had said the poor child had died a natural death; mayhap Alwynn had hoped that Kambria could use her powers to save the little girl, even heal her. Perhaps Alwynn had been the one to bury the baby beside her.

"No power is strong enough for that," she said aloud, stretching the deer hide slowly over a rock, smoothing it each time it began to roll up again.

"What?" Gavyn was tossing the final shovelfuls of dirt onto the grave, tamping down the soft earth.

"I was just thinking about Kambria," she said, grimacing as she tried to force the leather to flatten.

"About why, if she was such a great sorceress, she couldn't save herself?"

"Aye."

"Some things can't be explained," he said. "Like talking to a dead woman or dreaming of someone you haven't yet met."

"You know of my dreams?" she asked, confused.

He sat on a rock next to her and watched as she worked the leather, her fingers stretching and moistening the deer hide. "Nay, Bryanna," he admitted. "I only know of my own. So where is the dagger?" She looked up from her work. "Let me do this. You put the stone where it belongs."

He took over for her, pressing his thumbs into the leather as she unwrapped the dagger. "An opal for the northern point," she said and carefully rotated the stone over the top hole in the dagger. As the opal clicked into place, she felt a sensation ripple through her fingers and run up her arm, warming her from the inside out. A flash of light sizzled upon the hilt of the dagger and the stone was suddenly affixed firmly in its position.

"By the gods," Gavyn whispered. "It's set."

"As if it had always been imbedded in the handle," she said. The old dagger seemed to shine now, the opal glowing pink and pale blue, though she was certain it was a trick of moonlight.

Gavyn's eyes narrowed. "I don't believe in magick."

She handed the knife to him and he tried to wiggle the gem

from its place on the knife's hilt, but it was solid. Gavyn shook his head slowly back and forth, then handed the knife to her.

"You might have to change your mind about your beliefs," she said.

"Humph." His brow still furrowed, he handed her the ragged piece of doeskin. "Mayhap we should look at this and try to understand it. Kambria went to great lengths to hide it."

By the firelight they placed the three pieces on a long, flat rock, turning them and twisting them until their jagged edges meshed and the etchings made some kind of sense. "This is the way it goes," Gavyn said, studying the symbols and weird hieroglyphics. He ran a finger from the spot that indicated Kambria's grave to the edge of one portion, where, again, it looked as if the doe hide had been etched. "East," he said, eyeing the surrounding hills. He glanced up at the sky, then nodded toward the steepest cliffs. "That way."

Bryanna followed his gaze to the dark craggy hillsides covered in trees.

"An opal for the northern point, an emerald for the east . . . Tomorrow, I'll head in that direction," she said.

"And I'll come with you."

"Will you?" she asked, not certain that he should join her. As much as she missed him when he was gone, as much as she wanted his company, she was not sure he should be a part of her quest.

"Won't you need a hunter, and a tracker, and a grave digger, and a bodyguard?"

She nearly laughed. "A bodyguard with a price upon his head, riding a stolen horse that belongs to a nobleman. Is that what I need?"

"Aye," he said with a nod. "I think you do."

"And what about the rest?" she asked, still sore enough to be reminded of their lovemaking.

"The rest?" His words sounded innocent, but his eyes glinted in the moonlight.

"Between us. You know." The bastard! He was going to

make her say it. "What happened last night . . . between us. What about that?"

"Since you think I was too rough with you, mayhap we should wait."

"How long?"

"That, m'lady, is up to you. I am always ready."

Cursed man! Was he laughing at her? His quicksilver eyes gleamed in the moonlight.

A retort was on her lips when, quick as a cat pouncing upon a mouse, he grabbed her and pulled her close to him. Byranna dropped the knife from her hands as he lowered his mouth to hers, his lips hot and hungry. She gasped as his tongue thrust between her teeth, toying and touching, flicking upon the roof of her mouth.

"Ooh," she whispered, her arms wrapping around his neck. Her flesh was instantly fevered. "Gavyn . . ."

Holding her firmly to him, he pulled back his head. "What, lady?"

"I—I . . ."

"I know. Me, too. But I think it's best if we wait"—his smile was wicked as the night as he let go of her—"until you're bloody well ready."

It had taken every bit of willpower to allow her to sleep alone, but he had done it. He'd stretched out on the ground, swaddled in his mantle, and watched as she, exhausted, had fallen asleep.

Sweet Jesus, he ached for her. The night before had been pure bliss, and then today, her odd accusations had left him cold. Had she not responded to him? Had she not kissed and loved him with warm hands, wet lips, and willing body?

He stared at the dying fire while she lay so close to him he could touch her if he but reached out his arms.

Do not do it.

'Tis unlucky to bed a witch.

His jaw clenched at the thought, and he leaned over the log he was braced upon and spat. He didn't believe in witches or sorcery or spells or magick or *any* damned thing he didn't understand. Sometimes, when he witnessed incredible cruelty, even God was difficult to trust, though he did try to believe.

Dragging his gaze away from her, he stared up at the watery moon and finally dozed.

When he awoke, the sun was already rising, clouds starting to gather. He stoked the fire and waited until she roused to tell her that he would leave to hunt for an hour or so. By the time he'd returned with a duck and squirrel, she was just finishing stitching the map together with the heavy leather needle and thread she'd found in Gleda's sewing supplies.

He skinned the squirrel, plucked the duck, and placed the carcasses on a spit that Bryanna had created with her knife and several sturdy sticks. Smoke billowed into the sky, where high clouds were collecting. As the scent of charred flesh wafted on the air, he noted that Bane was back, poised intently at the edge of the forest.

"Can't you catch your own damned meal?" Gavyn asked.

Bryanna turned her head to spy the beast seemingly beseeching her.

"You're a wolf, for God's sake. You should be bringing game to us," he complained.

Bryanna chuckled. "She's not a hunting hound," she chastised, rotating the spit.

"Lazy, that's what she is." Sitting on a rock, Gavyn studied the pieces of leather now bound together. Some of the scratches on the doeskin made sense to him or sparked a memory of a place he'd visited, but many of the marks made no sense. "This appears to be a road," he said, "and this"—he pointed to a barely discernible scratch—"could be a keep or village. 'Tis a building."

"An abbey?" she asked, and he noticed the faint outline of a cross. "Mayhap a cathedral?"

"Or graveyard. See here there's a dark spot, mayhap another grave site, only this one marked with a cross."

"Oh, do not tell me I have to dig up another grave."

Shivering at the thought, she rubbed her arms and glanced past the fire to the freshly turned earth.

"Maybe Isa will tell you."

She sent him a scathing look. "We can only hope. Elsewise we know not where to go."

He frowned. "I think if we follow the map, we will come to some of these places that are marked. We'll probably recognize certain landmarks as we go. But it looks like it is a far ride over tall mountains. A journey. It could take a long time."

Turning the meat again, she eyed him through the wafting smoke. "You do not have to accompany me. Why would you want to make a difficult journey that will take too much of your time? You can go your own way."

He felt a smile tug at the corners of his mouth. "You cannot get rid of me that easily."

"Was I trying?" she asked, arching an eyebrow and licking the grease from a finger.

"You tell me," he said, ignoring the sudden burst of longing that raced through his blood. "You tell me."

"So let me understand this," Deverill said, clasping his hands behind his back and pacing the length of the large chamber in Agendor's gatehouse. The men, usually clustered in groups laughing, talking, and bragging, were stonily silent, as if the baron's rage were palpable and holding each of their tongues.

Deverill stood in the midst of a small band of his soldiers—incompetents, all of them. The very men he'd sent to track down Gavyn had returned less than an hour earlier, while there had still been light in the sky. They were tired, dirty, and grumbling, swords in scabbards clinking while they gathered around an odd-looking little man who, if Deverill could believe him, was more efficient than any man in the army of Agendor.

"You think you have seen my horse being ridden by Gavyn of Tarth," Deverill went on. The skinny little man with the oversized features started to interrupt, but Deverill held up a gloved finger. Obviously brighter than he looked, Cael held his tongue. "He was riding with a woman you claim is a sorceress. A wolf of incredible proportions was with them and attacked you, is that right?"

"Aye, m'lord," the runt said, nodding his head up and down so quickly it seemed about to bob off his thin neck. " 'Tis just as you said."

"You're certain of this?"

"Does not your steed have white stockings against his black coat and a crooked blaze running down his nose?" Cael asked, using a grubby finger to scrape down the middle of his own face to illustrate his point.

"Many people know this, but it seems incredible to me that you, one small man, observed so much when my own men, trained soldiers, warriors, found nothing. Not a trace of Gavyn or the horse."

Cael lifted a bony shoulder and offered a humble smile that didn't quite reach his bulbous, crafty eyes. "Mayhap they were looking in the wrong spots, m'lord. Or then again, it could be I just got lucky."

"Not so lucky if you were attacked by their wolf. Did they order it to lunge at you?"

"Nay, I was just sneakin' up on their camp, peerin' through the brush, I was. So quiet they didn't know I was there at all. Then, all of a sudden, this beast with jaws like none other and teeth the size of a man's fingers leapt at me from out of the darkness! 'Twas horrible." He glanced around the room to see that the other men were listening. " 'Twas fortunate, it was, that I was able to get away with me life."

"Yes, yes, so you said." Deverill didn't know whether to believe this little man. "Where are you from?"

Suddenly the little man's voice matched his stature. "Chwarel."

A servant of Hallyd. Deverill had never met the Baron of Chwarel, an odd man, and that was being kind. Once a priest, Hallyd had hung up his cassock many years ago. Rumors had circulated about him for years, tales of a man afraid to leave his own keep unless under the cover of nightfall. A nocturnal creature.

Deverill persisted, asking, "You came across my men at an inn, isn't that right?"

Seamus nodded. "Aye, m'lord. He came out right after us, claimed he'd seen Gavyn."

"How so?" Deverill asked.

"I was on my way to tell you. I, uh, I heard there was a reward for his return."

"And where is he now?" Deverill asked.

The runty little man had the audacity to hold his tongue, as if he had any power, as if he, this little insect of a man, could barter with a man as powerful as the Lord of Agendor. "You will be paid your reward if we catch him, but I do not give money to anyone on rumor," Deverill warned.

"Of course," he replied, shifting from one foot to the other.

"And your Lord Hallyd knows of this?"

"Aye, but he thought you would want to know."

"Thoughtful of him," Deverill said, unable to hide his sarcasm. "Tell your baron that I thank him for his concern." He pointed to the captain of the guard. "Send soldiers on fresh horses to Tarth. And you," he said, returning his gaze to this eager little bug-eyed informant. "I'll have the physician look at that leg of yours. The steward will see to it that you have food and drink from your long travels. You can rest this day and sleep in the guardhouse tonight. I'll dictate a message to the scribe, so that it bears my seal and Lord Hallyd knows that you truly did arrive here. You can ride with my soldiers in the morning, show them where you saw the murderer who stole my horse. Perhaps your valuable tracking skills will get my men back on his trail."

Cael shifted, using a cane for balance. "But my duty lies with the Lord Hallyd."

"Fear not, Cael. My men will see that you return home safely, once they've proven your story true." He leaned a bit closer to the man, who reminded him of a gargoyle. "But if you are lying to me, Cael, if you have come here with a tale of monstrous wolves, witches, and the thief and that tale proves to be false? An untruth? Only a means of extorting money from my coffers?" He watched as the smaller man swallowed hard, but those big eyes never wavered as the spy held Deverill's gaze. "If you have lied to me, you will pay for the crime with your life. Do you understand?"

"Aye, m'lord . . . and it's thanking you, I am, fer yer hospitality. But I lie not. I saw the thief with your horse. He and a witch and that beast from hell were heading to Tarth. If they are not there, I know not where they've gone, but surely someone will know."

"Aye." Turning back to his men, Deverill didn't bother to hide his disapproval as his gaze settled on the captain of the guard. "Take this man with you in the morning. Find the thief and my damned horse. And this time, do not let him slip through your fingers!"

CHAPTER TWENTY

Gavyn had been right, Bryanna thought as they came upon a small mountain village. The journey had been long and arduous, over mountains so sheer she'd thought the animals might slip down the rugged slopes. They had crossed rivers where there had been no bridges, and traveled down canyons that, when the clouds rolled in, had appeared bottomless.

Mixing charred wood, mud, and water, Bryanna had tried her best to make a dye that, when applied to Rhi, disguised his white markings. The coloring washed off, of course, and had to be reapplied each morn, but she hoped it helped make the horse appear less noticeable, less likely to be recognized as Lord Deverill of Agendor's steed. She called herself Brynn, a common enough name, and Gavyn introduced himself as Cain. Although there was little they could do to alter their appearance, Bryanna tucked her hair inside her hood and prayed that no one recognized them.

Although she wasn't a wanted criminal as Gavyn was, there was still the matter of Harry, the horse she'd stolen. Likewise, it would be highly suspicious that Gleda and her husband had been killed the day she'd arrived in their village for a visit.

The fewer people they encountered, the better.

They had traveled for more than thirty days, but progress had been slow, as they had to interpret the map while battling the elements. Twice they had taken the wrong turn and had been forced to backtrack, losing several days in the process. They had stayed only occasionally at an inn and had often found shelter in abandoned, decrepit huts that housed rats, spiders, and all kinds of insects. The weather was still cold and bitter, but, she guessed, it was because they were in the mountains. In the lower valleys there was evidence that spring was on its way. The first shoots of leaves were visible, a few flowers dared open their blossoms, and more often than had been the case at the beginning of her quest, the sun chased away the afternoon clouds.

The wolf was never far away, though there were periods when the beast had gone missing for several days before showing up again. Just when Bryanna had been certain the animal was gone for good, she would catch the glimmer of her gold eyes watching from the shadows, or spy a big paw print in the mud, or notice that Harry's eyes were wide and white-rimmed, for the packhorse hadn't gotten used to being in the company of his natural predator.

"Worry not about losing her," Gavyn had teased Bryanna one night when she'd asked him where the beast had gone. "She knows where the food is. When she's hungry enough, Bane will return."

She hadn't shared Gavyn's certainty. But the next morning, when she'd opened her eyes and stretched her cramped muscles, she'd spotted the great gray beast curled up in the dirt beneath the drooping branches of a rough-barked pine, her nose hidden beneath her tail. She'd lifted her head at Bryanna's movement, staring at her with those eyes that rarely blinked.

"Didn't I tell you?" Gavyn had needled her when he'd caught her staring at the creature. "There is no way to get rid of that lazy cur."

"As if you'd want to. You like having her around."

Gavyn's smile had widened as if admitting she'd spoken the truth. "So it's true. You *are* a witch, Bryanna," he'd teased, his quicksilver eyes sparkling in the morning light. "You can read my mind."

She'd feigned indignance, then laughed aloud and

wondered when he would kiss her again. Touch her. Make love to her. Though they'd had an unspoken understanding since the night at Kambria's grave, she couldn't help the wanting that surged deep inside each and every night.

And with each passing day his wounds healed. His bruises finally disappeared, and the whites of his eyes became clear and pristine as new-fallen snow. He no longer winced from too many hours in the saddle or too much time spent in any one position.

Along the journey Gavyn traded furs for food or money or arrow tips. In the early dawn hours, while he was away hunting the deer, squirrels, rabbits, and birds, Bryanna practiced her spells and chants or dug for roots and gathered needles, bark, and cones from the forest. Once she surprised him with two toads she'd killed, and another time she caught a fat trout in a shallow creek.

But she'd never divulged her secret, one that he would soon know. For, she was certain, she was pregnant.

Her time of the month should have arrived over a fortnight earlier, and in the last few days she'd been queasy. Although she'd tried to attribute her nausea to the rigors of the journey, a voice in the back of her head reminded her regularly of the night of lovemaking.

She knew how babies were conceived.

She'd lived on the castle grounds and had heard the gossip between the twittering laundresses or the bragging of the soldiers. And, of course, she'd seen the act for herself, be it the rams and ewes or stallions and mares, or even the dogs in the kennel. So she shouldn't be surprised. Never in her life would she have imagined she would be with child and unmarried, however, roaming the forested hills on a mysterious quest of unknown destination. Absently she rubbed her flat abdomen.

She thought of Gleda's talk of a baby born of Darkness and Light, a child in danger. Surely the child of the prophecy was not this little one in her womb? Nay, she would not think of it, of the lunacy of it all.

But the stone . . . Gleda's instructions had led her to find the stone and the baby in the casket—Lenore's child. Did that not give Gleda's words a ring of truth?

Bryanna refused to think on it. She would not consider that she could be the mother of the ruler mentioned in the prophecy.

They rode into a village, and while Gavyn bartered his hides for bread, grain, and cheese, she found an older peasant woman who was more than eager to offer a bowl of thick pottage, some hard bread and cheese, as well as a roof for the night and a little gossip. All for a sleek stoat pelt that the old woman kept rubbing with hands that showed knotted knuckles and dark spots as they ate.

The thick soup tasted of garlic and onions and pork fat with beans, and Bryanna swore it was the best she'd ever eaten. A widow, Rosie glowed under the compliment. The woman was as hungry for company as Bryanna had been for food. After the meal, while Gavyn tended to the horses and chopped firewood, Rosie sat by the fire with Bryanna, eager for woman talk.

It was nearly dark outside, the fire and one candle offering warmth and light in the small hut. Through the thin walls, Bryanna heard Gavyn working, his ax thunking as it bit into chunks of dry firewood. Another crack and the piece cleaved, two pieces spinning and hitting the outside wall.

"A strong one, he is," the old lady observed. "Like my husband, long ago." She sighed sadly. "So Brynn, where are ye and yer husband headin'?" She was staring at the flames while still stroking the pelt.

Husband.

The word echoed in Bryanna's brain.

Surprisingly not an uncomfortable thought.

And not one Bryanna hadn't considered.

"You must be goin' somewhere," Rosie prodded, her friendly smile showing a broken front tooth.

"East. We're really not sure," Bryanna finally replied. "Cain, he has family over the hills. A brother. I've never met him and . . . and it's been a long time since he traveled this road. I'm, um, not really certain where we're going. I leave that up to Cain." Oh, for the love of God, she sounded like an utter goose, the kind of woman she detested.

Rosie scowled, looking as if she'd just sucked on a tart crab apple. Using a walking stick, she poked at some charred bits of wood that had fallen near the edge of the fire. "Surely there is a name to this place." With a well-placed push, she sent a bit of blackened wood back into the fire pit.

"I'm really not sure—"

"'Tis a village not far from the river," Gavyn said as he walked through the door carrying an armload of wood and the woman's ax. "This needs sharpening," he said of the blade. "Duller than the village idiot, it is. I'll sharpen it if you have a whetstone."

"Let's see." She struggled to her feet. "My husband, God rest his soul, he took care of keepin' the tools sharp." She found a whetstone upon a shelf, then handed it to Gavyn before stirring the pot hanging over the fire pit. Bryanna's stomach growled as Gavyn began sharpening the ax. Rosie set a few more knives beside him, then settled onto her stool again. "What is the name of the village?"

"'Tis called Allynwood, and not too far from Connah's Quay."

"Never heard of it. Allynwood." She scratched at her cheek.

"A very small village," Gavyn assured her as he spat upon the stone and worked on the ax. "Smaller than this one."

She laughed at that, a quick cackling sound. "Hard to find one smaller than this one," she joked. He winked at her and she blushed, then offered them ale. As the night wore on, she spoke of her dead husband and the fact that she had no children.

"So if I were going to Allynwood, which way would I travel?" Gavyn asked when the woman began to yawn. "I mean east, of course."

"I know not where Allynwood is. You say it's near the quay? Hmmm." She was shaking her head, her brow furrowed. "My husband, he was a mason before the accident that crippled his arm. He traveled some. Spoke of towns he'd visited. But Allynwood? Nay, I don't remember it."

"I know it was near a larger town," Gavyn said. Watching his exchange with Rosie, Bryanna realized anew what a skilled liar he was. "But I don't recall the name. It had an abbey or cemetery or cathedral in it, I think."

"Oh, my, let's see." She looked up at the ceiling and sighed. "He talked of . . . Wrexham, but that's south and east, and Caer . . . oh, come now . . . Caerwys, it's not far from Holywell." She shook her head, graying strands of hair brushing her shoulders. "There's St. Asaph, south of Rhuddlan, of course, but it's not near Connah's." She rolled her lips over her teeth and cocked her head to one side. "Sorry, Cain. 'Tis all I remember."

"Worry not. We'll find our way," Gavyn assured the woman, though Bryanna didn't know how. Unless Isa, who had remained uselessly mute in the last month, decided to speak again, Bryanna wasn't certain where they should head or where their destination might be.

When at last it was time to sleep, the peasant woman found a pallet hardly large enough for the two of them and offered up a tattered blanket, while she took her own bed in the back of the single room.

Keeping up the falsehood of their marriage, Bryanna lay beside Gavyn and didn't protest when he flung his arm about her abdomen and pulled her close. Shutting her eyes, she attempted to ignore the warmth of his body, the strength of his arms, the way her back molded so perfectly to his chest and abdomen and legs. The front of his knees touched the backs of hers and the top of her head fit into the crook of his shoulder.

Oh, this was dangerous.

She sensed him in her nerves and her muscles. Though she tried to relax, she was highly disturbed by his warm breath ruffling her hair and sweeping over the back of her neck.

Images of making love with him again flashed through

her oh so willing mind. It was all she could do to keep from turning, wrapping her arms around him, and kissing him wildly. Passionately. With all the abandon that she'd felt on that one night they'd spent together in the castle at Tarth.

She wiggled a little, trying to put the slightest distance between their bodies, but he only held her tighter and chuckled. "You're not going anywhere, wife Brynn," he whispered against her ear.

"I'm not your—"

"Uh, uh, uh," he warned softly as one hand slipped upward from her waist to touch the underside of her breast. "Tonight, Brynn, I can touch you anywhere I please."

She felt a tingle deep within her at his words. "We are not alone."

"Matters not." He flattened his hand over her breast and she gasped. His fingers splayed and her nipple hardened. Though there were layers of fabric separating his skin from hers, she reacted and bit down on her lip to keep from moaning in pleasure. He found that little bud and through the bodice of her gown he played with it, toyed with it, making her squeeze her eyes shut so hard they ached.

"You're a miserable, insufferable cur," she whispered. "You're taking advantage of our circumstances and—oooh!"

His lips found the shell of her ear and his tongue rimmed that sensitive spot. All protests died on her lips. His breath fanned the place his tongue had moistened and she thought she would go wild with wanting.

Dear God, her blood was pounding through her veins, her skin hot and wanting. The desire deep within her was pulsing and hot, hungry, knowing that it would take but a few deep strokes of—

"Stop," she hissed, trying to control herself. This was ridiculous!

"You want me to?"

"Yes!" she said breathlessly. Her words were a lie; she and Gavyn both knew that.

One of his hands splayed across her abdomen, the tip of his

thumb tucked beneath her breast, his smallest finger reaching just above the juncture of her legs. Her world swam with sensation. As he shifted, she felt his hardness settle against her. 'Twould be so easy to turn over, let his hands push her skirt up over her thighs and hips, while she unlaced his breeches where so hard a bulge was now straining.

If they were quiet . . .

If he just slipped inside her slowly, in deep and out with painstaking deliberation . . .

She slammed the image from her mind, pushed the seductive thoughts far away, and kept her eyes closed. She did not turn over, did not wrap one leg around his, did not offer herself to him.

Not tonight.

This night, damn it, she would sleep on this tiny bed, pressed intimately against him. And not for a second would she acknowledge that her body ached to be loved.

Carrick was tired. He'd followed the woman he now knew was Bryanna to Tarth. The rumors there had been varied, and with each telling, he suspected, they'd been greatly embellished. According to gossip, sometimes she'd been with a man; other times riding alone. One woman had said she'd bought a tunic, but others had said she had several new dresses. Everyone had agreed that she'd come to visit the keep while Father Patrick was in charge, though now Lord Mabon had returned.

Father Patrick had been no help. He'd said that the woman, Bryanna of Calon, was trouble, and that he was glad she was gone. He even wondered aloud if she might be at least partly responsible for the deaths of poor Gleda and Liam, the beekeeper and her husband.

The woman Bryanna had been seen with, the beekeeper Gleda, had ended up dead in a creek soon after Bryanna's arrival. Gossip and rumors regarding the beekeeper and her deaf husband ran rampant through the muddy streets and dark inn. Everyone for miles around Tarth seemed to agree that Gleda and her husband might well be alive today had it not been for the red-haired woman on her white mare.

Bryanna.

Traveling alone.

Her trail cold as winter.

Rubbing his bad shoulder, he glanced up at the surrounding hills. Since he'd left Tarth he'd been riding for thirty days now, thirty sunrises in which he'd head off looking for the coldest trail of her.

Where would she go? Father Patrick, tight-lipped and sanctimonious, had provided no help. The serving girl in the inn and her mother proved more helpful, the old woman claiming that Bryanna was "near identical" to another red-haired woman who had lived in Tarth years before. The beautiful young mother who'd been known as a sorceress had been killed some sixteen years ago. A stoning, some said. Her blood on the hands of a man who had once been a priest himself, Baron Hallyd of Chwarel.

Carrick climbed upon his horse, glanced once more around the empty yard, and clucked to his horse. Sixteen years was a long while, and truly, Bryanna had little more in common with this dead sorceress than her curly red locks.

It was little more than hearsay, words from idle tongues.

So Bryanna looked like the woman.

It meant nothing.

But he had no other ideas. His search of the countryside had turned up no sign of her, and he'd promised Morwenna he'd find her sister.

He'd look under Hallyd's rock and see what he found.

Besides, Carrick decided, it might be interesting to find out what Hallyd, the rumored witch killer, had to say for himself.

She was awakened by the sounds of off-tune humming, the heavenly scent of baking bread, and the discomfort of a decidedly full bladder. Bryanna opened an eye and realized she was lying face-to-face with Gavyn, his nose touching hers, her arm flung carelessly over his shoulder, his gray eyes staring deeply into hers.

"God's teeth!" she cried, her skin suddenly flushed and warm.

She rolled off the pallet and scrambled to her feet, only to find Rosie dutifully stooped over a cauldron of beans and onions set over the fire.

"Mornin'," the old woman said, her dark wooden paddle moving the soup in the large pot. "I'm thinkin' you might want some breakfast before you leave."

Gavyn stretched, making an ungodly sound.

Bryanna felt her teeth clench, but Gavyn managed a grin for their hostess. "Aye, that would be good," he said. "It smells like a castle cook has been baking."

Rosie's cheeks reddened, either from leaning too close to the fire as she tasted her soup or from Gavyn's compliment. "Ye can freshen yourselves out back," she said.

Bryanna took a few moments to relieve herself and wash in the pails behind the hut. She returned to find Gavyn already eating, engrossed in conversation with the woman.

"I'll be hating to see you go," Rosie said. "It gets a little lonely up here, though recently we've seen a few more visitors than usual." She ladled the beans into a wooden bowl, then placed it upon the small table between her guests.

"Is that so?" Gavyn said, eating a slice of the grainy dark bread.

"Aye, just a few days ago three or four soldiers came through wearing the colors of Chwarel. Black and silver."

"Chwarel?" Bryanna paused, a morsel of bread lifted halfway to her mouth. "Lord Hallyd's keep?" It stole her breath away to say the name of the man, the so-called man of God, who had murdered her true mother all those years ago.

"Aye." Rosie nodded, stirring again to make certain the beans didn't stick and burn on the bottom of the old iron cauldron. "People say he doesn't go out, except at night. That he's been cursed for most of his life. Me, I've never seen him, but then, what is the chance of that? A peasant like me meetin' a baron of his ilk."

"Why were the soldiers in the town?" Gavyn asked, his silver eyes glimmering with danger like the blade of a sword.

"They were lookin' for two travelers, a man and a woman," Rosie said, sliding a glance toward Bryanna. "The woman, she was supposed to have wild red hair. Small of stature, she was. And the man, he was a warrior. He'd stolen himself a big black warhorse with one white stocking and a crooked, starlike blaze." She stirred her pot. "The woman's horse was white, with black mane and tail." Rosie looked up from her pot. "Too bad I hadn't seen the travelers, because there's supposed to be a price upon the man's head. Hallyd's men claim that this man is a bastard son of Deverill of Agendor. That he not only stole the lord's horse but killed the sheriff as well."

Bryanna felt goose bumps rise on her arms. How could Hallyd's men know this? Had the alarm spread that far across the countryside?

Gavyn's smile had faded, his expression hardened. The cords at the back of his neck, above his tunic, were pronounced as he remarked, "Is that so?"

"Aye. Too bad for me that I hadn't seen the two. A widow like me, I could use the money a reward would fetch. But, as I told the soldiers, I hadn't seen any travelers fittin' their description."

"What did you tell them?" Bryanna asked, working to keep her voice steady.

Rosie lifted a heavy shoulder. "Nothing. There wasn't anything much to tell, now, was there?"

"I guess not."

"But, if I were you two, I'd be careful. Some people, they'd do anything to get a little coin in their pocket. And you two, travelin' alone, the way ye look, the horses ye're ridin', you might attract notice." Rosie lowered her gaze and went back to stirring the cauldron. "Just watch yer back. Lord Hallyd has a reputation in these parts. A bloody history, if ye know what

I'm saying. When he wants something, he stops at nothing to get it."

"As is the case with many a lord," Gavyn said, pushing back his stool. "Thanks for the warning." As he gathered his things, he tossed two more pelts to Rosie. "For the hospitality and advice," he said.

Her old fingers held fast to the rabbit and squirrel as she tipped her head to Gavyn. "Thank you. I'll be sure to tell Lord Hallyd's men if they return that I saw nothing of that couple," she said, winking at Gavyn.

As they rode away, Bryanna felt herself sinking into a panic.

Already someone had recognized them.

A peasant woman, no less.

She'd known they would have to be on the lookout for spies and soldiers and mercenaries, anyone who knew that Gavyn was a wanted man, but she'd thought she could trust an aging widow who lived in such a small and isolated village.

Thankfully, Rosie had proven trustworthy. . . .

But what of the league of soldiers searching for them?

As soon as they were out of earshot of Rosie's small cottage, Gavyn shot her a warning look.

"Don't be crumbling to bits now, Brynn," Gavyn said, his horse trotting easily alongside her. "We've made it this far, and I'm not about to get caught by an old woman in want of a few gold coins."

"But did you hear what she said?" She struggled to control her voice, not wanting to reveal the panic that coiled inside her at the mention of his name. "Lord Hallyd's soldiers are looking for us. *Hallyd,* the man who murdered Kambria. What would he want with us?"

"Mayhap he's looking for the ransom everyone else on earth is vying for. Or hungry for excitement," Gavyn said. "What other pleasures are available to a man who remains confined in his own keep?"

Staring at the jagged landscape rising ahead, Bryanna

wondered if Gavyn was right. Could it be just a matter of one nobleman supporting another, lending out his men to join a search . . . or was something else driving Lord Hallyd?

He couldn't possibly know that Bryanna was the daughter of Kambria. She herself hadn't discovered the true facts of her birth until a few weeks ago. It wasn't possible that this nobleman who had seen fit to murder her mother could know that she was the sorceress's daughter.

Was it?

Soon after they rode away from Rosie's little house, they reached a narrow stretch of road where the horses had to climb single file. A high cliff rose on one side of the cart path; on the other the landscape dropped down to a deep ravine.

Bryanna's teeth were on edge, her heart in her throat as she watched Gavyn, astride Rhi, lead the packhorse. This narrow ridge, winding its way along the side of the mountain, was too familiar.

Just like the mountain chasm in her dreams.

Her heart thundered in her chest at the memory of the chase along the rocky spine of a snow-covered ridge, horses' hooves pounding.

Throughout the ride she remained tense, every muscle clenched as she rode along the pass. She couldn't free herself of the urgency she'd felt in her dream, the strong sense of evil lurking behind every outcropping of stone.

Astride Alabaster, she brought up the rear, her worried gaze upon Harry's uneven gait, her ears trained for the sound of approaching horsemen—Deverill's men or Hallyd's soldiers, who were now searching for them.

The riders in black racing behind her, bloodlust in their souls.

Beware the dark horseman. . . .

But they were alone.

Not even the wolf appeared on the treacherous cart way. The beast had been missing for nearly three days now. Although Bryanna assured herself the wolf would return, she couldn't help but think the lone animal had sensed their deepening danger and decided to go her own way.

Eventually, the narrow path opened to a wide meadow at the summit of the mountains.

Bryanna finally let out her breath. The air was crisp and clear, sunlight parting the clouds. A few flowers dared peer between blades of grass that were darkening to rich, verdant green with the spring.

Gavyn pulled his mount to a stop at the crest and Bryanna rode close to him. For as far as she could see, green tree-covered mountains surrounded them. Sunlight danced over the dewy grass and thin clouds scudded across the sky.

"We're lost," she said, taking in the terrain that bore no distinction, no landmarks that matched the map. "We're lost, and under siege. Hallyd's men are looking for us. Deverill's soldiers are probably searching for you. We're following a map that we're not even certain is leading us anywhere, and even if it is, we could have taken a wrong turn."

"You have no faith," he accused.

She glanced over at him and caught the devilment glinting in his silver eyes as he dismounted in one fell swoop and dropped the reins of both horses, allowing them to graze on the sweet grass.

"What?" She let the reins slide through her hands so that Alabaster could pick at blades of grass. "What is it you know?" she demanded, climbing off the mare. When he didn't immediately answer, she followed him to the highest point of the meadow. "Gavyn?"

"You have the map?"

"Of course."

"Open it."

"Oh, fie and feathers." She hiked back the few yards to Alabaster, unlaced one of her leather bags, and hauled it with her up the hill to the spot where he stood gazing over the mountainous terrain. "You think you know where we are."

"Mayhap."

"I'd prefer to hear, 'Of course I do, Bryanna. Worry not.'"

She handed the sewn leather pieces to him and waited, arms crossed over her chest, while he unrolled the doe hide with its odd-shaped etchings.

Eyeing the position of the sun, he moved to a patch of earth that afforded him a view across two mountaintops. "Look this way. East," he said, wrapping the arm with the map around her middle and pulling her in front of him. With his free arm he pointed over her shoulder. "See that mountain that appears to have a broken top? It's jagged and without trees."

She nodded.

"Here. Look at the map."

She took the doeskin and stood nestled against him as she studied the map she'd nearly memorized.

"On the eastern portion," he said, and touched the doeskin where the drawing was of three mounds. The two on either side were rounded, the one in the middle was jagged.

She trained her eyes on the mountains again, examining the vista. "You could be right."

"Could?" he said, pulling her close and kissing the top of her head. "What was it you wanted me to say?"

"That you knew where you were going. That I shouldn't worry." She turned to face him. So close. Only a hairsbreadth separating them, so near she could feel the heat of his body, see the barest outline of a bruise upon his cheek. "But you still don't know where we're going."

"Of course I do, Bryanna," he said with a wink as he threw her own words back at her. "Worry not."

She felt the icy panic of the mountain crossing slip away in the glow of his confidence. "Where?" she asked. "Where are we going?"

"To Holywell."

"And why are we going there?"

"Because, as Rosie told us, it's to the east, and if you look at the map, you'll see the dark spot with a cross upon it. We thought it might be a grave or a church, but I think we were wrong."

"You think it's a holy well?" she asked, as the wolf

climbed into her line of vision. She slunk just beyond the first layer of trees rimming the spot of grass.

"Not only that, wife Brynn," he said, nettling her. "I believe that somewhere in the town we'll find another piece of this bloody map and another stone, the damned emerald for the east."

CHAPTER TWENTY-ONE

"I don't want to hear one more excuse! Not one!" Hallyd's patience was as frayed as one of Vannora's blankets as he stood in the great hall with this ragged group of men who were part of his army, such as it was. Still sweating from his daily sparring ritual, he looked from one man to the next, most of whom avoided his eyes. Because they were ashamed, or because his discolored eyes set people on edge? Son of a cur, why did he have to trust his fate to imbeciles, idiots, and incompetents?

And Vannora. You put your faith in a woman who molds your mind into believing she possesses great power. Maybe she does, or maybe everything she does is only an illusion, a creation of your weak, willing mind.

Who's the idiot?

The imbecile?

The bloody damned fool?

He tossed his sword to a page with instructions to have it cleaned, then mopped his brow with the back of his hand. Bloody hell, the men were still staring at him like the morons they were.

One gloved fist clenched, and he would have liked nothing more than to slam it into Frydd's reddish face, yet he knew it would serve no purpose. The men were tired, having ridden for weeks in search of her. And truth to tell, he knew his rage burned not because of his inadequate patrols but because *she* was with another man. He burned for Bryanna. Each night he itched to find her again.

This was not the way he had foreseen his release. But then, Vannora had misled him.

While one servant replaced candles and another swept the floor rushes away from the fire, he glared at his pathetic lot of warriors. "You found nothing? No sign of them?" he asked, pacing in front of the fire. The men stood in a semicircle around him, shifting from one foot to the other, their swords clinking at their sides, their uniforms dirty, their faces unshorn and haggard.

"Our company headed east," Galton said. He was the tallest of the soldiers and the smartest, a man whose allegiance Hallyd doubted, but whose brains he did not. "We searched the mountains and hills. Though at times there was rumors of a man and woman who had been traveling through the countryside, she on a white jennet, he a black steed, the stories were few. A traveling musician in one town swore he'd seen their camp. A woman selling eggs in a village saw them stopping at the well. One innkeeper swore a couple had spent the night there." Galton shrugged at that point, and Hallyd wanted to reach down the man's throat and drag the words over his damned tongue.

The thought of Bryanna with the bastard Gavyn caused his blood to boil, and he nervously scratched the side of his face, irritating a spot that was already raw.

"Ain't ye gonna tell 'im about the grave?" Afal asked.

"What grave?" Hallyd's impatience manifested itself in a tic near his eye.

"The one we discovered east of here, long ago. We thought it might be where the witch was laid to rest," Galton said, his eyes dark as a bat's wing. "There were rumors that Kambria was buried in a pauper's grave, though no one knew the exact location."

"You found it?"

"We found a mound of freshly turned earth, two days after

the man and woman upon the distinctive horses had passed through a nearby town."

"How long ago was that?"

"Weeks."

"And I was not told?" he roared, and mopped his brow once more with the back of his glove. Christ, he could use a cloth.

Galton had the audacity to take a step forward. "You ordered us not to return until we had found them . . . m'lord."

Hallyd's teeth gnashed together. He wanted to cuff the insolent pup with the back of his hand, for there was defiance in Galton's stance, a challenge in the set of his jaw. They both understood that he was the smartest, strongest, and most daring of any of Hallyd's soldiers.

"You will take me there," he said. "Tonight. We'll travel at sunset."

"The men are tired."

"They can rest now. There are still a few hours of daylight." Hallyd eyed the soldiers, who dared not grumble but were clearly unhappy. Had they no vision? No desire? No damned understanding of how important this pursuit was? "Stay here and the cook will see that you are fed, your thirst well quenched." He snapped his fingers at a page, and the boy took off at a dead run to the kitchen.

Let them rest, simpleton soldiers. They had no idea of the scope of their task—the immense magnitude of the victory Chwarel would know once they recovered the dagger.

It would soon be in his hands. He could feel it.

The rise of power.

So this is Chwarel, Lord Deverill thought as he gazed up at the huge keep made of dark stone. Astride a great dappled steed that was far inferior to Rhi, the Lord of Agendor was followed by a small army, as well as Hallyd's greedy little spy.

On horses of differing sizes and color, they clustered together on a hillock that rose above the road leading to the massive castle. Deverill narrowed his eyes upon the wide wall walks and barbicans. From the highest watchtower the black and silver standard snapped in a stiff breeze as steely clouds, cut by shards of sunlight, slid across the sky like the underbelly of a great serpent. The entire keep seemed gloomy and dreary, a fortress devoid of color.

Deverill watched as men and women—peasants, peddlers, soldiers, and tradesmen—walked into and out of the main gate, a wide mouth yawning open that showed just a hint of the edges of the portcullis like brittle metal teeth.

'Twas an ugly castle.

"This is where your lord resides?" he asked the spy. "Day and night?"

"Aye."

"But he only leaves the great hall after the sun sets?"

Cael nodded. "Or if the day is dark with clouds."

Deverill had learned much about Lord Hallyd, the night marauder, from this runt of a man. A spy who couldn't keep his mouth shut and was forever searching for a way to get into Deverill's good graces.

'Twas a sign that Lord Hallyd's judgment was skewed. Even a blind man could see that Cael was untrustworthy, the kind of soul who would sell his services to the highest bidder.

"Nay, he stays inside if there is too much sunlight. As I told ye. 'Tis cursed he is."

"Gut rot." Deverill didn't believe in curses or spells or anything that could not be seen. Oh, he pretended to be a pious man, for it was expected. Being the baron, he had to at least appear to be a believer, but the truth of it was that he wasn't convinced there was a God. Not the pagan gods of his ancestors, nor the Christian God who demanded such a price in blood for His Crusades.

That Hallyd had gone from priest to baron only reinforced his opinion. If the man were a true believer, a disciple of God and Christ, why would he lay down his vestments and don the armor of a warrior? Why sacrifice piety for physical reward?

"So let us visit your lord," Deverill said, urging his horse forward. "You go on ahead and tell him I seek an audience with him."

"That I will." The spy kicked his mule of an animal and took off flying down the lush grass of the hillside, heading toward a creek's swollen current.

Deverill and his company followed at a slower pace, allowing time for Cael to bring word of their arrival to Hallyd and his men.

By the time they reached the main gate, they were allowed to pass. Pages collected the reins of the horses and the captain of the guard promised care for the animals, as well as food and drink for Deverill and his men.

Inside the gloomy keep, the soldiers were offered roast pig, salted eels, and tarts of mince along with cheese, wine, and jellied eggs. Deverill was brought to the main table, where Hallyd, a big man in a black tunic, stood and greeted him.

As pages poured wine and the men ate, Hallyd discussed little other than running the keep, the trouble with servants, a bad crop of hay, and the weather. Only when their trenchers had been pushed aside and they were sipping wine did he say, "Cael told you what we discovered, about your horse and son."

"You mean the murderer and thief," Deverill corrected him. "I do not think of Gavyn as a son." He made a broad you-understand-this motion with his hand. "He was the result of lifting one too many skirts. Though I do not doubt he is the product of my bedding his mother, I do not think of him as my son. A bastard he is and will always be."

"You only want him brought to justice." Hallyd drank from his cup and looked at Deverill with eyes that appeared oddly owlish, dark centers with the tiniest ring of color about the huge pupils.

Those eyes . . . like chambers in hell. Deverill had seen much in his life—anomalies and hideous injuries, a man run through with a lance, another beheaded during battle, a family lost to fire—but never had he looked at a man and sensed such a darkness as that which seeped from this man. It was as if Hallyd was devoid of a soul.

'Tis only his eyes, his mind insisted, but he knew Hallyd's evil ran far deeper. For the first time in a long, long while, Lord Deverill of Agendor felt more than a drip of fear.

"My interest is not in your son . . . er, the murderer," Hallyd said, leaning back in his chair. "He can live or die or be banished and I care not."

"But the woman?"

"Ahh, yes, just as you and the man have a conflict to re-solve—"

Deverill snorted. Conflict? 'Twas not a conflict. Gavyn had been a burr in his side from the moment Ravynne had borne him. Deverill enjoyed a conflict, looked forward to a battle. Gavyn, the killer and horse thief, was far, far worse than a simple conflict.

"—I have a score to settle with the woman. You know I am a man of great faith and spent many years in the service of God and His Holy Son. So it pains me that the woman is ru-mored to be a sorceress, and she has something of mine of great value. Just as the murderer has your horse, this woman has a dagger that belongs to me. My men and I were prepar-ing to ride this evening, to a place where the thief and woman were spotted. Mayhap we can strike a deal to run them to the ground. If we ally together, combine our armies, split them into small companies that can canvass a greater area and flush them out"—he appeared to warm to his topic—"then, when we finally find them, we'll divide the spoils." His smile was pure evil. "You take the bastard to face justice, and I'll deal with the witch. Together, we will divide and conquer," he sug-gested in a tone that made Deverill's blood run cold.

The Lord of Agendor hesitated.

Intuitively he knew that any connection to a soulless being like Hallyd was a mistake. And yet, the man was right, they could help each other. He offered his hand, and Hallyd shook it firmly while motioning to a page with the other.

"More wine," Hallyd insisted. "We have much to celebrate with our new alliance."

The page, a pockmarked boy with floppy brown hair, scurried from the great hall.

Releasing Deverill's hand, Hallyd fixed those eerie eyes upon him and said solemnly, "Now, I'm going to tell you a tale about a witch, a dagger, and a curse. And then, my friend, we'll ride."

Holywell was bustling, the town crowded and flush with peddlers and farmers' carts. Children ran through the streets chasing dogs. Geese honked, goats bleated, and cart wheels creaked.

The trek to this village had taken longer than Gavyn had anticipated, the travel slow and treacherous. It had been nearly a fortnight since they had stood on the mountain and decided to travel here, that day when he'd deciphered the symbols on Bryanna's doeskin map. Though the distance itself had not been great, the terrain had been nearly impassable, the weather ranging from snow to sleet to sunshine promising spring.

Slowing their journey even more, Bryanna had wearied often and developed a ravenous appetite. Fortunately the forests had been rife with game. Now, as the horses made their way through the gates of Holywell into the town, the packhorse was carrying the skins of many animals that had given up their lives to Gavyn's arrows. He had collected a nice bundle of fox, weasel, badger, rabbit, and mink skins, the lot of which he would barter for food, shelter, and wine.

"Come," he said to Bryanna. He hitched his chin toward an inn with horn windows and thick shutters. "Let's find you a room."

He thought she might protest, but instead she offered the tiniest of smiles, the first he'd seen in nearly a day. Once inside a small establishment that smelled of wood smoke and roasted meat, he paid the innkeeper, a dry, spindly man, for the room, then carried their pitiful few pouches up the stairs.

His "wife" followed slowly behind him. As they had since the onset of their journey, they claimed they were a married couple, Cain and Brynn, and though he'd never considered himself the kind to settle down with one woman, a part of him wanted to be with Bryanna always.

A stupid thought, he told himself as he left her alone to rest while he saw that the horses were stabled, fed, watered, and groomed.

From there he found a tailor, whose face softened when Gavyn began pulling soft animal pelts from his satchel. After some discussion, Gavyn ended up with coins in his pocket and a new tunic of deep forest green for himself. He also purchased a warm woolen mantle trimmed in rabbit for Bryanna, along with another tunic that cost him more than he could afford to spare. Nonetheless, he was pleased with his purchases, especially the mantle, as the cowl could be drawn about her face and the fur would be soft against her skin.

He returned to the inn with his prizes, then, before climbing the stairs, ordered them bread and cheese, a platter of sliced, roasted boar, and a jug of wine. He'd started for the steps once again before another thought struck him. Turning back to the innkeeper, he requested that a bath be brought to their room.

But it was too late.

When he opened the door of the room, he found Bryanna already asleep, her small body curled under the blankets of the bed. She looked so peaceful, he hated to disturb her. He tiptoed around the room with his purchases, unable to resist stealing glances at her resting form. Red curls tumbled over the pillow, and her skin glowed pale as a summer moon in the shadowed room.

"By the gods, what are you staring at?" She opened one eye and he laughed aloud.

"Were you trying to trick me by feigning sleep?" he asked.

"I was just dozing, resting my eyes. I thought you would be gone a while. . . ." She sat up and yawned, stretching one arm over her head before she spied the bundle in his arms. "What have you done?"

"I've been bartering. I bought myself a new tunic." He held up his purchase.

"At last!" She grinned. "Now we can finally wash the one you're wearing. 'Tis smelly."

He rolled his eyes. "And one for you." He held up the long gown and she gasped, a hand covering her mouth. "It's beautiful, but how did you—"

"It seems a mink skin or two is worth much." Holding up the mantle, he said, "This will keep you warm. Yours has been worn thin."

Her eyes rounded and she threw back the covers before she realized she was wearing only her chemise. "Oh." She blushed to the roots of her hair and hurriedly reached for her old mantle, tossed carelessly on the foot of the bed.

"Don't," he said, approaching her and slowly wrapping the new cloak over her shoulders. The soft folds fell nearly to the floor and he drew the laces tight enough that the fur tickled her chin.

"Thank you, but, really, you should not have spent your money on this." Tears touched the corners of her eyes.

"I wanted to."

"Gavyn—"

"Cain," he reminded her. As she gazed up at him, he couldn't resist. For the first time in what seemed like a lifetime, he kissed her, drawing her near, feeling her supple, yielding lips. The breath of a sigh escaped her as her knees gave way and he caught her in his arms.

Closing his eyes, his arms wrapped around her small body, he felt lost in her. His mind swirled with erotic images of making love to her, of lying on this bed and feeling her writhing beneath him. He imagined her fingers sliding down his chest and reaching lower to his abdomen. . . .

A rap sounded at the door.

"Someone is here?" she asked, pulling away.

"The innkeeper," he said, his head still reeling despite his empty arms. She reached for her tunic, but he shook his head. "You're fine."

He opened the door to the two boys lugging a wooden tub. Gavyn stepped back as they carried it in, then hurried back downstairs for buckets of warm water. As the boys filled the tub, a young girl who resembled the stern innkeeper lined it with towels and placed a cake of lavender soap nearby. As the boys lugged in the final buckets of steaming water, the innkeeper's daughter delivered their wine and a tray of smoked meat and cheese, along with eggs, apple tarts, and dark bread.

Bryanna, who had sat poised on the bed, her hands folded in her lap as the servants hustled about, thanked them as they finished up and filed out the door. "This is quite splendid, Cain," she teased, taking in the food and steaming tub. "Who knew one could be treated as royalty in the town of Holywell?"

Gavyn couldn't help but return her smile as he poured her a cup of wine. "Bathe first. The food will wait."

"And what will you do?"

He eyed the size of the wooden vat. "Watch, of course."

"Gav— Cain!"

"Well, 'tis too small for both of us. You go first."

"In front of you? Are you daft?"

"I'll turn my back."

"If you think that you can give me a nice new mantle and then I'll let you . . ." Her voice trailed off.

"I think we've come too far to worry about impropriety, don't you?" He poured himself a cup of wine and sat on a stool near the fire. "Hurry, now. 'Tis not getting any warmer."

"Fie and fiddlesticks," she grumbled, walking to the tub, then waiting until he dutifully turned away from her.

He could hear the rustle of her new mantle falling to the floor, then the sounds of water splashing. There was no reflective metal or piece of glass in the room, so once he was certain she was inside the tub and had a few minutes to clean off some of the grime from the journey, he turned again so that he was facing her.

"Gavyn!" she nearly shrieked, and he grinned wickedly as he watched her cover her breasts with her hands. "Leave!"

He took a sip from his cup. "Never. And it's—"

"Cain. Yes, I know." With one slick, dripping arm, she pointed to the door. "Leave, now. If you were a gentleman—"

"You would hate it. You wouldn't be here with me. Trust me, Brynn, 'tis not just fate that put us together. You like being with me. You'd be bored to death with a gentleman."

"You arrogant son of a cur! I've never heard anything so inane in my life. I do not *like* being with you. At the very least I wouldn't feel the heated compulsion to wring a gentleman's neck every step of this quest."

"Nor would he help you dig up graves in the middle of the night, or hide the fact that you stole a horse and who knows what else from a woman who was murdered. Nay, I think you prefer to be with a ruffian like me. You enjoy my lack of propriety."

He leaned back on his stool, took another sip, and enjoyed the view. Her wet, curling hair ruffled around her flushed face. Her greenish eyes narrowed at him in fury. And her body, white skin visible beneath the shimmering surface.

"For the sake of decency . . . ," she tried again.

But he felt his grin grow wider at the anger in her eyes, the way she tried to hide her nipples, pinkish disks that slipped through her fingers.

Suddenly she snatched up the slippery cake of soap and threw it at him. He ducked as it screamed past. The soap hit the fireplace, fell with a clunk, then skidded across the floor. "Turn around, damn it!"

"Now, wife, is that any way to talk to your husband?"

"You are not—"

He hadn't intended to do anything but watch her, but the soap gave him inspiration. "I think you'll need this," he said, picking up the wet cake. Rather than tossing it to her, he placed his leather cup on the mantel and crossed the few feet that separated them.

"Oh, for the love of Rhiannon!" She tried to cover herself with one arm while stretching out the other and opening her palm, as if she expected him to just drop the slick bar into her hand and leave her be.

But he had other ideas.

To her horror—or was there a bit of interest in those angry eyes?—he rolled up his sleeves.

"What are you doing?" she whispered, as if anyone else was in the room. "Gavyn, don't you dare—"

But he was already on his knees, dipping one arm into the warm water, the soap in his hand.

"You wouldn't!"

He rubbed the bar along her back, his eyes devouring the silken curve of her shoulders, his hands smoothing down to the curve of her waist.

"Oh, no!"

"No?" he mocked her, amazed at the soft texture of her pale skin.

"You're—you're evil!"

He laughed, leaning forward to take in her face and the glimmering sheen of her breasts. "As I said, 'tis what you love about me."

"What?" Her mouth dropped open. "I don't love you."

"Sure you do." He ran a finger along her shoulder.

"No."

"And I love you, Bryanna." He winked, as if he were teasing, though it came from his heart. "I always have."

"No . . . but . . ."

"Shhhh."

"Gav . . . Cain," she said in protest, but as she gazed into his eyes and saw that he was serious, he saw her swallow hard.

"I . . . I don't think . . ."

"'Tis good. Don't think."

With a sigh, she closed her eyes. "Oh, damn you. . . ." It was a whisper as much as a curse.

At that she relaxed beneath his fingertips, and he began to wash her body carefully.

Just as she was immersed in the water, he felt himself becoming immersed in Bryanna. Seeing her womanly legs folded beneath the water's soapy surface . . . smelling the scent of lavender in her newly washed hair . . . spying the red thicket at the juncture of her legs.

His cock came to hard and immediate attention.

"Oooh . . ." Her head lolled back as he washed her, his hands running over her back and arms before he laved her breasts. He watched in fascination as her nipples hardened and her entire body flushed. When he slipped one hand lower, across her abdomen, and over that fiery mound, her legs parted. He kissed her as he washed her, his soapy hands skimming her skin, his fingers exploring the wonder of her.

Her eyes opened just a bit. "Do you really love me?" she asked.

Rather than answer, he leaned down to encircle her body with both arms and carried her to the bed, where he showed her just how much. She didn't protest as he stripped off his clothes. Her own fingers seemed anxious and eager as they explored his chest and shoulders, then pulled him down upon her. She kissed him with a fever that infected him as he kissed her back.

She tasted of soap and water and all things feminine. His tongue and teeth scraped along the side of her neck, down her breasts. While he paused to suckle, his hand found that intimate little slit between her legs, and once again, he loved her. Never did he lift his mouth from her breast, not even when she bucked in anticipation, not when she yelled, arching, then shuddered. Still he kissed her pink nipple, tasting, teasing, toying until she was whimpering for more, her woman juices hot.

And then he knew she was ready. He came to her, rising above her. Their eyes were locked upon each other as he skimmed her legs wide with his knees. The tip of his cock rested against her and he thought he would go mad as he brushed it across her, watching her pupils dilate, hearing her gasp with anticipation.

"Husband," she whispered, and he leaned down to kiss her as he plunged. Deep inside her. Feeling her body sheath him. Slick. Hot. Eager. She began to moan, to feel the swelling wave, and he was with her. Holding back, fighting the mounting pressure, extracting every bit of pleasure from her, not letting go until . . . she cried out, her body convulsing. With a cry he spilled himself in her and collapsed upon her, his own body covered in sweat.

Lost in afterglow, he wondered vaguely how he would ever be able to let her go.

CHAPTER TWENTY-TWO

"So you dance with the devil," Vannora accused, her present guise vibrant and full of life. Her dark hair gleamed around a face that was no longer lined. Her lips were full, her body nearly seductive in its purple tunic that appeared as soft as velvet. Yet, there was still an opaqueness to her eyes. He thought it strange how they resembled his own cursed eyes.

She stood within the circle on the floor of her cell-like chamber. The cauldron was bubbling again, though oddly there was no fire. Thick steam rose to the cavernous ceilings, where, he was certain, bats roosted in the darkness. "The Lord of Agendor is not to be trusted," she said.

"Nor am I."

She nodded. "But you are planning to leave the keep, in daylight."

"My eyes are . . . The light of day does not burn them as much as it once did," he admitted, a phenomenon he'd discovered in the past few weeks.

"So she has found one of the gems, an opal." Vannora nodded, as if confirming something she already knew. "You must not do anything to stop her, Hallyd. For the curse to be lifted all of the stones must be located and inserted into the dagger." Vannora rubbed her neck and her eyebrows drew together, as if she were actually perplexed.

Never before had he seen her so worried. It gave him pause, needling at him. Had he been wrong to band with

Deverill? By all means, he did not want to risk losing the modicum of daylight sight that had been restored to him. He did not want the searing pain to return. . . .

"Listen to me. Do not let that dog Deverill interrupt the search for the stones, for if you find Bryanna and stop her from her quest, then all is for naught." She looked him squarely in the eye, her opaque orbs mystifying.

"Deverill wants his bastard son, that is all," he said, trying to dismiss her concern.

"But you must intervene to be certain that Deverill's crusade does not spoil yours!" she growled, her voice raspy as a snake. "Nothing must get in the way of the sorceress finding all of the stones. As for Deverill, use him to locate her, to follow her. Let him have his damned bastard son, but, if you want this curse lifted, do not interrupt her quest."

Bryanna woke to sunshine streaming through the open slats of the window. Stretching on the bed, she recalled the splendid night with Gavyn . . . making love to him, eating and sipping wine while he bathed in the tepid water, then returning to the bed for more lovemaking and finally sleep.

She'd barely stirred earlier when he'd leaned over and kissed her forehead. Now the room was empty and cold, the bare platters and tub of cool water the only reminder of all that had transpired.

She dressed in her new tunic, smiling as she touched the embroidery. A rich, vibrant brown trimmed in gold, it felt good upon her body. Clearly she remembered that he'd told her he loved her and then had gone about proving it in the bed. Oh, what a wanton woman she'd been! Even now, she trembled inside at the thought of his body joining with hers.

"Think not on it," she told herself as she quickly braided her hair. Intent upon finding him, she hurried downstairs, where the innkeeper's wife, a rotund woman with breasts that rested upon her protruding stomach, glanced up at her.

"Ye're the missus, are ye not? 'Tis Theone I am."

"Brynn," Bryanna said.

"Ever been to Holywell before?" the woman asked, and when Bryanna shook her head, she added, "Then ye may not know the legend."

Before Bryanna could stop her, Theone happily launched into the tale of St. Winefride, who was slain here, her head severed by a prince who could not persuade the unwilling virgin into his bed.

" 'Twas horrible." Theone's eyes grew round with horror, as if she'd witnessed the event rumored to have happened centuries before. "He pleads his case, he does, Prince Cradoc. And when she denies him and tries to leave, he lops off her head." Theone made a brandishing motion with her broom.

Bryanna pressed a hand to her roiling belly, but Theone didn't seem to notice, so enraptured was she with her own story.

"Well, the head, it rolls along and eventually stops in a bit of a hollow and, lo and behold, a spring, that very spring that still spouts today, erupted from the ground right there. Winefride's uncle, now that would be St. Beuno, he saw the whole damned thing. Quick as a fox, he grabbed up Winefride's head, crammed it onto her body, draped it in his cloak, and prayed to the Father that Winefride be allowed to live, that she be as one again, that her head and body be whole." Theone leaned upon her broom as she added, "And that was when the miracle occurred. Winefride, she got to her bloody feet. Alive, she was. Oh, aye, but from that day forward she had a thin white scar around her neck." Theone ran one large finger along the base of her own thick neck, and Bryanna cringed at the awful tale, which she assumed the woman had embellished.

"This is true?"

"Oh, aye! Every word of it."

Bryanna swallowed hard and touched her own throat, where only recently a ring of bruises had appeared.

Coincidence?

Or prophecy?

"People come from miles around to bathe in the waters

from the spring, they do. Rich and poor, noblemen and peasants—it matters not who they are, because they are all healed, their crutches and canes left at the well as a testament to the miracle."

"And what happened to the prince? The one who tried to kill Winefride?"

"Cradoc?" Theone snorted in disgust. "I heard he was struck by lightning. Others believe he was swallowed by a great hole in the earth. Either way, he was kilt dead! And he deserved it, too." She took up her broom again and chased a spider across the stoop. "Git," she muttered as Bryanna left, heading through the village.

She strolled down the hill past people on foot and horseback until she came to the well at the center of town. As Theone had said, a spring bubbled clear from the ground, a few shafts of sunlight reflecting in the shiny ripples.

Bryanna searched the streets for Gavyn. Although she did not find him, she did observe a man dressed in black hanging around the edge of the buildings, staying in the shadows.

'Tis just your imagination running wild, she told herself as her heartbeat increased. *You're just nervous because you can't find Gavyn.*

And yet, the man in black reappeared as she strolled past the tailor's shop, then again outside the tanner's hut.

In fact, the somber-robed man never disappeared.

Who was he?

She circled the spring, searching for Gavyn, telling herself not to panic. Mayhap she should have stayed at the inn. Even now he could be returning.

She glanced around the small buildings again, then wondered where a witch would hide a gem.

Deep in the well?

Of course not.

Buried nearby in the hill leading to the village?

Trying to calm her uneasy pulse, she paused and surveyed the area. People, crippled and whole, prayed at the spring's edge, touching the clear, healing liquid in an attempt to restore

their bodies as well as their souls. In a town always stirring
with villagers and travelers seeking a cure, there would be no
proper place to hide a gem.

"'Tis impossible," she said, and a man in a monk's robe
standing nearby turned to her.

"Nothing is impossible," he said. "Is not the miracle of St.
Winefride of Holywell proof enough of that?"

She managed a small smile for the religious man, then
quickly turned away before he could launch into a speech
about faith and piety and trusting in God. Not today, not when
she had a bloody emerald to find. Not when she was being
watched by a strange man in black.

She glanced around, searching for him, but the dark figure
was now nowhere to be seen.

Had he existed?

Or was he a product of her frightened mind? Her own fears
crystalizing?

She could not think of it now, not when she was so close
to fulfilling another part of her quest. Shading her eyes, she
looked up the hill to the village, where carts, horses, and people on foot traveled the old road. One woman sold eggs near
the side of the cart tracks, another peddled rounds of cheese,
and a tinsmith loudly clanged the bells he hoped to sell.
Horses neighed and geese clucked. A boy rolling a wheel with
a stick flew by, a younger girl with golden hair chasing after
him. Both children giggled madly as they raced down the hillside.

Bryanna pressed her lips together, thinking of the child Isa
kept mentioning. Could it be any child she saw, skipping
down a lane?

"He is the Chosen One," Isa's voice flowed, cool and familiar as the spring that bubbled through Penbrooke.

"Isa?" she whispered, weak with gratitude that the voice
had come to her again.

*"Sired by Darkness, born of Light, protected by the Sacred
Dagger,"* Isa's voice echoed through her head, right in the

center of the crowded village. *"A ruler of all men, all beasts, all beings. It is he who shall be born on the Eve of Samhain."*

Bryanna folded her arms across her chest defensively at the realization that her child was due to enter the world around Samhain. But no . . . 'twas impossible. And wasn't it like Isa to rattle off an ancient prophecy when she had more pressing matters at hand . . . like how to find the emerald?

"Aye, so I'm to protect the Chosen One with the dagger." Hard to believe, but even if it were so, how was she to find him? "I can't even find the second stone," Bryanna rasped loud enough to attract the attention of a passing woman.

With a carry cot slung over one shoulder to hold her swaddled infant, she was clinging to the pudgy fingers of her toddler with her free hand. The young mother looked up sharply, and then quickly shepherded her children to the other side of the lane.

Bryanna didn't blame her.

Certainly she sounded and looked like a madwoman chattering to herself. Reflexively, she touched her own flat abdomen. A child grew within her and she understood the cause of the mother's anxiety. Bryanna's babe had not yet come into the world, and yet she would do anything she could to protect it.

Clouds collected overhead as Isa's voice rang clear. *"That is why you were chosen for this journey. To save the child. Do not be cross! Do not run in circles! Forestall all evil. Find the gem and leave. Danger abounds."*

"Danger?" Bryanna repeated, softly this time, so that she would not startle the passing villagers. "Danger abounds? Isa, what are you saying?" Bryanna hated these cryptic messages that only she could hear. "Isa!" She was edging out of the crowded street so as to attract little attention, when she noticed Gavyn running from the village toward her, concern evident in his gray eyes.

Her heart leapt at the sight of him, his hair catching in the breeze, his new tunic stretched over his broad shoulders. She'd been right when she'd first tended to his wounds, months earlier. His bruises and cuts had hidden his strong jaw, sharp features, and deep-set silver eyes.

"Thank God you're safe," he said, grabbing her as if he expected her to vanish into the air. He hugged her tightly and she drank in the musky male scent of him. Immediately her mind was filled with flashes of their lovemaking, no longer savage or brutal, but not gentle either. Fierce and urgent, it was, and she knew deep in her soul she would never get enough of this man or his sensual touch.

Holding her against him, he whispered into her hair, "I went back to the room and couldn't find you and I thought . . . I thought that you might have . . . Oh, hell, it matters not."

"Might have what?" she asked, tears of relief burning behind her eyes.

"Been taken or harmed or . . . Bloody Christ, it doesn't matter."

She thought of the dark figure she'd seen loitering nearby, then dismissed it. 'Twas nothing. Twaddle. Managing a sly grin, she asked, "You were worried?"

"About you?" he asked, his arm slung around her shoulders as they walked toward the inn. "Always." Glancing over his shoulder, he said, "You have always had a way of getting yourself—and me—into trouble," he reminded her. "Even as a girl. But I thought you would sleep long and be safe until I returned."

"I am safe."

"Humph."

"Why did you not wake me?"

"Because I thought that in slumber you wouldn't be able to find trouble. And"—he touched the tip of her nose with a finger—"you are damned adorable when you sleep."

"Unlike you," she teased, and his eyes flashed as they skirted a puddle drying on the street.

"Best avoid the mud," he said. "The bathwater in our room has gone stone-cold."

"We could wash in St. Winefride's well."

"And have the parish priest draw and quarter us? Nay, I think not." But he did manage a smile at the thought of it.

She linked her arm through his. "So tell me, husband Cain, what did you find?"

"Nothing. As I said, rather than wake you I decided to canvass Holywell and try to locate the gem. But no one I talked to remembered a sorceress from sixteen years earlier. Nay, most looked at me as if I was without any brain at all. Others were scared, many making the sign of the cross before scuttling away to hide like insects beneath rocks."

Clouds began to block the sun as they reached the gates of the village and joined the procession of people on foot or horseback. Gavyn narrowed his eyes on the buildings and streets, squinting as he looked up at rooftops, frowning as he stared at gutters, peering hard into the open doors of shops.

"The bloody stone could be hidden anywhere." Vexed, he shoved his hair from his eyes and scowled.

"I know. I looked for the emerald, too, if only briefly."

They reached the inn, much to Bryanna's relief. These days she'd found the child within slowing her down, consuming much of her strength.

"It might take us months to find it," Gavyn said as he held the door open for Bryanna. "Or worse, we might never find it."

"Aye, I felt the same hopelessness, wondering where to start. 'Twas overwhelming," she said in a whisper as they climbed the stairs to the upper hallway. Her mind flashed back to Isa's recent words, though they were no help at all. What had she said? Not to be angry or run in circles. To get the gem and leave.

If only it were that simple, Bryanna thought.

He touched her shoulder, his fingers warm through her new clothes. "We can't very well tear the town and the well apart, stone by stone."

She stepped into their room, where all evidence of the bath and food had been removed. The freshly made bed was ample reminder of how they'd spent the previous night.

He glanced at the mattress, then back at Bryanna.

"Don't even suggest it," she warned, though she was more than a little tempted to lie with him again. "We have too much to do."

"And no way to do it." He sat on the foot of the bed, as if he hoped she would join him. Instead, she went to the window and looked out into the street. Was it her imagination or was there a man in dark clothes lingering in the shadowed doorway of the shop across the way? Her skin prickled in fear.

"What?" Gavyn asked. When she wasn't quick with a response, he repeated himself. "What, Bryanna?"

Grudgingly, she said, "I—I don't know. I wasn't certain. I mean, I dismissed it, but earlier there was a man on the street. He seemed to be following me," she said, remembering Gleda's dire warning. Poor Gleda, who had died within hours of meeting Bryanna. "Mayhap I'm just imagining things, but both Gleda and Isa, they have warned me of some 'dark warrior' who wants to harm me."

Gavyn crossed to the window and placed a large hand upon her shoulder. "And you think you see him?"

"I don't know. Look there, under the eave of that shop." With one finger, she indicated the wattle and daub building across the narrow street. "You see?"

He frowned. "Aye, there's a man there, but he's not hunting you down. It looks to me that he's a drunk who is relieving himself against the bole of a tree."

She squinted, saw that Gavyn was right, and turned away. "I am going out of my mind. Just today, while at the well, I heard Isa's voice again. Right in the middle of the street! Never before has she talked to me when I was in the midst of people. I was so surprised I called out to her and caught the ire and curiosity of everyone near the healing springs."

"And what did she say?"

"Oh, bah! She always talks in riddles. Let's see . . . oh, that danger abounds."

One side of his mouth lifted in amusement. "*That* we already know. See there." He hitched his chin toward the window. "The dangerous and deadly tree pisser is nearby."

Bryanna elbowed him and said, "You asked."

"Yes, yes, go on."

"She reminded me of my quest about the child I am supposed to save. She mentioned the old prophecy about the Chosen One. You've heard it before, I'm sure."

Gavyn nodded. "Sired in Darkness, born of Light . . ."

"Aye. The Chosen One, the next ruler of Wales. As if that's the child I'm supposed to use the Sacred Dagger to protect."

He scratched at his forehead and pushed a crop of dark hair away from his eyes. "What else did Isa say?"

"She told me not to keep running in circles and not to be angry. . . ." Bryanna let the words fade. "No, she said not to be cross—that was it. An odd choice of words. Why would I be . . . Oh, dear God, let me see the map."

She opened her leather pouch and withdrew the rolled deer hide, spreading it open upon the bed and tracing her fingers over the etching. "Look, over here, just a small distance from the well where the spring is? See the long stick with a circle on it and a cross within that circle? Like a wheel. . . . Could this be what she meant? Don't get *cross* with me. Don't run in *circles*?"

Excitement sizzled through Bryanna's nerves. She was right—she knew it! She could feel it in her bones. Quickly, she began packing her few things, stuffing them into her small leather pouches, forcing them inside. "Why would Kambria, a supposed witch, come to a religious place like this? She was running from a priest, and yet she chose to hide the gem here, where a Christian saint's miracle took place. That doesn't make sense, does it?"

"No. But then neither does hiding a map and opal in your own body to be buried with you." He rubbed the back of his neck. "And perhaps it was her attempt at supreme deception, hiding the very thing her enemies wanted right under their noses."

"No, no. I think not! Just listen." After another quick read of the map to assure herself of her own convictions, she rolled up the deer hide and stuck it into her pouch. "Didn't we pass something on our way here? A few miles north or west, wasn't it? We were a little lost at the time, I think. We rode past some kind of tall stone shrine?"

He touched his chin, trying to recall.

"Remember? 'Twas ancient and topped by a cross in a wheel . . . or mayhap a circle." She stared long and hard at Gavyn. "That's what Isa meant. When she said, 'Do not be cross' and 'Do not run in circles.'"

He looked at her skeptically, clearly unconvinced. "We passed by the Maen Achwyfan wheel cross," he said. "The stone of lamentations. No one is sure if that shrine was built to honor the Christian God or pagan rites."

"Perfect! Don't you think it is what she meant?"

He hesitated. "If truth be told, I'm not even certain her voice exists, Bryanna."

She froze, staring at him. What would it take to shake some sense into that mule head of his? "Then mayhap you would like to make a wager?"

"You want to bet on it?" He blinked, as if he couldn't believe what she'd just said.

"Aye, because I'm certain I'll win."

Gavyn's lips twitched. "All right, woman. What would I win if there's nothing there?"

"What?" She met his teasing gaze with her own, saw the dare in his eyes and was reminded of the time when they were so much younger. At Penbrooke, when he was the stable boy, he had often challenged her—to jump across a creek, to catch a frog in her bare hands, to ride a horse without a saddle, to steal a tart from the cook. Of course, she had never backed down. And he knew it.

He, too, was remembering. She saw it in the glint in his eyes, the smile he couldn't quite hide.

Bryanna arched a seductive eyebrow and whispered in a low voice, "What is it you would win?" she repeated with a slow wink. "Mayhap anything you want, husband."

"You mean it?"

"Mmm. That I do. But if you lose, then 'twill be me who can ask any favor from you."

" 'Tis a bet."

"Good. Then come with me and we shall see, shan't we?" She was already starting for the door, her new mantle billowing behind her. From the corner of her eye, she saw him grab his own leather pouches before following her down the stairs, his boots ringing loudly.

Outside the weather had changed. Gray clouds were rapidly chasing across an ever-darkening sky. Bryanna pulled her mantle a little tighter about her as she hurried to the stables. The horses had been groomed, fed, and watered. Alabaster nickered at the sight of her, and she rubbed the mare's nose fondly. She even took the time to scratch Harry behind his ears as Gavyn found the animals' saddles, bridles, and packs. Harry, devoid of a thick bundle of furs, was still loaded with tools and supplies.

Within minutes they were on the road again, the first fat drops of rain spitting from the sky and splattering against the ground.

They made their way down the steep hillside, then, once they were on flatter ground, picked up speed. Bryanna urged Alabaster into a gentle lope, keeping up with Rhi and Harry, who, despite his awkward gait, was able to gallop easily.

As they rode, the rain increased, sporadic drops turning into a heavy downpour. The sky turned dark as night, and far in the distance lightning flashed and thunder rolled. The road, already worn and furrowed from dozens of cart and wagon wheels, became a slick thick ribbon of mud.

Despite her new mantle and tunic, rainwater slid down Bryanna's neck, chilling her skin. Her teeth chattered, but she didn't doubt herself.

Surely this, the ancient monolithic cross, was the place where the stone was buried.

It had to be.

They pressed on through the curtain of rain along a road

that seemed abandoned. No sane person would brave this miserable weather.

At last they saw the stone monument, standing alone—a monolith with a wheel cross at its apex. Bryanna sent up a silent prayer to Morrigu that this, indeed, was where Kambria had buried the second stone.

Blinking against the rain, Bryanna dismounted. Gavyn slid to the ground, approached Harry, and untied the shovel. The horses' ears were flattened, their nostrils wide as they lifted their noses to the raging storm.

"It'll be all right," Bryanna said, patting Alabaster's withers.

"So where do you think we should start digging?" he asked, his gaze sweeping the grassy terrain.

"East, I would guess."

"No guessing," he said, tipping his head up to the sky, where another blaze of lightning sizzled over the mountains.

"Please, just dig," she said, pointing to the monument.

He threw his shoulders into the task, digging around the base of the stone monolith as thunder cracked and the wind began to rush around them.

One hole.

Two.

Three.

She helped, prodding the wet soil with her knife, searching for resistance.

But they found nothing.

He tried in another direction, cutting through the grass to turn up earth. Dark holes circled the statue, but to no avail.

"Oh, hell." Disgusted, Gavyn threw down his shovel. Using his sword, its blade far longer than her knife, he too began to test the ground. In the long blade went, Gavyn leaning heavily upon it. Then out again. In once more. Around the statue in ever-widening circles. Over and over while the rain lashed at them.

Finally, he looked up at her through the rain, dirt running

from the blade of his weapon. "It's not here," he said as thunder clapped.

"It has to be."

He shook his head and tried to wipe the water from his face, only to leave a streak of mud on his cheek. "It's no use."

"We can't stop yet."

He glared at her, looked up at the sky, then said, "You just don't want to pay your debt, wife."

"Oh, that's not it."

"Bryanna, this is the wrong spot. Whatever Isa said to you, it was wrong." He yanked his sword from the ground and started for the horses.

"No, wait!" she shouted. "It's here. We just haven't found it yet."

"Woman, what do you expect me to do? Dig up the entire damned field? Or perhaps I should topple that huge stone?" He was already at Harry's side, and she was left standing in the rain.

She'd been so certain, so sure this was Kambria's second hiding place.

Ignoring Gavyn for the moment, she stooped over the small mounds of dirt, digging around the base of the monolith. Although the wind and rain lashed at her, she tried to remain calm, to reason it out. *Think, Bryanna, think!* What was it Isa had said? *Where would Kambria have hidden the gem?*

"Well?" Gavyn called, his words tinged with impatience. He'd already taken the reins of Harry's bridle into one hand and was standing next to Rhi.

"I don't know. I thought it would be here. I *knew* it would be!" Rain washed down her face and neck, soaking her to the skin. Her clothes were heavy, the smell of wet wool adding to the scent of mud.

"We need to find shelter."

She turned from him and stared up at the sky. "Isa, what did you mean?" she demanded, holding her arms wide. She couldn't give up! Wouldn't. Looking at the threatening heavens, she remembered Isa's words:

Do not be cross! Do not run in circles! Forestall all evil! Find the gem and leave! Danger abounds!

Once more, she ran them through her mind.

Do not be cross! Do not run in circles! Forestall all evil! Find the gem and leave! Danger abounds.

Through the curtain of rain she stared at the stark monolith. There was the cross and the circle. That part was correct!

"Bryanna, come," Gavyn insisted.

She would not heed him. Not yet. "Forestall . . . danger abounds," Bryanna said, the words swirling through her mind like a chant. "Cross, circle, forestall, danger abounds." Faster and faster the words spun until they blended and she whispered them and . . .

With a rolling peal of thunder, she understood. *Oh, for the love of Morrigu*, she thought, piecing Isa's cryptic instructions together. "Wait! Gavyn, please." Turning, she saw him already astride his big steed. "No . . . we have to try one more thing," she pleaded.

"Bryanna, no. We came. We tried. It's not here."

"Please!" Bryanna insisted. "I think it's on the east side, but . . . but we were too close to the statue. I think Isa meant it's buried four leaps to the east."

"What?" He stared at her as if she'd finally gone stark, raving mad. Rain plastered his hair to his head and dripped from the tip of his nose. "Leap? Like a toad?"

"That's what she meant by *fore*stall and a*bound*ing."

"You can't be serious. Come on! You're soaked to the skin, and so am I. If we ride now, we can make the next town by nightfall."

"Not until we search one last time." Spinning so hard she nearly slipped on the wet grass, Bryanna strode back to the monolith and took four long jumps to the east. This was right. She was certain. "Oh, Isa, do not fail me," she whispered. "Here." She jabbed a finger at the wet ground, blinking against the rain. "This is where we need to dig."

He didn't move. What was wrong with him?

"Come on!" When he didn't move to help her, she muttered, "Very well," under her breath. She marked the spot by yanking a tuft of grass out by its roots, then marched to Harry and began untying the shovel.

"No," Gavyn said, but she ignored him, pulling her gloves off with her teeth so she could untie the laces securing the shovel to Harry's harness. "Bryanna—"

The laces came free, the shovel falling into her waiting hands. With one dark scowl at Gavyn, she strode back to the spot where the grass was uprooted.

"For the love of St. Peter," Gavyn said as lightning forked across the sky. "Bryanna . . . oh, bloody hell!" He dismounted quickly.

As she started slamming the shovel into the ground, he reached her and dragged the handle from her hands.

"I can do it," she insisted.

"It'll take all day."

"Really, Gavyn," she argued, "I can do it."

"And I can do it faster." And to prove his point, he jabbed the shovel's blade into the ground and began turning the earth, digging and tossing mounds of mud all around the spot where Bryanna had pulled up the grass. One hole two feet deep, then another.

"You know," he said, tossing another dripping shovelful of dirt to one side, "'Twould really help if that voice in your mind was a little more precise." Again he thrust the shovel deep, the blade cutting into the grass and soft loam. "I mean, if Isa's going to all the trouble to talk to you from the grave, the least she could do is speak so that you could understand her." He glanced over his sodden shoulder at Bryanna as he discarded another shovelful of mud and grass.

"That's not how it works."

"How it works isn't very well," he grumbled.

"We have three pieces of the map, don't we? And one jewel." Why she was defending Isa, she didn't know. But it wasn't any more ridiculous than digging around an ancient statue in a downpour.

"Well, this time we need more instructions. So why don't

you see if you can talk to her and tell her to bloody well let us know what she means?" He rammed the shovel into the earth angrily.

And the blade struck something that sounded like metal.

They stared at each other for a split second.

"Holy Jesus," Gavyn whispered. He redoubled his efforts, kicking out more dirt with his shovel and exposing the top of a small hammered tin box.

Bryanna held her breath as she knelt beside the hole and lifted the rusting box from the ground. She could barely trust her trembling hands to unlatch the lid.

With a creak, the lid opened.

Inside, winking upon a bed of doeskin that was being peppered with raindrops, was a perfectly cut emerald.

"So, husband Cain," she said, a note of triumph in her voice as she blinked against the rain. "It seems as if you just lost your bet."

Gavyn never thought he would be a believer. Not in a million years. But too many unexplained occurrences had happened on this trip for him to doubt Bryanna. Standing in the rain in this field, with lightning sizzling from the sky and thunder resounding, she'd pointed him to the very spot where the gem had been hidden.

It was not mere happenstance.

Something unworldly was happening here.

Something that made him rethink all of his previous beliefs.

Just as she'd predicted, they'd found the emerald, which, of course, was nestled upon the next piece of the map.

When they spread the ragged, torn bit of leather and, blinking against the rain, fit it into the existing pieces of the map, it indicated that they were to travel south.

"A topaz for the southern tip," she said.

But what bothered him was the map itself. It was etched on a much larger piece of deerskin, and upon its crude surface was a rudimentary drawing of the sea.

"Does that mean the *southern tip* of the dagger . . . or of Wales?" he asked.

Bryanna looked at him with eyes that were only slightly bluer than the brilliant green stone they'd found in the rusted box.

"Both," she said with what appeared to be newfound conviction and strength. Lightning flashed again, and raindrops drizzled down her face. "I fear, Gavyn, we're in for a very long journey."

CHAPTER TWENTY-THREE

Morwenna stripped out of her riding clothes, though the fresh scent of spring still clung to her mantle. This morning, with the sun shining upon rooftops and fields, she had not been able to stay within the keep. So she'd ridden upon a little bay gelding and seen the signs of the changing season. Farmers had been plowing their fields and sowing oats and wheat and rye. Frisky spindly-legged foals had frolicked at their mothers' sides. The river had been swollen from the melting snow and days of rain, and she'd even spied a fox with kits.

Renewed, she'd asked her serving woman to send for her husband. After changing and combing her hair, she now waited for him in the solar at Calon. Outside the window swallows and wrens sang, while inside the fire burned cheerily.

Her stomach was in knots.

"I have something to tell you," she announced as he strode into the room. Wearing a black tunic with leather and silver tooling, he was certainly the most handsome man in all of Wales. His hair was thick and dark, with the hint of a curl, his eyes intense and clear as he studied her, his jaw angular and strong.

Morwenna wanted to wring her hands. How she wished she'd spoken up earlier! She stiffened her spine, squared her shoulders, and took a deep breath.

"You're pregnant," he said before she could utter a word.

"You knew?"

"I can count, Morwenna, and we do sleep together. We do make love." He walked to the fire, where he warmed the backs of his long legs. "Your time of the month has not come for a long while. Three? Mayhap four months? I have seen how you devour food, then often throw it up. Other times you are weepy, still others extremely tired. How would you think I could not know?"

She sat on the chair near the wheel where she was supposed to take pleasure in spinning, which she did not. She'd always been more interested in riding and hunting, any activity in which she could compete with a man. Tending herbs, spinning, keeping track of the castle accounts, and even, aye, taking alms to the poor, though all worthwhile, did not fill her with the same sense of excitement as riding through a winter forest at a full gallop or chasing down quarry.

Slowly she turned the spinning wheel, hearing it hum. "I tried to speak with you about it earlier, but it never seemed the right time. You were preoccupied with learning the ways of this keep, of ruling it and making alliances, and I . . . I admit it, I've been worried about Bryanna." She nodded, as if finally acknowledging a fact she'd tried to deny. A stupid spate of tears burned the back of her eyelids. Again! Damn it all. She'd never been a weepy woman, never had such strange feelings, but with the coming of the child, she seemed forever either uproariously happy or unspeakably sad.

"This should be a time of joy for us," he said as he left the fire to come to her.

"It is! Oh, husband. I want nothing more than to bear this child and as many more as you would like." She was sincere, smiling up at him through eyes wet with tears. "The babe is due soon after the new year dawns. Aye, not even half a year away, and I care not whether it be a son or daughter, just as long as it's healthy and strong."

"And so our child shall be."

"And, of course," she said, sniffing back her infantile tears as she took his hands and stood, "if it is a girl, I am hoping for a strong one, like those of Penbrooke."

"Like Bryanna," he said.

She nodded, for it was true. Of all of her brothers and sisters, Bryanna was the least like the others, both in spirit and in looks. But Morwenna would not be saddened at thinking about her sister at this moment, not when she and her husband were close again.

"You may have a son."

"*We*," she said, "*we* may have a son, and would that he not be as strong-willed as his father."

"*Or* his mother."

She laughed and felt as if a cloud that had settled over them had been lifted. "I am sorry for hiring your brother to work as our mercenary. He has wronged both of us in so many ways, and—"

"Carrick is a black mark upon the House of Wybren," her husband interrupted. "He's a consummate actor, skilled in the art of half-truths and lies. A rogue and a violent blackheart. And yet this is the man you hire to find your sister?"

"He's also an excellent tracker, and if truth be told, he seemed eager to gain some modicum of forgiveness."

"Forgiveness?" His lips curled in a sardonic smile. "That does not sound like my brother."

"Husband, I was just out riding past a farmer sowing oats into his field. A field that was barren and overgrown last summer. But just because a field has been fallow does not mean it cannot be turned over to reap a plentiful harvest."

"I married a lady of wisdom," he said, his hand sliding over her belly to find the slight swell of their baby. "You'll be a fine mother, Morwenna."

"I will never do anything behind your back again. I swear it on my life." She wrapped her arms around him and kissed him hard on the lips. His arms wrapped around her body, holding her close in that perfect fit that she'd always found so magickal. "I love you with all my heart," she vowed.

He squeezed her close. "As I love you." His voice was

rough and raw—nearly cracked—and she felt new tears fill her eyes again. "And, wife, I trust you with everything I own, as well as my life."

She nearly sobbed as she clung to him, grateful for the relief that washed away her guilt. She kissed him again and her knees went weak. Then, suddenly releasing him, she stepped back a pace, grabbed his hand, and placed it upon her abdomen again.

He smiled. "Thank you," he said, and his eyes seemed to shine.

She shook her head. "Thank you for"—she lifted a hand to indicate all that surrounded her—"everything."

"I have a gift for you," he said, "though not as great as this—" He flattened his hand over her belly. "'Tis something you've been waiting for."

"What?"

From within his tunic, he withdrew a scroll. "This came by messenger today, from Tarth. 'Tis, I think, from your sister."

With a cry, Morwenna took the scroll, untied it, and scanned the short message. "Aye," she said, her voice cracking. "She is safe! And on a quest." Finally she let the tears roll down her cheeks as her husband's strong arms surrounded her.

Bryanna was safe.

Morwenna's husband loved her.

Of course he did, and she was going to bear them a child.

All was good with the world.

And yet, as she held her husband close, she crossed her fingers for good luck.

Deep in the forests of South Wales, Gavyn sat at the fire and smelled the scent of the sea. Overhead stars shone bright and a breeze stirred the highest branches of the surrounding trees. Three months they'd traveled to hear these unfamiliar sounds of rippling water and frogs croaking. He knew they were alone, and yet, he sensed someone, or something, nearby.

You are imagining things. All the talk of sorcery and dead witches has burrowed deep in your soul. You are safe here. You know it.

Still his eyes searched the darkness. He wished the wolf were out there, but the damned beast had been missing the past few days. Mayhap she'd given up a trek that had taken her far from her home.

A twig snapped and he shot to his feet, only to see that Alabaster was the culprit.

Calm down, he told himself as he returned to his position, propped against his saddle.

Tonight he and Bryanna had made camp in a clearing that wasn't that different from the one where he'd first seen her railing at Isa.

Had it been four months past?

She was washing in the stream, just out of the circle of flickering light cast by the fire. They'd traveled a long way since Holywell, the tightness in his muscles a testament to days, weeks, and months in the saddle.

Gazing toward the creek where she was washing, he remembered being stunned that she'd known where to find the emerald. That was when he'd realized that mayhap Isa, the dead woman, truly did visit her.

He'd been shocked beyond belief when his shovel had struck the tin box. Moments later, when they'd discovered the stone and map tucked inside . . .

He'd been wrong. So wrong.

Bryanna had looked up at him, triumphant and smiling, her face and hair bedraggled and dripping with rain. Later, when they'd taken shelter in an abandoned, dilapidated shed, where they'd managed to build a fire, she'd taken out the knife and placed the emerald into the open space in the eastern side of the hilt. The stone had fused with the metal surrounding it, the dagger warming in her hand. He'd snorted when she'd said as much, but when she'd handed him the damned blade, it had been hot. For a few seconds, the bloody knife had seemed almost alive, pulsing with a vibrant heat for the slightest of seconds.

After the stone was affixed, she'd laid out the map, and they'd scrutinized the worn doeskin together. As he'd guessed, it was fairly clear that their search for the next stone would take them far to the south, to the sea.

An arduous journey.

It had taken three months.

They'd traveled over mountains and through valleys, followed rivers and cut through deep forested chasms. The terrain had been rugged and their progress slow. With each ragged ravine and twisting river, they'd done their best not to leave a trail. Fires were well extinguished, hoofprints best left on the riverbank, where the swelling waters would cover them. They couldn't chance leaving hints for Deverill's men—or any other mercenaries, like Lord Hallyd's soldiers, who might be hunting him down for ransom.

On the run and crossing a no-man's-land . . . he had to marvel at Bryanna's determination. She had taken the time to send a missive to her sister, though Gavyn wondered if it would ever reach Morwenna at Calon.

At night when they camped in the forest, she practiced her spells and chants, the rituals Isa had taught her when she'd first embarked on this trek. Ofttimes she tried to reach Isa, casting herbs to the wind, speaking to the stars, scratching runes in the ground—all to no avail. He'd watched her each night, intrigued that he could be so beguiled by a woman whose actions he'd once thought daft.

His dreams of Bryanna upon Alabaster, riding through the sky as it rained jewels, came frequently now. The darkness that followed her, the umbra, was still behind her, ever chasing her. Sometimes it was close on Alabaster's tail, other times it remained at a distance, lurking, waiting. Somehow he knew it was dark and shifting, always dripping evil.

Those nights, when the dream had torn through his brain, he'd found it difficult to sleep. He would awaken terrified under the stars, and he would hold her more tightly against him, silently vowing to keep her safe.

As the days had passed, winter had finally abated and spring was now blooming into summer. Often now the sky was clear and blue, migrating birds returning, insects beginning to hum.

To their good fortune, game had been plentiful and they were fed. And until the past few days, the wolf kept pace, disappearing whenever they came upon a village, only to reappear when they were in the woods. When meat was roasting on a spit, he could always count on Bane to arrive in time for dinner.

Bryanna, who had come to rely on the wolf's distant company, now wondered if she wasn't a guardian angel.

"I doubt many angels come to the earth as wild snarling beasts," Gavyn had said. Admittedly, he'd enjoyed watching as she bristled astride Alabaster, the sunlight catching in her fiery hair.

"If not an angel, then at least a protector, a spirit that is with us in the guise of a wolf."

"Or mayhap she's just a wild beast who is too lazy to kill her own food."

She'd laughed and sent him a wink then, telling him she knew just how he felt about the bloody animal, then urged her horse to a faster clip, leaving Gavyn and Rhi slowed by the pack animal behind them.

"Bloody wench," he'd said upon catching up with her.

She'd tossed back her head and laughed softly again, her eyes a bright verdant color that bordered on blue, her face flushed.

"And you love it."

He hadn't been able to deny what he felt for her. Aye, the truth of the matter was, he thought now as he gazed up at the stars, he did love her. More than he'd ever thought possible; more than a man should love any one thing, including a woman. 'Twas dangerous. To love something so much made a man vulnerable, perhaps even overly protective and afraid.

Which made his fears that much worse.

He suspected they were being followed.

'Twas nothing he was certain of, and he certainly hadn't spotted any soldiers wearing the colors of Agendor. . . . Still, he had the uncanny feeling that he and Bryanna were but one step ahead of a pursuer.

Could it be Deverill, the son of a cur who had sired him? Or Hallyd of Chwarel, the hideous priest-baron who had killed Kambria, if the stories Bryanna was spinning were true. Considering his vicious history, Hallyd might add up to be a worse enemy than Deverill. 'Twas worrisome.

Clearly, the pursuers had descriptions of them and their horses. Gavyn had suggested selling Alabaster and Rhi, but Bryanna had refused. She loved that little white jennet, a gift from her sister, and Gavyn himself had a fondness for Rhi. The black destrier was not only a good fast steed but a symbol of Gavyn's disregard for his father. Old lame Harry was also distinctive. No doubt Gavyn and Bryanna would be safer on three old farm horses, all brown without any identifying markings, even if they were slower.

He'd gone along with Bryanna's wishes, however, a fool-hearted decision because he, too, liked the horses.

He picked up a stick and tossed it into the fire, watching the greedy flames burn away the bits of moss, crackling and snapping, sending bright sparks heavenward.

He wasn't a believer in all things mystical, but then again, he couldn't deny that there was more than a bit of witchcraft in the air. Witchcraft, or even magick.

He saw movement in the darkness beyond the ring of flickering light cast by the fire, and Bryanna appeared, the hair around the edge of her face wet where the water still clung to it. She dabbed at her face with the corner of her mantle and he couldn't help but grin. Aye, she was beautiful, to be sure, but there was something more than outward beauty to her. An inner spark often lit her eyes or tugged at the corners of her lips or pulled up an eyebrow, as if a bit of the devil was in her spirit.

"So . . . have you figured out where we are going?" she asked, plopping down upon a rock near the fire. The map was stretched out on a flat stone, its hieroglyphs visible in the firelight, but still an enigma. She'd stitched the last piece onto the others months ago, but still the specific location of the next stone was a mystery. They'd followed rivers and streams, roads and trails, always heading south, not knowing their ultimate destination.

Gavyn pushed himself upright and walked to the spot where she was seated.

"We must be getting close," she said. "We've traveled so far."

"Aye, that we have." He squatted beside her and traced their progress on the map, his finger following the path they'd taken. Just as he had every night since they'd first discovered this scrap of doe hide and Bryanna had attached it to the other pieces. The symbols never changed. In fact, he had committed the weird scratchings and hieroglyphics to memory. The flat hills, the rushing river, the steep cliffs and small villages. And at the lowest, most southern tip of the map, the markings that could only mean the sea.

"Look, here," he said, and indicated another cross scratched upon the map, a drawing nearly identical to the one that had led them to the monolith in the east. "We should be passing this landmark soon."

"Aye," she agreed, nodding her head.

"Would it not be the place she would hide the stone?" He hated to ask the question, because it wasn't the first time he'd posed it.

Bryanna's face was drawn into a knot. She chewed on her lower lip in deep concentration, but shook her head, her deep red curls catching the firelight. "I think not. I know you think it would make sense and, I have to agree, aye, this cross is similar, but I think it may be just a landmark. I don't have the same feeling I had about the first one."

"You have a different feeling," he said. They'd been over this before. Instincts and feelings, or a witch's intuition?

"Aye. It seems too obvious for Kambria to mark precisely where she buried the stones. And why would she choose the same kind of statue?"

"So that we could find them," he said.

"Not just us, but anyone else who stumbled upon the emerald and this piece of the map. It makes no sense. No sane person would do it."

"This is a supposed witch you're talking about. Her actions have little to do with sanity." She sent him a glare that he thought might just turn him into a stone sculpture, yet he reminded her, "The opal was not buried at a monolith."

"Nor will this one be," she said in frustration and drew her finger along one edge of the map. "This line, it's a river, is it not?"

"It seems."

"And if this edge is to be believed, it flows to the sea at this point." She indicated a square upon the map.

"Yes." The square, usually drawn to indicate a keep, was one of several scattered upon the leather. The map was full of squares and rectangles interspersed with etchings of circles and crosses and mounds and runes, none of which, it seemed, meant a wink to Bryanna.

"What is the name of this river?" she asked.

"I don't know, but we can ask someone in the next village," he said, rotating his neck so that it cracked. "You think the river is important?"

She shook her head. "I know not." But she stared at those crooked markings as if they were significant.

"Isa . . . she hasn't come to you again?"

"Nay," she admitted, scowling. "I've not heard her voice in a long while." With a disgusted sigh, she rolled up the map and tucked it into her pouch. "What good is this stupid 'gift' if I don't know how to use it?"

"I know not." Standing and stretching, Gavyn took her by the hand and glanced into the black depths of the forest where the light didn't quite touch.

Was there something out there? Something watching?

He saw nothing, but he *felt* hidden eyes upon them, and he sensed it wasn't Bane the wolf. He'd sleep very little tonight, he thought. And he would be certain to have Bryanna snuggled close and his dagger in his hand. "Come. We'll sleep on it."

He was not far behind.

Riding through the night, the mercenary Carrick knew he could catch them. But he knew not where they were going. Only one thing was clear: they were forever riding south.

He knew not why they traveled so far, but he'd caught their trail at Holywell and had spoken with an innkeeper's wife who was as loose with her tongue as had been the tavern wench in Tarth.

He was not alone in his pursuit of Bryanna and the man she traveled with. He'd heard the gossip, seen the small bands of soldiers, and overheard their mission. The soldiers, it seemed, were more interested in Gavyn, the bastard son of the Lord of Agendor. Word was that he had not only murdered a man—a sheriff, no less—but he'd also had the balls to steal his father's prized steed. According to the soldiers, Baron Deverill was more infuriated by the thievery than the loss of his sheriff's life.

But there were other forces involved, another group of soldiers who sometimes joined the first. Having listened from a darkened corner of a tavern, he'd discovered they were from Chwarel, and they cared little about the murderer. Their orders were to follow Bryanna, whom they referred to as a witch and a sorceress.

One night Carrick made it known to the soldiers from Chwarel that he was tracking Bryanna of Penbrooke and her traveling companion.

"What's your business with them?" one of the soldiers had asked, his yellowed teeth glinting dark in the dim light of the tavern. Afal, the others called him.

"Strictly for the ransom," the mercenary had said. "I'm in

it for the prize offered by Lord Deverill for the safe return of his bastard son."

Afal had tossed back his ale, then nudged the soldier next to him. "This mercenary's tracking the same quarry," Afal had said.

"Then my advice to you is not to harm the girl," the other soldier had warned. "Lord Hallyd issued strict orders. No one is to impede her—at least, that's what he's saying this week."

"I have no quarrel with the girl," Carrick had said. "I'm just a hunter in search of a prize."

Over a few mazers of ale Hallyd's soldiers had warmed to him, sharing tales of their exhausting journey of the last few months. When Afal asked, the mercenary said his name was Edwynn.

"So, Edwynn the mercenary, here's how it shall be," Afal said, a bit of spittle on his chin. "We'll let you close enough to capture Deverill's bastard son, assuming you be kind enough to leave our charge alone. Elsewise Lord Hallyd will have our heads, he will."

"'Tis a plan that can work to mutual advantage," Carrick agreed, oddly comfortable at living a new lie.

"Besides," Afal droned on, "you're best off leaving the daughter of Kambria alone. A sorceress and a witch, just like her mother." He lowered his voice. "Killed at Hallyd's own hands, Kambria was. You'd best stay away from this witch, Bryanna, if you knows what's good fer ye."

Carrick knew Bryanna from his youth, if only slightly, and thought her beautiful, impertinent, curious, and a bit of a ninny. There was talk that as a child she'd had pretend friends. Foolishness.

But now . . . all this speculation that she was a witch with magickal powers. He didn't believe it.

But, he thought, as a bat swooped over his head and a million stars twinkled in the black sky, he did believe that fate could offer as many twists and turns as a winding road.

The mercenary had more on his mind than Bryanna.

Carrick of Wybren was wondering if this assignment from

Morwenna might prove to be his chance to turn the tables. What might his future hold if he returned to Wybren a hero?

He smiled in the night and urged his horse to a quicker pace. He couldn't risk letting them get too far ahead of him.

Isa's voice invaded Bryanna's mind just as dawn streaked the sky in pale shades of pink and lavender. This time, not only did she speak, but as she did Bryanna was given a vision. . . .

Pictures of a river estuary guarded by a keep with two rounded towers facing outward. Situated on the mouth of a great river, this castle had an upper bastion as well as a lower bailey.

"From your ancestor who is great, you will find the stone past twin towers. Deep inside, hidden in a square. Pray to the Mother Goddess. Use the dagger."

"Holy Morrigu," she whispered, pushing on Gavyn's shoulder.

His snoring interrupted, he sputtered and snorted. His eyes flew open, his hand quickly finding his weapon. "What?" he said, instantly awake. "Is something wrong?"

"Just the opposite," she said, excitement coursing through her. "I know where we're going."

"You do?"

"Yes!"

"Where?"

"I do not know the *name* of it, but I will recognize it when I see it. I had a vision," she said, describing what she'd seen and telling him what Isa's voice had said. "The ancestor who is great must be Llewellyn, you see, and the stone is the topaz."

Gavyn seemed skeptical as he climbed to his feet and stretched, one arm lengthening over his head, showing off his buttocks as his tunic was pulled high. He cast a glance over his shoulder, caught her looking, and grinned wickedly.

Swiftly, she looked away and gathered her things. They made love nearly every night, and sometimes in the morning as well. This was what Bryanna had won from their bet—mayhap what they both won.

"No," she said a bit reluctantly before he could suggest that they spend a few more minutes kissing and touching and exploring each other's bodies. She felt her skin grow hot and tamped down any desire that dared heat her blood. Oh . . . she pushed those thoughts aside and hurried to cinch the saddle over Alabaster's back.

They were quick about it, their routines of making and breaking camp now second nature. Bryanna took the time to relieve herself and wash her face while the horses were given a measure of grain and Gavyn, too, made himself ready. They usually shared a piece of salted meat or fish, and then began their journey with the coming of the dawn.

The days were warmer now, fog lifting early, rain frequent, but snow and sleet long past. Once in a while they got caught in a downpour or thunderstorm, but they rarely suffered severe, toe-numbing cold or ice-crusted puddles and roads.

Bryanna had been able to mask her pregnancy because, though her waist thickened a bit, her abdomen had remained flat. That had begun to change this week, and she noticed the beginning of her rounding belly, which now would quickly become apparent. By her own calculations she was into her fourth month and the babe wouldn't arrive until sometime between Samhain, at the end of October, and Yule, before the Christmas Revels.

She didn't like to think that her child might be born at Samhain, or summer's end, the time of year when spirits and fierce, dark beasts could walk the earth. According to the lore of the old ones, Samhain was the time of year when the thin veil between the two worlds was lifted, blurring the line between the spirit world and the tangible world. When she was a child, Bryanna had gone off with Isa at Samhain to bury apples along the roadside. "For spirits who are lost, or those who have no descendants to provide for them," Isa had explained. Thinking that apples weren't quite enough, Bryanna had once slipped some quail eggs into the ground before covering the hole with dirt. If Isa was right, her spirit would be passing through this Samhain, journeying off to the Summerland. Gleda's, too . . .

She shuddered at the notion and turned her thoughts elsewhere. She must focus on the castle in her vision, the keep at the river delta, where, she silently prayed, they would find the topaz.

"Hurry," she said to Alabaster, letting the reins slip through her hands as she urged her horse into an easy canter.

The roads were smoother now, but oftentimes the mud gave way to packed earth and dust. They guided the horses along the river, stopping at the first village for feed for the animals.

While Gavyn spoke with a man in the stables about trading his fur pelts for grain, Bryanna caught the eye of a woodcutter walking through the village, carrying a large bundle of sticks upon his back, an ax over one shoulder. Once he'd greeted her, she couldn't help but ask him a question, which he seemed all too happy to answer.

" 'Tis the River Towy," he said, indicating the deep, wide waterway. He set down the ax, pulled off his cap, and wiped at his hair, brown tufts that stood straight up. "It flows to the bay at Llansteffan Keep."

River Towy? Had she not heard of it somewhere recently? It seemed familiar, but try as she might, she couldn't recall where. She asked, "And there's a castle at the mouth of the river?"

"Aye, I've lived here all me life and it's a beautiful place, it is. From the battlements you can see across the bay to the arm of land that juts into the water."

Bryanna pressed her lips together to suppress the thrill of recognition that flashed through her. This had to be the castle in her vision. It had to be the place where the topaz was hidden. "And the keep," she asked the man as Gavyn joined them, a sack of grain on his shoulder. "Llansteffan, you say. Does it have a gatehouse with two towers that are rounded on one side and flat, or square, on the other?"

"So you've been there?" he asked with a grin.

"Nay," she said, meeting Gavyn's silver eyes, "but someone told me of it."

"They were right. 'Tis just as they said." He shifted his load and admired the pelts strung across Harry's back.

Excitement bubbled up inside her. The vision was true. Maybe all the chants she'd said and runes she'd drawn and herbs she'd flung to the wind hadn't been for naught.

"Some very nice skins you have there," the woodcutter said, nodding at Gavyn. "As I was telling yer wife, you can't ride through here and not get a gander at Llansteffan, grandest keep in all the land, I say. As strong as she is, she's forever been fought over."

"By Llewellyn the Great?" Bryanna asked, her fingers knotting in the reins. Astride Alabaster, she tried not to appear nervous and anxious, but she could barely contain her anticipation. They'd ridden so long, and now they were so close!

"Llewellyn, aye, he was one. Claimed her back for the Welsh, he did. But there were others, of course. Now, if you keep to this road, you'll find the castle. 'Tis but half a day's journey, straight on. Don't veer from the river."

"Thank you," she said, feeling heat rush to her cheeks. They were almost there!

" 'Twas my pleasure." With a wave the woodcutter was off, walking in the opposite direction.

Bryanna couldn't help but smile. "Half a day," she said. "Let's hope there's an inn with wine, a bath, cinnamon tarts, and roasted eel."

"And a bed?" he asked, riding next to her.

"A canopied bed with a feather mattress and velvet curtains and crisp linen sheets."

" 'Tis a lot to ask for."

"Is it?" She shook her head, then urged her horse into a full-blown gallop. " 'Tis time to collect an amendment on that wager, husband," she called over her shoulder, her voice floating on the wind. "Me and the babe, we deserve it."

CHAPTER TWENTY-FOUR

By the time he caught up with her, the weight of her words had sunk into his brain. "You're pregnant?"

"Aye. Very." They were riding more slowly, the horses walking side by side along the river flowing deep and dark beside them. Seagulls cried loudly, whirling and floating overhead. Signs that they were approaching the sea.

"How?" He was thunderstruck. Not that he hadn't known it could and probably would happen, but he'd thought she would have told him. Now that he thought about it, all the signs were there. She'd become tired early in their journey. Queasy, too, and she ate like . . . like she was eating for two. How had he not seen it?

"How?" she repeated, both of her eyebrows shooting skyward.

"No, I mean, when?"

"From the first night, I think. I've never had my cycle since."

Another signal he'd missed. "But you said nothing and we've been riding for months and . . ."

"And what?" she asked, tilting her head defiantly. "You're not going to treat me differently now, are you? You're not going to start thinking I'll have to be treated as if I'm made of pottery and might break."

"No . . . I . . ." He was still trying to get his bearings. A father? He was going to be a father? "But, why did you wait? I mean, you should have told me." It was not often that he became rattled, that his concentration slipped, but this. . . .

"I just did." Her eyes gleamed. "And you should be happy."

"I am," he said, new emotions roiling inside him. A child? There was a child on the way? "When?"

"I'm not certain, but I would think near Samhain, maybe before." She bit her lip as she turned to him.

At that moment he thought she was the most beautiful woman in all of Wales.

The thought was wondrous to him: he was going to be a father. Have his own son or daughter. He thought of his own childhood, his relationship with his mother and the fact that he was nothing more than a burr in his father's side. "Then we must marry."

"What?"

"Aye, at the next town. No child of mine will be raised a bastard."

Some of the joy left her eyes and her smile faded. "Is that how it is? We *must* marry? Because a child is on the way?"

"Aye," he said vehemently. "Don't you agree?"

Her chin jutted out a fraction as she gathered up her reins. "'Twould be nice, I think, if we were to marry because we loved each other. I know sometimes love is dismissed as foolish and not practical, but 'tis what I think should be between a man and wife." She sighed. Tears shimmered in her eyes, but she quickly looked away, as if she realized he was still staring at her.

"I do love you. You know that." He felt foolish saying it atop a horse while she was ten feet from him on her own smaller mare. He should be gathering her in his arms, twirling her off her feet, laughing with sheer joy at the thought of their child.

"Do I? Know that you love me?" she asked, bristling again. Eyes the color of the sea stared over at him harshly. "Then, tell me, Gavyn, why does it take a baby for you to ask me to marry you?"

"What? Because . . . I . . ." He couldn't believe they were

having this conversation. "We've been busy with this quest and—"

"And yet we pretend to be married, don't we?" she charged. "At every town we visit. The happily married couple, Cain and Brynn, going from inn to inn, village to village."

" 'Tis a disguise."

She looked at him again, and her face was suddenly cold as a deep well in winter. "Precisely." Jaw set, she dug her knees into Alabaster's flanks, and the little mare took off as if shot from a crossbow.

"Christ Jesus," he swore, and clucking his tongue at the damned packhorse, urged Rhi forward. He wasn't even married yet and he was already understanding why some men complained about not understanding their wives!

Hallyd strode across the bailey, startling a goose that had been searching for slugs. Flapping and honking angrily, the creature scurried away.

"Shoo," he said to the irritating bird and thought he might request the stupid thing be served for the evening meal.

He'd spent hours walking the bailey, observing for the first time in sixteen years what the keep looked like in daylight. His eyes still burned a bit by day, but fortunately there were enough clouds blocking the sun that he was able to see where the roof had rotted over the stables, where the stones had begun to chip from the mortar of the north tower, and where the posts supporting the pentice were beginning to rot, either from the weather or pests. He didn't mind seeing the flaws. At last, he could actually see for himself the sorry state of the keep. The steward, it seemed, hadn't been completely honest with him. Repairs were in order.

Squinting as the clouds parted, he felt a jab of pain. He knew better than to think that his eyes were mended, for he still had to turn away from a bright reflection. When bright rays ricocheted off a polished sword, he was nearly blinded. And if the day was cloudless, he still had to hide like a weak-eyed bat inside the great hall. Nonetheless, his eyes were better. Less sensitive. They seemed to be healing, though unfortunately their owlish appearance hadn't changed. Yet.

He spent a few hours discussing repairs with the master carpenter and mason before the pain became too severe and he returned to the keep. As soon as the guard shut the door behind him and he was in semidarkness again, the headache began to dissipate.

He hurried down the stairs to Vannora's lair, a path he'd traveled nearly every week. For the past few months, ever since his discussion with Deverill of Agendor, he had obeyed Vannora's counsel. As agreed, he'd sent his armies to join Deverill's men and he, himself, had stayed within the stony wall walks of Chwarel. As ordered, his soldiers had searched the countryside, sending one man back each week with news of their progress.

There had been sightings of Bryanna and the murderer as far to the east as Holywell, where, he assumed, they had found a gemstone for the dagger. He suspected as much since his eyesight had markedly improved three weeks before the sentry had returned from Holywell. Hence he was attempting patience, but in truth, sixteen years seemed more than enough time to wait.

He hurried down the stairwell and unlocked the door to Vannora's room. 'Twas dark in the chamber, no candles or torches lit. For a moment, he thought she was hiding from him, playing a game. He wasn't in the mood.

"Vannora!" he called, squinting into the darkest corners of the room. "Vannora!"

He stopped and listened, hoping for some sound other than the drip of water. But there was nothing, and the air within this tomblike cavern smelled foul and dank. "Vannora? Where the hell are you? My eyesight is better and I think I should aid in the search."

He glanced to the empty cot and the circle by the altar, now stone-cold, the cauldron empty, the candles unlit.

She was gone?

Where?

Why?

He felt a trickle of fear. He'd trusted her and now she had abandoned him, after having insisted that he stay imprisoned in his own keep. His fists balled at his sides and cold sweat beaded on the back of his neck. He'd been a fool.

Well, no longer.

Swinging around, he started for the door, only to find her blocking the way. She was taller than he remembered. Stronger. Her skin white, her lips bloodred, her body seeming vital, her eyes as opaque and shining as a full moon.

"Where were you?" he demanded.

"What does it matter? You brought me no drink?" she asked.

He looked at her full lips and shook his head. "Nay. I think . . . I think mayhap you can get your own goat's blood."

"Do you?"

"I'm leaving. Joining the hunt for Bryanna."

She shook her head. "Then all will be for naught," she reminded him, walking past him fluidly, as if her old joints no longer ached. "You are feeling stronger. Your sight is somewhat restored. Why is that? Because the stones are being returned to the dagger and with each jewel the curse is reversing. But it won't be complete until every gem is once again in the dagger. Let your foolhardy soldiers chase after her and keep you informed. Allow Deverill of Agendor to track his murdering bastard down, but you must do everything in your power to ensure that the stones are retrieved and placed in the dagger's hilt. 'Tis of no use to us until its power is complete."

What she said was the truth; he knew it, and yet he was anxious, eager, his lust running as hot as his need for revenge.

"She is still with the murderer," he said, thinking of Bryanna and remembering their one night together. Oh, that there were more, that she was trapped in this dark keep with him, that she would warm his bed until he was tired of her and had no further use of her.

And when would that be?

Ever?

One night with her and you could not get enough. How do you know that if she were here, the tables would not be reversed and you would be the one begging for favors from her? Mayhap the witch would become the master.

"Ah," Vannora said, as if she'd just read his thoughts. With a cunning smile, she added, "What do you care? You have done your part, have you not? Is Kambria's daughter not with child?" Before he could protest, Vannora lifted a finger to her own eerie red lips. "Shh. Do not argue. She is far to the south, but will be returning. We both know where it all ends, do we not?"

He didn't answer.

"So we wait. And we make certain she is not thwarted in her quest."

Not the answer he wanted to hear.

He frowned as she stepped past him to stare into the empty cauldron. He followed her gaze, horrified. For a second he thought he saw liquid within reflecting her face, but it was not the image of the beautiful dark-haired woman in front of him. Nor was it the visage of a feeble old crone. . . . No, the flash of the face swirling in the depths of the cauldron that held no water was something else, something dark and vicious and completely without a soul.

The image was gone in an instant, and he found her staring at him, the cauldron once again empty. Her voice was the barest of whispers when she said, "I believe that patience is a virtue. And, I think, Hallyd, you need all the virtues you can get."

Llansteffan Castle, a great stone fortress with twin towers guarding the main gate, had been built on a hill that overlooked the River Towy where it drained into a wide bay. The sun was lowering in the sky when Bryanna and Gavyn approached. Shadows lengthened upon the ground as they hid their horses in a copse of oak, then walked, leading Harry with his load of furs, to the castle gates.

Bryanna had nearly forgiven Gavyn for his reaction to her pregnancy. Was it so awful that he wanted to marry her? She did trust that he loved her, didn't she? And she loved him. So she tried her best to push her childish emotions aside as they joined the traffic threading into the great keep. Cart wheels rattled over the rutted path and impatient horsemen loped around the slower pedestrians. Fishermen sang shanties as they lugged buckets of fish and shellfish, water sloshing over the rims to the great keep.

As they passed into the lower bailey, Bryanna checked for soldiers, but none of the uniformed guards or horsemen wore the colors of Agendor or Chwarel. She felt a bit of relief, but she reminded herself that just because she didn't see the uniforms of Hallyd and Deverill didn't mean there weren't spies lurking about. If one of these men recognized either her or Gavyn, he would most certainly forestall them or report back to his leader. She could never let herself forget that Gavyn had a price upon his head.

"Where do we start?" Gavyn asked as they walked along the pebble-strewn path of the lower bailey.

"Well, not here, where the towers are rounded. Not like the ones in the vision," she said, eyeing the interior of the castle walls. What had Isa said? Something about being hidden inside a square.

It was crowded and loud, people talking, chickens clucking, hammers pounding, wheels creaking, all punctuated with a bark of a dog or crow of a cock or bleat of a sheep. She grabbed her leather pouch, where the dagger and maps were hidden. "I'll search the square towers while you sell the pelts. We'll both watch for soldiers. And keep an eye out for anything that looks like it could be what Isa meant. You remember, don't you?"

"Aye, aye. Squares, twin towers, daggers, and prayers to the Mother Goddess."

'Twas as good as she could ask. "I'll be back soon."

"And what if someone sees you?"

"I'll tell them I'm only looking about," she said, "admiring the castle while my *husband* sells the hides of many a sleek and unfortunate animal." She smiled sweetly at him and started along a path to the upper bailey.

But suddenly he caught up with her. Gavyn grabbed her arm with his free hand while Harry hobbled behind. "No, you must wait for me. Do not go anywhere alone!"

"You have to stay with the horse," she insisted.

"I'll find someone to care for him," Gavyn said as she glanced through the main gate and saw the river behind, dark water moving slowly toward the sea.

"The River Towy," she whispered, and the conversation came back in a flood. "I know where I heard it. 'Tis the river where my grandfather Waylynn died. Gleda said as much. He was an apothecary. I wonder what he was doing here." Her heart was beating faster, her memory clear. Now she was certain they'd traveled to the right place. Surely her grandfather had come here—mayhap to hide the stone, then lose his life? "He must be buried nearby. Yes, this is the right place."

"Oh, for the love of God, don't tell me we have to dig him up, too."

"I know not." She had no answers, but felt they were closer to finding the topaz than ever. "See what you can find out about him. If anyone remembers him."

"Wait, Bryan—*Brynn*. I think we should stay together."

"Say, is that a fox pelt?" a merchant said, approaching Gavyn and eyeing the pack tied across Harry's back. "And a weasel and a stoat? You're selling these? How much?" The man, who had a long beard and a rotund girth, was already stroking the hides.

Gavyn released her arm. "Yes, all of them," he said.

Bryanna took advantage of the distraction. With a quick wave to her "husband," she dashed away, continuing up the gentle slope to the upper bailey. She felt Gavyn's gaze upon her backside and knew he was willing her to stay and wait for him, but she couldn't. She was too eager, and, she felt, time was running out. No matter where they went, how far they traveled, Hallyd or Deverill's men seemed to be about. For months, she'd heard rumors of small companies of soldiers riding through the forests of Wales, searching for a wanted man and the woman pretending to be his wife. More than once she'd spied the colors of both keeps on the uniforms of soldiers in the villages where they had stopped.

It seemed there was no getting away from them.

Nay, she told herself, they couldn't tarry. Not here at Llansteffan. Not anywhere.

She walked briskly along a path strewn with crushed oyster shells and pebbles. A fire burned bright in the farrier's hut as a boy pumped the horseshoer's bellows and the brawny man banged on a piece of glowing steel, his hammer clanging loudly with each strike as he molded the metal.

Elsewhere carpenters were shoring up a sagging roof, their hammers in quick counterpoint to the farrier's. A tanner was scraping a deer hide that was stretched tight upon a frame and a potter was busy at his wheel.

From the kitchen the smells of burning wood, baking bread, and roasting fish wafted in the air. Bryanna's mouth watered, as she was forever hungry these days.

Rounding a corner, she passed by girls checking the nests for evening eggs, then shrieking and laughing as boys toting buckets of water tried to splash them. For the first time in a long while Bryanna longed for her sisters and the comforts of Calon. It had been months since she'd seen Morwenna and Daylynn, and she missed the friendship, the camaraderie, the feeling of belonging that she always shared with her sisters. Oh, aye, they fought when they had the chance and they'd made fun of her when she was a child, but who else, aside from Gavyn, did she have to share the news of her pregnancy with? Who else would be as excited as she at the prospect of a new babe? Who else would tend to the child and care for her after the birth? Who else could she tell her most intimate secrets to?

They are only your half sisters, she reminded herself, but ignored the thought. Her sister bond with Daylynn and

Morwenna was strong, no matter how diluted their blood connection might be. Oh, to see Penbrooke or Calon again!

She nearly stumbled when she thought of her sister's keep and the husband from whom Bryanna had fled.

As if hit by a stone wall, she stopped short.

Morwenna's husband.

Bryanna hadn't thought of him in a long while. Now when she did, she felt none of the ridiculous feelings she'd had for the man while watching him and Morwenna at Calon. Was it possible? Had she lost all her fantasies of him?

'Twas true. Morwenna's husband was no more intriguing to her than the pockmarked stable boy leading a horse to the stables.

Sudden relief slid through her veins. As she cast a glance downward into the lower bailey and spied Gavyn, still bartering with the tailor, he happened to look up. He caught her eye and her silly pulse jumped. How had she ever thought she was falling in love with Morwenna's husband? The feelings she'd had for her brother-in-law seemed trite and ridiculous, a spate of girlhood silliness when compared with the depth of her emotions for Gavyn.

She'd been such a fool, a goose of a girl.

Gavyn glanced up at her, this supposed criminal, with his sharp features, brown hair shining with a bit of gold in the fading sun. Her heart squeezed at the sight of him. She waved, then turned and headed straight for the tallest of the square towers.

"Isa, do not fail me," she whispered.

The stone structure was immense, but surprisingly unguarded. She stepped inside the darkened doorway.

Should she climb up or descend down?

All of the gems had been buried in the ground, so she took a chance and headed down the spiraling dirty stairs into an abandoned dungeon that smelled of rot and mold and all things foul. No wonder this place was unguarded. No one would want to be anywhere near it.

"Please let this be the right spot."

She was alone, with only a little illumination from a rush-light that was burning out quickly. Proof enough that some sentry had been here recently and could be returning at any second. Mustering her strength, she pulled the torch from the wall. Nerves strung tight, she held the pitiful rushlight aloft and was able to see that the cells were empty, their rusted gates hanging open.

Just then a scraping noise cut through the abandoned chamber.

She froze.

Her throat was dry as dust.

A rat scurried across the tip of her boot.

"Aaagh!" she cried, but bit back a scream as her knees nearly gave way.

Do not panic. 'Twas only a rat. You've seen them before.

"Sweet Morrigu," she gasped, placing the hand clutching her pouch over her heart.

Now was the time to follow Isa's instructions.

Please let them work. . . .

Swallowing back any lingering fear of rodents, she un-laced the leather bag and extracted the dagger with its two winking stones. How was she supposed to use it?

"Isa, please, help me," she whispered. She slung the pouch with its leather strap over her shoulder. Then, with one hand tight upon the dagger's hilt, the other gripping the torch so hard her knuckles were white, she walked slowly from cell to cell. Her stomach churned as she recognized the remains of bones and scraps of cloth on the floors covered with rotting straw, smelling of stale urine. Hoping to God that the bones were the remnants of food left for whatever prisoner was ill-fated to have been locked down here, and not actual pieces of human carcasses, she kept searching.

Water dripped from the ceiling and rodents' claws scraped over stones. She eyed every inch of this horrible dank hole, her skin crawling as she spied a nest of furry spiders clinging to the ceiling.

"Where?" she whispered, holding her flickering, fading light aloft. "For the love of God, Isa, *where?*"

But the dripping, grimy walls offered no clues, and the small dagger seemed useless.

Swallowing back a mounting sense of dread, Bryanna tried to recall Isa's exact words. She closed her eyes and imagined Isa's voice:

From your ancestor who is great, you will find the stone within twin towers. Deep inside, hidden in a square. Pray to the Mother Goddess. Use the dagger.

"My ancestor who is great." Was Llewellyn-ap-lorwerth really in these dungeons? Mayhap not as a prisoner . . . that was it. She'd thought the word "deep" had meant deep underground. But mayhap Isa had only meant deep in the interior. Hastily, she walked away from the cell and found the stairs again. She started climbing, upward, faster and faster, past the door to the bailey and higher still. That was it. It had to be. Llewellyn hadn't been a prisoner in those cells. He was a warrior. He'd reclaimed the keep.

Breathing hard from the climb, she reached the door that led to the sentry post at the watch turret. Thankfully, the turret was also empty.

"Now where?" she asked out loud, glancing through the crenels. From high above the bailey she could see far into the distance: the river, the bay, the ships, their sails furled and masts slicing into the air like skeletal fingers. The view extended to the ends of the earth, clear to the horizon and the sea.

Closer in, as she turned her attention to the bailey, she looked to the spot where she'd last seen Gavyn, but she couldn't locate him in the crowd. Nor did she see Harry. Heart in her throat, she moved to another area of the tower to stare through a different crenel that allowed a wider view of the inside of the main gate. Surely Gavyn hadn't taken the horse far from where he'd met the merchant. . . .

The dagger in her hand seemed to hum.

She nearly jumped out of her skin and glanced down at the odd weapon with its two jewels and two dark holes in the hilt.

What the devil? Had it been her imagination?

She took a step to one side.

Nothing happened.

No hum.

She stepped back to the spot where she'd been standing. Again she felt the tiniest of vibrations.

Her throat went dry and she doubted herself. But sure enough, with one more try, the bejeweled knife actually trembled in her hand.

"Sweet Jesus," she whispered. This area made the dagger sizzle—the gem had to be nearby.

Keeping her feet in place, she studied the inside of the tower. Her gaze swept the masonry, but there was nothing unusual about it. Pointing her dagger, she walked around the rim but saw nothing. "Please," she whispered, and then remembered the prayer to Morrigu. Wasn't that what Isa had said? Returning to the spot where she'd felt the knife vibrate, she closed her eyes and started whispering a low chant to the Great Mother.

"Morrigu, help me in my quest. . . ."

As she spoke, she felt the dagger heat and hum in her hands, the vibrations moving from her fingers to her soul. In her mind's eye she saw again the great crevice and snowy ridge as her horse galloped wildly. She caught a flash of the rosary and felt a ring of stones cutting into her own throat.

When she opened her eyes, the day had become night, with stars abounding and a moon riding high. The noises of the keep had disappeared. As she stared at the interior of the tower, one stone near the floor seemed a different color from the rest. Pointing the sacred knife at the square-shaped stone, she fell to her knees. A square stone! New energy sizzled through her as she used the dagger, cutting through the mortar as easily as if it had been soft cheese. How easily it crumbled away.

" 'Tis here!" Forcing her fingers into the spot where the

mortar had given way, she tried to move the stone. The rock wouldn't budge, not the barest of spaces. "Oh, rats and riddles, come on," she whispered, but still it didn't move.

"Use the dagger."

Isa's voice was with her again.

In the darkness the knife slid easily through the remaining mortar. With little effort, she pried the stone free. It tumbled onto the floor, exposing a tiny niche that held a flap of leather rolled and tied. "Sweet Rhiannon," Bryanna whispered as she extracted the deerskin from its hiding spot and untied the leather lace surrounding it.

In an instant, a blaze of light flared bright, its yellow warmth radiating from Bryanna's palms.

Snuggled in the deer hide was a brilliant yellow stone, a gem as bright as the sun.

"Waylynn? The apothecary?" the merchant repeated, as if he hadn't heard Gavyn's question. "Aye, I knew him. He was from somewhere up on the Isle of Anglesey. No, wait. . . . I think he was from Holyhead, which is really on a smaller island, if I hear right, from the sailors, you know. He's the man you're asking about?" The heavy man glanced back at Gavyn as he tucked the furs he'd purchased into a box on his cart.

"He seems to be the one."

"Of course I remember him. An odd man, always talking of magick and spells and the like. Bah!" The merchant waved the thought away as if it were a bothersome insect. "He was a fine man, but just a little different from the rest. I'll swear to it on the lives of my sons, Waylynn of Holyhead, he was the best there was with medicine." He closed the lid of the box with a clunk.

Harry, who had been dozing, started.

"A shame about Waylynn, it was." Glancing out at the River Towy, the merchant shook his head. "Got caught in the tides at the mouth of the river, he did." He pulled at his beard as a woman carrying a basket of herbs hurried past. "Some people say that he was fleeing for his life. Got into some trouble with a lord . . . or was it a priest? Funny, I can't remember, but someone powerful from the north."

Hallyd, Gavyn thought, and his heart turned to stone. The same murderer who had killed Kambria. A priest-turned-lord who dealt in evil. The noise of the castle turned into an echoing rush in his ears. Bryanna wasn't safe. Nor was his child. His lips compressed with the knowledge that he had so much to protect now.

"I think a mercenary tracked him down, and the poor man drowned trying to swim across the river." The merchant scratched his beard thoughtfully. "As I said, 'twas a long time ago and hard to remember. But whatever those soldiers were searching for was never found. Whatever secret Waylynn knew, he took it with him to the bottom of the river." The heavy man glanced again to the water and sighed. "No one knows what really happened. Old Waylynn, he might have been caught in his own magick, but I do know this: those soldiers, from the ruler in the north, they never go away, not completely. They've been here off and on ever since." Again, he nodded to himself as he adjusted the straps of his mule's harness. "In fact, I saw a small band of them just the other day, on the road to Kidwelly."

Gavyn felt his blood turn to ice. "And how did you recognize them?"

"By their colors, of course. Black and silver, the colors of Chwarel! That's it. The baron, he was once a priest, that's it. An oddity that. I think his name is Hayden or Harwood or . . ."

"Hallyd?"

"Aye!" The merchant snapped his fingers and grinned, showing off a mouthful of big teeth. "Hallyd, that's the scourge's name."

"The soldiers, they were heading away from Llansteffan on their way to Kidwelly?"

"Nay, they were riding west along the road. I passed them only because one of their horses had pulled up lame and they were working on his hoof. 'Twas two, three days ago. About a day's ride from here."

Gavyn couldn't help himself. He looked up and searched the bailey, his gaze scraping over men on horseback and foot soldiers.

"Thank you," he said, his mind spinning ahead. What if Hallyd's men were already here? What if they were nearing the gates? What if they'd found the two horses hidden in the forest?

Heart pounding with dread, he slapped Harry's reins into the fleshy palm of the surprised merchant. "Would you mind? I will be not a minute. I just need to find my wife."

"What . . . wait . . . no!"

But Gavyn was already running up the hill toward the upper bailey and the tower where he'd seen Bryanna disappear. They had to leave. Now. Hallyd's soldiers could arrive at any moment. The dark lord would surely think that Bryanna would follow the same path as her grandfather.

Suddenly he didn't care about the damned stone, the Sacred Dagger, or anything other than the safety of Bryanna and the babe. He flew into the tower, desperately wanting to yell for her, but holding his tongue. 'Twould be foolish to announce his presence, dangerous to reveal that she was searching the keep. He raced down the stairs, grabbed a rushlight, and found himself in a decrepit dungeon smelling of rot and filth. Surely she wasn't here. Heart pounding, dread screaming through his veins, he scanned the dark corners and saw only the remains of corpses and the smell of despair.

Mayhap she'd left this dungeon and walked to another tower. Oh, God, please that she was safe! Quickly he retraced his steps. At the door to the bailey he thought he heard her voice, a low familiar chant raining on him from above.

By the Gods, was she practicing her sorcery?

Here?

Now?

Attracting attention to herself when even now Hallyd's soldiers might be searching for her? What was she thinking? He took the circular stairs two at a time, his heart pumping in fear.

Dread sank upon him as he heard soldiers enter the tower below while Bryanna's soft voice chanted above.

No!

They were certain to be found out.

Upward, faster and faster, he raced, until he emerged at the top of the highest watchtower.

His heart tightened when he saw her there on her knees, holding a gem and leather map in her hands.

"Come!" he said in a sharp whisper.

"But I found it!" Her sea blue eyes shone with pride, her smile nearly angelic.

"Good, now, let us go."

"But, 'tis the stone. Are you not—"

"We'll speak of this later, Bryanna!" Panic swarmed through him. "Soldiers are returning to their posts, and I heard that Hallyd's men are on their way."

"Then they must already know I'm here," she whispered, fear rounding her eyes as she quickly wrapped the stone in its leather map and tucked it into her pouch.

"Why?" He was pulling on her arm, leading her along the wall walk, intent on reaching the next tower.

"Because of the darkness."

"What darkness?"

"When I began to chant, day turned to night."

"What?" He spun so swiftly she nearly slammed into him. "What are you talking about? 'Tis almost twilight, yes, but there is no darkness, not yet."

"Did you not see it?"

"No, I was in the dungeons," he said, nearly dragging her to the next tower, trying to make sense of her words. "If this is true, why is there not panic in the keep?" he asked, motioning over the crenels to the bailey below, where everyone was going about their tasks as if nothing were out of the ordinary. Carpenters and masons were working on the buildings, the potter was turning his wheel, and laundresses were busy taking down sheets.

"I—I know not." She followed his gaze to the inner courtyard as they hurried across the wide curtain wall. "The woman is at her loom and the horses are not spooked. Even the dogs are calm." Her usually smooth brow was furrowed with vexation as she eyed the bailey, where the long shadows of evening were stretching, but there was still daylight. "I swear to you, Gavyn, that bright sun turned to blackness."

"Swear later. Now we must flee." They had no time to tarry or talk. They had to get out of the castle before Hallyd's soldiers arrived.

He held fast to her hand as they reached the tower. Together, they hurried down the stone steps until they were once again outside on the matted grass of the upper bailey. "Come." He led her down winding paths between the huts and stables. Within seconds, they had reached the packhorse. Gavyn thanked the man as he retrieved Harry's reins.

"Glad to do it." He looked at Bryanna. "Your husband, he sold me some fine pelts."

"Good," she uttered as they briskly strode off.

They were already heading to the main gate when the merchant's voice stopped him cold. "Oh, those soldiers you were asking about," the merchant called as Gavyn turned to face him again. "The ones wearing the colors of Chwarel?" He motioned with a finger toward the farrier's hut. "They're here. And they're not alone."

CHAPTER TWENTY-FIVE

Panic seized Bryanna.

Hallyd's men had tracked them down? Within an hour of their arrival at Llansteffan? How? Turning her head, she saw the soldiers in the farrier's hut—three of them, it seemed, as she didn't dare let her eyes linger on them. As calmly as possible, she and Gavyn joined the throng edging toward the main gate with its soaring twin towers. Gavyn led Harry while she walked on the far side of the packhorse, her hair tucked into the hood of her mantle. Though the topaz and Sacred Dagger were tucked safely in her pouch, she felt as if she were wearing a sign, a mark that she was the daughter of Kambria, the sorceress Hallyd's men were searching for.

They were nearly at the gate when she heard a shout. "Hey!"

Her heart dropped like a rock.

"There she is!"

A glance back confirmed her worst suspicions: the soldiers were hurrying toward them.

There were three men, two in the colors of Chwarel, one dressed as a soldier from Agendor. "Halt!" one cried.

Oh, God! Bryanna and Gavyn swept through the gate, beneath the portcullis, and ran down the road. The soldiers shouted behind them, the pounding of horses' hooves joining the fray. Bryanna chanced another look, only to see a merchant's cart squarely blocking the gate. He stood beside the cart, pointing to a wheel that appeared stuck. The soldiers and their horses could not get by.

Gavyn helped her onto Harry's back, then ran beside them down the hillside, where they ducked into the woods and the gloom of the coming night. It was now too dark to see what was happening in front of the castle gate, but Bryanna suspected the soldiers had gotten past the cart. On their faster steeds, they would be upon them soon.

To think that they'd come this far only to be captured.

Hurry, she silently urged Harry. The instant they reached the fresh horses, she slid off the packhorse's back over the clamor of shouts and pounding hooves.

The darkness was so thick she could barely make out the trees now, and she prayed Hallyd's men would be equally hindered.

"They went this way."

"Nay . . . are you sure?"

"Yes!"

"By the Christ, it's so bloody dark!"

Beside her, she felt rather than heard Gavyn slide his bow over his shoulder, then noiselessly withdraw an arrow from his quiver.

Was he out of his mind? Was he going to shoot in the darkness, through the forest?

"Can you see the trail?" one of the soldiers said.

His voice was so close that Bryanna nearly jumped. Holding her breath, not daring to move a muscle, she silently prayed that none of the horses would nicker or move so that a bridle would jingle. Her heart pounded crazily in her ears and she held her dagger in a death grip.

Morrigu, be with us.

She heard a rustle in the trees beside her.

She nearly fainted.

"What was that?" one of the soldiers said, his voice not ten feet away. "God's teeth, Afal, is that you?"

She sensed Gavyn turn and train his arrow in the direction of the sound.

No one answered.

Bryanna concentrated, every muscle tense, her ears and eyes straining.

"Afal?" the soldier said again.

So close.

Nervous sweat beaded on her forehead.

Harry snorted.

Bryanna wanted to scream.

"What the hell was that? They're over here!" the soldier said.

Gavyn released his bowstring and an arrow sizzled through the air.

"Son of a cur."

Another arrow zipped through the night, this one from the darkness off to Bryanna's right.

"Holy Mother Mary!" the soldier said. "Where the hell are they?"

She saw him then in a bit of moonlight. A dark predator upon a huge steed, another arrow trained upon the soldiers.

Near enough that he frightened the horses. Harry pulled on his reins. 'Twas a miracle his bridle did not jangle.

"Gavyn of Agendor, show yourself," a second voice boomed from the other side of the copse.

They were surrounded! Dark rider on one side, soldiers on the other.

Gritting her teeth, she held fast to her dagger. If there was any magick in the blade, now was the time for it to perform.

A twig snapped and a soldier's horse snorted. She felt Gavyn move around her, closing in on the horse and rider.

"There, I see them," the deeper voice said. "Here, they're over—Bloody Christ!"

Suddenly, a wolf howled, so close that the hairs on the back of Bryanna's neck prickled in fear.

One of the soldiers' horses squealed in fear, the noise piercing the forest. "Whoa, there . . . whoa!" Hooves crashed and branches broke as the horse took off through the woods.

"What the hell?" another soldier said as Harry, spooked,

tried to bolt. Bryanna held tight to his reins, but the fool horse pulled so hard he wrested free of her grip.

"No . . ." Bryanna gasped as Harry ran into the darkness.

Panicked hooves crashed and thundered through the woods. Another horse neighed wildly and nearly knocked Bryanna over as it tore through the undergrowth, his rider swearing angrily.

And above the noise of a scuffle Bryanna heard the deep, ferocious growl of a wolf.

Bane! She knew it. The fool wolf had returned. And now, from the sounds of it, the creature was in for the fight of her life.

"Now!" Gavyn whispered, helping her onto Alabaster's back. The clamor in the forest was deafening. Swords rang from unsheathing and the wolf snarled and growled while men bellowed that they were being attacked. The soldiers' horses were obviously in a panic, rearing and whinnying in sheer terror.

Alabaster minced nervously, tossing her head, her muscles quivering. Rhi, too, shifted, backing into her, snorting and pawing the ground.

"Damn!" Gavyn mounted his nervous horse and pulled on the reins of the white mare . . . and at last they were off, racing through the forest, leaving the sounds of snarling, swearing men and screaming horses behind. Gavyn guided them until they reached the road, where he handed over Alabaster's reins.

The night was blessedly silent as they headed north, the River Towy flowing darkly beside them, the moon as their guide. Bryanna's heart was heavy as a stone. They had lost Harry and the supplies of grain and dried meat he carried. Though someone would surely find him and see to his care, she'd miss Gleda's lame packhorse.

She was also certain that Bane had been skulking in the forest and had attacked one of the soldiers. Had the wolf survived the ensuing fight? *Morrigu, be with them both*, she silently prayed.

They traveled miles upon the main road, then as the sun rose, veered onto a more deserted path. Only when Gavyn was satisfied that they weren't being followed did he find a small village with an inn and stables. Once in their room, they sat on the bed and retrieved the doeskin Bryanna had found at Llansteffan.

They fitted the piece of doe hide with the others. Then Gavyn watched in wonder as Bryanna placed the topaz in the lowest point on the dagger's hilt, a vacant hole. Upon touching the knife's handle, the brilliant yellow gem melded and fused with the steel. All three jewels glowed while the blade shimmered with new vitality.

"Three stones. But one to go," Bryanna said, her voice tinged with relief and exhaustion.

"First, sleep," Gavyn said, pulling her into his arms on the bed.

"Aye." Together they fell deep into sleep, far into the next day. When Bryanna roused in the afternoon, she kissed him awake and they made love, twice, then slept until the sun was low in the western sky.

"We need to return to Calon and marry, or marry and then return to Calon," Gavyn said, "so that you and the child will be safe." He was standing at the window, lacing his breeches, and she watched the fluid muscles of his scarred back as he worked. Oh, how she loved that back, loved running her fingers across it as he made love to her.

Just like their first night together when she'd touched the scars from the whipping he'd received at the hands of the stable master. Just like the first night they'd been together, when he'd first made love to her.

Still nestled in the bedclothes as the sun was setting and the room held the heat of the day, she watched him. A memory of that very first joining of their bodies at Tarth flashed through her mind. The heat. The desire. The wanting. And that woozy feeling, as if she could not lift her head. What had he said? *Daughter of Kambria, you are mine.* That was it. Then he'd added, *Forever bound.*

Never since that first night had he called her "daughter of Kambria." Never had he sworn she belonged to him and him alone, nor had he uttered such possessive, irreversible words as "Forever bound."

She sat up straighter on the bed and remembered the way her skin had crawled when he'd uttered the words, the sense of alarm that had sliced into her soul. And later, when he'd come to her again, he hadn't made such dark decrees. His voice had never deepened into an animal growl. Her stomach churned and for a second she considered the idea that someone else had been inside her bedchamber at Tarth, someone of his build, but not his manner. The dark warrior she'd seen reflected in the mirror the next morning.

Bile rose in her throat. She wouldn't think of it.

But as she gazed at his back, she remembered the man who had first taken her . . . the smooth skin, stretched taut over hard muscles. Without any scars.

Gavyn turned to face her and caught her staring at him. Misreading her vexation for desire, he returned to the bed and sat next to her, then slipped his hand under the covers to touch the rounding of her abdomen. As he did, a smile crept across his face. "I think it would be safer if we returned to your family's castle, where you can worry about nothing but preparing for our child's birth." He kissed her forehead and massaged her belly, and she sighed as she lay back upon the pillows.

"'Tis not that simple," she said as her darkest fears congealed. "I cannot abandon the quest. The dagger must be complete if the child is to be saved. And lately I've been wondering if our child is the one destined to be saved by the power of the dagger."

He'd been rubbing her belly, but now his hand stopped. "Ours? You mean our babe is the child of the prophecy?"

"Aye." She closed her eyes, miserable inside. If this were true, then her babe was not only in danger; it was probably not Gavyn's. The Chosen One was to be sired by Darkness, and

Gavyn was not possessed by evil. Unlike the nightmare lover who had come to Bryanna and taken her while she was dizzy with wine or sick with a potion.

Was it possible? Was the dream she'd had in her woozy mind real? Had a man with demon's blood impregnated her? Oh, by the gods, she could not explain that to Gavyn, would not believe it herself, nor think that her child was not Gavyn's.

"But our child is not yet born." Gavyn was still going through the arguments of denial she'd suffered many a time, not wanting their child to be the future ruler named in the prophecy.

"I know, but . . . I think this may be true." She tried to disguise her fear. Others had known that she would bear the child of the prophecy, the ruler of all Wales, an infant sired by Darkness. Gleda had warned her, though she did not mention the evil of her dark lover.

Why had Bryanna not been told?

Because they were afraid you would change the course of destiny. If you'd been watchful, you would never have mated with a dark lord, the very heart of evil.

And she could not regret it, even now. For she loved this child. *Her child.*

Trust the prophecy. Keep him safe. Raise him in love and light.

"When you first heard of your quest, of a child to save, you were not yet pregnant," Gavyn said. "You and I, we had not even met."

She nodded. "I have been telling myself the very same thing," she said, placing her smaller hand over his. "Trust me, Gavyn, we must finish this journey wherever it takes us."

His jaw worked in frustration. "It will take us far." He withdrew his hands and retrieved the map. "I think we are headed to Holyhead, off Anglesey Isle. . . . See here, those breaks between the land? Not rivers, but sea inlets. Your grandfather was an apothecary from Holyhead, according to the merchant who knew him. And it is west."

"But so far north. We will be traveling farther than all the

distance from Holywell to Llansteffan," she said, thinking of
the long, arduous journey as well as her growing belly. They
had agreed to travel slowly, and, to make certain that no one
found them, they would do much of their traveling at night.
Bryanna knew it would be harder for her as the baby grew.
Dispirited, she said, " 'Twill take us nearly until the baby's
birth, or maybe thereafter."

"We could go to Calon. 'Tis closer. Then after the baby's
birth, once you are healed and the child is weaned, we can
leave him with your sister and continue. Or bring him with
us."

"Or her," she reminded him, and he grinned.

"Or *her*. Another little red-haired sorceress who will beguile me."

"Remember that when she is crying at night and I am
cranky from lack of sleep."

He laughed. "So tell me again: how is it you found this last
stone?"

She'd told him the story in bits and pieces as they'd ridden,
but now she explained about the dagger thrumming in her fingers and the day turning to night as it indicated the rock that
was to be removed.

"This power the dagger has, it would have been useful in
Holywell," he said. "We could have saved much time."

"It didn't work then," she said. "I'm sure of it."

"So why does it thrum in your hand now?"

"Because it's become more powerful, I suppose."

"Well, let's just hope it helps us locate the next gemstone."
He glanced to the window. "We should leave. 'Twill soon be
dark."

Her stomach growled. "I think we need to eat first."

"Aye." His gray eyes twinkled. "The lass appears to be
hungry."

The gatehouse was silent.

Outside in the bailey the sounds of the keep filtered in with
the warm summer breeze: wheels creaking, axes chopping

wood, looms clacking, chickens clucking, and people talking. But inside, silence yawned. The men—those awaiting duty and the dirty soldiers who had returned from their mission—stood facing Deverill, defiance in the sets of their chins, defeat in their eyes.

"So!" the Baron of Agendor said, barely able to keep his rage in check as he scowled at his men. "You have been gone for nearly six months and yet you come back here empty-handed, with no prisoner and no horse? Is this what you're telling me?"

One man coughed.

Another looked away.

But Aaron, much thinner than when he left upon his mission, dared stare the baron straight in the eye. "'Twas a long journey, m'lord," he said, and again the silence was deafening.

"A *long* journey?" Deverill repeated, lifting a hand in disbelief. "You were only in Wales—is that not correct? Can that be so long?"

"Aye."

Deverill's nostrils flared. He clasped his hand behind his back to keep from clenching his fists and driving them into a wall, the table, or one of his men's faces. "Now the Crusades . . . they were long journeys—thousands of miles longer than your travels—and yet the men who went to fight with King Richard *found* their enemies. They located the Saracens. They did not come back with the Lionheart empty-handed and complaining of the length of the journey."

"'Tis not the same."

"You were assigned a mission. You failed. 'Tis that simple." He had no time for this, no patience for more pathetic excuses.

Aaron glared at him. "Forgive me, m'lord," he said without much contrition, "but I think we, and aye, you, may have been duped."

"Duped?" Deverill repeated, and felt that same worrisome sensation he had earlier, when he'd first met with Hallyd.

"Aye," Aaron asserted, though no others joined him. "I

think all of us here at Agendor have been lied to, mayhap manipulated."

"How?" Deverill waited in the warm room for the man to explain himself.

"Lord Hallyd and his men, m'lord," the captain of the guard muttered.

Frustration crawling through him, Deverill nodded to the one-eared man. "Go on."

"We had them, m'lord, at Llansteffan nearly three months past," Aaron said angrily, extending his gloved hand. "We had them right there." He closed his fist. "But they slipped through our fingers."

Deverill couldn't believe his ears. "What do you mean you had them and you lost them?"

The angry soldier scratched at his mangled ear. "We followed them as best we could, but we were slowed by injuries." He glanced to one side. "Badden, he was attacked by a wolf just as we tried to capture the murderer and his woman, that red-haired witch. I think she called up the devil, she did, and this beast of monstrous size came out of nowhere, snarling and growling and snapping. Wounded one of the horses and took Badden down. Nearly ripped off his leg and then . . . well, he didn't recover." His face had flushed with color as he shook his head. "His leg near rotted off. 'Twas horrible. A physician at Llansteffan wanted to take the leg. 'Twas too gnarled. Should have been cut off, but Badden, he wouldn't have it."

"So this is why you were duped?"

"Nay, nay," Aaron said angrily. "We were duped by the soldier from Chwarel who rode with us. Edwynn, his name is."

"Nay, Edwynn is a mercenary," one of the other soldiers said. "He's after your reward, m'lord."

"What of him?" Deverill asked.

" 'Twas as if he didn't want the two captured."

"What?"

"I know it sounds odd, and he's a good tracker. Helped us locate Gavyn and the woman at Llansteffan, but he held back on their capture. Allowed a merchant's cart to block our way. And then in the forest, while Badden and I were fighting the bloody wolf, this Edwynn let Gavyn and the sorceress escape."

"What?"

"I'm tellin' ya true. He let them go. Oh, he took off after them, he did, but lost them. Later, after we put old Badden to rest, we searched for the trail again and within two weeks, we found it, though by that time they were far ahead of us." Aaron spat through the open door. "'Tis vexing." He shoved his hair from his eyes and frowned. "'Twas as if Edwynn wanted to keep track of the traitors, aye. He followed them. But when it came to actually capturing them, 'twas almost as if he thwarted us. I don't think he called up the wolf. Nay, I won't lay that at his feet, but he damned well let them escape. And Badden's blood is on his hands as surely as if he'd run him through himself." He spat again, as if he couldn't get a bad taste out of his mouth. "Hallyd's men were just as bad, holding back. 'Tis true, m'lord, they let the bastard escape."

Deverill's patience had run thin. "Why would that be?" he asked, but felt a suspicion that had been with him ever since he'd spoken with the snake Hallyd, who had told him about a missing dagger. Deverill hadn't trusted Hallyd in the first place, and there had been gaps in the story. At the time, as Deverill had sat drinking the man's wine, trying not to stare at his odd eyes, he'd thought that something was amiss.

Now, months later, it seemed to have come back to haunt him.

He frowned at his men. If there was anything he hated worse than a traitor, it was someone who tried to double-cross him. Damn it all! He would have to do this himself.

"Get my horse, and I'll need my sword," he told a page. "Five of you"—he pointed to the men he wanted—"ride with me. And bring the spy." Cael would turn for the right amount of silver and the promise that his life would be spared.

And so, the spy would fare better than the Lord of Chwarel.

Deverill would see to that himself.

*   *   *

As Bryanna's belly grew, so did her fears. The summer months came and went with warm breezes, butterflies, flowers and dry grass. The shade of the forest became welcome respite from the heat of the day, and the streams that cut through the hillsides ran more slowly.

Sleep eluded her, and when she did finally fall into exhausted slumber, her dreams were peppered with images of a dark castle with mazelike corridors. She combed those twisted halls in search of a baby whose cries echoed in the vacant vault. No matter how many doors she opened, Bryanna couldn't find the babe. Panic-stricken, she ran faster and faster, through the intricate labyrinth, opening doors and seeing only darkness until she came to the very last closed door at the end of the long hall. It took her forever to reach it, as her feet seemed to be stuck in quicksand and the door seemed to move farther away as she approached.

When at last she reached it, the door was locked. She grabbed for her key ring but found she had hundreds of keys to choose from. Which one would unlock the door? As she frantically fumbled with the keys, the baby wailed helplessly. "I'm coming, I'm coming," she cried. Finally, the lock sprang open. The door swung free and she stepped inside, only to fall into a black abyss, a chasm that she knew led straight to the underworld. By opening the door she had just let all the creatures of Samhain loose on the world.

"Oh, by the Fates," she whispered, waking in the forest at dawn. Gavyn was snuggled close to her and the summer sun was streaking the sky in brilliant tones of pink and orange. She touched her swollen belly, felt the movement within, and drew in a long, shaky breath.

"'Twas only a dream," she said, but pushed herself upright.

She walked into the forest to relieve her forever full bladder, then washed her face in the stream. As she did, the water that had been moving in a lazy current began to swirl, slowly at first, a tiny eddy in the stream, then faster and faster. It spun into a vortex, the center of a swirling funnel, and within the very center she saw an image of two giant rocks rising from the ground. Between them, on a seamless field of grass, she saw the beginning of a crack. Small at first, then larger, as if the very earth were rending. With a horrible, shuddering groan there appeared a dark abyss, not unlike the one in her dream . . . and then the vision 'twas gone. The water no longer eddied and swirled, but resumed its lazy path through the exposed roots.

"Isa?" she whispered, for it had been months since the dead woman had contacted her. Not since Llansteffan had she heard the nursemaid's voice. "Isa, can you hear me?"

The woods remained silent.

While Gavyn slept, she retrieved her herbs and amulets and the Sacred Dagger, still missing a gem. Closing her eyes, she concentrated and thought of all the spells she'd learned, all that Isa had taught her. She pinched off some dried marjoram and ivy leaves for protection and healing, then quietly she cast her spell for an easy birth, for the safety of her child, for wisdom and protection in the coming weeks.

Soon her child would be born.

What then?

Would her babe be safe, or would the baby be in jeopardy as she feared?

The words of the prophecy played through her head. . . . "A ruler of all men, all beasts, all beings . . ." The Chosen One would have the ability to harness magnificent, vast power. But, oh, how she wished this child inside her were not destined to be the greatest leader the land had ever known.

Just a baby. Please, just allow him to be mine alone, not a great savior to be shared with the world, defender of all that is right and good from the demons of the Otherworld.

"Please, Morrigu," she murmured, her hands sinking into the moist earth along the bank of the stream. "Protect my child."

Opening her eyes, she noticed yellow eyes peering back at her. Across the stream, lapping at the water's edge, was the wolf. But the reflection flickering on the water's surface did not mirror the creature.

Instead, Bryanna saw the image of a woman with pale skin and red hair so like her own. 'Twas the woman of her dreams, seen charging up the steep cliff on horseback, though now her face was calm and full of peace. Where the wolf had a ruffle of black fur around her neck, the woman was marked with a necklace of small red welts, not unlike the bruises Bryanna had suffered from her nightmare.

The marks from Hallyd's rosary.

Bryanna gasped as the woman's emerald-green eyes met hers in the wavering reflection.

Kambria.

The wolf *was* a guardian angel of sorts.

The spirit of her true mother.

Morwenna's child came at dawn, when the apples were beginning to show streaks of red and the hay had been cut and the summer breezes were cooling with the nightfall. The labor took hours and she was exhausted, sweat-stained, and feeling as if she were being cleaved in half when she finally heard her daughter's lusty wail and the midwife brought the babe to her breast.

"Lenore," Morwenna sighed as she heard a cock crow thrice and felt the tiny lips upon her nipple, "a daughter." 'Twas a blessing, she thought, for there would be more babes, but this one, her first, would be closest to her until the others came, and their time would be special. "I shall teach you how to run a keep, and shoot an arrow, and ride like the wind, and plant a garden." She sent up a prayer for her new child's health as the midwife took the baby to a nearby pallet to clean and swaddle her. Meanwhile Frynne, the freckle-faced serving girl, quickly changed the sheets and helped Morwenna wash. Only then would Morwenna allow her husband to see his daughter.

She heard him in the corridor, speaking to a guard, no doubt anxious and worried.

Finally, just as Frynne was finishing with the plaits on Morwenna's hair, the Lord of Calon muttered loudly enough for his wife to hear, "Oh, for the love of God," then shouldered open the door. He burst inside, then stood stock-still at the side of the bed, staring down at his infant.

"'Tis a girl, m'lord," the midwife said, "and a beauty she is."

"Like her mother." He came to the bed and watched in wonder as the baby suckled hungrily at his wife's breast. One large hand reached out and he tenderly touched the crown of black curls.

His gaze found Morwenna's and, just for a second, his blue eyes shone. "She's a miracle," he said, his voice husky.

"I've named her Lenore. After my mother. Unless you have another name you would—"

"Lenore is perfect," he said with a smile. "As is she."

He kissed the child's crown, then did the same to his wife.

"Oh, nay," Morwenna said. Reaching up, she grabbed the laces of his tunic and pulled his head down to hers. She pressed her lips to his and felt a sizzle of desire pass from her body to his. He moaned and she felt her tired body respond. Finally, she let go of the laces and pulled her head away. "None of those little innocent kisses for me, husband." She saw one side of his mouth lift in surprise. "I will not be treated ever, do you hear me, not ever like the dutiful wife on whom you bestow a quick kiss and be off and about your duties. If you're going to kiss me, m'lord, then you damned well better mean it."

"So that's the way it is?" he said with a lift of one dark eyebrow.

"That's the way it is."

"Well, then, so be it." And he kissed his wife as if he'd never stop. Only when his newborn let out a little cry did he lift his head. "Aye, wife," he said, pressing another soft kiss to his daughter's curls. "That is the way 'twill be."

CHAPTER TWENTY-SIX

The map seemed useless again. And Isa, damn her already dead soul, had remained mute. Though the journey west had taken most of the summer, as Gavyn and Bryanna no longer had a packhorse and spent much of the time in hiding, they had reached the western shore, where they'd found a farmer who promised to look after the horses, and a fisherman who was willing to ferry them across to Anglesey Isle.

Over Gavyn's protests, Bryanna insisted they keep going. Aye, her back hurt, aye, her ankles tended to swell, and aye, if she had her choice she would not be out searching for a bloody ruby on a small island surrounded by the sea. But Bryanna felt she had no choice. As the days had passed she was more certain than ever that she was not only piecing together the Sacred Dagger but somehow saving the life of her child.

Two days later, as they voyaged on yet another boat to Holy Island, the fishing captain eyed Bryanna with concern. "Ye won't be havin' that baby right here on me deck, now, will ye?"

"I'll try not." She felt awkward and queasy as the boat crossed the wide stretch of water, where sunlight glinted and shifted upon the surface.

She was large now, due to give birth soon, with autumn now upon them.

The pilot eyed her widening girth. "If ye need a midwife,

my sister, there in Holyhead, she's delivered more than her share of babes, including my own six. Her name is Ivey, and she's married to the innkeeper at Holyhead."

"If I need one, I'll ask for her."

The boatman pulled a face. "As I said, I've got six of me own. Ye'll be needin' her and soon."

Bryanna tried not to bristle, but the man bothered her with his gap-toothed grin and his knowing expression.

"Yeah, well, you tell her Morley, he brought you over to the island, now, will ya?"

"We will," Gavyn cut in, as if he read Bryanna's rising irritation and was afraid that she might offend the man. "So, Morley," he said, "did you know a man named Waylynn? An apothecary."

"'Course I did. Anyone who lived here twenty years back knew him. Worked with me sister he did. Why?"

"A relative," Gavyn said.

"Well, his old shop is still where he left it—in ruin it is. Shame about him, drownin' an' all." Morley sniffed and ran a sleeve under his nose. "Don't know what he was thinkin', swimmin' in that river so far from home. Though I did hear a rumor that he was robbed and left for dead. Nigh seventeen years ago, that was."

Bryanna suspected that her grandfather had not been robbed at all. The men who tracked him down were more likely Hallyd and his cronies, searching for the stones Kambria had given him to hide. Like Kambria, Waylynn had died protecting the dagger.

Morley docked the boat and Gavyn, with their packs slung over his shoulders, helped Bryanna ashore.

Morley gave them directions to his brother-in-law's inn. "It's but a short walk," he assured them.

At the clean little inn, the woman who greeted them looked like the feminine version of the scrawny man who had rowed them to Holy Island. She introduced herself as Ivey.

"Well, look at you," she said, beaming. "Did you come

here for the birth?" Ivey looked from Gavyn to Bryanna and
back again.

"We've been on a long journey," Gavyn said, "and we need
a room."

The midwife nodded. "But the babe is due soon."

"Yes," Bryanna said. "Soon." She'd thought about finding
a midwife often enough but had never known where she
would be when she was ready to give birth.

"I would be glad to help you. I've delivered dozens of little ones. In fact, just about any child you see in the town
who's less than twelve, I probably helped bring 'im into the
world."

"Then I'll call for you," Bryanna said, "if the babe decides
to come." The woman seemed friendly enough, and it was
comforting to think that someone so experienced at bringing
babies into the world was nearby.

"Now, go on up to the room. You rest up and I'll bring you
something to eat."

Bryanna took Ivey's advice, climbing the stairs, finding
their room, and, though it was only late afternoon, falling onto
the bed with a soft straw mattress and thick down pillows. She
struggled out of her clothes and fell into a deep sleep. She
didn't awaken when the food was brought up, didn't want to
even think about the damned ruby. In fact, she didn't raise her
head until the following morning.

When she finally awoke, Gavyn was nowhere to be found.
The impression of his body remained upon the cold mattress.
A platter of leftover cheese, dark bread, an apple, and a piece
of salted fish were placed upon a small rough-hewn table. Her
stomach grumbled with hunger.

She sat up in the bed and felt a crick in her neck, then
stretched. Ungainly, she climbed out of bed and ignored the
pain in her lower back. She felt cranky and, despite all
the sleep, still sluggish. Gavyn had probably been right. She
should have gone to Calon to have this child and, yes, gotten married by the priest who resided there. She laughed at
the thought. She was on a quest, thinking she might be the

daughter of a sorceress. . . . She doubted a priest would bless her marriage.

Gavyn was adamant on the subject, swearing he loved her, that he wanted to marry her, though, of course, they both knew the true reason was the child.

Her head pounded; she couldn't think of this today. She ate a little of the cheese and a bite of bread, then pulled out the map. As she ate, she studied each section of deerskin, the symbols upon it, the way it connected to the others. With her dagger in hand, she prayed, asking Isa to come to her, asking the Great Mother to bless her, but the knife remained cold and lifeless in her hands. Again, she tried. Again she failed.

Oh, 'twas useless.

And where was Gavyn? She washed her face and adjusted her hair and clothes. She was about to go searching for him when he arrived, his face ruddy, as if he'd been on a brisk walk by the sea.

"I found Waylynn's hut," he said without preamble, "or what's left of it." He pointed to a spot on the map. "Right there. The place has a view of this ancient fort, Caer Gybi."

"Good." Ignoring a sharp twinge of pain in her lower back, she gathered up the map and dagger, stuffed them both in her pouch, and started for the door. "Show me."

"You're certain they were going to the island?" Carrick of Wybren asked the farmer, a man as thin as his own scarecrow. He scratched at the earth with his rake while his family—two older boys, a toddler, and the farmer's wife—worked in the garden behind him.

"Aye, that they did. Said they'd be back within the month and asked me if I could board these two here." He hitched his chin toward the horses grazing in a field nearby: a black destrier with dirty gray markings, and a sleek white mare with dark mane and tail. Bryanna's horse, that much the mercenary recognized.

"And you let the animals graze in the lord's field?"

"I pays me taxes, I do. I got me no fight with the baron.

You ask anyone if Farmer Reece pays his bodel silver, chiminage, agistment and wood-penny. Fodder corn, too. And when they lay me bones in the ground, aye, my wife, Ellynna there, she'll pay heriot, and give the lord me best animal. So Baron Laython, he's got no argument with me." The farmer propped his rake into the dusty soil, then swatted at a bee as he slid a glance at the two horses. "So what is it ye want? I canna sell the animals. I promised the man I'd look after them."

"Then would you watch mine as well?" Carrick asked.

Beneath the stubble on his narrow chin, the farmer's grin widened. "For the right price."

"I'll pay you what the others paid, and when I'm back, we'll see. Mayhap you'll end up with a new animal."

The farmer frowned, thoughts spinning in his head. "I'm an honest man, I am, and God-fearin'. We tithe, stay within the law—I pride myself so."

"I understand, but it could be that one of those horses, the big one there, is stolen, from a lord no less."

"Saints be," the farmer whispered.

"And the man who stole him has a price upon his head. Accused of killing a sheriff. If I locate this murdering criminal and find that indeed this is the man Lord Deverill seeks and bring him back to justice, there will be a reward in it for all of us."

"And what of his woman? She's heavy with child, she is." The farmer hazarded a glance at his own wife, pregnant herself, stripping dried vegetation from her garden.

"Worry not. I know the woman as well as her family," Carrick said, his jaw growing tight as he thought of Morwenna and the man she'd married, the brother he'd betrayed. Would all these days and nights spent riding and gathering clues in inns amount to anything? Any chance of mending fences? "The woman and her child will be cared for."

Leaning on his rake and squinting into the hot sun, Farmer Reece wiped the sweat from his brow. "When you return, we'll see about all this. In the meantime, aye, I'll tend to your horse, but you must pay me up front."

"Of course." Carrick paid the agreed-upon price, then offered up another coin. "Do not release my animal to anyone else who might arrive. The horse is mine, bought and paid for." He saw the woman looking over at them and she quickly turned away and made the sign of the cross over her chest.

Farmer Reece saw the movement as well and looked up to the sky, as clear and blue as the sea surrounding the Isle of Anglesey. "Me wife, she 'feels' things. And this mornin', one of my sons, the eldest, Thomas there, he swore he saw a wolf swimmin' across the channel just at dawn." The farmer snorted and spit. "A wolf, swimmin'?" He shook his head and picked up his rake again. "Women," he said, as if any man would understand his comment. "And pregnant women, wanting to eat such odd things, havin' 'feelings' and believing a lying boy who had better be confessing his sins to the priest."

A thin-faced boy with the beginnings of a beard paused beside a row of corn, his hoe suspended as he listened for a moment, then hung his head in shame and hacked at the ground.

"Thomas there, he's not backin' down on the lie," the farmer explained. "So maybe he saw himself a seal and *thought* it was a wolf. Who knows? The lad's got a good imagination, that he does. I only hope he's not givin' up his soul to the devil." He shot his older son a glance and the boy merely set his jaw in defiance and continued his task.

"Sure, I'll look after yer horse," the farmer said, squaring his cap upon his head, then taking the reins from the mercenary's hands. "And I'll see to the saddle and bridle, too. Thomas, he can oil the leather. It'll all be here when ye return."

Cael, the spy, turned easily. For a few pieces of silver and gold and a guarantee of his freedom, he gladly spilled more than enough information. As they rode west nearing the coast, the little runt of a spy nearly talked Deverill's ear off. The salty smell of the sea was in the air as the weasely man spoke of odd, magickal things, the same Sacred Dagger and stones Hallyd had mentioned. He also spilled rumors of a locked room in Hallyd's keep where a witch as thin as vapor resided. And of Hallyd's curse and obsession with the daughter of a woman he'd killed.

" 'Tis true, I'm tellin' ye," Cael insisted, riding next to the lord and puffing out his chest with his newfound stature. "I knew one of the men who was with Hallyd that day, when he was but a priest. He chased the witch Kambria through the mountains, upon a ridge in winter. When he finally caught her, she cast a spell that blinded him, caused his eyes to take on the shape of an owl's, banished him into being a creature of the night."

Part of the story was true, Deverill knew. He'd seen Hallyd's face himself, the odd eyes. And he'd seen the obsession with Bryanna, as well.

"Why did she not just cast a spell upon him and kill him?"

"Ah, well, she didn't have the Sacred Dagger with her now, did she? Her power wasn't as strong as it could have been. She had just given birth to her child and hidden the babe, then dissembled the dagger and had those who believed in her scatter the jewels. 'Tis said she'd drawn a map and cut it into pieces, one piece hidden with each of the stones."

"Then she hid the map."

"Or had a trusted individual hide each piece. That's why Waylynn, the apothecary, was in Llansteffan."

"Hiding a piece of the map."

Cael nodded, his head bobbing on his weedy neck. "Only a witch with powers as great as Kambria's own would be able to piece the dagger together again, and only after she had found each of the missing jewels and affixed them to the dagger."

Deverill found himself intrigued by the weaselly man's story of the magickal dagger. His pulse quickened at the thought of getting his hands on such a treasure. Not to mention the added satisfaction to be gained at besting Lord Hallyd, who obviously knew of the dagger's value and sought to snatch it up behind Deverill's back. The owl-eyed swindler! Deverill would take great personal delight in wresting the dagger out from under him.

But was the spy reliable?

"How do you know all this?" Deverill asked reluctantly, for the little man loved to hear himself talk. Thank the gods they were nearly at the coast, the seabirds circling overhead attesting to their close proximity.

Though Deverill questioned him, he believed the man, for the spy knew that his tales would earn him more than money—his very life hung in the balance, as well.

"I know it because I listen," Cael bragged.

"You listen at keyholes?"

"When I have to. Not only to what a man says, but what a man is not saying, what he doesn't want you to hear. That's the truth of it." His face clouded up a bit and his big eyes narrowed, as if he didn't know if he should continue.

"What is it?" Deverill prodded.

"'Tis something I shouldn't talk about."

Though Deverill questioned him, hadn't thought there was any subject that was taboo for a man so in love with the sound of his own voice. "Tell me," Deverill insisted. "We have a deal, do we not?"

A bead of sweat rolled down the spy's temple and, for the first time since Deverill had met him, fear shone on the little man's face.

"All was not as it seemed in Chwarel," he admitted.

This was no surprise. The place had an aura of gloom and death to it. "You mean, aside from the talk of sacred daggers and hidden maps and dark obsessions?"

"Aye. . . . You know, 'tis my talent to hear and see things others do not."

"Of course." *The man was a spy, for God's sake*, Deverill thought as he shifted in his saddle and felt the heat of the day sink into his bones. How long had they been riding west?

"Well, at a keyhole I was, as you said, in the deepest part of Chwarel, where no one goes. No guards dare roam there, no one except Lord Hallyd. He goes there often, sometimes carrying a mazer of goat or pig's blood. So I follows him one night, I do, and I look through the damned keyhole, but I see nothing. 'Tis dark on the other side, well, you know, because the baron, he likes it dark. But I hear a voice. His voice."

"Just his?"

"Aye."

"So? Mayhap he goes down there to pray," Deverill said, but he felt a frisson of fear slide down his spine, despite the heat. He glanced ahead to the vast blue sky, where seagulls wheeled over the road leading toward the sea.

"Oh, he prays and he talks, but no one's there. I stole his keys once and went into the chamber when he was sleeping and there was nothing inside. 'Twas empty and dark and smelled of rot. And one time when I followed him, he forgot to close the door fully behind him. I slipped the door open and peered in to find him raving like a madman. Talked to someone—he called her Vannora. He brought her a cup and he set it on a table, but there was no table."

"So it fell to the floor, spilling the blood?"

"Nay." Cael shook his head and swallowed hard. "It sat in the air it did, as if it were upon a table I couldn't see. He talked to this Vannora and he was vexed with her, and I felt a coldness in my soul like none other. I slid out the door as quietly as I could, because though I think Lord Hallyd, he did not hear me, I swear as God is my witness that the spirit within did."

"Vannora?"

"Yea. I felt her eyes burn through me, but, as I said, 'twas not from heat, but as if knives of ice had been stabbed through my very soul." He looked up at Deverill on his taller steed and genuine fear shone in the man's eyes. "I know not who she is, or what she is, but she is not of this world, m'lord, and I swear she never has been."

"Or Hallyd is mad," Deverill said, trying to make some sense of it all as he looked ahead to a spot in the road where a crow was tearing apart the innards of a dead rodent. Spying the horsemen, the crow cawed in irritation and flapped away, its shining black wings a dark spot in the clear sky.

"Aye, Hallyd is no longer sane, 'tis true."

Deverill looked down at the spy again.

The little man made the sign of the cross over his chest. "But 'tis not just his madness, nor the curse of a witch that is a part of this. Nay, Lord Deverill, 'tis something from the very depths of hell, his demon inheritance. Pure and cold. Evil at its core."

"'Tis time," Vannora said from within the circle at her altar. Candles burned low, the scent of fragrant herbs filled the chamber, and mist rose from the cauldron upon her altar. No amount of smoke or incense could disguise the hungry aura that shimmered around Vannora. The dank air Hallyd breathed was rife with wickedness. "Step into the circle."

She was young again, youth and vitality thrumming through her. Even her eyes seemed clearer, offering a view of gold orbs that had at one time, he suspected, been heart-stopping. In this guise she was a beautiful woman. "Tarry not. The baby is coming. The final stone is about to be found."

"Where is she?" Hallyd asked.

"Far to the west."

"How far?"

"Too far to ride," she said, and he felt a niggle of dread. "Near the western sea. Step closer. . . . Hurry!"

He glared at her, his muscles tense. "Near the sea?" he repeated. "'Tis miles from here, a week's journey, at least." Sudden fury boiled through his blood. "I should have been with her when she found the stone. I should be there when the child is born."

"What care you for the babe?" she demanded. "You don't want a child. You only wanted to rut with Kambria's daughter, to rape her, to show her your power, to get back at the woman who blinded and cursed you." She jabbed a long finger at her own chest. "*I* was the one who told you to see that she was pregnant. *I* was the one who arranged your mating.

You want the curse lifted. You want the dagger. You want its power. You want to bed the woman until she is gasping for her last breath. But the child, he is mine."

He felt tricked.

Betrayed.

The back of his scalp prickled with dread.

"Nay, Vannora. You lied to me. Used me."

He witnessed a flare of defiance in her golden irises. A fury as wild as a raging storm.

"Who used whom?" she snarled, her voice rising in the cavelike chamber. "Listen, Hallyd, I have done my part. Your curse will be lifted. You will see again, and you will rule all of Wales with the dagger. But the babe is mine. Now"—she grabbed his hands with her own surprisingly strong fingers—"step into the circle and we will claim what is rightfully ours."

Swallowing back his denials, he forced himself to take one step forward, his boots touching the circle drawn upon the stones. "What is it, Vannora? What is it you need to claim?"

"You don't know?" she asked, her lips pulling back to show beautiful white teeth. "After all these years?"

"Why do you need the Chosen One?" Nervously, he took another step forward. "Tell me."

"I want to go back."

"Back where?" he asked, though a part of him didn't want to know.

She tugged on his hands and stared deep into his eyes. "Come!"

"But you . . ." Hallyd stepped into the circle completely. "Where are you going?"

"I am going home to the Otherworld." She reached for a handful of crushed herbs. "The child will ensure my passage."

"But on Samhain spirits move freely from one world to the other."

"Not spirits who have erred," she said, hissing with annoyance. "'Tis my fault the dagger slipped into this world. To return there without the babe would be a fate worse than the roiling pits in Hades. But I can set it all aright by bringing the babe back to the Otherworld. He will be raised among demon spirits, taught the ways of the dark arts."

"How do you know he is the one?" he asked as her fingers swirled the mist over the cauldron.

"The prophecy. Sired by Darkness, born of Light . . . he will be the child of an amoral mortal and a moral sorceress. Good and evil, blended together."

He felt beads of sweat on his brow. Her ministrations set his nerves on edge. "Wasn't Kambria born of mortal man and sorceress?"

"So many questions now, when it is time to go through the passage!" Vannora whirled on him, furious. "Think of the prophecy. Kambria's father was not depraved like you, not willing to go to the murderous lengths that thrill your soul. Waylynn would not have killed innocents like Gleda or Liam or Kambria, as you have. But then, you must know that, as he died at your hands."

Hallyd felt a new surge of confidence, feeling his plans and desires on the verge of fruition. His eyes were healed. He had sired the Chosen One. The sorceress would soon be his to defile and punish for pleasure. And the dagger . . . he could almost feel its power swelling his stature.

"Come, now," Vannora said firmly, " 'tis time. Samhaim, the day of the child's birth, is upon us."

Bryanna stared at the interior of what had once been her grandfather's hut. Situated near an old Roman fort, there was little left of the building. The roof had sagged and rotted through, the walls were falling down, and the circle of stones where he'd once built fires had scattered so that they no longer formed a ring. Sunlight streamed through the cracks and gaps in the walls.

So this was where he had lived and worked. Her grandfather, a man who had lost his life in the cold waters of the River Towy.

Now they were all dead, the brother and two sisters. Gleda and Isa had died within months of each other.

Isa, please come to me.

"Let's see if this dagger works," Gavyn suggested, unwrapping the knife and handing it to her.

Her fingers circled the hilt with its three winking stones. Refusing to think of the pain in her back, she squatted down and drew a rune in the dust of the floor, scattered her herbs and closed her eyes. Her chant to the Mother Goddess was soft as she turned slowly in the small space, the knife cold and lifeless in her hand.

Increasing her prayers, she felt the tiniest of movements, a vibration, when she pointed toward the sea. She moved in that direction and the dagger seemed to hum.

"Is it working?" Gavyn asked curiously.

But his words faded to the back of her mind as she took a step toward the briny scent of the sea. The words of the old riddle of the stones filled her head.

> *An opal for the northern point,*
> *An emerald for the east,*
> *A topaz for the southern tip,*
> *A ruby for the west.*

Isa's voice or her own? She knew not. But as she moved toward the western wall the air in the hut darkened into sudden night and the dagger suddenly slipped from her fingers and fell. She gasped as it tumbled to the floor, where it drove into the ground, the blade disappearing in the hard-packed dirt floor.

Gavyn watched in wonder as she knelt at the spot and wiggled the dagger to and fro, loosening the earth in the darkness, removing dirt until the blade hit something. Digging with her fingertips, she exposed a round, narrow disk—the top of a vial.

Gavyn used the dagger to pry the vial out of its grave and lift the pottery carefully out of the ground. "The stone is stuck inside," he said, shaking the vial.

With gritted teeth, Bryanna swung the dagger and smashed the vial.

The little bottle shattered, shards raining to the ground. A twisted piece of doeskin bound with a leather lace fell to the dirt floor. Heart in her throat, Bryanna untied the string and unfurled the final piece of the map to reveal a bloodred ruby glittering against the deer hide.

With trembling fingers, she grasped the stone and dropped it into the last hole on the knife's handle.

The ruby glowed warm, sending heat through the hilt of the dagger. It penetrated Bryanna's hand and thrummed down her arm.

Immediately she sensed the uncanny stillness, the quiet of eternal rest. In her mind's eye she saw a tomb, a private place of worship, and there, inside, was safety.

She lowered the knife.

"I know where we must go," she said to Gavyn and realized that the night had not existed for him. The vision was hers alone.

"Where?" he asked.

But before she could answer, the first pain of labor brought her to her knees.

CHAPTER TWENTY-SEVEN

Gavyn carried Bryanna back to the inn and barked an order to the boy stacking firewood near the grate. "Send Ivey to our room," he said to the skinny boy as Bryanna felt another wave of pain sweep through her. Clenching her teeth, she clung to Gavyn and fought the urge to scream.

Help me, Isa, she thought as the pain subsided and she could breathe again.

He carried her up the stairs and settled her into the bed. Nothing she'd ever been through before had prepared Bryanna for labor and childbirth, the pain that came in huge, intense waves. Ivey came and sat with her, tending to her with warm, wet cloths and watching the baby's progress.

"He's turned," she said at one point, hours into the labor, while Bryanna gasped, covered in sweat, her hair damp ringlets. "'Twill be faster now."

Spent, Bryanna hadn't responded, but just waited for the next sharp pain. When it came she breathed as the older woman had instructed. Although Bryanna knew this torment would be over eventually and she would have a baby, she had trouble seeing beyond the pain. Gavyn had been pushed outside the door, though every once in a while popped his head into the room, only to be smartly reprimanded by Ivey. "Your part's done," she told him at one point. "Let your wife do hers."

Wife, Brianna thought miserably, her hands twisting in the bedsheet. *Not yet.*

The sun went down and Bryanna, soaked in sweat, labored on. Only when it was near morning did she feel a shift, and the older woman instructed her how to push. *Gladly,* Bryanna thought, letting nature take over.

And then he was born.

After all that work, after several hard pushes, Truett arrived, lifting her heart with his lusty cry and a hungry appetite. Despite her pain and all the effort, Bryanna was instantly charmed by this perfect little baby, who seemed as exhausted as she was and happy to lie upon her breast.

"Welcome, little one," she whispered, cradling him close. "I'm so glad you are finally here." She kissed his tiny head and felt near tears. Tired to her bones, her emotions a jumble, she thought that of all the miracles she'd seen lately, none compared to this little boy.

Ivey had proven to be an adept midwife. She managed to clean Bryanna a bit and change the sheets while Bryanna held her new little infant.

"We've been waiting for this one for a long time, we have," Ivey said, smiling down at the baby.

Bryanna, surprised, didn't think she'd heard correctly. "*We've* been waiting?" she said, suspiciously. "Who is *we*?"

"Those to whom the child rightfully belongs," she replied with a kind smile. "Those who believe."

"Believe in what?" But she knew. Bryanna's heart, which had been so light, now felt heavy, sodden with dread. She pulled her child closer to her breast.

"In the ways of the old ones. 'Tis Samhain this night, you know. Starting at dusk. And it was foretold that he would come on the very day before the Samhain, with the light of a full moon."

Ivey whispered an ancient chant, then pressed her fingertips to her forehead to recite the prophecy. "Sired by Darkness. Born of Light. Protected by the Sacred Dagger. A ruler of all men, all beasts, all beings. It is he who shall be born on the Eve of Samhain."

Bryanna felt as if she were tumbling into a bottomless chasm. She would not lose her child. Would not!

"Why are you waiting for him?" she asked, her voice hoarse with fear.

The woman's face wrinkled a bit. "Do you not know? You who are the sorceress?"

"He's my child." Bryanna inched backward on the bed, clutching the boy as if he might disappear.

"Aye, but you cannot alter his destiny, that he will be the leader of those who believe in the gods and goddesses—"

"What are you talking about? Leader? Gods and goddesses. Nay," she said. "This is but a little boy child. A normal, innocent babe. Do not attach any destiny to him." But in her heart, she knew the hated truth. Had she not realized that the baby's birth was tied to her quest? Had not Isa told her she had to save the child? Had she not known the very child Isa mentioned was her own? Fear struck deep in her heart.

Her throat went dry as desert sand. "This is *my* child," she said, and her arms wound around her baby a little tighter. "Do you hear me? Mine and Cain's. He is ours and ours alone."

"Of course he is," Ivey agreed amiably, but the glimmer in her gaze unnerved Bryanna.

Oh, dear God. Anxiously she licked her lips and told herself to calm down. Mayhap she was just overwrought with the birth, or perhaps all of Isa's talk of saving the child had set her on edge. Or could it be that as a new mother she was already overprotective and bristly with anyone who showed any interest in her baby. But no matter how she tried to talk herself into being calm and resting, fear penetrated her heart.

"Where's Ga—Cain?"

"Outside the door."

"Let him in. Now."

"Of course." Ivey turned to the door, but paused, a serene smile on her face as she gazed at the downy baby. "He's flawless," she said, and her beatific smile was more frightening to

Bryanna than had she scowled. "He will rule well," she said, opening the door.

"He's not ruling anything."

Ivey cast one look over her shoulder, a look that said louder than words, *You'll see.*

Bryanna let out a horrified squeak.

"Finally!" Gavyn said striding in. "Does not a father have any rights to see—" He looked to the bed and all of the irritation left his voice. "By the gods."

" 'Tis a boy," Ivey said as she passed, then walked out of the room. The older woman hadn't congratulated Gavyn, hadn't told him *he* had a son. Nay, just " 'Tis a boy."

"And a fine one he is," Gavyn said, eyeing the baby's tiny body. A tuft of red curls sprouted on an otherwise bald head and large blue eyes stared up at the man who looked down on him. Bryanna felt pride swelling in her heart.

But it disappeared as the weight of everything Ivey had said reverberated through her brain. "We have to leave here."

Gavyn nodded, winking. " 'Tis beautiful, you are, Brynn," he said, joking. "We will, when you're fit to walk and ride."

She had no time for this! "Nay. Soon. Right now."

"Now?" he repeated. "You and the boy here, you need care. Time to rest and recover and . . ."

"I don't trust Ivey."

"Why not?" Gavyn was thunderstruck. "She tended to you, helped you with the birthing."

" 'Tis how she acts, what she says," Bryanna said, her voice rising frantically with her fear. "We . . . we have to leave." She was already climbing out of bed. "With Truett. Now."

"Truett?"

" 'Tis his name."

"Have I no say in this?"

"Nay. Right now, you don't. We'll speak of it later."

" 'You're serious about leaving?" Gavyn shook his head in bafflement as her feet touched the floor. "Whoa, Bryanna . . . slow down. You . . . the babe? Are you suddenly daft? No, I'll not risk it, not now. In a week, mayhap, when both you and the child are stronger."

She pinned him with her frightened gaze. "No, Gavyn, trust me. We have to leave and leave now."

Her child squalled and Bryanna took him to her breast again, leaning back on the bed. Oh, sweet little innocent thing. He suckled heartily and Gavyn stared, fascinated.

"I mean it," she said, managing to keep her voice down. "We must leave. Trust me."

"But—"

"Must I prove myself to you yet again?" she asked, moving her infant from one breast to the other. "Has not everything I said about the jewels and the map proved true?"

He nodded.

"And still you doubt me?"

Gavyn's expression turned from bewilderment to understanding. "You're right. If you say we should leave, then we shall, but it would be so much better if you could just wave that magick dagger of yours for the babe's safety."

"That's not the way it works—you know that. Just bring me the map." Her newborn nodded off, but she refused to let him go, even in his slumber. "And the dagger. Please."

"Now you should rest, for just a little while."

"Gavyn, do not argue," she insisted, frantic. She felt it, the swelling darkness, the pulsing terror that someone might steal or harm her child. It was near, an umbra that was chasing her, long clawlike fingers extended, ready to rip her child away.

Gavyn looked at her as if she really had gone mad, but he did as asked, unrolling the map. With his help, Bryanna inserted the new piece. The ragged swatch of deerskin fit perfectly into the remaining gap. While the baby slept, she used Gleda's needle to stitch that final piece in place. When she was finished, the map complete, she realized that the final shape was that of all Wales. The places they'd visited were clear now; the symbols, runes, and marks made some kind of sense now.

Across the middle of the map, where all the pieces connected, the hieroglyphic lettering she hadn't been able to read now became one single word: "Coelio."

"Coelio," she whispered, touching the etched letters with the tip of one finger. "Believe." She let the map drop onto her lap and picked up the Sacred Dagger.

Closing her eyes, she held the knife with both hands, her baby nestled between her arms. Slowly, over and over, she whispered the word, then chanted the riddle of the stones.

Coelio.
Believe.
An opal for the northern point,
An emerald for the east,
A topaz for the southern tip,
A ruby for the west.

And again. As the words spilled over her tongue, she felt a warmth invade her. Renewed energy generated by the bejeweled blade flowed quickly through her body, coursing through her veins. Exhaustion seeped away, replaced by a new vigor, a power she'd not felt before.

For a second, she heard Isa's voice as clearly as if the dead woman was standing next to the baby. *"Take the babe and run. Now. Trust no one. There is a demon after him, a dark spirit who will stop at nothing. The evil one needs the Chosen One in order to return to the Otherworld. You cannot let this happen, Bryanna. Go! Run!"*

"You knew this and you didn't tell me?" Bryanna charged. "All this time, you did not tell me?" Fury burst through her.

"The prophecy must be fulfilled."

"Damn the prophecy!" she cried, suddenly filled with a fear as black as all the underworld. "This is my child we're talking about. My baby!"

"Then save him," Isa ordered. *"Go now to the sacred place. Do not tarry. Save your child."*

"Isa . . . wait!" Bryanna cried, but the voice had died. Bryanna looked up at Gavyn and lowered the knife.

Throughout her ruminations, her baby had slept. "We're leaving," she whispered. "Our son's life depends upon it." She climbed out of the bed, and with one hand began stripping off the bedsheets. "Tear the linens."

"What?"

"Make a sling and blankets for our son. I'll have to carry him."

"Bryanna, this is mad. I don't think—"

"Isa just warned me, Gavyn! She said we have to leave. Not to mention that Ivey told me she has some sort of designs on Truett, thinking him cursed to lead a kingdom of sorcerers. Our child's life is in jeopardy." She handed the boy to his father, then finished tearing the sheets herself. As Gavyn held the babe, she crafted a sling in which he could be toted. Other pieces of the sheets would be used for Truett's swaddling.

Her body, though aching, was remarkably strong, filled with vigor. With purpose.

"What else did Isa tell you?" Gavyn asked as she wrapped her baby in a bundle.

"To save our baby, we must take him to the holy place."

"What holy place? A church?"

"Not as you would call it."

"So why are you so frightened? Who would want to harm our boy?"

"I know not," she said as she slipped the sling over her shoulder and around her neck, "but I swear on all that is holy, if anyone tries to stop us or hurt my child, I will kill them myself."

Hallyd felt as if all the breath had been sucked from his lungs. His heart was near bursting, the sensation of swirling so fast he felt sure his eyes would fall from his head. He opened his eyes and found himself on a mound of earth with the scent of the sea in the air and twilight approaching.

His eyes were healed. He looked straight into the sunset, where streaks of red and gold were striping the horizon over the calm ocean waters, and he felt no pain, no aches, no vestige of the damned curse remaining.

But his heart was beating like a drum, and he had trouble catching his breath. He fell to his knees, then sank onto the ground in a sitting position, all the life seemingly drained from him. What in the name of Hades had happened to him? How had Vannora, in the blink of a cat's eye, thrown him body and soul from Chwarel to wherever he landed? Her powers always surprised him.

Hadn't he been clinging to her as hard as he could, screaming into the wind and riding in a maelstrom with her, gasping for air while he'd heard her laughter? By the gods, 'twas lucky he had not pissed himself.

Nay, fool. 'Tis lucky you are still alive.

He knew of demons and witches and those who flirted with Satan. Had he not been a priest, learned of both the good and the bad in the world, of heaven and hell, of light and darkness? Had he himself not dabbled in sorcery?

Of course, he'd long suspected she wasn't what she seemed and had believed that her motives weren't pure . . . but then, whose were? Certainly not his own.

But this . . .

What he needed right now was a huge mazer of ale to calm his jittery nerves, for he was still shaking inside, his muscles quivering from his bones. Gulping air, telling himself to somehow find his composure, he furrowed his hands through his hair and managed to catch his breath. There was time enough later to try to understand the inexplicable.

For now, he had his own mission.

Bryanna was here.

On this solitary island where the sound of the ocean crushed the shore.

With a newborn baby, *his* child, the one Vannora wanted so desperately.

And with a man who claimed Bryanna for his own.

Along with the dagger.

Now complete, the jeweled magickal knife was restored.

He rubbed his fingers together in eager expectation and threw off his fears and doubts.

Vannora had been right. He looked around for her, for she had come with him, had she not? 'Twas her spirit that had cast him to the west, but it seemed he was alone atop this steep mountain. As he gazed to the vast waters, he knew where he was. Holy Island. Of course. Where it was rumored the practice of the old ways had existed for centuries, mayhap longer.

He dusted himself off and searched for her. "Vannora!" he called, more than a little irritated, for she'd brought him here, *somehow*, but he had little with him. At least his sword was strapped on, and he was lucky to have that.

So now, to find the place where the old rituals took place.

Vannora be damned.

As if she wasn't already.

Deverill and his small company had landed at Holyhead with a new mission. Aye, he still wanted his damned horse back and that bastard son of his brought to some kind of justice, but also, he wanted to make Hallyd of Chwarel pay for his greed and trickery. If the spy were to be believed, Hallyd was also due to arrive here on this godforsaken scrap of land.

Which was fine with Deverill.

What better place for a liar and a blackheart to meet his maker than an island where the wind blew fierce and waves crashed three hundred feet beneath a sheer cliff? 'Twas a fierce place, this rocky patch of land cast into the sea. A place of old ruins and tombs and bloody rituals of the ancient ones.

Deverill of Agendor wasn't afraid of much in this life, but 'twas the things he didn't understand, the talk of dark arts and witchcraft, that bothered him. He professed to be a nonbeliever of the dark side of things, but a place like this, so raw and wild that old chants fairly sang on the roar of the surf, gave him pause.

Worse yet, 'twas dusk on Samhain Eve, the night when, according to the old ones, spirits of the underworld were allowed to walk the earth. On this night there was a ripple in time and the wall that kept the two worlds apart, the invisible veil, was opened, if only for a little while.

Long enough, Deverill thought, his bones suddenly cold. But he would not think of Samhain just yet, not allow himself to be distracted. He had vengeance to serve.

And then there was the matter of that precious dagger.

Whether it had magickal powers or not, it was valuable.

Deverill figured he deserved it for his trouble.

What was a wolf doing on a small island? the mercenary wondered as he climbed a steep slope toward the apex of the mountain. From atop this rocky crag, Carrick surveyed the island and could, he hoped, decide which way he should search. He'd visited Holyhead, learned of a pregnant woman, a traveler giving birth in the inn, but other than that he found out little more. The innkeeper had been silent on the matter, his wife, the town midwife, also tight-lipped. But in the alehouse he'd heard the rumor started by another guest that a woman had labored the previous night through and her muffled cries had kept him awake.

But she and the baby and the man who claimed to be her husband had left. 'Twas odd, he thought as he eyed the wolf, moving between the rocks, nose to the wind, fur ruffling. There had been talk of Samhain in the village, that it was to start this very night, the new year beginning in the span of a day.

'Twas twattle. Of course it was.

But as he saw the dark shape of the wolf prowling through the shadows, he doubted his own nonbeliefs. This could be the first monster to come from the Otherworld.

Or from the sea.

Had not Thomas, the farmer's boy, insisted he'd seen a wolf swimming in the channel?

He glanced down the hillside to a spot lower than the crown of the mountain, a place where there was a mound on one side of the grassy lea and the sheer cliff face on the other.

Far below was the angry roiling waters of the sea, and on the other side a trail leading from the village.

There he saw her. She was struggling up the steep path. Bryanna carried the baby in some kind of sling. Beside her was the man he'd seen her with, a man about the same size as he.

He watched for several minutes as they continued on their climb, obviously heading for the mound rising from the grass. Why in God's name would they be out walking so soon after the birth?

Squinting, he saw something else. A shadow darting between the rocks, but following them closely. A flash of silver. Then a dark shape.

A wolf.

For the love of Christ, what was a wolf doing on this bit of land? His jaw hardened when he thought that the hungry beast was no doubt tracking down his next meal, smelling the blood from the birthing, intent on attacking.

Damned cur.

It slunk back into the shadows.

But it wasn't gone. Not yet.

Silently, Carrick reached into his quiver and pulled out a long arrow. If he saw the beast again, he would be ready. And it would die.

Bryanna refused to give in to the fear as Gavyn, the baby, and she climbed the gentle slope of the path leading up the mountain. So her child was born the day of Samhain night. So it was now dusk, when the Otherworld creatures were to be set free. She would not be afraid. Would not.

If this was to be her destiny, if this was how she would save the life of her child, so be it. She would follow the map and Isa's instructions to search for a holy place.

Isa's amulet was still near her, hanging from a leather cord around Bryanna's neck. As she carried her baby up the hill rising so high above the sea, she felt the old woman's presence.

"Be with us," she said, and sent a prayer to the Great Mother for the safety of her child.

Though Bryanna had expected a fight from Ivey upon leaving the inn, the woman hadn't even shown her face. After the birth, the inn had become silent, as if no one were about. Bryanna tried to convince herself it wasn't because of Samhain, though she knew in her heart there was no other reason. She'd been brought here to this island on this very night for a reason. 'Twas no coincidence of her child's birth upon the very day.

She clung to her newborn with one hand and clutched the dagger in the other. Would she be able to protect her son?

"You do know where we're going?"

"Yes." She was breathing hard, her legs tired from the effort, her eyes scanning the hillside as it rose over the sea. Every once in a while she looked over her shoulder, so certain she felt someone following them, intent on doing them harm. Perhaps Ivey had gone to get others, and now those who claimed to be believers were tracking them down.

"Coelio. Believe."

Night was falling fast, stars emerging in the purpling sky. The surf echoed as it pounded the rocks far below, the cries of seagulls fading.

"Tell me about this holy place. What are we looking for?" Gavyn asked.

"A tomb."

Gavyn glanced at her as if he'd heard incorrectly. "Again, we have to dig up a body?"

"Nay, we have all the gems. We don't need to search any longer," she said.

"Then what are we doing?"

"Saving the life of our son," she said as they reached a fork in the path, and she chose the trail leading ever upward. "I'll know it when I see it." How could she describe the vision she'd had at her grandfather's hut and again in the bed? "'Tisn't like a huge church, for it's hidden below the ground and—Ahh." They rounded a corner and the path ended in a wide meadow where the grass was now patchy and huge stones, giant rocks as tall as a man, were interspersed across the lea. As the wind whipped past the cliff face, she noticed a rise beneath the dry grass, a spot most people would assume was just a little hillock set upon this steep mountain.

"What?" he asked.

"Look on the map," she told him, and as the light faded he unrolled the deer hide and scanned the stitched leather. "Well?"

"Aye," he said, nodding slowly as his gaze scraped the raw land with its sheer cliffs to the sea. "At the ocean's edge, these stone giants. 'Tis some sort of outdoor temple."

The holy place. At that moment, Bryanna felt a shift in the air. A current as cold as demon's blood whipped by in a gust of wind that ripped at her hair. Shivering to her soul, she turned her back to the wind and held her baby close. "Come, mayhap we can find shelter."

Gavyn started searching. "I don't understand."

"Neither do I. Not yet."

"What is there to understand, murderer?" a voice boomed from the shadows.

A frisson of fear skittered down her spine. She spun, holding her baby close with one hand, her dagger in the other.

In the gathering darkness, Gavyn's face grew hard as steel. Hand on his sword, he turned to face the sound.

A man stepped out from behind a pillarlike stone. Even in the gloaming, Bryanna saw the resemblance between father and son.

"So 'tis true what they say about Samhain," Gavyn said. "About all the monsters and beasts rising from the Otherworld. You, *father*, must be the first."

Deverill of Agendor bristled. "Your tongue will be the first part of you I dismember, bastard."

"Good." Gavyn smiled as wickedly as a devil. Sword drawn, he stepped between his father and his child. "So you are not alone, are you?" Gavyn asked. "You are not brave enough to come without your thugs."

"That's where you're wrong. They are scattered about this island, guarding the port, searching for you. Nay, bastard, this is just you and I." Deverill lifted his sword high. "I have waited long for this," he said over the roaring sound of wind and surf.

Gavyn charged.

"Nay, please! Do not," Bryanna said, and again she felt the coldness sweep by. *"Isa, help me,"* she whispered, holding the dagger high.

And then she saw him.

The dark one, appearing from behind the rise.

Hallyd of Chwarel had found them.

Her soul became ice.

His sword was raised, his eyes centered upon the dagger.

"Stop!" Bryanna ordered, but he edged toward her, sword drawn.

Distracted, Gavyn turned.

"Give it to me," Hallyd ordered, one hand outstretched, fingers wiggling in invitation. "The dagger, 'tis mine."

"Nay." She thrust it in front of her to ward him off. At that moment, Hallyd lunged toward her. In an attempt to protect Bryanna and Truett, Gavyn threw himself in front of the dark one's sword.

"Nooooo!" she screamed, and from her lips came a spell, as deadly and dark as all of Hades. She cast it at Hallyd and felt the ground shift beneath her feet, the earth rending as night fell and the moon glowed bright. The chasm of the spirit world was opening wide.

Samhain!

The dead were coming.

Gavyn fended off Hallyd's strike.

Behind him, the Lord of Agendor seemed to forget his son for a moment and turned to see the newcomer who had risen from the shadows, the Lord of Chwarel.

"You shrivel-balled liar," Deverill yelled. "You who ask me for an alliance, and then thwart my men? Use them for your own purposes? Lie to me?" He was advancing on his new enemy, his feud with his bastard son temporarily forgotten. He held his sword high, death beating a tattoo at his temple. "You shall die first, liar," he said, lips curled in disgust. "Before all others, you are going to die."

Hallyd took one look at Deverill and his jaw tightened in a snarl of pleased fury. "Petty baron," he muttered, "taking the word of a greedy spy. Oh, yes, I know this," he said, his odd eyes glowing with the night. "You are mistaken, cur. 'Tis your time to leave this earth." He held his ground as Deverill charged, wielding his weapon high.

Gavyn leapt. Intent on protecting his family, he planted himself between Bryanna and the two swordsmen.

Metal clanged.

Men grunted.

The wind howled.

"Run, Bryanna. Take the babe and run!" But even as he uttered the words, Gavyn knew there was no place to hide. The forces of evil were forever near.

Instead of running, she actually stepped closer. Gavyn grabbed one arm, but she held the dagger in front of her, pointing the blade toward the sea.

"Coelio," she whispered over the howling wind. "I believe." Chanting the word they'd seen on the map and the legend of the stones, she stood tall, dagger extended toward the howling ocean.

Gavyn felt a rumbling deep in the earth, a slow shudder that shook the ground.

The wind came up ever faster, wild gusts whirling around them. In the fury Hallyd leapt high into the air, holding his sword with both hands, and drove his blade deep into the body of his enemy.

The Baron of Agendor let go of life in a bloody howl.

But Hallyd didn't wait for the man to breathe his last breath. Using his foot against Deverill's chest for leverage, he withdrew the sword and turned to Gavyn.

"You're next," Hallyd promised, his eyes narrowing. "Do you know that you've been bedding my woman? That I was the one before you?" he said, hooking an angry thumb at his chest. "I took her virginity and warmed the bed that you later slept upon. That child is mine."

The words burned her ears. "Nay!" Bryanna cried, her chanting broken by Hallyd's horrid proclamation. She couldn't believe, wouldn't. . . . She glanced down at her babe, so perfect and pure. That this hateful, vile spawn of the devil would dare claim him!

She swallowed back her denials as he glared at her.

"You know, do you not?" he said. "You remember the rutting. How I took you from behind. Claimed you. Ripped you apart to plant my seed."

She shuddered, nearly dropping the dagger.

"You lie!" Gavyn yelled, starting for Hallyd, his sword ready, every muscle tight.

"Gavyn, no!" she cried as darkness fell and the stars in the sky winked red. The wind was whistling now, and an opening had appeared upon the mound, a hidden entrance to the chamber where long before the old ones had crossed to the Otherworld.

Where there might be safety, a passage that could lead them away. . . .

But it was too late. Gavyn was ready for battle. He swung his sword and Hallyd spun away. Another strike, another blow to empty air.

With a snarl of triumph, Hallyd twisted.

His blade found Gavyn's arm and sliced hard. A river of blood spurted and flowed.

Oh, nay, nay, nay! She had not come this far to lose him.

Gavyn lunged again, and this time Hallyd's sword clanged against his opponent's weapon so hard that the younger man lost his grip.

"Wait!" Bryanna cried. Whatever power was in the knife, 'twas not worth losing this man she loved, who was already bleeding. "Is that all you want?" she asked, as the storm swirled around them and the hole in the hillock widened, a dark yawning crevice. "The dagger? Then take it. Leave us!"

"You would give it up for him?"

"Yes. Take it!" She held the knife toward him, offering it with one arm while clutching her child with the other. Suddenly, Isa's voice rose above the howling wind.

"Do not let it go, child. Do not! All of the death and destruction that will come of it, that blood will forever be on your hands."

Her heart squeezed in terror. What could she do?

"Give me the dagger . . . or I will take the child," Hallyd ordered, looking away from the man at his feet for an instant.

"What?" she screamed.

In that heartbeat, Gavyn retrieved his sword and sliced upward.

Hallyd leapt backward, his eyes still on Bryanna.

"You heard me. I want the baby."

Gavyn thrust forward.

Hallyd spun quickly, his sword finding Gavyn's flesh again. More blood appeared on her beloved's shoulder, running down his arm. Hallyd sprang forward, sword wielded high.

"No!" she cried as his blade caught in the moonlight. She pointed the dagger at Hallyd and screamed a spell as dark as the dungeons of the Otherworld.

"That's right," Isa whispered. *"Use the dagger. It's your son's only protection."*

From the shadows came a growl, a low, wild snarl, loud as the ocean and deadly as a plague.

Hallyd hesitated.

The wolf sprang.

Long fangs flashed in the night.

Hallyd's sword glinted as he tried to whirl and face the new menace.

But he was caught off guard and the wolf's teeth found his neck, ripping at the soft flesh as Hallyd's sword clattered to the ground. He fell to the ground and wrestled the beast with his bare hands.

Horrified, Bryanna backed away from the snarling tangle

of man and beast. She held Truett closer as she cast spell after damning spell of darkness upon Hallyd, the nightmarish demon-man who claimed to be the father of her precious child. No, no, no!

Gavyn appeared at her side and extended a bloody arm, shepherding mother and child past the open door of the underground tomb.

Then a wolf's bay, as deep as the night, curled to the heavens. She looked over her shoulder to see Bane, her head thrust back in triumph. Blood dripped from her snout onto the lifeless body at her feet as she cried to the moon.

The wolf's cry cut through the air, and then the soulful howl was carried off in the whistling wind. Bryanna was conscious of the thundering of her own pulse and Gavyn's labored breathing beside her as they stared at their angel.

The creature possessed by her mother's spirit.

Kambria.

Now a mother herself, Bryanna felt tears sting her eyes at the heroics of the wolf. That her mother had reached out from beyond to save her life, to save the child in her arms and the man she loved . . . 'twas an enormous relief, a miracle.

She turned to Gavyn and noticed him swaying from the pain. "Come," she said, her eyes searching his cuts, assessing the wounds she would need to treat with an herb poultice.

"Help me," she heard, a soft little cry.

An old woman stood shivering in the wind. Her clothes were tattered, her teeth yellowed, her eyes white with blindness. "Help me," she whispered again. "I'm scared. How did I get here?"

How indeed? Bryanna stared beyond the crone, along the rising hillock. Where did this woman come from?

"Don't trust her."

Another voice? Bryanna looked over her shoulder to see an approaching warrior, bow drawn, arrow pointed at the little woman's shrunken chest.

"Carrick?" she whispered when he was close enough for her to see his features. "What are you doing here?"

"Saving your hide, so it seems," he answered, his eyes trained on the fragile woman. "Your sister Morwenna thought you could use some assistance. And mayhap she was right. This one, she is not what she seems."

"Carrick of Wybren?" Gavyn asked, stepping toward the man.

Bryanna's heart clenched at the sight of Gavyn, bloody and wobbly, his legs about to give out. Oh, dear God, how could she save him? There was so much blood.

The little birdlike woman turned opaque eyes toward Bryanna. "Who is this man?" She pointed a bony finger toward Carrick. "Why is he saying this about me? I'm a bit addled and I wander . . . and I was trying to get out of the storm."

Bryanna's baby cried and the woman's face softened.

"A babe? You have a babe? Oooh, how perfect." She inched closer and the chill that Bryanna had felt earlier swept by again. "Can I see him, your son? 'Tis a boy, is it not?"

How could this woman know that her child was a boy? This shivering little stranger, who appeared blind.

"Nay." Bryanna glanced at Carrick and stepped back from the harmless-looking crone. "I need to tend to Gavyn's wounds," she said as Gavyn's face turned white and he fell to one knee.

"You watch her!" Bryanna ordered Carrick, her heart ripping as the lifeblood began to seep from Gavyn. "And you, don't you dare die on me. Not now, Gavyn. Not ever." She refused to lose him. "You will live, Gavyn, do you hear me?" She pointed the dagger at him and began a spell for safety and healing and—

In that instant, the woman struck, reaching for the child. Carrick let loose his arrow and it pierced the crone, sinking deep into her chest. Her face didn't so much as flinch, but her guise melted into the night.

No longer was she a sickly old hag. Her withered body was now a spiraling wraith, a wildfire whipped into the wind, hovering over them. Fury exploded in her white eyes, which glowed like the luminescent sheen of the moon.

The child wailed, and Bryanna held her baby close as she staggered back, away from the looming monstrosity.

Save the child. . . . Take the babe and run. . . . There is a demon after him, a dark spirit who will stop at nothing. . . . Isa's words thundered through her head now, all the warnings that had seemed ludicrous but now made sense in the shadow of the heinous demon that had sprung to life from the shell of an old crone.

This was the demon Isa had warned her about.

This was the moment she'd been preparing for her entire life. All the visions and warnings, all the chanting and spells and the long journey to collect the gems throughout her quest . . . everything in her life as a sorceress had brought her to this struggle, staring up into the jagged jaws of an ethereal demon.

"Give me the child," the demon raged. "The child for your life."

"Never!" Bryanna jabbed the dagger into the air, the stones humming in her hand, and the wraith recoiled.

"Don't even come close to him!" Gavyn dragged himself up and held his wavering sword aloft. Despite his noble effort, he could be no threat to the beast. 'Twas a wonder he stayed on his feet in his weakened state.

"Did I not say the old crone would prove troublesome?" Carrick said, aiming high at the hovering wraith.

Bryanna watched as the man sent to protect her shot another arrow through the beast, which only made her roar in rage, turning those vile eyes upon him. Like a snake striking, she grabbed at his body with her bony talons, claws that were strong though they seemed to have no more substance than a thin veil.

Fighting free of the monster's grip, Carrick shot another arrow through her, and again she roared and writhed.

Bryanna began to chant with an intensity that burned her soul. She would not give up. . . . She could not! She was summoning the Mother Goddess when the wretched beast swatted at Carrick again and snagged him in her talons. Bryanna gasped, her words caught in her throat as the terrible creature swung him high into the night sky. He dangled in the air, higher than the tallest tower at Wybren Castle.

"Release him!" Bryanna cried, pointing the dagger at the beast. "Set him free, now!"

A raspy roar sounded, like a rumble of thunder—the beast was laughing. But despite her evil mirth, the monster seemed to be lowering Carrick. Bryanna held her breath, hoping against hope.

The beast held him aloft, then tossed him into the air.

Horror washed over Bryanna as she watched his body arc against the purple sky, then descend over the cliff to the swirling dark water below.

Her eyes followed him until it was too late. Carrick was dead.

"Morrigu, be with him," Bryanna whispered, stricken with remorse for the man who had ridden here to protect her. She had unleashed this raging she-demon on this sacred night of Samhain. She was to blame.

Overwhelming despair stole through her heart.

Then something stirred against her chest. Truett kicked again, moving in his sling. Her son, the child she had to save. There was no time to wallow in despair.

"I believe," she said, her heart heavy. Deverill was dead. Hallyd, too, had died, and now Carrick's body was crushed on the rocks below. She could not let this demon claim another being. "Leave us!" she cried to the heinous she-beast. "Get thee back to Arawn, the king of hell, and never return!"

She sensed the magick flowing from her body, through the dagger toward the malevolent creature that loomed before her, claws outstretched to take her child.

The wraith screamed in rage and pain, but still bent near her, reaching her abhorrent claws toward her child. "You cannot stop me," she hissed.

"I believe," she said, lifting the blade toward the heavens, which seemed to pain the beast.

Writhing in agony from Bryanna's words, the wraith shot forward, intent on the child.

But Bryanna would not surrender. "Die, demon!" Summoning all her strength, she hurled the dagger into the gaping mouth of the horrendous monster.

The momentum of the dagger sent the monster reeling back. With a tormented howl, the creature wriggled into a coil, withdrawing upon itself like a snake slithering into a dark hole. Smaller and smaller the wraith shrank until, once again, she took the shape of the tiny haggard woman.

Bryanna stared down at her, keeping her distance, not trusting the evil within.

"Where's the dagger?" Gavyn gasped, pushing himself up. "What happened to it?"

"I think it's in the belly of the beast," Bryanna said. Holding Truett with one hand, she dropped to the ground to search the midnight-blue hillside. But as soon as her palm touched the cool blades of grass, she knew. There was no shimmer of magick here, no vibration or warmth of glowing gems. "It's lost," she said, and in her mind she could see the small knife tumbling down, end over end into a world festering with evil.

The Sacred Dagger was gone from this world.

Mayhap 'twas for the better.

"Oh, please," the old woman moaned. She lay in a huddle on the ground, her cloudy eyes fixed on Bryanna and Truett. "Please, I cannot go back there." Her bony hands pointed to the chasm in the ground, the puckering, oozing wound in the earth that led to the Otherworld. "Without the child, I'll be doomed to the darkest reaches, imprisoned in the gruesome pits of the Otherworld, a slave to Arawn. . . ."

Bryanna's teeth clenched; she would not fall for this woman's pathetic ploy, though she wondered at her own strength to stave the she-demon off without the dagger. Were her powers diminished?

"Return you must," she said, carving a rune in the earth before her with one fingertip. "Coelio," she chanted. *Believe.*

"Please help me . . . ," the crone cried, pushing herself up onto weak elbows, even as the winds sent her sliding along the hillock toward the crack in the earth. The Otherworld was drawing her back into its glowing mouth, pulling her with an invisible hand the crone could not fight.

"Coelio," Bryanna repeated, and the sound of the word made the old woman cringe with pain. "Coelio . . ."

"His powers will dwindle under your guidance," the old woman shouted hoarsely. "What can you teach the Chosen One, you, a girl yourself? You son needs a skilled advisor."

He needs his mother, Bryanna thought, though she said only, "Coelio."

"No! I will not go!" the demon howled, her bony fingers tearing into the dirt, raking up grass as she was dragged through the darkness, sucked toward the oozing entrance to the Otherworld.

Gavyn knelt beside Bryanna, placing a hand on her shoulder. They watched in silence together, unwilling to turn away until the shrieking demon had been sucked into the crevice in the hillside, consumed by the Otherworld.

As the glowing chasm began to settle, the ragged edges of earth began to mend. The winds died and the stars seemed to shine brighter overhead. In the new silence that blanketed them, Bryanna was grateful for the quiet of Gavyn's sword being sheathed and the sweet stir of Truett's breath.

The sounds of peace.

EPILOGUE

Castle Calon

Bryanna sat on the garden bench, feeling the warmth of the June sun. Beside her Truett was trying his best to stand upright while watching an ant carry a tiny crumb across the path. To keep his balance, he held on to the edge of the bench and looked up at her, wobbling, but proud of himself.

"Oh, what a strong, smart boy you are," she said as the summer air ruffled her hair and brought scents of fresh-baked pyes and roasting pork from the kitchens. Off in the gardens, Morwenna was plucking herbs and flowers from the lush bushes, humoring her daughter, Lenore, with a ticklish blossom.

A shadow passed across Bryanna's feet and she twisted, looking up sharply to spy Gavyn approaching. "Husband," she said with a wry smile.

Gavyn grinned, for finally it was true. Upon returning to Calon, they had married and now were planning to return to Agendor, where Gavyn, the only son of Deverill, would become baron. The villagers had requested that he return to Agendor, where a surprising number of his subjects had been glad to be free of Deverill's rule. Deverill's wife, Marden, always frail, hadn't survived an ailment over the winter after the loss of her husband.

Bryanna couldn't wait to become lady of her own keep,

to be at her husband's side as he ruled. Who would have thought they would come to this?

"Come, I have something to show you," he said.

"What?"

"Oh, 'tis a surprise."

She was instantly wary. "A surprise?"

"Mmm. You'll like it, I swear. Come." He grabbed Truett and placed him upon his broad shoulders. Balancing his son carefully, he led Bryanna down a winding path past the candlemaker's hut and the farrier's forge to the stables. Truett giggled gleefully, patting his father on his head.

"What's this?" she asked, but her heart skipped a beat. She knew.

Gavyn's grin widened as he slid his son from his shoulders and curled him in his arms. He led the way beneath the overhang of the stable roof and inside, where the smells of horse and dung and hay greeted her.

"Shh," Gavyn whispered as they eased their way to a stall where Alabaster stood. Beside her, lying on the straw, was a newborn foal, black as night with one white stocking. It looked up at them with wide eyes.

Bryanna couldn't help but smile. "So he's come," she said. "Rhi's colt."

"Aye. You knew it to be male?"

"Of course."

His eyes narrowed as if he didn't quite trust her. "Listen, witch," he said, "what is it you know? Can you foresee the future?"

"I thought you didn't believe."

His grin slashed white in the darkness. "You made a believer of me."

"Is that so?" Bryanna rubbed Alabaster's velvet nose.

Nickering, the mare turned away, took a step toward her newborn, and nudged at him with her face. Still wet from the birth, he struggled several times before his spindly legs finally perched under him. When he was finally on all fours, he pressed his nose against his mother's white flank and found her udder.

Truett gazed at the animals in fascination. He pointed at the black foal and smiled widely.

"I think he's claimed the foal as his own."

"You can't be serious. He's not even walking."

"But he'll need his own steed."

"First his own two feet. Then we'll talk about putting him upon a horse," she said skeptically, though she knew it would happen. She could see it laid out before her as they walked out of the stable and into the heat of the summer day. Horseflies buzzed, the sails of the windmill turned with the breeze, and the sound of hammers rang through the bailey. She knew a lot more than she admitted to her husband, for though her vision of the future was limited and sometimes unclear, she knew that their son would grow strong and healthy, thriving in the arms of his two loving parents.

As if he knew that she was thinking of him, Truett turned his gaze to her. He was a handsome boy with red hair, rosy cheeks, and blue eyes, though one held a spot of brown in it, a reminder of his heritage. Hallyd.

She knew that her son had been conceived in the union of Dark and Light spelled out in the prophecy. But she also realized that his was an innocent soul, one that could be guided and taught, brought up in love.

Of course Gavyn knew the truth, but once, when they were in bed together and she lay awake worrying about the boy, Gavyn levered himself up on one elbow and stared deep into her eyes. "He is my son, Bryanna. Whether of my blood or not, I will raise him as my own. There will be other children, if we are fortunate, and they will all be as one family." His jaw hardened and she realized then that he meant it. Having lived forever without a father's love, he would not pass that rejection to another generation. "Now," he said and kissed her forehead, "we will speak of this no more. We will raise him to be a good, fair man. 'Tis the best we have to offer."

Now, as she plucked her son from his father's arms, she sensed that their years together would be long and happy. She also could foresee that Truett, conceived of good and evil, would have many tests, many choices, many battles. He would struggle. He would make mistakes. But his true destiny was not yet decided. In the end it would be up to Truett, the Chosen One, to decide which path he would follow.

"You are worried, wife," Gavyn said as they walked past a hayrick, where a wheelwright was mending the spokes of a broken wheel.

"'Tis a mother's fate."

"And a father's, but," he said, his eyes twinkling with devilment, "worry not. Today, while I was out hunting, I saw an old friend hiding behind a rotted stump."

Her head snapped up. "The wolf? Bane?" she asked, disbelieving. Could it be?

"She was there."

"You're certain it was Bane?" She thought he might be teasing her.

"Aye, 'twas no other."

Bryanna thought of the mother she'd never known. Could it be true? She hadn't seen the beast since that final battle at Holyhead, and had feared she would never lay eyes upon her again.

"I have a feeling the wolf will follow us to Agendor."

"Do you?"

"Aye, wife, I do," he said. With their son nestled between them, he drew her into his arms as the sun sank lower on the horizon.

"It seems impossible."

"Many things do," he said, whispering into her ear. "But you, sorceress, of all people, should know that above all else, there is one thing you must do."

"Is there? And what is that?" she asked, amused.

"Have faith, Bryanna," he said. "Do as you taught me."

"As *I* taught you? And all that time I felt sure you were turning a deaf ear to me."

"Aye, 'tis all you must do." He kissed her, then lifted his head and winked. "'Tis simple, wife. Just . . . believe."

Penguin Group (USA) Inc.
is proud to present

GREAT READS—GUARANTEED!

**We are so confident that you will love
this book that we are offering a
100% money-back guarantee!**

If you are not 100% satisfied with
this publication, Penguin Group (USA)
will refund your money!
Simply return the book before
December 1, 2007 for a full refund.

New York Times bestselling author

Lisa Jackson

Temptress

A bloodied warrior is brought to the Castle Calon, battered, nearly unrecognizable. And yet Morwenna sees that he resembles Carrick of Wybren, a man who not so long ago broke her heart. Is he friend or foe? Lover or enemy? As the days pass and the unknown soldier revives, Morwenna senses that, together, they will face a new peril. For the Redeemer, a mysterious man who stalks the halls of the castle is moving now——and in his wake he brings with him destiny, desire and death.

Available wherever books are sold or at penguin.com